TREGARON'S DAUGHTER

At the turn of the century, young Cadi Tregaron has lived the hard life of a fisherman's daughter in a small Cornish coastal village. The dream that often recurs as she grows up, of a great house standing amidst water and of the faceless man who awaits her there, is both wonderful and terrifying. At the age of sixteen, by a cruel blow, she is suddenly orphaned. As a result, she is taken into the family of Mr. and Mrs. Morton who live in a large house in Kent with their son and daughter. Cadi finds it difficult to adapt herself to the new life of luxury but she is a determined girl and too self-reliant to become spoiled. In her new environment she finds mystery, danger, and a hidden enemy. Can it be young Richard Morton? Or Lucian Farrel, the Mortons' nephew? Or is it the mysterious grey-eyed stranger who always seems to be watching her? The haunting dream becomes a nightmare, for the house standing in water is a reality to which she is bound by ancestry, and there she comes to know grief and heartbreak, and also learns the truth about herself and her hidden enemy.

TREGARON'S DAUGHTER

*

MADELEINE BRENT

THE
COMPANION BOOK CLUB
LONDON

THE COMPANION BOOK CLUB
The Club is not a library; all books are the
property of members. There is no entrance fee
or any payment beyond the low Club price of
each book. Details of membership will gladly
be sent on request.

Write to:
The Companion Book Club,
Borough Green, Sevenoaks, Kent

*Made and printed in Great Britain
for the Companion Book Club
by Odhams (Watford) Ltd.*
600871525
9.72/252

Chapter One

ON THAT DAY IN SUMMER, the day that Lucian Farrel came into my life, I awoke in the morning with a strange sense of uneasiness that was close to fear. There was no reason for it. For all I knew, this would be just another ordinary day, and in any case it was not my nature to be nervous, even for some cause, but as soon as I opened my eyes it seemed that all my senses were unnaturally keen and vivid that day, the world was sharper, more clear-cut than usual, yet curiously unreal.

Once or twice in my life this had happened to me before. It happened on the day that my mother and grandmother were killed, and again on the day of the two accidents; that was a black day in Mawstone, for within a few hours a drifter was wrecked on the rocks and one of the undersea shafts of the Polbren tin mine collapsed. Our little village lost seven men on the day of the two accidents.

Now I had the same feeling upon me. It is hard to describe, except as a kind of special awareness. I saw dust-motes dancing in the shaft of sunlight that slanted between the curtains of the small window and reflected from the big brass knob of the narrow bed, to throw a globe of golden light on the white-washed wall. I heard the ticking of the magic lantern clock that Granny Caterina had given me on my tenth birthday, seven years ago, and saw the picture of the dial thrown on to the wall by the lamp inside.

I felt every lump and wrinkle of the tired old mattress under my back. The blend of fishing-village smells, salt and fish, tar and good clean air, seemed as sharp and new to me as if I had lived my life in some big town far from the coast.

I saw that the hands of the clock stood at half past six. It was time to get up. I shook myself, trying to throw off that strange feeling of tautness, then got out of bed and poured water from the jug into the bowl. Ten minutes later I had washed and done my hair. In the little cupboard where I kept my clothes there were three dresses, two for working and one for Sunday best. I was lucky this year. Fish were plentiful and my father had a few shillings to spare. Two years before, in the year that the Old Queen died, there had been only one dress in the cupboard. That had been a bad year for the fishermen of Mawstone.

I put on my best working dress, the one in blue linen, turned out the lamp in Granny Caterina's clock, drew back the curtains, and went to knock on the door of my father's bedroom.

'Just going down to get the breakfast, Dad.'

'Right, m'dear. I'll be down-along with 'ee by seven.'

My father was a Cornishman and spoke like one. But though I had been born in Cornwall and spent my life there, I knew that I would always be regarded as something of a foreigner by the Cornish folk. Granny Caterina, my mother's mother, had come from Italy. The way in which my grandfather had found and married her was a wonderfully exciting story, and a mysterious one, too. I often used to day-dream about it, remembering the many times I had listened to Granny telling me the story when I was little, but there was no time for day-dreaming now.

I raked out the range and fed wood to the glowing ashes until there was a good fire under the big kettle that was still warm from the night before. It was a joy to me that I would be able to put a decent breakfast in front of my father, eggs and ham and piping hot potato cake, followed by a pint mug of strong, creamy sweet tea.

In that bad year, when the huer watched day in and day out for the red glint on the sea which told of schools of pilchards in the bay, when the weeks went by and not once could he lift his speaking-trumpet to send out the longed-for cry of 'Heva! Heva!' to the village, then like most Cornish fisherfolk my father and I saw little of meat or eggs or cheese. It was kiddley broth for breakfast, dinner and supper. I was younger then, only fifteen, but I remember that sometimes my eyes stung with tears as I poured boiling water into a basin holding a few lumps of bread with pepper

6

and salt and a scrap of butter. It was tasty, but no meal for a man to eat three times a day, and I grew to hate putting it before him.

My father came down the narrow stairs into the kitchen just as I finished the potato cake. I had boiled and mashed the potatoes the night before, so the cooking took very little time.

'That smells handsome,' he said, and gave me a kiss on the cheek, then stared down into the big skillet. 'Looks handsome, too.'

The feeling was still on me. The skillet in my hand felt strange, and the familiar heat-ripple above the range was something I seemed to be seeing for the first time. Even my father seemed strange to me. He stood beside me, Donald Tregaron, forty-four years old, six years a widower, a thousand years of Cornish blood behind him, his eyes blue, his hair as fair as mine was dark: a powerful man, who in his youth had wrestled Cornish style against the middle-weight champion; a quiet, strong, loving man, who spoke softly and not often.

His father had been a miner, and had died before I was born. That was in the day when a man went to work climbing down ladders for a thousand feet, and then, after a gruelling eight hours in heat that melted the flesh, he would have to make that sheer climb up the shaft-ladders again at the day's end. The miners died young, their hearts and lungs worn out. My father had seen too much of it, and so he turned to the sea. Even when kiddley broth was the only fare, a fisherman could tighten his belt and feel that at least he was not dying twice as fast as his fellows, and I know my mother was happier for it.

There had always been a great gentleness between my mother and father. Her name was Jennifer. She was a Pen-warden, and very beautiful. Though she had a lively spirit, I never heard them quarrel. Once a week, on Friday evenings, my father would go out to *The Fisherman's Arms*. When he returned he would be just a little unsteady, his tongue a little uncertain, but he was always as gentle as ever and full of affection.

Sometimes, crouched at the top of the stairs when I should have been asleep, I have heard my mother laugh as she helped him off with his jacket and settled him in his chair, saying to Granny Caterina, 'Well, here's a big old stray sheepdog come to bide with us the night, mother. Shall we let him stay?'

Once I asked her why she was never angry about it, and she stared at me in surprise. 'Why, what's to be angry for, then? With us three women in the house, it's good for your Dad to be out and taking a glass or two with his friends once in a while. Don't ever go for to hold a man too close, love.'

When nets were empty and money scarce, my father would give up his Friday evenings at *The Fisherman's Arms*. My mother would urge him to go, insisting that 'a few old pennies' wouldn't make any difference, but she always urged in vain. That was the nearest I ever knew them come to quarrelling.

After her death, my father gave up the old habit. Strangely, I felt sad about this. It seemed an added emptiness in his life. Then, when I was three or four years older, I became frightened that he might marry again. I knew it was wrong to feel like that, but I couldn't bear the thought of a new mother.

I need not have worried. One night after I had gone to bed I came down to the kitchen again because I had prepared some marinated pilchards and forgotten to put them in the slow oven where they would cook all night. It was hot, and my father was out on the doorstep talking with Jack Warren from next door. Neither of them knew I was in the kitchen. I heard Jack saying, '. . . 'Tes proper lonely for 'ee, Donald. Four years now since your Jenny's been gone. Don't 'ee never think o' finding some nice steady woman to wed?'

I froze, holding my breath. Then I heard my father speak. He was not a man to wear his heart on his sleeve, and his soft voice was quite matter-of-fact as he said slowly, 'Well, see now, Jack, I couldn't never do that. I'm still in love wi' Jenny.'

Those words came back to me two years later, on that

strange morning when all things seemed new and different and even the air seemed fragile. I stood there holding the handle of the big skillet, my father beside me, and I knew that he was the same and that all things were the same; the difference, the strangeness, lay within myself.

'It'll be a wisht ol' job if you burn that tetty cake,' my father said, and I lifted the skillet quickly and pulled myself together.

'That's you standing watching,' I said. 'Go and sit down now, Dad. It makes me all fussed to be watched serving up.'

He smiled and went to the table. 'That's just what your mother always said, Cadi.'

I was named after my grandmother, Caterina, but for as long as I could remember I had always been Cadi to everyone in the village. My mother once told me that it was Mr. Rees, the vicar, who first called me Cadi, and he said it was the Welsh form of Catherine. But however it started, the name stuck, and only one person ever called me Caterina now. That was Miss Rigg, the English lady who had been a governess in London until she retired to the West Country ten years ago.

Even though I had long left school, I still went to Miss Rigg for lessons three afternoons each week. My father insisted on that, even in bad times. 'If anything was to happen to me, Cadi love,' he would say, 'I'd want better for you than to be going into service and scrubbing other folk's floors. So you learn from Miss Rigg, and one day you'll be a governess in a fine family, just like she was.'

It was because of Miss Rigg and Granny that I had never really talked in the true Cornish way. Granny had always spoken to me half in her own rather strange English and half in Italian, so I had learned Italian as easily and naturally as only a child can. And then my lessons with Miss Rigg, which began well before I left school, helped to prevent me having too strong a Cornish accent and manner of speech. All this made me something of a freak in Mawstone, of course. Some of the folk felt I was giving myself airs, talking like some dainty English miss, but for the most part they were very friendly. In their eyes I was something of a

9

foreigner anyway, being one quarter Italian, and they were quick to forgive a foreigner something which might have irritated them in a true daughter of Cornwall.

While we ate breakfast I was thinking of what work I had to get through that day. There was no lesson with Miss Rigg, but I had quite a lot of washing in the hamper, and I had promised myself that I would turn out the attic room this week because I had missed that earlier in the year when I was spring-cleaning. I was trying to plan things so that I would be free in the afternoon to go out with the fishing boats. I thought that if I worked very hard, I could be finished in time.

'Can I come out with you this afternoon, Dad?' I asked.

'I'll be on mending the nets all today, Cadi.' He picked up his mug of tea and drank deeply.

'You're not going out with the others, then?' I was disappointed.

He shook his head. 'The nets need seeing to.'

'But there are still pilchards waiting to be caught, Dad. They're running fine this year.'

He nodded and gave a wry smile. 'Close to a glut, I'd say. If it's not one thing it's another. We'll not lose by spending a day on the nets, any old way.'

'You'll be home for dinner, then,' I said. 'I'll do a squab pie, and figgy duff for after.' My father nodded and smiled. Perhaps because I was not myself that morning it had been on the tip of my tongue to suggest beef and tetty pasties with pickled samphire for our supper. This had always been a favourite of his in years gone by, but from the day my mother and Granny Caterina died we had never touched pickled samphire. It was that cliff-growing flower, St. Peter's herb as some call it, that brought the tragedy upon us. Luckily I bit back the words before they were spoken, but I was shocked at myself and felt almost dizzy for a moment.

When my father had set off for the quay I got down to work, keeping at it busily in the hope that this would help to make the strangeness pass away. Mrs. Warren from next door looked in to say that her husband was taking his cart out to Penderrow's Farm, and did I want him to bring back a sack of potatoes for me. Later, Old Martha called to gossip. She had been known as Old Martha for twenty-five years, so my father told me, and nobody knew her real age.

Old Martha told fortunes with cards, tea-leaves and palms. People came fifteen miles from Truro to have Old Martha look into the future for them. Often she had offered to read my palm for me, '. . . an' nothin' to pay, Cadi.' But I would never let her do it. I wasn't sure whether she could really see into the future. For the most part I thought she did a lot of clever guessing and wrapped it up in hints and misty prophecies, so that whatever happened people would say she had been right. And if she really could see the future, I didn't want to know my part in it. I preferred to wait until it happened.

Perhaps I envied Old Martha a little, because if she had the sight at all when she was mumbling over her cards and tea-leaves, then I suppose she could at least see some sort of picture, however vague, in the future of the person whose fortune she was telling. With me it was different. I just had this strange, taut feeling that frightened me because it seemed to herald disaster, but I did not know what shape the misfortune would take, and I could do nothing about it.

Old Martha often tried to find out if any of the young men in the village had asked me to walk out with them. I would never give her an answer, because her inquisitiveness annoyed me. Another reason was that nobody had asked me. I would have refused, because I was not interested in any of the Mawstone boys, but I would still have liked to be asked. I believe the Cornish boys found me too different from most of the girls in our parts. I took after my Granny Caterina, who was small and dainty, and though I did not have her daintiness I was rather small and looked two years younger than my age. Also my Cornish blue eyes contrasted oddly with my Italian black hair. I managed to cut Old Martha's gossip short that day, and when my father came home for dinner I had got through most of the tasks I had set myself.

'Bob Rossiter was saying there's English gentry staying at *The Anchor*,' my father said as I put the figgy duff in front of him.

English gentry. I remembered how it had always amused Granny Caterina, the way Cornish people spoke as if England was a separate country. My father simply meant that gentry from another county were staying at *The Anchor*, which was a little hostel in Bosney, the next village along the coast from us.

'At *The Anchor*?' I was surprised. 'Gentry don't stay in the villages. In a big hotel up-along Newquay more likely.'

My father shrugged. 'You can never tell what foreigners 'll do next. Kentish folk they are, Bob says. Five of 'em. The man speaks pleasant enough, but the woman's full of flappin' and wailin'. Then there's two young 'uns and Lord Tom Noddy.'

'Who's he, then?'

'I'm not sure, Cadi. You know how Bob rattles on. Young feller with a different name to the family, I think. I were only half listening.'

I sighed. 'I wish you'd listen a bit more, Dad.'

'Ah, it's only ol' gossip, Cadi.'

'Yes, but it's—well, it's *interesting*. What else did Bob say?'

My father rubbed his head, frowning in an effort to remember, just as he used to when my mother asked him for details of some snippet of news he thought unimportant.

'Well . . . Bob said something about the man, the old 'un, hiring his brother Davey's boat to go sailing.' My father looked at me hopefully.

'Is that all you can remember, Dad?'

'Just about. Oh, Bob said he reckoned the old 'un just *pretended* he liked sailing on his own, but really it was to get a bit o' peace from the flappin' and wailin'.' My father grinned and looked pleased with himself for having remembered so much, then got to his feet. 'Well, I'll be getting back. You look fine in that blue dress, Cadi love. Proper handsome.'

He kissed me goodbye, and I set to with the washing-up. By three o'clock I had finished all the work I had planned for the day. I thought of going down to the quay, but then decided against it. With this strange feeling still upon me, I wanted to be alone. I took a book that Miss Rigg had lent me, called *Lorna Doone*, and walked up the cobbled street to the end of the village where a track led through hard, tufty grass to the top of the cliff.

This was my favourite place for reading. To the left I could look down on the little bay of Mawstone, where the village nestled between granite arms. To the right was a smaller bay, hemmed by tall cliffs. This was Mogg Race Bay, and was said to be named from the legend about some giant called Mogg. Even in the calmest weather it was a dangerous stretch of water. About a hundred yards from the western arm of the bay a great round rock, like the head and shoulders of a giant, lifted its glistening black bulk from the sea. This was Mogg. East of Mogg, all was safe, but beyond the rock there was a savage current, a freak caused by the formation of the sea-bed and the surrounding cliffs.

Even a six-oared gig was helpless in that current, and a little rowing boat was no better off than a cork. The race was circular in movement, but not a whirlpool. Whatever it gripped would be carried in a great circle between Mogg and the western arm of the bay, yet it was as if the circle became drawn out on one side into an oval. A boat taken by the current would swing round between Mogg and the cliffs perhaps three or four times, but always drawing nearer to the cliffs and farther from Mogg, until at last it was dashed upon granite fangs at the foot of the sheer height.

Mawstone folk took no chances with Mogg Race, but others were more foolhardy. A Bosney boy had been lost only last year, after being dared to go close enough to Mogg to toss a canvas bucket up on top of that massive wet black head.

I plaited some grass, and threw it down into the bay for Mogg. I always felt he must be lonely there, standing shoulder deep in the sea for so many centuries to warn people of danger. Looking down on the Mawstone side I could just make out the figure of my father as he sat working on his nets. There was nobody else on the quay. The boats were out at sea and far to the west, where the pilchard schools were to be found, letting down their nets in deep water. The shrimp boats were busy, too. Even in so small a village there was usually some coming and going by the slipway or the quay, but today, on this hot bright afternoon, it seemed that Maw-stone slept. To me it was all a part of the sense of unreality that had been with me from the moment of waking.

I tried to read *Lorna Doone*. It was an exciting book and I was halfway through it, but somehow my mind kept wandering, and in the end I gave up the attempt to concentrate.

'You're in a dream, Cadi,' I told myself, and then sat up sharply, for the words made me remember. Last night I had dreamt The Dream. It was one that came to me three or four times in a year, and it was always the same—no, not quite the same, because the dream had two different endings. There was a house, a big house more like a palace. Moonlight picked out the beautiful stone-carving over the great portico. Well forward of the splendid façade, massive railings rose to twice the height of a man. Strangely, the ground on which the palace was set rose up out of flat calm water, and also rising from the water were several tall striped poles, in line along the front of the railings. In my dream I came to the house in a boat, and went up broad stone steps which marched out of the water, between two pillars, and on to the great doors, which stood open. Beyond them lay darkness.

I was looking for somebody who was waiting for me in the house. In my dream I knew clearly who it was, but as soon as I woke the knowledge was gone, I knew only that it was a man. I was quite unafraid, and I made my way across gloomy halls, along broad corridors, and up a great curving staircase. He was waiting for me in an upper room, and I was eager to find him, longing to find him. While I was dreaming I knew every detail of the house, even though it was dark, but when I woke all detail had gone from my mind, everything was blurred.

I was calling as I moved along an upper corridor. A crack of light showed beneath a door at the end. The door opened and I saw a figure silhouetted against the light beyond. I ran forward gladly, and the man moved a pace or two back into the room, so that when I reached the doorway I saw him clearly.

It was here that the two dreams were different, right at the end. In the Good Dream I saw his face and knew it as well as I knew my own, and a great happiness swept over me as I went towards him. He held out his hands to take mine, and I knew all the joy in the world. Then I would wake up, slowly, reluctantly, feeling my limbs heavy and a great warmth within me.

But if it was the Bad Dream, the dream I had had last night, then when I saw his face, the same face, I was suddenly racked by cold, unreasoning fear. He would come towards me, reaching out his hands, and I would turn to run from him in terror. But my feet were rooted, I could not move, and as his hands touched me I would either wake up chilled and whimpering, or blackness would engulf me like a cloak, and the nightmare would end without my wakening, as it had last night.

I had never told anybody about The Dream. Sometimes it was Good and sometimes Bad. Perhaps I would have told my mother, or Granny Caterina, but the dreams did not begin until three years after they died, when I was fourteen and starting to change from a girl into a young woman. From what I had heard, all sorts of odd things could afflict young girls in those growing-up years, and I thought The Dream was just a part of it. In a way I wanted it to pass, because the Bad Dream was very frightening, but when the Good Dream came it was so wonderful that I never wanted to lose it.

Now, sitting on the cliff top in the soft warm air, I wanted to turn my mind away from last night's dream, so I decided to think about Granny Caterina and remember the story she had told me so many times, of how Robert Penwarden, the grandfather I had never known, had saved her life one day long ago in a faraway place called Naples. There was a wonderful mystery about the story, because Granny knew hardly anything of her life before that time, not even her family name. The thing that happened to her had taken away her memory, and she could only recall little dream-like scenes of her youth, like seeing a picture and wondering what happened before and after that frozen moment of time. She had remembered her Christian name, Caterina, and that was all.

To begin with I had to imagine her as she had been at

twenty years old. She could never be quite sure of that, but thought she must have been about twenty then. I pictured her in a long white dress with a tiny waist, and that much was true for Grandfather Penwarden had told her so. He had found her unconscious in the waters of Naples Bay at night, and she had been wearing such a dress then. But to conjure up a picture of her before that time, I had to use my own imagination. I saw her with her long black hair coiled at the back of her head, wearing a lovely velvet bonnet with a tall oval brim that framed her face, and perhaps carrying a parasol to protect her from the hot sun.

Then I had to imagine Robert Penwarden, a young seaman of twenty-six, on a fine sailing-ship, carrying a cargo of salted pilchards to Naples. I saw him as having a likeness to my mother, a man as powerfully handsome as she was beautiful, but with fair hair. The ship came gliding into the bay and took up its mooring.

And now . . . now I was free to concoct my own solution of the mystery to which nobody would ever know the true answer, the mystery of what had happened to the young Caterina on that bright day in Naples. Sometimes I would day-dream an old solution that I had imagined before, and sometimes I would try to think of a new one.

But suddenly my day-dream stopped short. I was staring down into Mogg Race Bay, and at long last a message had passed from my scarcely-seeing eyes to my dreaming brain, a message that brought me to my feet with a gasp of horror. There was a little sailing boat in the bay. It was east of the line where Mogg's Head lifted from the sea, and safe for the moment, but it was moving gradually closer to danger.

The boat was Davey Rossiter's, I knew it by the triangular blue patch on the sail. So the man in it must be the English gentleman from *The Anchor*. I could see that he wore a white cap of some kind, like a sailor's cap with a peak, and a blue and grey striped blazer with white trousers. For a moment I felt furious anger towards him for his foolishness, but as I shaded my eyes and stared harder, I changed my mind. It was not foolhardiness but bad fortune which had brought him into Mogg Race Bay.

Sailing was almost as natural to me as walking, and I could read all the signs. The slight wind was setting into the bay at an angle, shifting and gusting a little as it always did in the confines of the bay, and the man evidently knew of his danger, for he was trying to tack away from that dreadful and invisible line where the current would take him in its grip. But the boat's rudder was almost useless. I could not tell what had happened to it, but it gave very little steerage and the boat answered much too slowly. Twice I saw him swing the tiller to and fro, then peer over the stern, reaching down with his hand. Again he moved the tiller, and very slowly the boat came into the wind, but then it lurched and fell away again.

He was making the best use of the sail, handling it delicately to catch the shifting gusts in an attempt to claw his way to safety against the light breeze. I could tell that he was skilled in sailing, and I remember feeling a touch of surprise beneath my alarm, for being Cornish I had never thought that Kentish folk had much knowledge of boats and the sea.

Despite his skill, he was losing ground. With the rudder so faulty and erratic, he could not hold the boat on course and it was being pressed back slowly and remorselessly by that gentle wind, back towards the unseen race that swung swiftly and powerfully beyond Mogg.

I turned and began to run down the grassy slope towards the village, slithering and sliding in my haste. I had only one thought in my mind. If my father and I could pull out round the point and into Mogg Race Bay before the sailing boat was caught in the race, then we might be in time to save the stranger from certain death. That he carried no oars was only too clear, and he must be unable to swim, for otherwise he would have abandoned the boat long minutes ago, to swim round the point and into Mawstone Bay.

It was a long run down to the village, and by the time I reached the twisting cobbled street my heart was pounding and my lungs heaving so hard that I could scarcely see. Still it seemed that Mawstone slept. Everything was so quiet that for a moment I wondered if this was a new dream I was having. But my toe hurt where I had grazed it against a rock, and I could see a smear of blood between the open straps of my sandal. This was no dream.

Useless to call for help as I ran down the street. All the men were out in the boats. Suddenly I heard the clip-clop of hooves not far behind me. The pace quickened, and as I flung a glance over my shoulder I saw a man on a fine grey horse cantering down upon me. My vision was too blurred for me to see his face clearly. I had the impression of somebody young and slim, sitting the horse beautifully. He wore narrow grey trousers, not breeches, and a short matching jacket over a white shirt with a cravat.

I suppose he must have seen the distress on my face, for as I halted I heard his voice from above me say sharply, 'What's the matter?' There was a crisp authority in his tone, but no warmth. I pointed down the street, dragging breath into my lungs so that I could speak.

'I must . . . get to the quay,' I panted. 'Sailing boat . . . caught in Mogg Race Bay. . . .'

The voice said, 'Here, take hold.' Next moment a wiry hand reached down under my arm, and to my dazed astonishment I was plucked from the ground. As he swung me round I dragged up my skirt and flung myself astride the saddle, close behind him. He said, 'Hold on!' and spurred the horse to a gallop as I clasped him round the chest.

It was like riding a great roller of surf in a tiny boat as we thundered down the narrow street, and now Mawstone began to wake up, for from the corner of my eye I saw doors and windows open and startled faces appear. I could feel the fine material of his jacket against my cheek, and for a moment felt stupidly embarrassed at clinging so closely to this stranger. I tried to hold him more loosely, but he said, 'Hold *tight*, girl!' in an angry voice. It was as well I obeyed, for as we rounded the corner where the fish-cellars lay the horse's hooves slithered and scrabbled for purchase on the shiny cobbles. For a second the man's body seemed to turn to iron in my arms, and then as if by main strength he lifted the stumbling horse and we were galloping like the wind again as we clattered along the quay.

My father looked up from his nets, then came to his feet.

staring. We slithered to a halt as the rider reined in fiercely. I let go of him and slid sideways, almost falling, but my father caught me and set me on my feet.

'Sailing boat in Mogg Race,' I jerked out breathlessly. 'Davey Rossiter's boat. Rudder's gone. Trying to sail her out, but . . .' I ended with a gesture.

My father said softly, 'Dear God.' Then, 'We'll have to try. You take the tiller, Cadi.' I ran for the gig which lay moored to the quay, and as I jumped down into the stern I heard my father say, 'Can you row, sir?'

The cool voice said, 'Well enough. Can the girl steer?'

'Well enough.' My father echoed the words curtly. 'And better than most. Will you take the midship oars, then?'

A grey and white figure flashed past me as the man sprang down into the boat, jacketless now. Then my father was with us, dropping a long coil of rope at my feet. He settled himself on the stern thwart and ran out the long oars. I untied the painter and pushed off from the quay, bringing the boat round with a touch of the tiller. My father said, 'Give way,' and the four oars dipped as one. Then we were heading for the western point of Mawstone bay, a hundred and fifty yards away.

'Shave her close, Cadi love,' my father said, and I nodded, not taking my eyes from the point. I knew exactly how the sea swirled round and back there, and I knew how to use that backwash of current so that we would be carried swiftly round the point, close in, instead of being carried wide and away from it.

The gig glided swiftly over the smooth water. For a second I glanced at the rowers, but I could only see my father, for the stranger was behind him. He had said he could row well enough, and that was true, for I could see the working of his oars. He had neither the skill of a man who had spent his life in boats, nor the rare strength of one who had been a notable wrestler in his day, as my father had been; but for all that he was strong enough, he had lifted me as easily as a truss of hay, and he was keeping a good rhythm, feathering the oars nicely and not digging too deep on the pull.

I focused on the point again, and concentrated on the feel

19

of the tiller. Many times in the past I had steered round that point, but I had never before taken it as close as I took it that day, to win every scrap of advantage from the swirl of the backwash. Then we were round, and pulling hard into Mogg Race Bay, and my father panted, 'Good girl, Cadi.'

I looked ahead, and drew in a quick breath of bewilderment, for at first it seemed that the bay was empty. No sail was in sight. Then I saw what had happened, and my heart sank. Davey Rossiter's boat was in the race beyond Mogg; but worse than that, it had capsized. That was why I had seen no sail. No doubt the man had risked too much sail in an attempt to win free, and the boat had turned over as the race snatched it.

I was the only one who could see Mogg Race, the rowers had their backs to it and had not risked losing rhythm by looking round. 'Cadi?' my father said, still pulling hard.

'He—he's gone, Dad.' My voice was shaking a little. 'The boat's capsized and in the race—no, *wait*!' I stared as the overturned boat came swinging round in a great circle within twenty yards of Mogg, and now I could see the man clearly. 'He's hanging on to the side! He's still alive!'

The stranger spoke, his breath rasping but his voice still holding no emotion. 'You know best what to do. Give your orders, man.'

My father said, 'Cadi, take us twenty yards south of Mogg's Head, and the same east.' Then he spoke over his shoulder. 'We'll bide steady there, short of the race, see? And get a rope to the gennelman when he comes back-along past Mogg. You heave the line, sir—I'll stick wi' the oars.'

Two minutes later I called, 'Back oars!' and we slowed to a halt. My father heaved on one oar to swing us round stern-on to the race. There was a rumble as the stranger shipped his oars. My father relaxed, and kept the gig in position with gentle touches of the blades. I turned my head to seek the capsized boat, and saw it far over towards the granite wall of the cliffs. On the next circuit, or perhaps the one after that, it would be dashed to pieces.

There came a scramble of feet, and next moment the stranger was standing up on the stern-sheets astride me as I ducked down to make room for him and to secure one end of the rope he held. He lifted his voice, and in the deceptive peace of the bay his words would surely have carried to the far point, for they were barked out sharp and clear.

'Uncle Edward! Stand by for a line!'

Uncle Edward? Now I realized for the first time that the young gentleman rider was connected with the family staying at *The Anchor*. He must be the fifth one of the party, the one with a different name, as Bob Rossiter had described him. I tried to look up and see his face, but all I could see were the grey-clad legs above me, a stretch of white shirt, damp with sweat now, and the line of his chin.

A faint answering cry came from the wrecked boat as it circled inshore before starting to sweep round towards us. Then there was silence for thirty seconds, which seemed like as many hours as we waited for the moment. The sailing boat came curving round. In seconds now it would be as close to us as it would ever be again. I stopped breathing. From above me there came a grunt of effort as the grey-clad man cast the line.

He did it well, for I saw it snake out and fall across the hull, just aft of the keel. The man in the water was on the far side of the boat, and he must have caught the end of our rope as it fell beside him. I had expected to see him let go of the boat at once and cling to the line so that we could tow him out of the race, but fate had taken a hand, for the line slid down between the broken rudder and the stern and caught fast there.

It was then I realized why my father, in his wisdom, had stayed at the oars. There came a feeble cry from the race: 'Take care! Line's caught!' I heard my father swear softly under his breath, and in the five seconds before the line ran out taut he began to row with a madman's strength. Then came a smooth but powerful jerk as the full weight of the wrecked boat came upon us and began to drag us towards the race.

The young gentleman rider could well have been flung overboard by that sudden lurch, but evidently he had seen the danger, for before it came he had crouched down over me, holding the gunwale to brace himself. A second later he was up, and as my father leaned forward for the pull the stranger jumped clear over him in one long stride. I snatched at the tiller, and heard the rattle of the midship oars being slid into the rowlocks, then both men were pulling together with all the power they could muster.

I glanced to my left, and my heart lurched. We were almost level with Mogg, which meant that we were within a few feet of the current's invisible claws. And there we stood, losing a foot or two with the recovery stroke of the oars, gaining the same amount with the pull. But time was against us. For the moment we were standing still, but no man could keep rowing with that ferocious energy for long. The current would never flag, though; if we kept the capsized boat in tow, Mogg Race would have us, would draw us slowly into its clutches like a great fish on the end of a line.

More clearly now, from only thirty yards away at the end of the rope, a voice called, breathlessly and choking a little, yet astonishingly calm. 'I . . . cannot free the line. Cast off your end, please. Goodbye, and thank you for trying.'

They were the words of a brave man. I saw my father's brown face harden like teak with the stubbornness of his determination.

'Lash the tiller, Cadi!' he gasped as he leaned forward. 'Take bow oars!'

I slipped the twin nooses over the tiller-bar to keep the gig pointing steadily east, eased past my father quickly but carefully to avoid spoiling his stroke, then past the man beyond. He was bent forward, head down, as I jumped over the loom of his port oar, and again I did not see his face, only a mop of thick chestnut hair.

It was a six-oar gig, and my father had shortened the bow oars to make them a comfortable length for me. I unshipped them, slid them into the rowlocks, and took up the stroke. Then the ordeal began. While it was happening I had no idea whether we were winning or losing, for after the first few minutes my eyes were blind with sweat and there seemed to be nothing in the world but the increasing agony of straining every muscle against an unyielding enemy. But we must have been gaining just a few inches at a time. The extra power from my bow oars, small though it was, must have made that tiny difference which turned the tables against Mogg Race.

Through a blur I could see the soaking white shirt of the man who sat in front of me. It had split at one shoulder under the strain, and soon I felt the side of my own precious blue linen dress tear in a great rip as I lay back on the oars. I shall never know how long we fought Mogg Race that day, I think none of us ever knew, but it seemed to last for an eternity. My hands were slippery, and I could feel the strength draining out of me. Each time I swung forward I knew that I could manage only one more pull, but somehow I managed that one last pull again and yet again.

And then, quite suddenly, I knew that we were moving through the water. Moving, not just inching along. I heard a gasping shout from my father. 'Easy all!'

I hung forward over the looms. My limbs and my back seemed to be one huge fiery ache, and I could not draw air into my lungs without making a whooping sound. With a great effort I lifted my head. Astern, the line stretched out at an angle, vanishing under the water and emerging by the capsized boat, which was twenty paces on the safe side of Mogg now, clear of the race, out of danger.

We had won. I became aware of pain in my hands, and when I looked at them I saw that it was not only sweat which had made them slippery, but blood as well. It seemed of no importance now. I heard my father speak, and saw the white-shirted young man start to row again with easy strokes while my father crouched in the stern and hauled on the line to draw the capsized boat alongside. I managed to focus my eyes, and made out the head and shoulders of the man who still clung to the wreck. By some freak of chance the white peaked cap was still on his head. He was holding on to the useless rudder now, and I saw that he had a small pointed beard.

A sudden new wave of relief swept me, for now—now of all times—I felt normal again. The strangeness of the day had dissolved and vanished. I no longer felt as though I was

23

walking an invisible tight-rope of brittle air. No doubt this was because the disaster I feared had come, and so the spell was broken; but in the end there had been no disaster because we had won.

The sailing boat was drawn alongside, and my father helped the bearded man as he dragged himself over the gunwale of the gig. He collapsed against the stern-sheets, gulping in air. The young man still had his back to me as he pulled with slow easy strokes to keep us moving away from the race. He said, 'Good afternoon, Uncle Edward.'

'Good afternoon, Lucian.' The voice was breathless still, but quite calm. I judged the man to be in his middle fifties. He had come well through his ordeal. 'I hardly expected to see you here, my dear boy,' he went on. 'Thought you were out horse-riding. Please introduce me to these good people.'

'We haven't yet found time to introduce ourselves to each other,' came the reply. 'There have been distractions, my dear Uncle. May I recommend that you learn to swim?'

'Odd that you should mention it,' Uncle Edward said politely. 'It's a matter to which I've been giving no little thought quite recently.' I saw a glint of humour behind the exhaustion in his eyes, and wondered if it was reflected in the eyes of the young man called Lucian. It seemed to me that their calm politeness to each other was a pose which amused them both.

The older man looked at my father, who was making fast the wreck on a shorter tow-line. 'My name is Edward Morton,' he said, 'and this is my nephew, Lucian Farrel.' He paused, and the humour faded from his eyes. Quietly he went on, 'I'm sure that better men than I have failed to find words for those who have saved their lives. I can only say that I thank you from a full heart.'

My father smiled a little and gave a nod of his head in acknowledgment. I could tell that he respected this man. 'Our pleasure, sir,' he said in his slow Cornish burr. 'I'm Donald Tregaron, and there's my daughter, Cadi. It's her you've to thank, I reckon. She was the one that turned the scales.'

Mr. Morton looked past Lucian Farrel to where I sat on

the bow thwart, nursing my sore hands. 'She did indeed turn the scales,' he said soberly. And then he did something which brought the colour to my cheeks from a mixture of surprise, embarrassment and pride. Still looking at me, he took off his peaked cap, revealing a head almost completely bald, and somehow contrived to give a polite bow from his half-lying position. 'Your servant, young lady,' he said quietly. 'I am most truly grateful.'

It was the first time in my life that any man had raised his cap to me. I could find no words to make an answer, but only smiled stupidly in reply.

My father and Lucian Farrel rowed back round the point into Mawstone Bay at an easy pace. I was vaguely aware that Mr. Morton was talking with my father, but I was too tired to take in what they were saying. Then Lucian Farrel and his uncle were talking again, in that odd, mock-courteous manner that they seemed to use with each other. A few phrases penetrated my weary mind.

'You'll need dry clothes, Uncle. If you've finished sailing for the day, that is.'

'I feel that the call of the sea has waned within me for the moment, my dear boy,' Mr. Morton said reflectively. 'As for my clothes, I'm sure they will shortly be dry in this capital sunshine, and I would rather risk the scourge of rheumatism than trouble your Aunt Helen with an account of this mishap. It might give rise to prolonged reproaches.'

'It might well do so,' Lucian Farrel agreed gravely, and I remembered Bob Rossiter's description of the Kentish lady as 'flappin' and wailin' '. Lucian Farrel continued, 'But you will need some means of conveyance to Bosney. It's a long four miles.'

'A pleasant walk, Lucian. Just a pleasant walk, no more. You'll enjoy it, my boy. I shall ride the horse, as befits the weight of my years.'

I heard Lucian Farrel laugh as he leaned forward into the stroke, and as I looked at his back, the broad shoulders and the narrow waist, I realized that through all this adventure I still had not truly seen his face.

We were almost home now. Word of the trouble had

spread, and there were a dozen women and two old men on the quay as we drew near. One of the men was holding Lucian Farrel's horse.

'All's well, don't fuss,' my father said impatiently as we climbed from the gig. He waved the chattering women away. 'Get along back to your homes now, there's good folk.'

My legs would scarcely support me, and I found that I was trembling. It angered me that I should feel as weak as a robin in this way, particularly in front of the two Kentish gentry, so I sat down on a bollard to hide my foolishness. Mr. Morton came over to me and gently picked up my hands, turning them to look at the raw palms.

'You must have ointment and dressing for these at once,' he said sharply, and turned his head. 'Lucian! This young lady must be taken to the nearest doctor without delay. Her hands must be seen to.'

Lucian was crouched on the edge of the quay, staring down at the stern of the capsized boat, and he seemed so absorbed that he did not hear his uncle's words. I said quickly, 'They'll do well enough, sir. I'll have Mrs. Mansel, the midwife, dress them with her special salve. She's better than doctors.'

Mr. Morton looked at me doubtfully for a moment, then smiled and nodded his head. 'Very well. I expect you know best.'

Lucian Farrel called, 'Will you come here a moment, Uncle Edward?' Now I saw that my father was crouching alongside Lucian Farrel, gazing down with him. Mr. Morton said, 'Excuse me, Cadi,' and turned away. He had remembered my name, and he behaved to me as if I was a fine lady. Tired though I was, something made me rise and follow him. The three men stared down, and I peered over my father's shoulder as he crouched on the edge of the quay. It was easy to see why the rudder had failed. The lower pintle, one of the two square iron hooks which secured the rudder to the stern-post, had snapped off.

'That's rather what I thought must have happened,' said Mr. Morton. Lucian lay flat for a moment, gripped the rudder and drew it up a little higher so that it was level with the quay. Kneeling, he pointed to the bright and un-

26

weathered face of the metal where the pintle had broken off. 'It didn't just happen, Uncle Edward. It was caused to happen. Somebody sawed halfway through the pintle.'

I could see it clearly, and I was horrified. Even if it was only a prank, it was a mad prank for anyone even to think of. I could not imagine any of the Bosney lads playing such a practical joke. Those born to the sea would never wilfully risk life by damaging a boat.

There was a long silence, and then at last Mr. Morton said in a strange, quiet voice. 'We must not let imagination run away with us, Lucian. The pintle was flawed, no doubt, which made it break in that curiously suggestive way.' He turned to my father. 'I hope that you and your daughter were not shocked by my nephew's very natural mistake. Please put all thought of it out of your minds.'

My father hesitated, his lips tight. He had seen, as clearly as I, that what Lucian Farrel said was true. 'If that's what you wish, Mr. Morton,' he said at last.

Lucian Farrel let the rudder fall. It swung loosely on the single bent pintle that now held it. He stood up, wiping his hands on his torn grimy shirt. Then he turned, and for the first time I saw his face as he looked through me without seeing me. It was a rather long face with a very square chin, and held none of the usual pallor of the city-dweller. There was a short white line of scar on one cheek. The ears were small. In contrast to the dark chestnut hair, his eyebrows were black. They were strange eyebrows, and his most noticeable feature, for they flared up slantingly above light blue eyes to give him a faintly satanic look.

Lucian . . . Lucifer. The likeness of the names struck me even while my mind swayed dizzily. The cold anger in his face as he gazed sightlessly through me was frightening, but it was not this that shook every nerve in my body.

Lucian Farrel's face, which I had never seen before, was the face that I knew in The Dream but could never recall while awake. It was the face of the man who waited for me in an upper room of that palatial house surrounded by water, the man whose presence brought me either intense joy or nightmare fear.

27

Chapter Two

LUCIAN FARREL'S rage faded, and he moved his shoulders in a little shrug. His eyes focused slowly, and he looked at me.

Strangely, stupidly, I almost expected him to recognize me from The Dream, but his look held no emotion now except perhaps for a vague curiosity as he saw me for the first time. I must have looked an unsightly picture. My face was streaked with sweat, and no doubt with grime from my hands where I had wiped it. My dress was torn. My hair hung about my face.

The sky suddenly seemed to lurch sickeningly over my head and there was a great rushing noise in my ears. As if from a long way off I heard my father's voice crying out anxiously, 'Cadi!' An instant before darkness enclosed me I felt strong arms catch me as I fell.

I know that I came somewhat to my senses in only a few seconds, and I could hear my own voice assuring everybody that I was quite all right. My father wanted to carry me home, but I would not have it. I remember Mr. Morton's anxious voice, and my father answering, and then there were just the two of us walking slowly home, my father with his arm about me to steady me.

Some time later I found my hands were bandaged with a cool salve on the palms, and Mrs. Mansel was putting me to bed, clucking and murmuring about menfolk being 'Proper gate buffleheads,' which meant that they were stupid. I slept until well after dark, when my father woke me and gave me a dish of rich broth, then I slept again, all through the night and into the morning until the sun was three hours risen.

It was Sunday morning, and I did not simply feel recovered, I felt wonderful. The strangeness, the fear, the tiredness had all passed away, and there remained only the excitement of yesterday's adventure to think about. My hands were still stiff and sore, but Mrs. Mansel's salve had done its work well, and I no longer needed the bandages.

I got out of bed, opened the window and stood gazing out over the sea. Everything was beautifully normal. I could laugh at myself now for imagining that Lucian Farrel's face was that of the man in The Dream. The fact was, I told myself, that I did not know the face of the man in The Dream. At that moment on the quay I had been utterly exhausted both in body and mind. After the fear and the urgency and the frightful effort of the rescue, I had been in a daze, and because of that my mind had played a trick. By chance I had been with Lucian Farrel for perhaps half an hour without really seeing much more than his back. Deep down in my mind he had become a faceless man to me, like the man in The Dream. And then, when at last I saw him, I was half asleep from weariness. His was an unusual face, even startling, and in that moment my mind had confused The Dream and reality. There was nothing more to it than that. I felt pleased with myself for reasoning things out so sensibly.

There was a tap on the door, and my father came in when I called. He was carrying a big jug of hot water.

'I heard the window open,' he said. 'You feelin' better, Cadi love?'

'I'm fine, Dad. Sorry I went all funny like that. It was exciting yesterday, wasn't it? I mean, Mogg Race, and the boat, and everything.'

He smiled. 'We can do wi'out too much o' that kind of excitement. I'll have your breakfast ready by the time you're down, m'dear.'

'Oh, Dad. I should be getting it for you. I'm sorry.'

'You earned it, I reckon.' He put the jug down, kissed me good morning, and went out. I spread a square of canvas on the floor, stripped off my flannel nightdress and had a good wash all over. I was sad when I looked at my torn blue dress, all dirty and salt-stained, but I put on my best one and went down to the kitchen.

My father had made me a special breakfast, and I ate hungrily.

'Them gentry from Kent, they'll be calling this afternoon,' he said, filling his pipe. 'Mr. Morton and young Mr. Farrel.'

I stopped eating and stared at him in alarm. 'Dad! Calling *here*?'

'That Mr. **Morton** wants to say his thank-you's proper, I reckon. There's no need, but he wouldn't have it so. We'll have to offer 'em tea, Cadi. You make a sheet of saffron buns and some cream. They'll never taste the like in Kent, I shouldn't wonder.'

'But Dad, they can't come *here*.'

'They're going to, love.'

'But they're gentry!'

'Ah.' My father nodded agreement and drew on his pipe thoughtfully. 'But they wanted to come, and we've naught to be shamed on, have we? He wouldn't want us to feel bad, not that Mr. Morton. Gentry or not, he's a good brave 'un, him. Kentish or not, too,' he added with faint reluctance.

'What about Mr. Farrel?' I asked, scarcely knowing why.

My father pondered. 'He's quick and handy, the young 'un,' he said slowly. 'Like a soldier, maybe. A cool one, and he's not afeared. But after that, I don't know. He could be any old way.' He shrugged. 'You'd best get the good china out and wash it, Cadi.'

I didn't just wash our few pieces of good china that day, I washed almost everything in sight, and scrubbed and polished the tiny parlour until it shone. Meanwhile the buns were cooking. I had intended to make them anyway, the evening before, and in the morning I had set a drachm of saffron, the dried stamens of crocus, to steep in a cup of warm water, so this was ready to be mixed in with the dough.

For good measure I made some splits to go with our home-made jam, and then begged from Mrs. Warren some strained milk which had stood for twelve hours, for making the clotted cream that foreigners to Cornwall always marvelled over.

I had changed into my old working dress for all this, but at three o'clock I washed again and brushed my hair and put on my Sunday dress once more. It was in fine cotton, a creamy colour, with crochet-work at the neck, the sleeves puffed at the forearms. The skirt fell a little short, reaching only to the middle of my calves, but I liked it and was still young enough to wear it that length. With an inward sigh I realized that it was probably years out of fashion in London, but there was nothing I could do about that.

Now we had only to wait, and I grew more nervous with every minute. My father was fidgety, too, not because he was overawed by a visit from two gentlemen—as a Cornishman he was too independent for that—but because they were coming to renew their thanks, and this embarrassed him greatly.

'You mind you keep 'em eating and drinking, Cadi,' he said, frowning at his pipe. 'I don't want 'em chattering on and on with their thank-you's. Makes a man tongue-tied, that does.'

I felt the same way, but I said, 'Mr. Morton won't make us feel embarrassed. I'm sure he's a very understanding man. And you won't be hearing much chatter from that young Mr. Farrel. He's sparing enough with talk.'

'He talked free enough with his uncle when we were rowing back. Jokey-like, it were.'

'I know, Dad, but I think he only spoke to me once from start to finish. That was when we were galloping down through the village and he nearly snapped my head off telling me to hold on tighter.'

My father pondered, consulted his pipe, then smiled. 'Weren't much else to say, I suppose.'

'Mr. Morton found something else to say. And he raised his cap to me.'

'T'other one didn't have a cap, Cadi.'

I remembered my mother telling me that sometimes it was a waste of good breath to argue with a man, so I changed the subject. 'Dad, it was a queer thing about that pintle, wasn't it?'

'Main queer.' He shook his head. 'Looked half-sawn through to me, like the young feller said.'

'But who would do a thing like that? I know nobody could have *known* it would break while he was in Mogg Race Bay or even that he might be sailing there, but even so . . .'

'Weren't nobody in these parts,' my father said. 'That's sure.'

'But Dad, there aren't any strangers here except his wife and children, and it wouldn't be *them*.'

My father nodded. 'Well, I don't know, love. Maybe the ol' pintle broke in a funny sort of way, like Mr. Morton said. No use fretting about it now.'

At four o'clock they came. We heard a rumble of wheels and a jingle of harness, and then through the window I saw a small pony phaeton draw up outside. Lucian Farrel was driving, and Mr. Morton was beside him. My father dropped his pipe, muttered an oath, picked it up and put it on the shelf over the fireplace, then started for the door.

'No, Dad!' I whispered. 'Wait for them to knock!'

'Eh? What's the sense o' that?'

'I don't know,' I said desperately. 'I think Miss Rigg told me. It's polite, or something. And anyway, I think *I* have to answer the door because—because you're the master of the house.'

'Dear God,' he said softly, looking bewildered. But Miss Rigg was the voice of authority as far as my father was concerned, and when a hand rapped on the door he said, 'Go on then, Cadi!' and stood in front of the fireplace, clearing his throat.

I opened the door and Mr. Morton looked down at me with quick pleasure coming into his eyes as he took off his hat.

'Ah, so you've recovered, Cadi. I'm so glad, my dear.' He took my hand gently to shake it, then looked at the palm. 'That looks better, but you mustn't do any rough work for a while.'

I thought of all I had been doing that day, and said, 'Yes, I'll be careful. Won't you come in please, sir?'

'Thank you, Cadi.' He came in, with Lucian Farrel following him and saying in his rather cool voice, 'Good afternoon.' As I led the way through to the parlour I decided that I did not like Mr. Farrel. He was lofty and arrogant, and it seemed to me that he thought himself much too good for our little home. That made me angry, and though I did not let my feeling show, it helped me to forget my anxiety about entertaining these two gentlemen.

I liked Mr. Morton very much. I think I had liked him from that first moment when he lay half-drowned in the boat yet had taken off his cap to greet me with courtesy. He quickly put my father at ease, and in a few minutes they were chattering about boats and sailing and all the tricks of the local waters, as if they had been friends for years.

Lucian Farrel hardly said a word. I tried to make conversation with him once or twice. This was something I had practised with Miss Rigg. But he only answered briefly and then lapsed into silence, listening to Mr. Morton and my father.

When I brought in tea and set it out on the table for passing round, Mr. Morton ate heartily and really seemed to be enjoying himself. He had never tasted saffron cake before. Few people outside Cornwall had tasted it, I think, and he was very complimentary to me. Lucian Farrel ate half a split, with jam and cream, and drank one small cup of tea.

Then there came an odd change in the atmosphere. Mr. Morton seemed to be distracted and grew rather silent. The conversation became stilted and awkward. At last Mr. Morton said, with many hesitations, 'I—er—I find myself in great difficulty at this moment. Mr. Tregaron, Cadi, you saved my life at the risk of your own yesterday, and the more I have thought about it the more I have realized how . . . how very brave you were. I want to thank you again more fully, and yet I—I have a strong feeling that this will embarrass you. . . .'

'It would, sir, it would,' my father broke in hastily. 'All's well, and we're glad you're safe, and let that be an end of it.'

Mr. Morton looked down at the floor. 'There is one other thing . . .' he said slowly, and then stopped as if not knowing how to go on. There was a dragging silence, broken at last by Lucian Farrel.

'If I can speak for my uncle,' he said almost brusquely, 'the matter which troubles him is this. You saved his life and he is in your debt. It is a debt that cannot be repaid, certainly not with money. But money has its uses, and my uncle is not a poor man. He longs to recognize what you did for him, but he knows that the Cornish are proud people, and so he hesitates to offer the only recognition he can make. But it would give him very great pleasure if you would accept.'

My face felt crimson. I had never dreamt that there would be any question of a gift for helping him, and yet I could dimly see how Mr. Morton must feel. He would know that sometimes, in bad years, we had to go hungry, and the thought that he could so easily help us had compelled him to speak—but when it came to the point he had been so afraid of offending us that Lucian had spoken for him. I stole a glance at my father, expecting to see anger in his face, but to my surprise he was smiling a little as if to himself, studying first Lucian Farrel and then Mr. Morton, who kept his eyes on the floor.

'Yes, we're proud,' my father said at last, speaking softly, 'but we're never stupid, I hope. You're a man, Mr. Morton, and a man likes to pay his debts, so there's no offence taken at what you've said. I'll ask one thing, for I think it'll please you.' Mr. Morton looked up hopefully, and my father's smile broadened as he went on, 'Cadi there ruined her best working dress with the rowing. If you've a fancy to give her a new one—nothin' special, mind, just a linen dress with good wear in it—then I'll be happy to accept for her.'

Mr. Morton's uneasiness had gone. He fingered his little pointed beard and smiled ruefully. 'It's not what I had in mind, but at least I haven't offended you,' he said. 'You're an understanding man, Donald Tregaron. Give me your hand.'

My father laughed as they shook hands. There seemed to be some mysterious male communication between them that I could not fathom. Lucian Farrel was smiling now, too, and when he smiled he was a different person. But his smile was for my father, he still did not seem to be aware that I was in the room. Mr. Morton turned to him and said, 'Thank you for explaining matters, Lucian. I've always regarded articulate speech as being among the least of your very few accomplishments. You've surprised me.'

Lucian Farrel inclined his head with that touch of affectionate mockery I was growing to expect between him and his uncle. 'It's the duty of the young to assist the elderly in their failing years, Uncle Edward,' he said solemnly.

'Quite so.' Mr. Morton leaned back in his chair with a sigh of relief. 'Thank heaven that's over,' he said fervently, and looked at me. 'Cadi, my dear, do you think I could beg another saffron bun and a fresh cup of tea?'

I served him quickly, feeling very pleased, and then somehow he was talking to me while Lucian Farrel talked with my father. I decided that Mr. Farrel was not really a snob, as I first thought, because he seemed to be quite at ease with my father. It was just that he looked on me as a child, and couldn't be bothered with me. So I liked him a little better then, but not much.

Mr. Morton was as much at home now as if he had been part of the family, and he talked to me so easily and naturally, quite unlike a gentleman talking to a fisherman's daughter. I was no longer at all nervous, and really enjoyed myself.

Twenty minutes later, when our guests rose to go, Mr. Morton paused in the doorway and put his hand on my father's shoulder. He had been very merry, but now his face was serious. 'I won't thank you again, Donald, nor Cadi either. But I'll leave you my address.' He took a card from his pocket and put it down on the little shelf by the door. 'If ever you need a friend, write to me. I've a long memory, and I'll not forget you.'

When they had gone we talked about them all evening. I told my father what I thought of Lucian Farrel, but he shook his head, smiling. 'You make up your mind too quick, Cadi. They were proper uncomfy, both of 'em, for wondering how to speak of money to us. And when a young man's not easy, he sometimes shows up hoity-toity and a bit sharp-spoken.'

'You think he's nice, then?' I challenged.

My father shrugged. 'That'd be making up *my* mind too

35

quick. It's easy enough to tell with Mr. Morton, but I just don't know about the young 'un. Seems to me he might be six of one and half-a-dozen of t'other.'

Two days later the dress arrived for me, brought by messenger all the way from Newquay. It was exactly right, not too expensive but the best of its kind, and the same blue as the one I had ruined. It fitted perfectly. With the dress was a short note:

Dear Cadi,
Lucian assures me that this is the right colour and size. Please remember me kindly to your father. I hope we may meet again before our holiday ends.
Your sincere friend,
Edward Morton.

I was astonished. 'Lucian Farrel picked it out!' I said to my father as I showed him the note. 'Now would you ever believe it!'

'He took more notice of you than you reckoned then, Cadi love. It just shows.'

I didn't quite know what it showed, but I was very pleased with the dress and wrote a little letter of thanks, which I posted to *The Anchor*. I looked forward to seeing Mr. Morton again, but that was not to be. On the Wednesday, Bob Rossiter reported that Mrs. Morton had been 'took bad' and that there had been a lot more flapping and wailing. Next day a note arrived for my father. It was from Mr. Morton again, saying that he had to return home with his family as his wife was unwell, and regretting that there would be no time for him to visit us before they left.

There had really been no need for him to take the trouble of writing, and I thought it very kind.

After the excitement of those few days, life seemed rather flat for a little while, but there was always work to be done, keeping the home, helping my father on the boat or the nets, lessons with Miss Rigg, books to be read. The slight feeling of emptiness soon passed, but something was left behind. I had always had a longing, a hopeless longing, to break free from our little village and taste something of all the strange and different ways of life in the world beyond.

I loved Mawstone, but I knew it was only a very tiny part of the world. Most people in the village were content to live out their days there, rarely going farther than Truro or Newquay, but to me it seemed a pity to spend a whole lifetime in the world without seeing more of it than a man could ride in a single day. It was like seeing exactly the same sunset every night, beautiful perhaps, but always the same.

I loved to listen to the seamen talking, the men who had sailed to India or America, or even just across the sea to France, and now the meeting with Mr. Morton and Lucian Farrel, who came from another county and another way of life, had strengthened my longing to experience more than Mawstone could ever offer.

We had never seen a motor car in our village. My father had seen only two, one in Falmouth and one in Truro. Yet Miss Rigg, who read every word of *The Times*, had told me that there were nearly nine *thousand* cars in the whole country. It was hard to imagine so many. During an arithmetic lesson one day we worked out that if they were all lined up like railway coaches they would make a solid line from Mawstone to Truro.

As summer gave way to autumn, as the purple-pink fox-glove and the yellow celandine sank into winter sleep, I often thought of Mr. Morton, and sometimes of Lucian Farrel, especially when I put on my blue dress. Then winter was upon us. The sea rose, pounding the granite cliffs. Snow sheeted the grey slate roofs of the cottages, and no boat moved out to sea.

Twice that winter I had The Dream about the house that stood in water like a moated castle; yet this was no moat, for the house was like a palace, and palaces are not hemmed by moats. Once it was the Good Dream, once the Bad Dream. In both, the face of the man in the room was the face of Lucian Farrel. I had strangely mixed feelings about this. It seemed to make the Good Dream better, but the Bad Dream worse. On the whole I think I felt foolishly indignant towards him for intruding on my dream.

37

Slowly the days grew longer, and soon, when in London and the North the skies were still bleak and grey, the early daffodils and irises turned the flower gardens of Cornwall into carpets of mauve and gold. There were clumps of rose campion and yellow cat's ear along the lanes, and pink valerian on the stone walls.

That was a poor year for fishermen. Throughout the summer I wondered if the Mortons might visit Bosney again for a holiday, but we heard no word of them. In one way I was glad, for there was little enough in the house to offer guests, but in another way I was sorry, for I would have liked to see Mr. Morton again. In the short time I had known him I had grown to have a great affection for him.

The seasons turned, and it was in the next year, as the tulips came to their best, that the blow fell and my life was suddenly shattered. On a May night, after a calm day, a freak gale sprang up and swept our shores. A drifter from Penzance was dismasted two miles off Bosney. My father was one of the crew of the Mawstone life-boat, and they pulled out through thunderous waves on the black and moonless night to save what souls they could. The drifter itself was doomed.

Hours later they returned. The sea had quietened and the first light of a grey dawn was in the sky. I stood with those who had huddled on the quay all night, waiting. The life-boat was full, overladen with the crew from the drifter. We learned later that some had been transferred to the Bosney life-boat and that all had been saved. But my father was not there.

As the men came from the life-boat I saw their drawn, weary faces, and the way they avoided meeting my eye. Then Mrs. Warren put her arm round my shoulders and I heard her say with a sob, 'Oh, Cadi. . . .'

Her husband, Jack Warren, came towards us, soaked and exhausted after the night-long struggle. 'Come back home wi' us, Cadi,' he said, and shook his head wearily. 'Your Dad . . . he's gone round land.' That was our way of saying that somebody had died.

I wanted desperately to cry, but I could not. The grief

38

was too deep for tears. We walked back to Mr. Warren's house in silence, and I remember being given something hot to drink. At last I was able to speak, though my voice did not sound like my own. I said, 'How did it happen, Mr. Warren?'

'Ah now, don't 'ee torment yourself wi' it, Cadi——'

'Please. I'd rather know.'

His eyes went blank as he remembered. 'Drifter were breakin' up fast. We couldn't get a line to 'em, nor could the Bosney boat. There were terrible big seas. Couldn't go close enough, see, else we'd be smashed agen 'un. Then Donald, your Dad, he says he'll tek a line an' swim. We didn't like it much, but he were fixed on it.'

I could imagine the scene. In that turmoil and nightmare, with the sea lunging and battering at its prey, my father would be as placid as ever, but unyielding in his decision.

'I never thought he'd get there,' Mr. Warren went on slowly. 'Seems like a miracle even now. But your Dad got the line to 'em. They made fast, an' they came along one by one, wi' your Dad waiting till last. Hours it took, wi' the old life-boat tossing like a cork an' the men going deep under an' coming up again. But they had the line, see, an' we got 'em all safe across.'

He rubbed a hand over his eyes. 'There was . . . there was just your Dad left, Cadi, when this big wave took us. Like a cliff fallin' on us, it were. Life-boat almost turned over. The line snapped. Drifter were caught beam-on, an' over she goes, breaking up like some ol' pilchard crate.'

He pulled the blanket closer round him and stared into the empty fireplace. 'We never saw him again, Cadi. I reckon maybe he took a bang on the head when the drifter turned over. But us and the Bosney boat, we stayed till first light, searchin' and callin'.'

There was nothing to say. I did not cherish any faint hope that my father still lived. The life-boat men would not have returned until they were sure beyond all doubt that he was lost.

Mrs. Mansel, the midwife, came and gave me something else to drink. It had a bad taste, but I didn't care. Later I was put to bed and slept for a few hours, but everything was confused and I remember nothing very clearly of the next two days. Everybody was kind to me, but I knew that I was alone now. Eight years ago, my mother and Granny Caterina had been taken. And now, in the same kind of way, suddenly and without warning, my father was gone.

Gradually I came back to life and was able to think. On the fourth day, although it troubled the Warrens, I moved back into our own little house. That night I was able to cry for the first time. In the morning I was limp and exhausted, yet in a way I felt better.

My father would never have wanted me to mope and wail, or to be dependent on other people. I had to think of the future, and what I would do. The people of Mawstone and Bosney took a collection for me. Though they were generous, they had little enough to give, but at least I found myself with a few pounds which would keep me for a month or two. I went to see Miss Rigg, and asked if she thought I could get a job as a governess. I had in mind to put a small advertisement in a newspaper, but I didn't know what to say or how much it would cost.

Miss Rigg listened to me, her fingers busy as she absent-mindedly kept tucking in little wisps of grey hair, a habit of hers when she was flustered.

'I'm sorry, Caterina,' she said at last, looking quite distressed. 'It won't do, my dear. For one thing you are too young, and for another you really haven't the qualifications to offer yourself as a governess.'

'But I've kept up my lessons, and you said I was very good, Miss Rigg.'

'Perfectly true, Caterina. You are far ahead of most village girls of your own age, and I'm proud of you, but that is not enough, child.' Even now that I was nineteen she often called me 'child'. I still looked younger than I was, perhaps two years younger than other girls of my age. 'What the gentry want in a governess,' she went on, "is education, experience, and *background*.' She gave a sympathetic smile. 'I've known governesses with perhaps less education than you, but they invariably came from a family of impoverished gentlefolk, my dear. I did so myself. That's the trouble, really. Your background is not right.

'You mean because my father was a fisherman, Miss Rigg?'

'Yes. I'm sorry, and I am not saying that things *should* be this way, but that is the way they are, Caterina. The gentry do not just want to have their children taught lessons, they want them *brought up* in a particular way, a way that you know very little about. You have learned something from me, of course, but not enough. I'm sorry if my opinion is disappointing to you.'

It was certainly disappointing, but I wanted the truth and Miss Rigg had given it to me. I could hardly complain because the way of the world did not happen to suit me. I had learned that long ago.

'I won't go into service, Miss Rigg,' I said. 'I know my father hated the thought of that. There's another idea I might try, though.'

'And what is that?'

'Something where background doesn't matter. I thought I might try to rent a little piece of land and grow spring flowers. They have to be packed properly and sent up by train to London, but the city folk pay an awful lot of money for them.'

'Not "awful"—that's quite the wrong adjective,' Miss Rigg said automatically. Then she stared at me in some bewilderment. 'Running a flower garden? You are an extraordinary child, Caterina. Flower-growing is a *business*. I hardly think a young girl like yourself could cope with it.'

'I can rent a small piece of land for a few shillings a month, Miss Rigg, and I've got green fingers. The garden at the back of our cottage is only tiny, but it's easily the best in the village. The crates won't be any trouble, Mr. Warren says he'll make them for me. And tomorrow I could go into Falmouth and find out all about the trains.'

Miss Rigg took off her glasses and blinked. 'Quite extraordinary!' she repeated. 'Such a—a *practical* attitude is almost unbecoming in a young girl.' Suddenly she smiled. 'But I really think you might succeed, Caterina. And if you find you need a *little* money to tide you over, well, I have

41

a small pension and I think perhaps I could spare a few shillings.'

'Thank you, Miss Rigg, but I wouldn't ask that. I can always earn a little extra on the nets if I need it.'

For the next two days I did nothing but work and plan for my flower-growing adventure. I soon realized that it was going to be a lot harder than it seemed at first. Whether or not I should ever have got started I shall never know, for three days after I spoke to Miss Rigg there came an event which changed everything, and which was to lead me into a different life, where I would know great happiness and great distress, a life in which strange shadows from the past would loom over me and blot out the sun, so that amid mystery and danger I would suffer torments of doubt, not knowing friend from enemy, or in whom I could put my trust.

I was sitting at the kitchen table, composing a letter to Mr. Dobson of Bosney, who owned the piece of ground west of Mawstone that I hope to rent. I was feeling a little upset, because the day before Miss Rigg had pointed out to me a small paragraph in the newspaper, telling of the lost drifter, and of my father's brave action which had ended in his death. I had refused to read the paragraph. It was foolish, I know, but the grief belonged to me and to Mawstone. I hated the thought that strangers in other parts would read about what had happened and then go about their daily affairs without giving it another thought.

There came the sound of hooves and the clink of harness in the street outside. I was trying hard to concentrate, so I scarcely noticed when the hooves clopped to a halt. The tapping on the front door made me jump. I knew it could not be any of the village folk, for the door stood open and they would simply have walked in, calling to me.

I put down my pen and went to the door. Mr. Morton stood there, his soft felt hat in one hand, gloves and walking-stick in the other, wearing a dark, waisted overcoat with side pleats. His expression was grave and troubled as he said, 'Cadi, my dear. Do you remember me?'

I was so startled to see him that for a moment I was tongue-tied.

Then I stammered, 'Oh! Mr. Morton—yes, of course I remember you. Please come in, sir.' I led the way through to the parlour, still feeling bewildered, and said, 'Will you take your coat off and sit down? Can I bring you a cup of tea? I'm afraid my father isn't here. He . . . he——'

'I know, Cadi,' Mr. Morton said gently. He did not sit down. 'That is why I'm here. I read what had happened in the newspaper, how the life-boat went out and how your father saved the others but lost his own life. I can't tell you how distressed I am. I came down by train this morning.'

I felt so strange inside. This was not just the local squire riding a few miles to offer his sympathy. In fact the local squire had not yet troubled to do so. But Mr. Morton, a gentleman I had met only twice before, had made a journey of over two hundred miles.

'Yes . . . it was in the newspaper yesterday,' I said, trying to collect my thoughts. 'It's so kind of you to come, but you should never have made such a journey, sir.'

Mr. Morton moved closer and put a hand on my shoulder. 'Donald Tregaron was my friend,' he said simply. That was all, but as he spoke the words something seemed to break inside me and I began to cry. Desperately I tried to stop, but it was hopeless. I thought I had done with weeping, but now the sobs racked my chest.

Next moment Mr. Morton had put his arms about me and was holding me against him. He had thrown open his coat on entering the room, and my cheek was resting against the fine silk of his waistcoat. 'There now, there. Cry all you wish, child,' I heard him saying, 'it's best for you.' But all I could think of was that my salt tears might stain his waistcoat. I stammered something about it, but he only said, 'Never mind, never mind. Weep your grief away, Cadi. It's a woman's gift to do so.'

I gave up the struggle and let nature have her way. It was as if a hundred springs were uncoiling inside me, and soon, because I did not try to resist, I began to feel better. I must have looked so ugly, with my face all blotched and my eyes swollen, but Mr. Morton did not seem to mind. After a little while he made me sit down on the couch, and

he sat beside me holding my hands. 'Do you have any relatives, Cadi? Any uncles or aunts? Or are you alone now?'

'I'm alone now,' I said, and I was glad to hear my voice
growing more steady. 'But I'll be all right. I'm sorry about
the crying, Mr. Morton, but you needn't worry——'

'Listen, Cadi,' he broke in quietly. 'Two years ago you
saved my life, you and your father. But when I ask you, as I
do now, to make your home with me and with my family, it
isn't simply because I wish to pay my debt to you; that's
only a small part of the reason. And I'm not undertaking
a burdensome duty, please believe me. I want you to come
and live with us because I like and respect you very much,
and it would make me happy.'

I felt quite dazed. 'Do you . . . do you mean that you want
me to go into service in your house, Mr. Morton?'

'Good heavens, no.' He looked quite shocked. 'I want you
to become one of my family, Cadi.' Sadness touched his face.
'I think it would have pleased your father. I can never replace him, I know that, but I'll gladly do my best.'

It was all too much for me to take in at once. I could leave
Mawstone, with its constant reminders of my sorrows, and
travel far away to live in Kent, under the care of a man who
had won my respect in the first moment of meeting and who
had then gained my genuine affection by the warmth and
kindness of his whole manner. The house would be a big
house, no doubt, very splendid and comfortable. Perhaps I
would have pretty dresses to wear, and there would certainly
be books to read, a new world to explore and a new way of
life to be learned.

I was a little nervous at the thought, but my excitement
was much stronger than any fears.

'I'm sure I would be very happy to live in your home,'
I said at last, rather shakily, and Mr. Morton smiled with
pleasure. 'But there's your wife and your children, sir. They
might feel I was an intruder.'

'At the moment,' Mr. Morton said slowly, 'my wife is full
of enthusiasm for the idea. But . . . she is a rather highly-
strung woman, and her enthusiasms are inclined to wax and
wane.' He hesitated, and as if by instinct I understood his

difficulty. It disturbed him to hint at any fault in his wife, but at the same time he did not wish to paint for me a rosy picture that was false. After a moment humour crept into his eyes and he went on. 'For myself, I don't take her good moods too seriously, and then I am not disappointed when she is perhaps not at her best. You're a steady girl, Cadi, and I think you could easily do the same.'

I nodded. If I was going to plunge into a new way of life it would be foolish of me to be too sensitive about other people's funny ways. 'And your children—would they mind, Mr. Morton?' I asked.

'I have only two,' he answered slowly. 'My elder son, John, died a few years ago in an accident . . . a shooting accident. My other son, Richard, is twenty. My daughter, Sarah, is seventeen.' He paused, thinking. 'Sarah will be shy at first, and this may make her seem unfriendly, but she will very soon become fond of you, because you have a strong character and she is attracted by this. As for Richard . . .' Mr. Morton smiled wryly. 'I regret to say he is not a *sincere* young man. We find it very difficult to know his true feelings. To me he seems withdrawn and reserved, yet he has just been sent down from University four weeks before term's end for an escapade I've avoided inquiring into too deeply. But I'm sure he will not resent you, Cadi. He may well enjoy having the company of somebody with whom he can feel at ease.'

Mr. Morton stood up, and seemed relieved to have finished with the subject. 'So there you are. There may be small problems at times, as there are in all families. But on the other hand you will lack for nothing, you can pursue whatever studies or interests you wish, and . . .' he turned to stare out of the window and added after a little pause, 'you will be as my own daughter.'

At that moment I felt a strange pang of pity for him, though it was hard to tell why. Perhaps I sensed that he yearned for something that his family had been unable to give, for suddenly he seemed to me a very lonely man. I had the impression that when I cried in his arms it had made him glad because he was needed.

45

'I'm a fisherman's daughter, Mr. Morton,' I said, and looked at my work-roughened hands. 'If I go with you I shall have new ways to learn, and I shall make mistakes sometimes. I couldn't bear it if you were ever ashamed of me, and I'm a little frightened of failing you.'

He remained staring out of the window, and answered in a whisper, almost as if speaking to himself, so that I could only just hear the words. 'You did not fail me on the day when Mogg Race had me in its grip, Cadi Tregaron. With your lungs close to bursting and the skin tearing from your palms, you did not fail me then.'

'You make too much of it,' I said desperately. 'You must have many friends, and if they laughed at you behind your back for taking me in, I'd never forgive myself.'

He turned sharply to look at me, and there was anger in his face, but it was not for me. 'What people may do behind my back we'll never know, Cadi, but if anyone smirks to my face then by God they'll regret it!' The moment of anger passed, the fierceness faded from his voice, and his eyes were warm as he gazed at me. 'You have courage and heart, child, and that is what matters. All the other frippery of becoming a young lady can easily be learned. I was proud of you that day two years ago, and I have no doubts at all that I shall be proud of you in the future.'

I felt so hot with embarrassment that it was almost like a fever. Mr. Morton thought I had been very brave that day. He did not realize that I had been concentrating so hard on the rescue that I had not given a thought to my own danger until it was all over. But I knew it was no use trying to explain this to him. He would only laugh and brush it aside. All I could do was try hard to be as he believed me to be. I said, trying to keep my voice steady, 'Then I'll be happy to come with you, Mr. Morton . . . and I don't know how to thank you.'

'Splendid!' he cried, and I could see that he was truly delighted. 'Now let me see,' he went on, pacing across the little parlour. 'We must work to a programme. I shall stay at *The Anchor* tonight, and that will give you time to pack. If we make an early start we can catch the 8.30 train from

46

Plymouth. It has a restaurant car and will bring us to Paddington Station by two o'clock. But today we must see your teacher, Miss Rigg, isn't it? And also your vicar, so that they know everything is in order.'

He stopped pacing, and ran a hand over his bald head. 'Now, what else? Ah, yes. You must have some clothes. We could go shopping in Plymouth tomorrow, and catch a later train. But no. Better if we catch the 8.30, then we shall have plenty of time to do our shopping in London before we take the train down to Sevenoaks.'

I knew Mr. Morton lived near Sevenoaks, in Kent, because I had studied the card he had left with his address: *Meadhaven Wealdhurst, Sevenoaks, Kent.* I had looked up Sevenoaks in Miss Rigg's atlas.

'I don't suppose either of us is very experienced in buying clothes for young ladies,' he went on, his eyes twinkling, 'but we'll manage somehow. If we place ourselves in the hands of the ladies at Mr. Harrod's emporium, we can't go wrong.'

My head was muzzy with excitement. I felt eager yet nervous, happy yet a little scared. A dozen pictures flashed across my mind as I imagined the new life awaiting me, and with them came as many half-formed questions. But I asked only one question, and I was startled when I heard it, for I had not even realized that it was in my thoughts.

'Does your nephew, Mr. Farrel, live with your family?'

'Lucian?' A shadow seemed to dim Mr. Morton's pleasure. 'No. He has a flat in town, and he travels quite extensively. We have an occasional visit from him, usually unheralded, but . . .' He frowned with a troubled air, and hesitated as if trying to decide whether to say more, then gave a little shrug and simply concluded, 'but he does not live with us.'

My curiosity must have been stronger than I realized, for it was to encourage Mr. Morton to speak further that I said, 'I don't think he liked me very much.'

Mr. Morton laughed, but there was more sorrow than humour in it. 'Or perhaps you did not like *him*, Cadi?'

'We've hardly spoken, so I don't know. But . . . he didn't seem very friendly.'

Mr. Morton nodded, and looked past me with distant

eyes. 'There are some who reject friendship rather than suffer the risk of being rejected,' he said quietly, and gave a little sigh. 'It is the way of the outcast, Cadi.'

Outcast? Lucian Farrel? I could not imagine what Mr. Morton meant. It was on the tip of my tongue to ask, but he seemed to be musing on his own thoughts rather than speaking to me, so I kept silent. Miss Rigg had warned me many times that to be inquisitive was a great fault in anybody, particularly a young lady.

Next day was the most exciting I had ever known. I took with me only some personal mementoes, in a small case which Mr. Morton bought for me, and I wore my best dress. It was the same creamy cotton dress, but I had lengthened it last year by sewing on a very wide pleated hem. We travelled in a First Class compartment of the train, and halfway through the journey we went to the restaurant car for dinner; at least, I thought of it as dinner, but Mr. Morton called it luncheon, and I remembered that for the future.

I could not take my eyes from all the fascinating sights as we roared through the countryside. It was like glimpsing a series of wonderful pictures flashed before the eyes; a man in a hayfield, sharpening his scythe; a woman calling to a dog from the window of a farm cottage; a windmill set on the slope of a hill, its sails turning against a sky of bright blue with mackerel cloud. And most exciting of all, a motor car passing under a railway bridge as we rattled above. I just caught sight of the motorist himself, in his cap and huge goggles, clinging to the steering wheel.

Mr. Morton made a point of telling me each time we passed from one county to the next, through Devon and Somerset and Wiltshire. I must have asked a hundred questions, but I did not feel shy. He was very easy to talk to, with no trace of that stilted manner which some older folk have when they are talking to young people, and he seemed to enjoy my excitement and curiosity immensely.

Soon after luncheon we reached the county of Berkshire. In all my life I had never been so far from the coast before. Here there were no sea-washed cliffs and windswept moorland, but silver-birch, and sweet-scented pine and great stretches of green bracken, with drowsy villages nestling between, and here and there a busy town.

At last the train brought us into Paddington Station, and the roar and bustle of London was all about us. The air smelled smoky, and everyone seemed to be hurrying. We took a hansom-cab, and as we rattled along the busy streets we saw two motor cars and one of the new motor-buses. I remembered my father saying that these noisy contraptions were just toys really, and that the fad for them would soon pass, but when I repeated this to Mr. Morton he shook his head.

'I think they will increase, Cadi,' he said with a touch of regret. 'I believe that in time even the tramcar will give way to the motor vehicle, which is a great pity, since electricity is so much cleaner than these petrol engines. But the motor vehicle will have its way in the end. And they will go faster all the time. Did you know that there is a new law raising the speed limit to *twenty* miles an hour?'

After the first ten minutes in a big shop called Harrods I was dizzy with confusion. Mr. Morton put me in the care of a very pleasant lady with greying hair, and soon I was trying on summer dresses, winter dresses, underclothes, bonnets, topcoats, gloves—so many things that I became almost tearful in my confusion. After two hours, one large trunk was packed with clothes to be sent by rail, and a smaller trunk containing all I should need for the next few days was carried out to a hansom-cab.

I was terrified to think how much money all this had cost, but Mr. Morton seemed to be enjoying himself enormously. He took me to have tea at a huge new hotel called *The Ritz*, which had recently opened in Piccadilly. The clothes I had worn at the start of the journey had been packed away, and I now wore a beautiful pale green dress with a bead-embroidered bodice. The petticoat beneath was of silk. The toes of my new black kid lace-up shoes peeped out beneath the hem of the dress.

The Harrods lady had been very distressed because she thought it improper that I did not want to be corseted. She had gone away to speak with Mr. Morton about it, and returned with a flustered look, repeating his words to me with some indignation. He had said, 'I don't care whether it's proper or not, madam. Nature and plenty of exercise have given that child all the corseting she needs, so don't start strapping her up in whalebone.'

The hat had been another problem calling for a conference. Mr. Morton thought that at my age I should have my hair up, but it was too short, and he really liked me with my hair down and tied back in a ribbon. Also, he did not like the big hats, all covered with stuffed birds and imitation fruit, which were the fashion just now. So in the end I had a bonnet which matched my green dress, a little toque with small feathers at one side, and two straw hats with shallow crowns and stiff brims, rather like a man's boater. I was wearing the bonnet as we took tea in *The Ritz*.

I did not think it a very good tea, particularly when I saw how much Mr. Morton paid for it, but I was glad to sit quietly for a while. Then, after I had forgotten my gloves and run back for them, another hansom-cab took us to Charing Cross, where we boarded a train for Hildenborough, one stop beyond Sevenoaks. I learned that the village of Wealdhurst lay the same distance from each, but Mr. Morton preferred Hildenborough because Sevenoaks was sometimes too crowded with carriages. The journey took just over an hour. Mr. Morton had sent a telegram as soon as we reached Paddington, to say which train should be met, and his own carriage was waiting for us when we arrived. The driver was very old, and I was surprised to notice that the two horses were not as well-groomed as they might have been. Mr. Morton looked at them and wrinkled his nose in a grimace, but said nothing.

I had been very sleepy on the train journey from London, for it had been a long and tiring day in every way, but now I was keyed up again because soon I would be meeting my new family. We trotted along a country lane for about two or three miles, gradually climbing uphill, and then at last we turned into a drive between tall stone pillars.

As we passed beyond the trees which screened the house from the road I caught my breath. I had expected a large house, but this was huge. It lay beyond a wide carpet of lawn, with the drive curving round the edge of the grass to an apron of cobbles in front of the porch. I learned later that it had been built when the Old Queen was young. The red bricks had mellowed over the years and were softened by ivy. As we moved round the drive I could see beyond the house and glimpse lawns and rose-gardens.

Mr. Morton tucked my hand under his arm and together we walked up the five steps into the wide porch. The door was opened by a butler, the first I had ever seen. He was a rather plump man with thin grey hair and a grave manner.

'Good afternoon, sir, and welcome home,' he said in a hushed voice, inclining his head.

'Good afternoon, John,' said Mr. Morton and took me into the lofty hall. 'This is Miss Cadi, the new member of our family.'

'Welcome, Miss Cadi,' John said politely, though I thought his eyes studied me sharply and rather disapprovingly.

'How do you do?' I said, in the way Miss Rigg had taught me. I looked round the hall. A broad staircase curved up to a gallery above, and a balustrade ran round the four sides of the gallery. The hall was beautifully furnished, with two long sofas, side-tables and carved chairs, a grandfather clock, a bust set on a marble pillar, and several small statuettes. I could not take it in all at once. And on the walls were at least a dozen paintings.

John coughed very quietly and said, 'Mrs. Morton, Miss Sarah and Master Richard are in the garden, sir. Shall I inform them that you have arrived?'

'No, don't bother.' Mr. Morton put down his hat, walking-stick and gloves on an inlaid side-table. 'We'll join them out there. Come along, Cadi.'

But I could not move, and his last words came to me faintly, as if through a wall of velvet. I was gazing at a picture which hung above the side-table, and though my head was pounding it seemed that my heart had stopped beating. Before me was a fine, detailed painting of a house set against a starry sky, an ornate and foreign-looking house, more like a palace. Dark water lapped its walls, and beyond tall striped poles lay stone steps rising from the water to the wide porch. I knew every detail, every pillar of the colonnade, every carving on the stone, for I had seen this house before, not in reality but in The Dream.

This was the house I knew so well, the house where joy or terror waited for me, and a man with the face of Lucian Farrel. It was a house that existed only in my dream. But somebody had painted it in detail on canvas.

Chapter Three

I FELT MR. MORTON'S ARM about me and heard him say anxiously, 'Cadi! Are you all right?'

With an enormous effort I pulled myself together, breathing deeply and tearing my eyes away from the picture. 'Yes. It's nothing, thank you,' I said. 'For a moment I felt dizzy, but it's passed now.'

He turned me towards him and looked at me curiously for a moment, then gave a little nod. 'After all the travelling and excitement, it's not surprising you should feel the effects. Most young ladies would have had swooning fits long ago. Come along, we'll sit in the shade and rest. John, bring Miss Cadi a nice tall glass of fruit juice, if you please.'

'Very good, sir.'

We moved across the hall, then through a huge drawing room and out on to a terrace. As we did so Mr. Morton looked down sideways at me with a droll air and murmured, 'Half these fashionable swoons are because ladies will insist on being encaged in whalebone. I'm very glad we withstood that sales-woman in Harrods.'

'So am I, Mr. Morton.' Miss Rigg had told me that it was indelicate for a man to speak of women's underwear, but it wasn't so with Mr. Morton. I felt we could always talk easily between us, not just because he was in a sense my new father, but because he was also my friend. And in any case, I fervently agreed with him about the corseting.

The garden was huge and beautifully kept, with neatly trimmed hedges, long flowerbeds full of tulips, and rosebeds where swollen buds gave nature's promise that soon there would be great splashes of colour against the green lawn. Beneath the surrounding screen of pine and sycamore, lime and oak, lay a dark green quilt of periwinkle.

On the croquet lawn a girl in a pink dress and a man a few years older were playing. Sitting in a swing chair under a tree was a rather tall lady in a long white dress. I judged that she was in her late forties, and much remained in her face of what must once have been a remarkable beauty. Her hair was still golden, with no trace of grey, her eyes were a startling violet. She rose to her feet rather dramatically as we approached, putting one hand to her breast, and on seeing her more closely I realized that there were little lines on her face which hinted at a discontented and long-suffering nature.

She hardly looked at Mr. Morton, but kept her beautiful eyes on me as he took her hand and kissed her on the cheek, saying, 'Helen, my dear, this is Cadi, of whom I have told you.'

Mrs. Morton gave a little gasp, swept forward and enfolded me in her arms. 'Caterina, my poor, poor child. Welcome home. I am so *glad* that we can help you in your distress, and truly *happy* that we can repay the kindness you showed my husband on that dreadful occasion when the water came into his boat.'

Half crushed against Mrs. Morton, I could see past her arm with one eye. Mr. Morton was looking towards us, and he gave me a slow, deliberate wink. I realized that he had given his wife some account of our first meeting, but that he had made it sound very much less dangerous than it was, to avoid distressing her—and perhaps to avoid endless reproaches for putting himself in danger. I was surprised that she called me Caterina, but then remembered Mr. Morton asking me about my name that day when he had come to tea with us, and I had told him my real name then. Mrs.

53

Morton was certainly a dramatic and highly strung person, and Bob Rossiter's description of flapping and wailing came back to me. I could imagine that the meagre comforts of *The Anchor* had been most distressing for her.

'It's very kind of you to have me, Mrs. Morton,' I said, my voice muffled since I was still smothered against her. She released me, smiling fondly, and I felt that she was rather pleased with the welcome she had given me. I saw that the girl and the young man playing croquet had stopped and were coming to join us. 'Now you must meet your new brother and sister,' Mrs. Morton said in a voice that shook slightly with emotion. 'Richard, Sarah . . . this is Caterina.'

Mr. Morton, who was looking on rather owlishly, said in a mild voice, 'I think she would prefer to be called Cadi, my dear. It will help her to feel more at home, perhaps.'

'Not at all, Edward, not at all. Caterina is her real name and a very beautiful one.' While Mrs. Morton spoke, Sarah had been waiting timidly with a hand half extended, looking at me with wondering eyes. She had a rather empty face, with neither her mother's beauty nor her father's intelligence in it.

I shook hands with her and said, 'How do you do, Sarah?'

Then Richard was presented. He had his mother's golden hair and violet eyes, and the face of an angel, rather pale, with fine delicate features and a warm sweet smile.

'We're so happy to have you with us, Caterina,' he said softly, and leaned forward to touch his cheek against mine. I was strangely moved by the gesture, and my eyes were pricking when I answered.

'Thank you very much, Richard. It's wonderful for me to be here.'

'We must call her Cadi,' Mrs. Morton announced in a decisive voice, much to my astonishment. She turned to her husband. 'That is the name she is used to, Edward, and she will feel far more at home with that name, you see.'

'Of course, my dear,' Mr. Morton said gravely. 'How very sensible of you to think of it. You hear what your mother says, Richard? Sarah?'

'Yes, Father.'

My astonishment passed as I realized that in one way Mrs. Morton was very much like Miss Rees, the vicar's sister in Mawstone. A good suggestion or idea had to be made her own before it was acceptable to her.

'Now let us all sit down,' said Mr. Morton, and as he spoke John appeared from the house with a tall glass on a tray. 'Cadi must have a cool drink to refresh her after our long journey, and then I expect she would like to rest in her room for an hour or so before dinner.'

Not surprisingly, the conversation was a little stiff at first. Sarah said nothing, but just gazed at me nervously. Richard, his angelic face interested and smiling, asked about our journey and the shopping. Mrs. Morton sighed and pressed a hand to her head, saying that Mr. Morton should never have left the selection of my clothes to the Harrod's lady, and that she herself should have been present.

'I'm sure we managed quite well, my dear,' Mr. Morton replied. 'And I was afraid the strain might be too much for you.'

Mrs. Morton gave a brave smile. 'I can always summon the strength to do my duty, I hope, Edward.'

'Of course, Helen. That is your great quality.'

When speaking to his wife, Mr. Morton did so with much courtesy and kindliness, but, it seemed to me, rather automatically, in a manner quite different from the way he talked to me. I felt that this came from long established habit. Mrs. Morton was a lady who liked to feel that the burdens of life lay heavily upon her, far more heavily than upon anyone else. A wrong word, an unwary phrase, and she would feel injured and unappreciated. Mr. Morton's manner was in a way a gentle sedative to prevent disharmony.

Tired though I was, I took note of this. Mrs. Morton had welcomed me warmly, and, despite her rather dramatic manner, even genuinely, but I sensed that there might be times when I would have to humour her in the same way that Mr. Morton did.

After a little while he said, 'I think you might take Cadi up to her room now, Sarah. Make sure she has everything she wants, and tell Betty to call her at seven-thirty. Then she

can have a bath and there will still be time for you to show
her round the house before we sit down to dinner.'

Sarah said, 'Yes, Papa.'

Once we were alone, going up the wide curving staircase,
some of Sarah's timidity faded and her face became a little
sullen as she watched me furtively. Mr. Morton had warned
me that she might be wary at first, until she came to know
me, so I was not upset. I made up my mind to be friendly,
no matter what her response.

'You can sail a boat, can't you?' she said, rather sulkily.

'Yes.' I smiled at her. 'My father was a fisherman, so I've
sailed since I was very small.'

'I can't do that.' Her voice was disconsolate. 'Papa
likes sailing, and sometimes we go down to Hoo or Sheppey,
it's not far, and he has a boat there. But I always feel sick.'
She paused, then added, 'So does Mamma.'

'It's only because you're not used to it,' I said as we moved
across the gallery. 'I felt sick in the hansom-cab, there's a silly
thing for you.'

'I suppose so,' she said uncertainly. 'Can you ride a horse?'

'I've ridden on a farm horse once or twice, but that's all.'

'I can ride a horse,' she said with pride. 'We have several
in the stables, and I've ridden for years.'

'Then I hope you'll teach me, Sarah. I'd love to try.'

Her face brightened for a moment, then fell, and after an
inward struggle which showed plainly she said, 'I'm not
much good at it, though.'

I could not help laughing, and for a moment she looked
almost tearful, but then she must have seen from my expression that I was not laughing in mockery of her, for her
face cleared and she gave a little giggle. 'I had to tell you
I wasn't much good, Cadi, because you'll soon see for yourself. Oh, I wish I could *do* things, like other people.'

'I expect you can do lots of things nicely,' I said. 'I mean,
the things a young lady *should* be able to do, like sewing
and embroidery and . . . and music and painting. I do hope
you'll help me, Sarah. I've such a lot to learn.'

She gave me a shy smile that suddenly made her much
prettier, and said quickly, 'I'm glad you've come, Cadi.

56

You'll be company for me.' She opened the door of a room, and stepped back for me to enter.

It was a beautiful bedroom, with pink walls and thick rugs on the floor. A maid in a dark dress with a frilly white apron had just finished unpacking the smaller trunk we had brought with us from Harrods and was hanging up the clothes in a huge wardrobe. My suitcase, carrying the few mementoes of my family that I had brought with me, remained unopened. One of my new nightdresses was laid out on the bed.

'This is Betty,' said Sarah, and the maid dropped a little curtsy. 'She looks after your bedroom and mine and Richard's. Betty, this is Miss Cadi.'

'Good evening, Miss.'

I just stopped myself putting out my hand, and said, 'Good evening, Betty.'

'Miss Cadi is going to rest for a little while,' Sarah said. 'Wake her at half past seven o'clock, Betty, and bring up hot water for a bath. Is there anything else, Cadi?'

'No . . . no, thank you.' Whether or not Sarah could sail or ride, she had plenty of experience in speaking to servants, and I had none.

'That will be all for now, Betty.'

'Very good, Miss Sarah.'

The maid went out. Sarah looked in the wardrobe and said, 'Oh, they're lovely clothes, they really are. I'm sure Mamma couldn't have done better.' She turned to me with sudden anxiety. 'But please don't tell her I said so.'

'Of course I won't.'

She gave a little sigh of relief. 'Oh, this is *such* an exciting day. I'm sure we'll have lovely times together, Cadi. But I'll let you rest now, you must be so tired.' She opened the door. 'There's a water-closet just along the passage here, first door on the right. That's all you need know for now, I'll show you the rest of the house before dinner.'

It was good to know that Sarah had taken to me so quickly. I think it was because I had asked her help. I had not done so to flatter her, but because I meant it, and she must have sensed that.

When she had gone I pulled the curtains to, then undressed and put on my nightdress. When I lay down on the bed my head was buzzing with a confusion of thoughts, and I felt sure I would not sleep. Mr. Morton and his family were all mixed up in my mind. I kept seeing their faces one after the other, and I kept going over the conversation in the garden, to make sure I had spoken and behaved in the correct way, as Miss Rigg had taught me.

Then I thought again of the picture which hung in the big hall downstairs. Had it really been the house that I always saw in The Dream? I tried to recall my dream, tried to recall the painting, but neither of them would make a picture in my weary mind.

It seemed only minutes later that Betty, the maid, was speaking to me and touching my shoulder. I sat up, amazed to find that I had slept, and said, 'What time is it?'

'Half past seven, Miss Cadi. Your bath'll be ready in just a minute.' The Kentish accent sounded strange to my ears. For a moment or two everything seemed strange.

I looked about the room, blinking, and saw that a hip bath had been drawn out from a big cupboard and set in front of the empty fireplace. I guessed that in colder weather a fire would be lit in the bedroom for bath time, but it was too warm for that now.

I heard footsteps outside the door, and the sound of something being set down, then a man's voice called, ''Ere's the 'ot water then, Betty.'

' 'Bout time, too!' Betty answered sharply as the footsteps retreated. She went to the door and carried in one at a time four tall hot-water cans of polished brass, each covered with a be-ribboned cosy. I watched, fascinated, as she half filled the bath, tested the water, and set out the soap and towels.

'Which dress shall I put out for you, Miss?'

'Oh . . . the—the pale grey with the white jabot.' I had only discovered what a jabot was that afternoon. She found the dress, laid it out, and said, 'Will there be anything else, Miss?'

With an effort I remembered what Sarah had said, and

found the right words. 'No, that will be all, thank you, Betty.'

I had slept soundly for two hours and now the bath was a joy, for it seemed that I washed all fatigue and sleepiness from my body. I had dressed, and was just brushing my hair, when there came a tap on the door. Sarah came in when I called, and five minutes later we began a tour of the house. The family had not yet come up to change for dinner, so I was able to see all the rooms.

Mr. and Mrs. Morton had separate bedrooms on the other side of the gallery. His was rather simple in style, but hers was almost too pretty, full of frills and ornaments and knick-knacks. I thought how much work would be needed to clean and dust, but then remembered that there were servants to do all this. Between the two bedrooms was a bathroom, with an adjoining water-closet. The bathroom was a wonderful sight. The walls were tiled, and on the floor was a cork carpet. The hand-basin and the bath itself were of porcelain crockery with polished brass taps. Sarah showed me that hot water could be drawn direct from the tap, and explained that this came from a new boiler which had been fitted in the kitchens.

'Father wants to put in another bathroom,' she said, 'and perhaps a third later on, for the servants' quarters upstairs.'

I was awed. 'It will surely cost an awful lot of money,' I said, then was angry with myself for two mistakes in a single sentence. I had used the word 'awful' wrongly, and I had spoken of how much something cost, which Miss Rigg had told me many times was impolite. But Sarah did not seem to mind.

'Yes, I suppose it will,' she said without much interest, and I realized that she had never had to count pennies and so was unconcerned about money.

Sarah's room was next to mine, and Richard's lay beyond, on the other side of the passage. Hers was full of souvenirs that she seemed to treasure greatly, dolls from her child-hood, a Coronation cup, and small ornaments brought back from holidays. Richard's room was at the front of the house.

We only peeped in for a moment. I was reluctant but Sarah insisted, giggling. I saw that it was very different from her room. On the walls hung ancient pistols, African spears, a witch-doctor mask, and other strange objects I could not identify. An elephant's foot stood by the door, and on a table was a collection of oriental idols, strange creatures carved in stone of all colours. It seemed like the room of a traveller who had collected souvenirs from all over the world.

The room seemed out of key with Richard's innocent, almost seraphic face. Sarah must have noticed my puzzlement, for she said, 'He likes strange things.'

We went up the back stairs to the servants' quarters, just so that I could see where they lay, then down again past the first floor to the kitchens. Here there was great bustle and activity as dinner was prepared. John, the butler, stood watching with sharp eyes and snapping out an order every now and then.

It was quite clear that here in the servants' hall he was the master, though I thought he would probably use his authority with great tact when dealing with the short stout woman who was working at the big range and was evidently the cook.

When we entered Sarah said, 'Carry on if you please, John. I'm only showing Miss Cadi round.' He nodded politely and resumed his keen surveillance of the staff.

I learned that the plump woman was indeed the cook, and that her name was Mrs. Beale. In fact she was the cook-housekeeper, and a very important person. I was introduced to her when she had a moment to spare, but there was little time for talk. A huge fillet of beef was turning slowly on a bottle-jack roasting screen, and half a dozen large sauce-pans were steaming on the range. The door of a vast larder stood open, and when I saw all the jars and bottles, the cheeses, the dishes of cold meats and poultry, it seemed to me that there was enough food in the house to feed an army.

A few curious glances were darted at me as the servants hurried about their business. Sarah told me that apart from John, the butler, there were two footmen and a hall-boy, a scullery maid, a between-maid, two under housemaids

(Betty was one of them) who also acted as chambermaids, and a head housemaid. The two footmen wore dark suits, not livery, because Mr. Morton thought livery old-fashioned and rather ridiculous.

When I looked about me I felt that Mr. Morton must be one of the richest men in the whole country. It was not until several weeks later that I realized there were many such households within a few miles of *Meadhaven* and that these were modest compared to the estates of the truly rich.

When we went up to the ground floor again and into the big hall, one of the footmen was going round with a long stick, at the end of which was a hook and a lighted taper. He was lighting the gas lamps throughout the ground floor, stairway and gallery. The gas jets were not simple flares, but incandescent mantles, and they gave a wonderful light, so different from the yellow light of oil lamps that I was used to. I watched the footman light the six mantles which formed the central chandelier in the hall, and then, holding my breath a little, I turned to look again at the painting.

Though I could never conjure up a clear vision of my dream when I was awake, now that I looked at the picture I knew that this was the house, exact in every detail.

'That's a lovely picture,' I said to Sarah, keeping my voice casual. 'Do you know who painted it? And where?'

'You like it?' Sarah said rather doubtfully. 'I remember my father bought it when I was little, but it frightened me because it always seemed so . . . so mysterious. At the saleroom they said it was about a hundred and fifty years old, but they weren't sure who the artist was, so I don't suppose it was expensive. It's a Venice scene, of course.'

Venice. Yes, of course. Why had I never thought of that? I had seen no photographs of Venice, but had read of it in one of Miss Rigg's books, an ancient city and one with a fascinating history, where the roads were waterways and the carriages were gondolas. I remembered her playing on her piano some of the music from an opera called *The Gondoliers,* one of the famous operas by Mr. Gilbert and Mr. Sullivan. The music had told me very little, yet in my mind was a hazy notion of splendid palaces and rich noblemen carrying swords, of masked balls, beautiful women and handsome men. Perhaps my impressions came from some oleographs Miss Rigg had once shown me, depicting scenes from *The Merchant of Venice*, with Mr. Henry Irving as Shylock.

'Is it a real scene?' I asked slowly. 'Or just from imagination?'

'Goodness, I don't know, Cadi. You'll have to ask Papa, but perhaps he doesn't know, either. It's pretty, isn't it? He says that one day he'll take us all to Venice for a holiday. Come on now, or there won't be time to show you everything.'

We went through the drawing room and into the dining room, where the long table was set for dinner. I was startled by all the knives and forks and spoons set out by each place, and wondered how ever I should know which of them to use.

There was a small sewing room, and here Sarah showed me some of her needlework. It was beautifully done, but her patterns and pictures were a little cloying for my taste. We crossed the hall again, and Sarah tapped on the door of Mr. Morton's study. When there was no answer she led the way in, saying that he must have gone up to change. The study was large, with a thick carpet and a very big desk across one corner of the room. All along one wall were roll-fronted oak filing cabinets. Beyond the study lay the library, and I gasped with pleasure as I saw the rows and rows of books on the shelves which lined the walls.

'Do you think your father would let me borrow a book to read sometimes?' I whispered.

'Of course.' Sarah looked surprised. 'But they aren't books you can enjoy much, Cadi. They're all about *subjects*, you know, history and politics and, oh lots of things ending in 'ology.'

'But subjects are interesting.'

'Mamma says young ladies shouldn't meddle with such things. I only read books about people, I mean people in novels. I like stories where they fall in love.' She sighed romantically. 'I always imagine that I'm the young lady heroine, and it's so wonderful. Have *you* ever fallen in love, Cadi?'

'No, not yet. I haven't really thought much about it.'

'Oh, dear.' Sarah looked concerned for me. 'You're quite old not to have done so. I've done it three times already.'

'Fallen in love *three* times? Who with? I mean, with whom?'

'First there was Mr. Latham. He's captain of the Sevenoaks Gentlemen's Cricket Club, but that was only for a little while. I stopped because I didn't like his wife, or his spotty little boy. Then there was that young under gardener who came to help Hoskins for a few weeks last summer. I never actually spoke to him, but I used to watch him from my window all day, and I cried when he went away.'

It was hard not to smile at Sarah's childish romances, but she was so artless and honest that I would not have hurt her for worlds.

'Who was the third?' I asked.

She hesitated, then said shyly, 'Lucian Farrel. Do you know him? But of course you do. You met him with Papa. Oh Cadi, I think he's so . . . so *wonderful*. I keep praying that he'll marry me when I grow up.'

It was the strangest thing, but I felt a sharp pang of jealousy. That was ridiculous, of course, as ridiculous as Sarah's rosy dreams. I was not at all sure that I even liked Lucian Farrel. Just then a gong sounded somewhere in the house, and Sarah caught my hand. 'That's for dinner,' she said. 'Come along, Cadi—and you won't tell any of my secrets to anyone, will you?'

'I promise,' I said, and we set off for the dining room.

Mr. Morton and Richard had changed into dark suits, and Mrs. Morton was now wearing a long navy skirt and a lacy white blouse. Peeping at the cutlery before me as Mr. Morton said grace, I felt suddenly very nervous.

Soup was served, and nobody spoke until the footman had withdrawn. Then Mr. Morton said, 'Well, Cadi . . .' and paused. When I looked at him he slowly picked up a big spoon from the right-hand side of his plate, giving me a quick encouraging glance. I picked up a similiar spoon, and he went on, '. . . do you feel rested and refreshed now, my dear?'

'Very much so, thank you, Mr. Morton.' My nervousness had gone. He knew my difficulties and would quietly guide me through them. I loved him in that moment, and could hardly speak. Fortunately there was little need, for Mrs. Morton launched into an anxious monologue.

'Edward, I have been giving serious thought to a number of matters concerning Cadi. We simply must get her a hat with a large brim, to shield her face from the sun. The poor child is so *brown* and a tanned face is quite unbecoming to a young lady. We must realize that she *is* a young lady now, Edward, which brings me to the matter of her hair. Do you not think she should put it up? The Mainwaring girl put hers up last week, did you notice in church last Sunday? And she is much younger than Cadi.'

Without a pause she changed the subject completely. 'And you will have to speak to Gertrude. Really, the task of controlling servants is enough to destroy one's nerves completely.' She heaved a martyred sigh. 'For the third time in as many weeks, Gertrude forgot to wash the small change from my purse this morning. It is hardly believable when one considers she is paid eighteen pounds a year to carry out her duties. Yet one cannot discharge her. Lucy Talbot has been seeking a new maid for weeks, and would simply pounce on her. . . .'

I glanced round the table. Mr. Morton was eating his soup placidly, his eyebrows slightly raised to indicate an interest which I doubted that he felt. Sarah was daydreaming, a faraway look in her eyes, not even pretending to listen, dreaming perhaps of Lucian Farrel. Richard was looking at me, and as our eyes met a warm smile illumined that handsome, delicate face as if from a light within. With his golden hair shining like a halo in the bright gaslight, he looked more than ever like some youthful angel.

Mrs. Morton paused for breath, and Mr. Morton said, 'Helen, my dear, your soup will grow cold.'

She made a helpless gesture and said plaintively, 'That is of small importance when there is so much to be discussed.'

'I don't believe there is very much to discuss, my dear,' he said amiably. 'Now, while you catch up with us, let me tell you my thoughts on the matters you have raised. First, it may well be fashionable for young ladies to have a becoming pallor, but it is quite definitely unhealthy. Fresh air, good food and healthy exercise do not produce pale faces. Cadi is a picture of health, and I wish her to remain so.' He glanced at me with humour in his eyes and added, 'Until she decides for herself that our nonsensical fashions override the importance of well-being.'

Mrs. Morton made to interrupt, but her husband lifted a hand and said mildly, 'If I may finish, my dear. As regards Cadi's hair, I agree with some reluctance that she should shortly put it up, but first she will have to let it grow a little. I suggest that our end-of-summer ball here at Meadhaven would be an appropriate occasion. Finally, on the matter of Gertrude's negligence, I will speak to her myself. I suggest it would help if you put your purse on your dressing table each night.' He smiled very gently. 'You have a habit of mislaying it in all sorts of odd places, and though I know this is because you have so much to do and to think of, perhaps you might give your special attention to the matter. I know you have a wonderful determination when you set your mind to anything.'

Mrs. Morton lowered her eyes and looked modest, saying, 'Oh, you flatter me, Edward.'

'Not at all,' Mr. Morton said blandly. 'And now that we have settled these troublesome matters, let us take the next course.' He rang a little bell which stood on the table near his plate.

That was the biggest dinner I had ever eaten. Wine was served with the beef, and after some mild protest from Mrs. Morton I was given half a glass and Sarah just a spoonful so that she could drink a toast that Mr. Morton proposed in honour of my joining the family.

Dinner ended with what I later learned was apricot condé, with cream, though the cream was poor compared with our Cornish cream, as Mr. Morton himself declared. When we rose and went into the drawing room, Mr. Morton and Richard remained, Mr. Morton to smoke a cigar and Richard to take a glass of port wine with him. Twenty minutes later Richard joined us, but Mr. Morton excused himself and went along to his study to attend to some urgent work.

Mrs. Morton sighed. 'He must constantly sacrifice his family for his work,' she said in a lamenting tone. 'Really, he must be longing for the day when this dreadful Mr. Balfour and his Government are thrown out.'

'It makes no difference to Father, Richard said with a smile. 'As a Civil Servant, he has no politics.'

'And a good thing too,' Mrs. Morton said thankfully. 'They cause nothing but trouble. Your father should retire. I really don't know why he goes on, since he has an ample private income.'

'He has an even more ample sense of duty, Mamma.'

'That is quite beside the point, Richard. I know his work is highly important, but surely they can find somebody else to do whatever it is he does at the Foreign Office.'

'Lord Lansdowne seems to think otherwise, Mamma. Do you remember the letter he wrote to Father last year? It was most flattering.'

'Oh, these Ministers,' Mrs. Morton said vaguely. She pondered for a moment, then went on, 'The fact is, your father has a very strong sense of duty, Richard, and knows that he is needed at the Foreign Office. That is why he continues his work. It's no good fretting and asking why he doesn't retire. You will understand these things better when you are older.'

'Of course, Mamma.' His face as serenely angelic as ever, Richard looked at me and rolled his eyes upwards. I had to turn my head away or I might have giggled, which would have been quite dreadful. Later that evening, when Sarah had played the piano for us—not very well, it seemed to my ear—and when Richard had given me my first lesson in chess, Mrs. Morton rose and said that it was time for me to go to bed, since this was my first night and I had endured a tiring day.

I was very ready to agree, for the refreshment of my short sleep had drained away now, and I could scarcely think for

66

weariness. I went to the study to say goodnight to Mr. Morton. He put down his pen and sat back in his chair with that curious half-mournful, half-humorous smile which was becoming familiar to me now.

'I won't ask you if you are happy, Cadi,' he said. 'It's much too early for that. But I would like to think, if I were suddenly plunged into a completely strange world, that I might do as well as you have done today.'

'Everybody was so kind, Mr. Morton. You all made it easy for me.'

He pursed his lips. 'Yes. But I'm sure you know that there may be difficulties.'

'I had much bigger difficulties before you came to Mawstone yesterday.'

He laughed, and there was approval in his gaze. 'Few human beings are clear-sighted, Cadi, but I think you are one of them. You see things as they are. That is the beginning of all wisdom, and rare in one so young.'

His praise made me feel suddenly anxious, 'Please don't think too well of me, Mr. Morton, it makes me afraid that you'll be disappointed.'

'Disappointed?'

'I mean . . .' I groped for words. 'I mean you've only seen me on my best behaviour. But I'm impatient, and if I'm in a bad temper I have a spiteful tongue, and I hate it if other people can do things better than I can, and that's envy really, Miss Rigg says . . .'

His eyebrows rose higher and higher as I stumbled on, and at last he threw back his head and drowned my words in deep, unrestrained laughter.

I stopped, flushing. He recovered himself and said with an attempt at gravity. 'I'm very glad you've warned me, Cadi. But if we know our faults it's much easier to correct them, so don't worry too much. I never expected perfection of you, you have too strong a character for that. Now . . .' The humour faded from his face to be replaced by a puzzled look, and it was a few moments before he continued. 'There's a question I would like to ask you. I may be wrong, but it seemed to me that when you suddenly felt faint this afternoon you were staring at the picture of Venice that hangs in the hall, as if it was familiar to you. Did you recognize it?'

I was half ashamed of my dream, and it was on the tip of my tongue to say no. But I would have been more ashamed to tell Mr. Morton even a white lie.

'I've seen the house in a dream,' I said awkwardly.

'A dream?'

'Yes. A dream that comes to me quite often.'

'I see. Does anything happen in this dream?'

'Not very much. I come to this house, this palace, in a kind of boat. It must be a gondola, but I didn't realize that before. Somebody is waiting for me in an upper room, and everywhere's dark. I don't know who it is, but it's always the same person. Sometimes I'm very happy, and other times I'm very frightened. But then the dream ends.'

Mr. Morton sat brooding for a full minute, fingering his little beard, then he rose and moved through the open door into the library, beckoning me to follow him. He did not take out a book, but ran a hand lightly along one of the shelves, fingering the bindings gently.

'There are many recorded instances of dreams of premonition,' he said thoughtfully, 'but I have never heard of a recurring dream that was premonitory, and yours is a recurring dream, Cadi.'

I only just understood his words, for I was so taken up with relief that he had not laughed at me.

'Mr. Freud deals at length with recurring dreams and their significance,' he murmured. 'Have you heard of psychology?'

'Only that it's about what happens in people's minds,' I said. 'Miss Rigg told me the meaning but said it wasn't a nice subject.'

He gave a short laugh. 'I doubt if Mr. Freud's books would be considered suitable reading for any lady in this day and age, perhaps rightly so, though I sometimes feel that our Victorian attitudes are unhealthy in this respect. Let us hope the new era will bring a little fresh air into our ways.' He turned away from the shelves. 'However, Mr. Freud's theories are hotly disputed by other explorers of the human condition, and certainly you are too young to be exposed to them for the present. In any event, to read his books calls for a knowledge of German; they have not been translated yet.'

He ran a hand across his scalp, smiling at me. 'We all have our dreams, good and bad, Cadi. Don't worry about yours. It can't harm you. And if Mr. Freud is right, it simply means that there is a deep-seated desire in you for fulfilment of some kind. Time will take care of all that, I think.'

He looked at me sharply. 'Goodness, child, you can hardly hold your eyes open and I'm keeping you from your bed.' He came forward and kissed me on the cheek. 'Off you go now.' I desperately wanted to thank him for all that he was doing for me, but could find no words, so I put my arms about his neck and hugged him for a moment. When he straightened up he blinked quickly several times and half turned away, but said nothing.

After a little hesitation I said, 'Goodnight, Mr. Morton,' and went to the door.

Then he spoke. 'I'm so glad you are here, Cadi,' he said in a rather muffled voice. 'Goodnight, my dear. God bless you.'

As I came into the hall I saw Richard. He did not smile but stood gazing at me with a puzzled air. 'I heard Father *laugh* a few moments ago,' he said. 'He never laughs like that. What on earth did you say to him?'

'I don't know, Richard.' I put a hand to my head, trying to remember. 'It wasn't anything special. I think it was when I told him I had a lot of faults.'

'He never laughs like that,' Richard repeated wonderingly.

There was nothing more I could say, so I wished Richard goodnight and went upstairs. Already my bedroom seemed familiar. The bath had been emptied and put away, the bed re-made and the covers turned down. I undressed, and five minutes later I was in a deep, dreamless sleep. I had drawn back the heavy curtains a few inches because I liked to have a shaft of sunlight coming into the room when I woke, but it was long before dawn when I roused suddenly from sleep.

I lay facing the window, and could see stars in a black

sky through the gap in the curtains, but there was a light from behind me that threw flickering shadows on the walls and ceiling. I turned, and my heart seemed to jump into my mouth. The door of my room was open. Mrs. Morton stood only a pace or two from the bed, holding a candle in a big brass candlestick. She wore a long white nightdress trimmed with lace and ribbons. Her wonderful hair hung loosely down on each side of her face. The candle flame was reflected in her eyes, to give a glittering blend of gold and violet.

She neither moved nor spoke, but stared down upon me with a strange and frantic gaze, and in her eyes there was no recognition at all.

Chapter Four

MY SKIN CRAWLED WITH SHOCK. In the light of the candle I could see that although Mrs. Morton was looking down at me her eyes were empty and unfocused. Then slowly the frantic look faded and her face softened.

'John?' Her voice was clear but not loud, and held great tenderness. 'Ah, you're back from the shooting, darling. I was becoming quite worried about you. Did you get any pigeons?'

I sat up slowly in the bed, shivering a little although the night was warm. 'It's me, Mrs. Morton,' I said in a croaky whisper. 'Cadi.'

'I'm so glad, John dear,' Mrs. Morton said, gazing blankly through me with a fond smile. 'What would you like for tea? The strawberries are really at their best just now.'

The feeling of horror began to lose its edge as my mind struggled to wakefulness and I realized that Mrs. Morton was sleep-walking. But still the eeriness of it all made my nerves creep.

'Strawberries would be very nice, thank you,' I whispered, fighting to keep my voice steady and getting slowly out of bed. My thoughts whirled as I tried to choose the right words. 'But . . . but I think you should have a little nap before tea——'

I broke off as a figure appeared in the open doorway beyond her, and with a great surge of relief I saw that it was Mr. Morton, wearing a dark silk dressing-gown over pyjamas. He made a little gesture with his hand to silence me, and said quietly, 'Yes, a splendid idea. You look rather tired, Helen, and a nap before tea would be just the right thing.'

He took her arm coaxing her towards the door. She moved obediently, and did not resist when he took the candlestick from her hand.

'I was getting quite worried about John,' she said.

'Nothing to worry about, my dear. Come and have your nap.' In the doorway he turned his head to me and mouthed 'Wait, Cadi,' without uttering a sound.

They disappeared along the passage, and I moved to the door feeling shaky inside. I could hear him murmuring as he coaxed her across the gallery and along the passage to her bedroom. Two or three minutes went by before Mr. Morton returned. I whispered, 'Is she all right now?'

He nodded. 'I'm sorry, Cadi. Such a shock for you.' His face looked tired and strained. 'John was our elder son, and this was his room.'

Now I remembered. There had been a son older than Richard, and he had died in a shooting accident.

Mr. Morton said, 'Cadi . . . thank you for keeping so calm and not waking her. Poor dear soul, it would have been very distressing for her. This hasn't happened for a long time now.' He shrugged, and a weary smile touched his lips. 'But, as you see, other people have dreams, too.'

'Yes. And I'm so sorry. About your son, I mean.' I had lost all my own family. It was easy enough for me to feel pity for those who had lost a son. 'Will Mrs. Morton remember in the morning?'

He shook his head. 'No. Say nothing, Cadi. And get back to bed now. You won't be disturbed again.'

I closed the door and climbed into bed, hugging the bed-

71

clothes around me, for I still felt chilled within me. It was a long time before I went to sleep again, and many weeks were to pass before I could close my eyes at night with my mind untroubled by the memory of waking to find Mrs. Morton standing over me.

Except for that nerve-racking incident in the dark hours, my arrival at *Meadhaven* had been much less of an ordeal than I expected. But as the days passed I found myself facing the challenge of putting down new roots, and this was not easy. At first the novelty of my new life carried me along as if on the crest of one of the big rollers that race into Mawstone Bay. Perhaps, too, my coming to the Morton family brought fresh interest into their lives and was stimulating for them. But then came the stage when I knew that the roller beneath me had broken into swirling surf. Homesickness struck hard, I knew times of great melancholy, and I felt renewed grief over my father.

Mr. Morton remained the same as always, he had not fussed over me to begin with, so I did not miss it now, but the rest of the family lost some of their warmth and enthusiasm, and I felt alone and unwanted. It was foolish, of course. They could not continue to treat me as a newly arrived guest for ever, neither could I continue to act as one. This was a natural in-between phase, but I did not realize it then.

I hated Kent. The countryside seemed soft and vulnerable after my native Cornwall, too pretty, and without sinews. Sarah irritated me. She did beautiful needlework and played the piano without too many mistakes, but that was all. She had never gutted a fish or cooked a meal in her life, and was a little awed by everyone and everything, whether it was the vicar, a barking dog or a furry caterpillar. Mrs. Morton changed from day to day, sometimes being quite kindly to me and at other times giving the impression that I was yet another burden life had laid upon her. Richard was always pleasant and courteous, but because I was depressed I chose to think that his manner to me was no more than false politeness. He was studying law at University, and spent quite a lot of time in his room. I imagined he was busy with his books, but Sarah only giggled when I said as much. Whatever he was doing, we had little companionship except for sometimes playing chess in the evenings. Despite my feelings, I was careful never to show any sign of unhappiness, and this must have made my own manner rather forced and unnatural, which did not help to improve matters.

I saw more of the others than of Mr. Morton. He travelled up by train to London on three days in each week, and worked in his study for two days. It soon became clear to me that he was a man of some importance in his profession, for sometimes messengers were sent down from the Ministry with urgent papers for him, and Mrs. Morton occasionally spoke with pride of 'Lord Lansdowne and my husband', or would casually mention, 'As the Minister was saying to Edward the other day. . . .' Also, there was talk of having one of the new telephone machines installed in the house, so that Mr. Morton could talk over the wires to his colleagues in London.

I always felt happy when he was about, and this helped me through the difficult in-between phase. He only once mentioned the incident that occurred on my first night at *Meadhaven*, and that was a few days later when he said, 'Are you sleeping well, Cadi?'

'Yes, thank you, Mr. Morton.' It was true, for although each night I wondered if Mrs. Morton might sleep-walk again, once I was asleep I slept soundly.

'Good.' He hesitated, then went on, 'Would you prefer to move to another room? I don't think my wife will disturb you again, but it is just possible.'

'No, I like the room, Mr. Morton. And I wouldn't be frightened again, now I know.'

He nodded, as if he had expected that answer. 'You're a strong girl, Cadi,' he said slowly. 'It's a gift from your forbears, and you must be grateful for it as that. Those who are strong must have sympathy and understanding for others who find life more difficult.' He was silent for a while, but I knew he had more to say and was searching for the right words. This was something he rarely had to do.

73

'My wife has good physical health,' he went on at last, 'but mentally she has always been rather fine-drawn.' He gave a little wry smile. 'That also is a gift from her forbears, though a less welcome one than yours. Her father was an eccentric man and became . . . somewhat unstable in later life, which distressed her greatly. I believe I helped her to overcome that distress, at least I like to think so. I love her dearly, and I try always to give her my support and understanding.' He shook his head and sighed. 'But life is sometimes harsh, as you well know, my dear. A great tragedy was to fall upon us with the death of my son John . . . such a wasteful, unnecessary death.' He closed his eyes for a moment. 'My wife used to be a very different person before we lost John. I wish you could have known her then.'

He looked at me, lifted his hands in a little gesture, and let them fall to the desk. 'I'll say no more, Cadi. I've only told you this because I feel the more you understand us the more easily you will settle down.'

'Yes, Mr. Morton, and thank you.' But I did not really understand. I had lost all my family, and it had not changed me into a different person. I had yet to learn for myself what Mr. Morton had told me only a few moments ago, that we are not all made in the same mould, and that those who are of stronger fibre should be truly thankful for this gift. But I was glad he had talked to me, for it helped me in the days to come.

After the first excitement of welcoming a new member of the family, Sarah went through a period of resenting me as an intruder. She did not put it into words, but was as brusque with me as her nature would allow her to be. I have no doubt I caused her resentment myself by being unable to hide my frequent irritation with her. When at last this dawned on me I became very angry with Cadi Tregaron, and asked myself how I would have felt if my father had introduced a sharp-tongued, irritable creature into the house.

I think I began to emerge from that unhappy settling-down period when I realized that in some ways I was more at home with Mr. Morton's family than he was himself. That seems a strange thing to say, but it was so. I was much quicker to anticipate Mrs. Morton's moods for one thing. At first, when she might gush fondly over me in the morning and put on a cold, injured air in the afternoon, I was very hurt and troubled. But soon I saw her moods for what they were, simply an outward reflection of what she happened to feel in her vague and muddled mind at any given moment, not necessarily connected with me or with anyone else. And as growing instinct helped me to anticipate her more difficult moods, I could often prevent them with the right word of sympathy, admiration, or apology, whichever was called for. Although I humoured her, I never sank into a milk-and-water attitude with her, I was too naturally stubborn for that, and sometimes I let my stubbornness show, which I think made her respect me.

My irritation towards Sarah grew rapidly less. She was an open book to me, a book with very little written in it, I fear, and I accepted her for what she was, an honest and affectionate girl, childlike in many ways, but good-natured. Mr. Morton was always rather awkward in his manner to her, and I realized that this was simply because he could not enter her mind and did not know what to say to her. He was a clever man and she was a rather dull girl. He loved her, but was at a loss with her. I felt very sad for him. With me, he could chat for hours on end, happy and at ease, ready to explain anything I did not understand, seeking my opinions and listening with a twinkle in his eye. But with his own daughter he could find little contact. If he made a joke, she would look blank, desperately trying to see it. If he commented on something in the newspaper, poor Sarah would get a hunted look in her eyes because she did not know what to say. I knew very well that compared with Mr. Morton I was stupid and ignorant, but I was not ashamed of it and at least I was eager to learn. I never ceased to be thankful for all the hours I had spent in conversation practice with Miss Rigg, for I am sure it was this which gave me confidence.

One thing I could not understand was Mr. Morton's attitude towards Richard. I can only describe it as wary. It seemed to me unfair and unkind, which was quite out of key with Mr. Morton's character. As with father and daughter, so conversation between father and son was oddly stilted, but for a different reason and one I could not fathom. They both seemed to be watchful and on guard.

As my homesickness and settling-down difficulties passed, I realized that Richard's manner towards me was not false, as I had foolishly imagined. His quiet friendliness, his courtesy, his seraphic smile, they were all genuine and quite unforced. I think the last barriers between us went down on the day I visited Richard in a small out-house where he had set up a workshop.

He enjoyed using his hands, it seemed, and the bench was covered with springs, coils, magnets, and many objects I could not recognize. He showed me a miniature steam engine he had made, which turned a little wheel at enormous speed; an ordinary clock with a fixture on the back which made it an alarum clock; a mousetrap with no spring or cage, but with what he called counterweights which operated a guillotine.

When I made a face at this last object he only laughed and asked if I thought a mouse would prefer to be killed by a spring rather than by a knife-edge. His new interest was wireless, and he had diagrams of a wireless receiver he planned to build, which he hoped would pick up signals from Mr. Marconi's machines. I felt very proud to tell him that I knew of Mr. Marconi, because he had come to Cornwall only two or three years ago and put up a wireless station at Poldhu, from which the first ever signals were sent right across the Atlantic.

It was watching Richard as he showed me his work which made me realize the final step needed to make me feel truly at home. The trouble was that I did not have enough to do. In Mawstone I had always been busy, for there was always work to be done. Now it was different. When I thought about it I concluded that most of each day was simply wasted.

How did I spend my time? I went riding quite often, and I was improving rapidly as a horsewoman, but I did not want to spend all day on a horse, particularly as it was always such a sedate affair. I was not allowed to ride alone yet, and either Old Kemp, the stableman, or Young Kemp, the coachman, had to ride with me. Young Kemp, the son, was over sixty, and I think nobody knew what age Old Kemp had attained; he was hardly ever awake, even on a horse, and Young Kemp was dour and lazy. So our rides were not very exciting, and when Sarah joined us it was even worse. She squealed if we broke into a trot, and would ride only Shamrock, the oldest and gentlest of the eight horses in Mr. Morton's stables.

Then again, if I wanted to occupy myself there were hundreds of books for me to read in Mr. Morton's library, but I did not want to read all day. In the afternoons I would often join Sarah in the sewing room, but although I could sew on a button or make a patch well enough, I had little skill in delicate needlework and quickly became impatient.

Earlier on, I had gone down to the kitchens in the hope that I might help with the cooking in some way, but I quickly learned that this was quite out of order. John, the butler, was horrified. He spoke to Mr. Morton about it, who later spoke to me. He seemed very much amused, but told me with regret that I must leave the kitchens and servants' hall strictly to the staff.

Most of our afternoons were spent in paying calls or receiving calls, and making polite conversation over cups of tea and cucumber sandwiches. I really hated that, but to Mrs. Morton and to most of the ladies of our acquaintance it was the most important part of their lives.

Paying calls and leaving cards was a very delicate and complicated matter. I discovered this one evening at dinner, soon after my arrival at *Meadhaven*, when Mrs. Morton was letting her soup go cold during the first of her dinner-time monologues.

'I really cannot think what is to be done about the new people at Little Grange,' she said, shaking her beautiful head in distress. 'The name is Hatton, I am told. But really. Do you know what occurred this afternoon, Edward? I shall tell you. Mrs. Hatton called *here*! Surely she must know that it is for the older resident to call upon the newcomer first. Not only that, but when her carriage arrived she descended herself and rang the doorbell instead of sending the servant with her card!'

Mrs. Morton closed her violet eyes for a moment as if from the stress of the experience.

'She asked John if I were at home. He hardly needed to consult me in order to tell her that I was *not,* of course. And then she left her card—but one *single* card, Edward.'

She turned to me. 'You must realize, Cadi, that a lady should leave *three* cards, one of her own, two of her husband's. That is because the husband is considered to be calling by proxy upon both the master and the mistress of the house.'

She looked along the table towards Mr. Morton again. 'I shall have to call upon her, naturally. But I shall *not* ask if she is at home, and will simply leave cards. That will indicate that I wish our acquaintance to be of the slightest. At least I *hope* she will have sufficient refinement to perceive what is intended, but really one wonders if she has ever been schooled in correct behaviour. Oh, I forgot! She attempted to place her card on the salver John was holding, instead of putting it into his hand. How could she not know such important things? Poor John was quite dismayed by the incident.'

'Your soup is getting cold, my dear,' Mr. Morton said placidly. 'I'm sure John will survive the experience. You know, I sometimes feel that our society rituals are much too rigid. A little healthy nonconformism would be rather refreshing, I fancy.'

I remembered those words of Mr. Morton's when I decided that I must find something useful to do. I had made up my mind what it would be. Old Kemp was very old indeed, and could only potter slowly about his work. The stables in his charge always looked slovenly, and though the horses were cared for they were never groo...ied as well as they should have been. Mr. Morton seemed resigned to this. He had little fancy for riding, and hated hunting, so until my arrival the horses were seldom used except for carriage work. We had a big carriage, a mail phaeton and a dog-cart. Young Kemp was responsible for these, but he took little trouble over his duties and seemed to begrudge whatever energy he expended on them.

I wanted to tackle the stables. I knew I could persuade Richard to make any repairs to the buildings. Then, with old Kemp's help, I would clean the stables and maintain them handsomely. I would groom the horses and make them beautiful. And with Young Kemp's help I would make sure that our carriages sparkled, and see to it that he did his work properly.

When I spoke to Mr. Morton about it one evening in his study, he blinked in surprise. 'But you can't become a stable-boy, Cadi!'

'I wouldn't be, Mr. Morton. I'd just be looking after the stables and horses. It means . . .' I watched him anxiously, 'it means I'd have to wear breeches for working, but I want to do that anyway, for riding. I hate side-saddle. And it would only be for an hour or two each day. Once I've got the stables all repaired and clean, Old Kemp can easily *keep* them clean, becuse I'll look after the horses. I'll make sure I don't get dirty, at least not very dirty, and I'll change as soon as I've finished each day.'

He began to chuckle, but there was doubt in his voice as he said, 'My dear, can you imagine what my wife will say?'

I could well imagine, but I pressed on pleadingly. 'I'll make the carriage horses really beautiful, and I'll see that Young Kemp does the same for the carriages. Mrs. Morton is always saying they're a disgrace.'

'She is indeed,' Mr. Morton agreed with a faint sigh. 'I have been meaning to do something about it myself.'

'But you haven't the time, Mr. Morton. Young Kemp is to blame. He's a lazy old scoundrel and he knows you'll never discharge him, so he takes advantage. But if you let me take charge I'm sure that everything will soon be fine.'

Mr. Morton pondered for a long while in silence, then a faint gleam came into his eye. 'What I simply cannot resist,' he said slowly, 'is the idea of turning you loose on Young Kemp. All right, Cadi, I'll make a bargain with you. You can be in charge of the stables, and you can wear breeches while you're about the job or riding. But you must only supervise the work, except for grooming. I'll let you have the gardener's boy for an hour each day, to help Old Kemp.'

I was so happy I ran to hug him. I was the only one in the house who ever made a fuss of him in this way, and I think it warmed his heart, but he pretended I was being a nuisance.

'Go away and don't pester me any more, child,' he said when I released him. Then he put his head on one side and looked at me strangely for a moment. 'I must stop calling you child,' he said slowly. 'You're a very beautiful young woman, Cadi. And very persuasive. Now be a good girl and let me get on with my work.'

I went to my room and studied myself in the looking-glass. I had one or two good features, but if I was honest with myself I felt that my looks were ordinary enough. It was a matter, I decided, of beauty lying in the eye of the beholder. Mr. Morton saw me that way because he was very fond of me.

Mrs. Morton was full of protest when he first told her that I was to be in charge of the stables. Mr. Morton allowed her to talk herself into silence, and then said amiably, 'You must not worry about what people will think, my dear. In a sense we shall be doing them a good turn by giving them something to gossip about, but it will soon pass. You'll see.'

Without dramatics for once, Mrs. Morton said quite gently and with genuine anxiety, 'But Edward, I don't want our Cadi to become one of these—these masculine tomboys.' I warmed to her for the way she had spoken of 'our Cadi'. Sometimes a glimpse of the woman she had once been peeped out from the depths.

'I hardly think Cadi could ever be called masculine,' Mr. Morton said, and patted her hand. 'I believe very soon you will have young men calling and leaving their cards, Helen.'

Sarah squealed with delight, and Mrs. Morton became quite pink and flustered. I felt no excitement myself, for although most of the young men I had met while visiting were quite pleasant, I was not interested in any of them, and I very much hoped that Mrs. Morton would not begin match-making. However, she had been diverted by her husband's words and made no further protest about my new project.

In three weeks I transformed the stables. There were several bitter and stubborn battles with Young Kemp at first, but in the end he saw that my mind was made up, and resigned himself to working harder. Mr. Morton was delighted, and called it a famous victory.

Then I found another occupation which pleased Mrs. Morton more. Two miles away was a small orphanage, and after talking with the vicar I began to visit the orphanage on three afternoons each week to teach a dozen of the younger children their letters and numbers. Because this was charitable work it was quite acceptable in our circle of acquaintances, and I think in a way it helped to make up for the peculiar behaviour of 'the Tregaron girl', who wore breeches for riding and actually groomed horses with her own hands.

And so, as the weeks went by, I found my own way of settling down in my new life. The strangeness of it all faded, and I was content. Now that the sharpness of my grief had passed, I could think of my mother and father, and of Granny Caterina, without the heartache becoming unbearable. I rarely spoke of them, because none of the Mortons ever asked me about the past. I think they refrained during the first few weeks after my arrival, to avoid making me unhappy by reminding me of my loss; and this became an unconscious habit which continued.

I did not mind, for in a way my memories seemed very private and precious to me. Often when I was in my bedroom at night I would gaze out over the moonlit garden and remember my own people. I still made up stories about the way my grandfather had rescued Granny Caterina so many years ago and brought her home to Cornwall, her memory a blank. Several times I tried to contrive a story about her which involved the palace in Venice, but I could never make the details fit together.

The Dream came to me only once during those early weeks at *Meadhaven*, and it was the Good Dream. Often as I passed through the hall I would stop and gaze at the picture of the palace in Venice. Was this really the setting of my dream? Perhaps it had only become so because the reality of the picture was imposed on the hazy memory of what I saw in the dream. Yet deep within me I knew that the memory

81

was not hazy. Could I, in some strange way, have dreamt the *same* dream as some foreign artist who perhaps had been dead for many years now and who had set down in paint on canvas the place of his sleeping vision?

That thought was settled when Mr. Morton called me into his study one morning.

'I have been making inquiries about the Venice scene from the dealer who sold me the picture, Cadi,' he said, his expression a mixture of amusement and bafflement. 'This had taken some time, since he had to write to a dealer in Venice, but apparently the picture was not painted from imagination. The house, or palazzo as it should be called, is some four hundred years old and still stands on the Canal Grande, near the Ponte di Rialto.'

'Then . . . it's *real?*' I said a little breathlessly.

'Very much so. It is called the Palazzo Chiavelli, and part of it is still occupied by descendants of Count Chiavelli, who built it in the sixteenth century. Does the name Chiavelli mean anything to you?'

I shook my head. 'No . . . I've never heard of it before, Mr. Morton.'

'Well . . .' He shrugged 'Apparently the picture is well over a hundred years old, so perhaps you once saw a copy of it in a book of Miss Rigg's, but have forttotten about it except in your dream, when it comes back to you.'

'Perhaps,' I said doubtfully. 'But I don't think so.'

He smiled. 'I would like not to think so. I find the mysteries of the subconscious mind most fascinating. It would be much more exciting if one day we discovered an explanation for your dream which did not simply depend on some forgotten picture seen in childhood.'

'But . . . what sort of explanation, Mr. Morton?'

'Heavens, my dear, I don't know. There are so many mysteries in life, so much to baffle and bewilder us.' He gazed musingly into the distance. 'Perhaps if we go to Venice next year we may be able to visit this palazzo of yours.'

I caught my breath, and felt a pang of simultaneous fear and longing. He looked at me sharply, saying, 'Does the idea alarm you?'

I hesitated. 'Yes, it does a little, but I don't know why.'

'Then you wouldn't wish to go?'

'Oh, yes! I'd love to, Mr. Morton. Being a little bit afraid doesn't make any difference.'

He laughed and said, 'You're a joy to me, Cadi. But let's not worry about Venice just now. We have the end-of-summer ball to think of.'

I had been thinking of little else, for the ball was only three days away now. I had spent hours in my bedroom while Betty practised putting up my hair, and preparations had been going on all week. Mr. Morton and Mrs. Beale, the cook-housekeeper, dealt with everything, but a dozen times a day Mrs. Morton clasped a hand to her brow and declared that it was too much, she could bear it no longer, her nerves would break under the strain of all she had to do.

I was so excited I could hardly sleep. A new dress had been specially bought for me, and I was almost in tears when I thanked Mr. and Mrs. Morton for it. Sarah danced with rapture. I snapped at her and reduced her to tears, then ran after her to her bedroom to apologize and comfort her.

At last the great moment came. The huge drawing room had been cleared for dancing, the furniture had been re-arranged in the hall, dining room and sewing room, so that the older people could sit out if they wished to. We had all prayed for fine weather, and we were fortunate. Twilight came with no cloud in the sky, and a magnificent buffet supper was set out on long trestle-tables in the garden, with white linen cloths and sparkling silver. Lanterns had been set in the trees, to cast a shimmering light over the whole magical scene. In the house there were cut flowers everywhere.

I stood in my wonderful new dress, gazing about me, remembering every detail so that I could write about it in my next letter to Miss Rigg. There would be the dress to describe, too. It was of cornflower silk, with long close-fitting sleeves of matching lace, and cuffs which fell over my hands in points. The neckline was wide, with a white bertha collar. My evening shoes were of satin, matching the dress. Betty had been thrilled with my hair. She had drawn back the front in a pompadour, with little sidepuffs over my temples, then taken the back hair up in a rounded puff and pinned it under the pompadour.

At the front of the house a long red carpet had been laid out and an awning set up. Soon the carriages began to arrive, and from within the house came the sound of the small orchestra playing *Valse Bleu* as we stood receiving our guests. It made my heart beat a little faster to think of them as 'our' guests. I was part of the Morton family now.

The early formalities seemed to go on for an age, but at last they were over and dancing began. For the past three weeks I had been practising every evening with Richard and Sarah, under Mrs. Morton's guidance. Most of the dancing would consist of waltzes, I was told, though there would be a polka, a set of lancers, and possibly a two-step. Mrs. Morton was uneasy about the two-step, but she had no doubts whatever about the new practice of reversing in the waltz. 'Should you be asked if you reverse, Cadi, you must say *"no"* in a slightly haughty tone. Reversing is considered to be rather *fast* by the best people.'

All the same, I had practised reversing with Sarah in my bedroom when we should have been asleep. I loved dancing. I suppose I was light on my feet, for I always felt as if I was floating, but Mrs. Morton's pleasure at my quick accomplishment was marred by certain doubts. 'If only you could move in a rather more *ladylike* manner, Cadi,' she had said several times. 'A little more controlled, dear, a little less free and exuberant, perhaps.'

But I could not contain my exuberance. My programme was soon filled, and I found myself dancing with one young man after another. I was hot, and knew that I was glowing more than was strictly correct, but I was having the happiest time of my life. The young men talked to me, took me out to the laden buffet tables, brought me fruit-cup to drink, and paid me compliments. I chattered furiously, and yet I hardly noticed them. They might all have been the same person for all I knew.

Then Mr. Morton was standing in front of me, his bald head gleaming in the gaslight, looking splendid in his tails and white tie. He gave me that funny, slightly mournful smile I had come to know so well, and said, 'I'm sure you haven't a dance left for me, Cadi.'

'This one, Mr. Morton.' I stood up and smiled at the young man who had been hovering over me. 'I'm afraid you will have to excuse me.'

To my surprise, Mr. Morton danced very well. 'How lucky I was to come along just at that moment, Cadi,' he said as we whirled across the floor. 'But I'm astonished that you had a space on your programme.'

'I didn't. I just told all the young men they could only write their names down provisionally, and that if *you* asked me to dance they would have to stand down.'

'You—you said *that*?' He held me at arm's length as we spun round, his eyes wide. 'Provisional bookings! Dear heaven, what will my wife say?' Then he threw back his head and roared with laughter so loud and long that people turned to look at us. I could see no joke, and felt he was laughing because he was proud and happy over what I had done, which made me happy in turn, though it seemed to me a very small thing to have kept a dance for the man I loved best in the world after my father.

It was almost midnight, and a young man had just returned me to my seat beside Mrs. Morton, when I looked across the thronged room and almost jumped out of my skin. Sarah was coming towards us, her face glowing with delight as she towed a reluctant man behind her, holding him by the hand. The man was Lucian Farrel.

'It's cousin Lucian!' Sarah was calling. 'He's just arrived! Oh, isn't it lovely!'

Mrs. Morton seemed pleased but at the same time flustered as he bent to kiss her cheek and said, 'Good evening, Aunt Helen.'

She flapped her hands about helplessly. 'Why, Lucian, my dear boy. What a surprise! How well you look. Are you staying for a while? I'll have a room made ready. Have you come down from London? You must be so tired. Perhaps you . . . perhaps you would like to have a meal sent up to your room now?' She said the last words almost hopefully.

Lucian said, 'If you wish. I don't want to be an embarrassment to you, Aunt Helen.'

Mr. Morton had joined us. He patted Lucian on the shoulder and said, 'Nonsense, my dear nephew. I'm sure you didn't arrive in evening dress to spend the time in your room.'

'O, my prophetic soul, mine uncle,' Lucian exclaimed gravely and shook hands.

'What was that about your soul, Lucian?' Mrs. Morton asked distractedly.

'He was quoting from Hamlet, my dear,' Mr. Morton replied. 'A Shakespearian play, you may remember.' Then, to Lucian, in that dry, half-mocking manner they used with one another, 'You must not be persuaded to withdraw from our merrymaking, Lucian. Think how disappointed all these good people would be.'

Lucian gazed round the room, his dark flaring eyebrows giving him a strongly satanic air. I noticed that glances were being darted at him, whispers were being exchanged, and I had an impression of some consternation among the company.

'I feel they should have the opportunity to show their pleasure,' Lucian said ironically. 'Do you mind, Uncle Edward?'

Mr. Morton waved a hand and smiled, but I saw that his eyes were serious. 'I am always fascinated by human nature, Lucian, and I think perhaps it is time you tested the atmosphere here once again.'

I could not understand the meaning behind their words, but before I had time to think about it Mr. Morton was saying, 'But first let me re-introduce you to the latest member of my family. You have met before, of course, and I wrote to tell you about her joining us. Lucian Farrel . . . Miss Cadi Tregaron.'

Lucian's eyebrows became straight diagonal lines as he gazed at me. 'Well I'm damned,' he said softly, and I heard Mrs. Morton give a little tutting gasp of protest. He put out his hand to take mine. 'Hallo again, Cadi. Did the blue dress fit you?'

'It was perfect, thank you, Mr. Farrel.'

'I was grieved to hear about your father. He was a fine man.' Though the words were sympathetic his voice was abrupt, and I could not judge how sincere he was.

'You're very kind, Mr. Farrel.'

'I've rarely been accused of that.' He was still holding my hand, looking down at me, unsmiling. 'Have you made any more rescues recently?'

'She has rescued us all from boredom,' said Mr. Morton. 'She gallops around in breeches, bullies Young Kemp into submission, has transformed the stables, teaches at Weald-hurst Orphanage, dances too exuberantly——'

'I must test that exuberance one day,' Lucian broke in, and released my hand. 'But it would hardly be fair to her tonight.' He looked speculatively around the room. 'Now, who shall the victim be? Mrs. Garner's red-nosed daughter will have her usual empty programme, I imagine.' He gave us a little bow. 'Excuse me, ladies.'

I wondered, with some annoyance at myself, why I had jumped so at sight of Lucian Farrel. He had not been expected, true, but there was nothing very surprising about his arrival. Yet seeing his face had made me start as if at some sudden danger, which was absurd.

The orchestra had begun a new dance, and a dozen couples were on the floor. I saw Lucian lead out Mrs. Garner's daughter, who was twenty-four now, and who, so everybody said, was very much on the shelf, poor soul. Then young David Steadman appeared, to claim me for this dance.

He was a rather nervous boy, and kept turning his head to look about him as we danced. I noticed with some surprise that the couples on the floor had dwindled by almost half, and as we turned I saw three more couples leave the floor, then another two. Everywhere there seemed to be rather grim, embarrassed faces, though the embarrassment was tinged by a kind of awed excitement. I glimpsed Mrs. Morton fluttering her fan furiously as if she were close to fainting. Sarah seemed about to cry. I could not see Richard, but Mr. Morton stood gazing at the scene with apparent calm.

There were only two couples on the floor now—ourselves, and Lucian with Dorothy Garner. My partner whispered anxiously, 'We . . . we'd better sit this dance out, I think.'

'Why?' I asked sharply.

'Well . . . you know.' He stumbled over my feet in his confusion. 'Because of Lucian Farrel.' Then without further asking he stopped dancing, took my arm, and hurried me back to where Mrs. Morton sat.

Lucian and his partner continued. He was smiling a little, a touch of arrogance in his expression, talking politely to her and seemingly unaware that they were alone. I saw Dorothy's scarlet, anguished face as her head twisted from side to side. Then she whispered urgently to Lucian and stopped dancing. He bowed to her, and as he did so she turned and hurried off the floor before he could escort her.

The orchestra played on. People gathered in little groups and began to talk with false brightness. Lucian stood alone, looking slowly round, his face without expression. I could not think why he had been treated in this way, though from his cryptic conversation with Mr. Morton I vaguely realized now that they had both half expected this.

Sudden anger rose up inside me, and my quick temper snapped. I was still unsure that I liked Lucian Farrel, but he was a member of the family, my family now, and I would not simply stand by and see him insulted in this way. Whatever anybody else thought, I knew deep down in my heart that this was a moment for Cadi Tregaron to stand up and be counted.

It took all the courage I could muster, but I tried to look quite calm and at ease as I began to move forward. I heard Mrs. Morton gasp, 'No, Cadi!' Then Mr. Morton's voice, soft but decisive, saying, 'Let her go.'

I walked out and stood in front of Lucian, my face fixed in what I hoped was a serene smile. He alone could have heard me above the music as I said, 'My partner has deserted me, Mr. Farrel. Would you care to take his place?'

Chapter Five

FOR THE FIRST TIME, and for a brief moment, I saw Lucian Farrel taken aback. Then, under the sound of the music, he said short and sharp, 'Don't be a fool, Cadi.'

Still smiling, I said through clenched teeth, 'I shall indeed look a fool if you refuse me, Mr. Farrel.'

I saw wonderment in his face, then he smiled, and again I jumped inwardly as if some nerve had been touched. The smile made him a different man, yet a man I knew, for this was the face of the man who awaited me in the house in Venice when I dreamt the Good Dream.

'Call me Lucian, please,' he said. 'After all, we're adopted cousins now.' He lifted his arms to take me into the dance. Then we were whirling round the empty floor, and it was as if I danced on air.

'My God,' he said softly, and laughed. 'You seem to make a profession of rescue work, Cadi.'

Mr. Morton had once spoken of him as an outcast, and now I had seen him treated as one. I wondered what lay behind it all, but at this moment I was too much taken up by the joy of the dance to ask questions, and I did not care that we were alone on the floor. But we were not alone for long. I saw Richard, his face tranquil and angelic as ever but a little paler than usual, cross the floor and lead Sarah out. Then Mr. Morton was dancing with his wife; her eyes were closed, her face stiff with embarrassment, and I knew that this was one of the very rare occasions when he had exerted his authority over her.

Mr. Holmes, who was a governor of the Wealdhurst Orphanage, took his wife on to the floor. He smiled at me as we passed. One by one, other couples joined us. There were still many people who stood firm and looked on, some disapproving, some hesitant and a little ashamed, but when the dance ended there were more than a dozen couples on the floor.

Mr. Morton was waiting for us when Lucian escorted me to my seat. 'As I was remarking, Lucian,' he said blandly, 'she is a most unladylike minx. But she has one or two good points, perhaps.'

'We are none of us all bad, Uncle Edward,' Lucian replied solemnly. 'And one must at least give Cadi credit for her knack of tipping the scales.'

Mr. Morton laughed and took my hand as I stood beside him, holding it so tightly that it almost hurt. I think he must have been very happy, for his eyes were glistening. 'She is a constant trial to me, of course,' he said, 'but I feel she initiated a modest swing of local opinion tonight.'

Lucian nodded, saying nothing, looking at me with an expression I could not read.

Mrs. Morton said feebly, 'I thought I was going to *die*, Edward. When Cadi walked out on to that empty floor, oh, the brazenness of it! My heart palpitated so, I was quite *sure* I would die.'

'We are all very glad you were mistaken, my dear,' Mr. Morton said soothingly. 'Sarah, run and fetch your mother a glass of champagne.'

The orchestra struck up a new dance, and my partner came to claim me. The buzz of excitement over the incident was dying down now, and soon all was normal once more. Mr. Morton and Lucian went out into the garden, and I did not see either of them dance again. An hour later, when the ball ended, I stood with Mr. Morton and the family as the guests made their farewells. One or two showed some signs of awkwardness, but only one made any reference to what had happened. That was old Colonel Rodsley, who, as he shook hands said, 'Sorry I had to call young Felicity and her partner off the floor, Morton. No offence to you intended, but if I'd known that nephew of yours would be here, we'd not have come.'

'I'll let you know another time, Colonel,' Mr. Morton said pleasantly.

I am sure that his meaning did not sink in at once, for Colonel Rodsley had reached the bottom of the steps before he stopped short, turned, and glared.

That night, when the house was quiet, Sarah crept into my room, as I knew she would. 'Wasn't it wonderful, Cadi?'

she breathed as she sat on my bed. 'And wasn't it simply thrilling that Lucian came? Do you think he likes me?'

'I'm not sure that Lucian likes anybody except your father.'

'Oh, they've always been good friends. But Lucian did bring me a plate of trifle in the garden. I'm *sure* he likes me.'

'What has he done, Sarah?' I asked. 'Why did everybody turn their backs on him and stop dancing?'

The corners of her mouth drooped, and she plucked at the bedcovers. 'Oh, it was because of that thing in the war,' she said sullenly.

'In the war?'

'Yes, silly. The South African war against the Boers. Lucian was a cavalry officer.'

I don't know why I was surprised. I had reason to know that Lucian was a superb horseman, and I remembered my father's impression that he was quick and handy, like a soldier. I knew about the war, too, for Miss Rigg had made me read some of the reports in *The Times*.

'What did he *do*?' I asked Sarah.

'He got cashiered from his regiment,' she said reluctantly.

'Cashiered?' I echoed. 'That means dismissed, doesn't it?'

'Yes. It was all very mysterious, and it wasn't in the newspapers. I think Papa had something to do with that.' Her eyes filled with tears. 'But it leaked out. And being cashiered is a terrible disgrace, Cadi.'

I was very shaken as I said, 'But you still haven't told me what Lucian did.'

'Oh, I don't know exactly.' She tossed her head petulantly. 'I don't think many people really know, but he was cashiered for being a coward, so everyone says, especially that old Colonel Rodsley.'

I remembered Lucian in the boat that day, when Mogg Race had almost taken us, and I shook my head. In many ways Lucian Farrel was still a mystery to me. For all I knew he might well be capable of misbehaviour over money, or over a woman, or over something to do with army discipline, but he was not a coward.

'They're wrong, Sarah,' I said.

She shrugged. 'I don't care anyway. I love him whatever he's done. Papa says people will forget in time, but it's been going on for nearly three years already.' She sighed heavily.

Now I knew why Lucian was an outcast, and I understood the incident in the ballroom. One or two of the guests had turned their backs on him and the rest had followed like sheep, but because I had danced with him there were a few who had been shamed into a show of courtesy, for Mr. Morton's sake if not for Lucian's.

Although it was so late I was a long time going to sleep when Sarah had left, for my mind was busy re-living every moment of the evening and wondering about Lucian Farrel. That night I had the Bad Dream. It was more clear than ever before, and I woke from it crying with fright. This made me angry with myself. I had no fear of Lucian while I was awake, so why should I be so stupid in my dream?

It was strange to have Lucian with us at breakfast, and I learned that he was staying for a few days. Apart from wishing me good morning, he did not talk to me but chatted quietly at one end of the table with Mr. Morton, while the rest of us listened to Mrs. Morton as she wondered how she would ever find the strength to get the house in order after the ball.

Sarah spent the whole of breakfast gazing adoringly at Lucian. Richard looked even paler than usual, and hardly raised his eyes from his plate, but when he did so I noticed that he was unsmiling, and that he darted a glance from Lucian to me before lowering his eyes again.

After breakfast I changed into a shirt and breeches, plaited my hair in two pigtails, and went out to the stables. My riding had improved so much that for over a fortnight now I had been allowed to take Pompey out on my own. He was a fine, spirited horse, but I loved the feel of him beneath me and we were good friends. Because of his fiery spirit he had to be held in when we galloped, but I had strong hands and wrists and could manage him easily enough.

When I had set Young Kemp to work I saddled up Pompey and led him out. I felt that I wanted a good fast ride, with the wind buffeting my face to blow the cobwebs away. There was a gate in the mellow brick wall which hemmed the grounds of *Meadhaven*, and from the gate a bridle path ran beside fields until it reached a long grassy slope which lay like a quilt of green on the hillside. From the crest of the hill I could look far out over the Weald of Kent, all gold and green at this time of year.

The ridge of the hill was over a mile long, and a beautiful place for a gallop. Pompey seemed to catch my mood, for when I nudged him with my heels he gathered himself and broke from an easy canter into a gallop that made my pigtailed hair fly out behind me. His hooves drummed on the turf as his powerful body was unleashed beneath me. But he was under control, and I heard myself laugh with exhilaration at the pleasure that came from feeling his obedience to a touch of the rein or pressure of the knee.

I reined him in gradually as we reached the end of the ridge, and walked him round in a circle for a few moments so that he could get his breath. To one side lay the slope up which I had come. On the other side was the far slope of the hill. I was not allowed to ride down there, for at the bottom lay a stretch of woodland. A horse entering the woods fast after a downhill gallop could easily dash its rider against a tree or an overhanging branch.

I sat easily in the saddle, thinking how lucky I was. Mrs. Morton had not wanted me to ride Pompey, and had not wanted me to ride unescorted, but Mr. Morton had prevailed against her, as he always did when his mind was made up. The land as far as the woods was his, and he saw no reason why I should not ride over his private land as I pleased in daylight hours, whether it was thought ladylike or not.

I turned Pompey to face along the ridge again, and as I set him to a gallop I glimpsed from the corner of my eye the figure of a rider coming up the hillside to my right, from the direction of *Meadhaven*. I thought it was Lucian, but had no time to stare, for Pompey was racing along, his body bunching and stretching in a joyous gallop.

It was then that something snapped, and the rein in my

right hand went slack. An instant later Pompey had veered to the left, almost unseating me, and then he was flying down the forbidden slope towards the woods below, out of control.

His speed was so great that it felt almost like falling down a cliff. I could not even see the end of the broken rein, much less reach it, and to tug only on the left rein would surely make him cross his legs on that slope and cause a dreadful fall. I clung to his mane, and could sense that he was in a panic now. Free of guidance, he could only plunge madly on, driven by his own blind fright.

I talked to him, trying to make my voice soothing and unafraid, my legs clamped fiercely to his ribs, but he was beyond all hope of stopping. The line of trees was very close now, no more than fifty yards away. Pompey was nimble on his feet, and might with good luck weave his way through the woods for a little while without taking a tumble, even at this speed. But a briar, or a root, or a hollow in the ground could trip him, and even if he kept his feet I could be scraped off against the trunk of a tree or by a low branch.

There was another danger, even closer. Ahead of us, a few paces from the woods, lay the remains of a demolished hayrick, a brown and gold pile of half rotted hay, which stood almost as high as Pompey's shoulder. He was racing straight for it, and I was certain he would attempt to jump it in his panic. He could never clear that obstacle. His feet would be caught and I would be thrown over his head, then he would fall, somersaulting perhaps, rolling on me.

Yet even as I braced myself hopelessly for the jump, Pompey swerved very slightly to miss the demolished rick. We would leave it close on our left as we passed. I cannot remember any clear thought, but instinct must have told me my one hope of escape. I kicked my feet free of the stirrups and let myself slip sideways a little, still clinging to his mane, my right leg hooked over his spine, my left knee drawn up against his flank.

As we passed within an arm's length of the pile of hay I let go with my hands and thrust against Pompey's flank with all the strength of my bent left leg, pushing myself away from him. Feet in the air, I landed on my shoulders and was engulfed in hay as I plunged down.

Then all was still. The hay was compressed beneath me like a cushion, damp here at the bottom of the pile, and rose up like a cocoon all about me. Faintly I could hear the fading sound of Pompey's hooves as he flung himself into the woods. For several moments I could not move, but lay there shivering as if from cold, marvelling at my escape, not wanting to emerge from this strange haven.

There came the sound of other hooves, thundering down the slope of the hill. Lucian's voice shouted, 'Cadi!' A moment before I had been cold with shock, now I was suddenly hot with shame. Lucian must have been well up the other side of the hill when the rein broke and Pompey bolted. He must have seen the end of my downhill gallop from the ridge. Surely no young woman could have been thrown in a more undignified way, hurling herself upside down into a pile of rotting hay.

'Cadi!' His voice was close now. I heard the slither of hooves as he wrenched his horse to a halt, and running footsteps as he came towards the hay. 'Cadi! Are you all right?' His voice was sharp as a sword, and seemed to be more angry than concerned.

Scowling, I found my feet and began to stand up. 'I'm all right,' I said. My head emerged from the hay, and I had to trample a lot of it under my feet before I could stand up waist deep, plucking dry wisps from my hair, my ears, my mouth. Lucian stared. When he spoke, the anger had gone from his voice but it still sounded strange.

'You're not hurt?'

'Of course I'm not hurt—I just said so!' I beat furiously at the hay that entangled me. 'Aren't you going to help, instead of just looking?'

He came forward, reached out and took me under the arms, then gave one heave which plucked me out of the hay and set me on my feet in front of him with a single movement.

'The rein broke,' I said, glaring at him.

95

I must have looked like a scarecrow, but I was too angry at knowing Lucian had seen me thrown to have any thought to spare for my appearance. His lips compressed, then suddenly he began to laugh, unable to help himself.

'Don't you *dare* laugh!' I said furiously. 'It would have been the same for you if your rein had broken!'

He shook his head and waved a hand apologetically as he tried to speak. 'I wasn't laughing because you took a fall, Cadi . . .' another convulsion of laughter, 'it was . . . look at you!'

I looked down at myself. My breeches and shirt were blotched by damp from the rotting hay, and wisps of dry hay were stuck all over me. I could imagine what my face and hair looked like, and the picture I must have made when I rose up out of the pile of hay.

I started to giggle, and then remembered Pompey. 'We have to find Pompey,' I said anxiously. 'He may be hurt.'

Lucian's face changed and he turned to Adam, a big roan and our second best horse, which he had taken from the stables. 'Will you rest here or come with me?' His voice was brusque once again.

'I'll come.'

He swung up into the saddle and reached a hand down to me just as he had done two years before in Mawstone. 'We seem fated to ride double,' he said with a dry smile as he lifted me.

I sat behind him in the saddle, and held his waist. It was strange to be in exactly the same position as when we had first met. Adam entered the woods at a walk, and I began calling. I had little hope that we would find Pompey unharmed, and as the minutes passed my heart sank lower.

Then at last we were through the belt of trees, and I heard Lucian exclaim. Pompey was trotting fretfully in a circle on the pasture which lay ahead of us. We rode towards him slowly, and I kept calling his name. When we were twenty paces away he stood still, poised for flight. I slipped from the saddle and edged forward, talking to him gently, soothingly. Suddenly he trotted towards me and nuzzled my shoulder.

'Poor Pompey, poor old boy,' I said, making a fuss of him.

'Did you have an awful fright? Never mind. Let's see if you're all right.'

'Hold him while I look,' said Lucian, who had dismounted now. With firm but unhurried movements he checked Pompey's legs one by one, and it was clear to me that he knew what he was about. 'Just this graze along his right flank,' he said at last, and I moved round to the other side of Pompey's head to look. It was more than a graze. A broken-off branch, or something of that sort, had made a long gash along Pompey's side. It was not serious, but I felt cold again when I thought what would have happened to my leg if I had been in the saddle.

'Never mind, Pompey love,' I said, patting him gently. 'We'll see to it when we get home.'

I heard Lucian catch his breath, and turned to look at him. He held the end of the broken rein in his hand, but the rein itself had not broken. The ring connecting it to the cheek-bar of the snaffle had snapped and been jerked free. The ring was still attached to the end of the rein, pulled slightly out of shape now, and with the gap in it showing clearly. Lucian twisted it away from the leather.

'I've never heard of a ring breaking,' I said in wonder, and reached out to take it. Lucian hesitated, and I sensed reluctance in him as he put the broken ring in my hand. I peered at it closely, thinking there might have been some hidden fault in the metal. Then I knew what had made Lucian catch his breath. At the point where the ring had broken it was very thin, unnaturally thin. But this was not from wear. It could not be, for wear makes metal smooth, and the brass at this point was not smooth but slightly rough, for all the world as if it had been filed down almost to breaking point.

I lifted my eyes to Lucian. He was not looking at me but was gazing past me, eyebrows flaring like a demon's over the blue eyes, and in his face that bitter fury I had seen once before. This was his face as I had first seen it on Mawstone quay, as he gazed at the broken rudder pintle which had almost caused Mr. Morton's death. 'Half sawn through . . .' he had said at the time, though Mr. Morton had brushed the idea aside as a mistake.

97

And now I had nearly been killed, or at least badly injured, because the ring on Pompey's snaffle had been filed thin. I could not begin to understand it all. I only knew that I felt sick inside.

'I've known these rings break before,' Lucian said, and took it from me. His face was impassive again now.

'But that didn't just break!' I cried.

He lifted a hand quickly to silence me. 'Please, Cadi. Don't imagine things. If anyone wanted to harm you, this would be a foolish way to do it. A weak ring could snap at any time, it was only by chance that it snapped when you were galloping. And besides, who in the world would wish you ill? Mr. or Mrs. Morton? Sarah or Richard?' He looked at me intently. 'Or me?'

I shook my head slowly, beginning to doubt what I had been so sure of a moment ago. Lucian's questions made the whole thing absurd. For a fleeting moment I thought of Young Kemp, and then was ashamed. Despite his sour manner and brusque speech, that surly old man had grown to like me over the past few weeks as much as he would ever like anybody, I was sure of that, and it was beyond belief that he would try to harm me.

'You must be right,' I said at last, and began to pluck away wisps of hay that still stuck to me. 'Have I got any hay in my hair? If I'm seen riding in, I don't want to look like a scarecrow.

'Keep still a moment.' He pulled some pieces of hay from above my brow, then turned me round and picked a few wisps from my pigtails and from the back of my shirt. I felt suddenly shy at the touch of his hands. 'You'll do,' he said at last. 'Are we going to tell Mr. Morton that you took a fall?'

'I'll have to,' I said, and sighed, wondering if my riding would be restricted in future. 'Not telling him would be like telling lies.'

'I see. And do you never tell lies?'

'Sometimes, I suppose. But not to Mr. Morton.'

One of those strange devil-eyebrows twisted up while the other remained straight, and Lucian laughed softly. 'You don't set limits on your loyalty, Cadi, do you?'

I did not understand what he meant, but without waiting for a reply he turned and led Adam forward. 'You'd better ride Adam. I'll walk with Pompey.'

'No,' I said quickly. 'I want to ride Pompey home, or he'll think I don't trust him any more. Can you mend the rein so it will hold if he just moves at a walk?'

Lucian hesitated, then gave a half smile and a resigned shrug. 'I expect so.' We walked the horses across the foot of the slope to where a wire fence ran down one side of the hill. There Lucian broke a short strand from the fence and made a makeshift repair to fix the rein to the snaffle. He gave me a leg-up, mounted Adam, and we set off for *Meadhaven* at a slow walk.

There was no more conversation between us. Lucian rode in silence, and when I glanced at him I saw that his mood had changed again. He was staring down at the ground ahead, brows low over his eyes, seemingly unaware of my presence. There was anger in him, a menacing anger that made him alien to me and a little frightening. I could see no reason for it, could not understand him, but then I had never understood Lucian Farrel in the few brief encounters we had had. Perhaps, I thought with sudden impatience, he was angry with himself for having been pleasant to me for a few moments.

With that, I dropped a pace or two behind and talked to Pompey all the way home.

This was one of the days when Mr. Morton had not gone to London, so I did not have to delay in telling him about the fall I had taken, but first I spent ten minutes soothing Pompey while Young Kemp and Lucian attended to his hurt.

Before going to Mr. Morton's study I washed and changed, undoing the pigtails I wore when riding, and putting my hair up in the new grown-up style, then went down to tell my tale.

'It was just one chance in a thousand that the ring broke,' I ended. 'Please don't say I mustn't ride Pompey again, Mr. Morton.'

He looked at me with affectionate exasperation. 'Really

Cadi, that's exactly what I ought to say, for your own safety. But I find it rather difficult to refuse you anything.' He wrinkled his brow as if wondering why. 'Now I come to think of it you very rarely make any requests, and certainly never for the things a young woman usually wants. Oh, you're delighted to have a new dress or new gloves, but you've never asked for anything like that.'

I was surprised. There had never been any need to ask. Mr. Morton always provided all I could ever want without asking.

I told him so, and he laughed.

While he was chuckling I said, 'I'll be very careful with Pompey, and I'll make sure Young Kemp inspects all the harness and saddlery.' I was trying to keep any hint of wheedling out of my voice. I had heard Sarah wheedling her mother when she wanted something, and I did not wish to sound like that.

Mr. Morton rubbed his head. 'All right,' he said at last. 'I'll make no restrictions, Cadi. Nobody can live a full life without some element of risk, and I sometimes think women are too sheltered and pampered these days. It's not good for them, and deep down they don't like it. Sooner or later we shall have an explosion from the female sex, mark my words. We have a new king on the throne and there's a new spirit in the air——' He broke off and shook his head, smiling. 'But you don't want a lecture on trends in modern society, I'm sure. You just want to know that you can continue riding Pompey. Well, so be it.'

Now I let my pleasure show, and ran to kiss his cheek as he sat at his desk.

'Off with you,' he said, but putting an arm round my shoulders to return the hug. 'I've work to do, and no time for fuss and nonsense. You only do it to annoy me.'

'I'll be better behaved next time,' I said as I released him, but he knew I did not mean it. He tugged at his little beard and gave me his funny owlish look. 'And what will it be next time, I wonder, young lady? Oh well, I'll say this for you, Cadi, you always do your fussing *after* you've persuaded me, not before. Now run along and be careful.'

As I reached the study door he called to me in a voice so sharp that I was startled. 'Cadi!'

I turned, and saw that he was standing up, looking at me with sudden anxiety. 'What is it, Mr. Morton?'

'The ring that broke.' He spoke casually now, but it seemed to me that he was making an effort to do so. 'Did you bring it home with you?'

I had to think for a moment. 'No . . . I believe Lucian threw it away when he mended the rein. Was it important?'

He shrugged. 'Not really. I was just wondering how it came to break. Did you examine it?'

I hesitated for a second. 'It just seemed to have worn thin in one place. That's what Lucian said.'

'I see.' There was a blend of relief and doubt in Mr. Morton's voice. 'Well, if Lucian said it had worn thin . . . He was silent for a few moments, then sat down and said, 'All right, Cadi, my dear. Thank you.'

I did not tell anybody else about the fall. Sarah would have oohed and ahhed for hours and Mrs. Morton would have made a great to-do about it. Apparently Mr. Morton shared my opinion, for nothing more was said in front of the rest of the family.

That night Sarah came to my bedroom looking tragic. 'Lucian is only staying for three days,' she said with a great sigh. 'Isn't it terrible, Cadi?'

'Not very. He doesn't make particularly good company while he's here. He always seems to be either angry or thinking of something else.'

'Yes, I know, and I could cry. I'm sure he's *tormented*, Cadi. I'd think it was because of you, except that he was like that before, anyway.'

'Because of me? What on earth do you mean?'

She sighed again. 'Oh, if only he'd sometimes look at me the way he looks at you. I'd be in *heaven*.'

'Oh, don't be silly,' I said impatiently. 'He hardly ever bothers to look at me, and if he does he usually glares.'

'But that's to hide his real feelings,' Sarah said eagerly, her romantic imagination hard at work. 'Perhaps he's madly in love with you, Cadi. Perhaps he'll ask you to marry him;

After all, you're old enough. You're older than Mary Lead-
better, and she got married this summer. I heard Mamma
say the other day that it was time you began to think
seriously about these things.'

Sometimes Sarah's childish ways made me irritable with
her, but tonight I could only smile. I had not even thought
about getting married, and the idea that Lucian Farrel
might be madly in love with me was something only Sarah
could have dreamt of.

'What does Lucian do all the time in London?' I asked.
'I mean, does he have a profession?'

Sarah looked glum. 'Well, he was a soldier,' she said miserably, 'but that's all finished now. I told you.' She brightened
almost immediately. 'I saw him in his uniform when I was
younger. Oh, he looked so handsome, Cadi. . . .'

She rambled on. Sarah's conversations were usually
rambling, because she kept interrupting herself with romantic notions and comments, but I had schooled myself to be
patient, and as I listened I learned more about Lucian.

His mother, Mr. Morton's sister, had died when he was
born. His father had died only a few years ago, and according
to Sarah had been a quite well-known architect. It had been
intended that Lucian, when he left the Army, should join
his father's old partners and study to be an architect, but
after being cashiered he was unwelcome among them. His
inheritance was small, for though his father had been a good
architect he had been a poor businessman. For a time after
the war Lucian had drifted, but then, two years ago, he had
suddenly set up stables near Epsom and gone in for breeding
horses. He often travelled abroad now, to France, Ireland,
and even Turkey and Syria, buying or selling.

'Papa says he does quite well now,' Sarah said. 'But I don't
think Lucian cares very much about money. He just enjoys
working with horses—as much as he enjoys sculpting.'

'Sculpting?'

'Yes, didn't you know? It's a hobby, really, and he sculpts
in wood, but he makes the most beautiful things. Horses, of
course, but people as well, sometimes just a hand, and so
beautifully carved. Or a bust. He wanted to do a head of

Mamma once, but she said the strain would be too much for her.' Sarah paused for breath and giggled. 'So he did a bust of an actress instead. Imagine, Cadi, a young actress! They're terribly fast. We saw it when we visited his flat in London, and the bosom was so . . . *exposed*! There wasn't any bodice at all really, because the carving stopped short before the bodice began. Poor Mamma was greatly shocked, but I wasn't. It seemed to teach me something because it was real and true.'

My opinion of Sarah went up a little. Sometimes she showed a surprising streak of her father's good sense. When she left to go to bed she paused at the door for a moment and looked back at me with a confiding smile.

'I've just thought, Cadi,' she whispered. 'If you do marry Lucian, I won't hate you, even though I'm madly in love with him myself.'

All the next day I felt strangely unsettled. I was glad that Lucian had gone to Tunbridge Wells to look at a mare. Although Sarah's words were foolish, I knew that I would be affected by them; knew that I would find myself watching Lucian to see if he was looking at me; and knew that I would feel awkward in speaking with him.

It was all quite absurd, and I felt impatient with myself, but in some strange way that day marked a quiet turning-point in my life. I realized for the first time that I was at an age when a girl should begin to think of her marriage, and I felt at a loss. How did it all come about? There was nobody I wanted to marry. I was certainly not in love with any man. Perhaps I was a freak . . .? Perhaps I would become a spinster like Miss Rodsley, the Colonel's sister. The thought of that made me feel quite depressed.

I remembered the Good Dream, and tried to recall as clearly as I could that warm, breathtaking sense of longing and joy that came to me when the door opened and I saw the man who awaited me. Surely that was love, for no feeling in the world could be more wonderful. But the man was Lucian, and in my waking hours I had no such feelings for him. Then again, it was also Lucian in the Bad Dream, when I was swept by fear.

That night when I went to bed I did something I had often done in my early days at *Meadhaven*, when I was passing through the unhappy stage of settling down. I took from my wardrobe the little case in which I kept the few precious mementoes of my own family, except for the magic lantern clock which stood on my dressing table.

In the case there were three photographs, one of my mother, one of my father and mother on their wedding day, and one of Granny Caterina and Grandpa Penwarden taken on the same day. I had a silver brooch and a tortoiseshell comb with a silver back, both belonging to my mother. There was a small gold tie-pin of my father's, and a filigree gold locket belonging to Granny Caterina. This was the only possession she had brought from her forgotten past. The locket had been on a chain round her neck when young Robert Penwarden had rescued her from the sea. It was oval, hinged on one side, and made to take a miniature daguerreotype photograph. The silvered copper plate of the daguerreotype was still there, fixed inside the locket, but there was no picture on it, only blurred patches. It seemed that salt water, perhaps held in the locket long after Granny Caterina was taken from the sea, had destroyed whatever image had once been there.

I sat holding the locket, wondering who had given it to the young Caterina almost half a century ago. We had often talked about it together. I had made up stories about it, and Granny had listened, smiling. She was never sad, never seemed to long for memory of her past to return. She was content with Robert Penwarden and the life he had given her, and I realized now how completely she must have loved him. Like all Italians she was Roman Catholic, but this had not prevented her marrying my grandfather, though I believe there were difficulties which they had to overcome.

The rest of the mementoes in my case were books and papers. There was a missal which my grandfather had given Granny Caterina, even though she had lapsed and attended our own church with us. There were some exercise books I had used for lessons with Miss Rigg, and there were certificates of births, deaths, and marriages. On Granny Caterina's marriage certificate the space for her father's name was marked 'Unknown'. She had been left with memory of her Christian name, and little else.

I put my box of treasures away and went to bed, feeling disturbed yet not quite knowing why. I was in a restless sleep when I woke suddenly to the touch of a hand on my shoulder. My first thought was that Mrs. Morton had walked in her sleep again, but when I turned I saw Sarah standing there in a pale shaft of moonlight that came through my slightly parted curtains.

She put a finger to her lips and said urgently, '*Shhh!*' then bent to whisper in my ear. 'Please—you *must* help me, Cadi!'

'What's wrong?' I whispered back in alarm. 'What time is it?' I sat up in bed, peering at her.

'It's after one o'clock.' Sarah's face twisted as if she might cry at any moment. 'You've got to help, Cadi. It's Richard —he can't get into the house.'

'Into the house?' I echoed dazedly. 'But . . . isn't he in bed?'

She shook her head. 'He went to the village tonight. He does, sometimes. And then he comes in by my window, because the ivy is thick enough to climb there. I leave it unlatched for him.'

I felt I must be dreaming, and took hold of Sarah's hand to reassure myself that she was really there. 'He's been to the village tonight, you say? But why?'

'He goes to see a woman there.'

'*Sarah!*'

She gave a little shrug. 'Oh, it isn't anyone we know. Just some woman who does dressmaking,' she said, vaguely. 'Young men have to sow their wild oats, you know.'

My astonishment deepened. Silly, squeaky Sarah had shown that she could actually keep a big secret, even from me. More surprising still, she was quite unshocked by her brother's behaviour, her only concern was that he could not get back into the house.

I climbed out of bed and pulled on my blue velvet dressing-gown, speaking as I did so. 'Some young men may sow their wild oats, especially in the books you read,' I whispered furiously, 'but don't you realize the terrible trouble Richard will be in if your father and mother find out? They don't know, do they? No, of course they don't,' I went on before she could answer, and then I stopped short for a moment, puzzled. 'How am I supposed to help? Why can't Richard get in tonight if he's done it before?'

'I—I don't know,' Sarah said tremulously. 'He threw some gravel at my window to wake me, and then he whispered that he couldn't climb up. He told me to go and let him in at the front door, but I—I *daren't*, Cadi! I simply daren't go downstairs to the hall. It's so dark down there, and—and awfully ghostly. Besides, somebody might hear me.' She was beginning to stammer with fright, and her voice was rising, so I took her by the shoulders and gave her a little shake.

'Go back to your room and go to sleep,' I whispered sternly. 'You'll have hysterics and rouse the whole house in a moment. Go on! I'll see to Richard.'

She said, 'Thank you, Cadi, oh *thank* you,' her voice shaking so much she could hardly speak. I saw her back to her room, closed the door on her, and then began to tiptoe across the landing and down the broad stairs. They creaked with every step, in a way I had never noticed before, and my heart was in my mouth as I clung to the banister rail with one hand and moved slowly down through the heavy darkness. It seemed to take an age to reach the foot of the stairs, and another age to cross the hall. I moved with my hands stretched out in front of me, dreading that I might bump into something and make a noise. Yet I dared not show any light.

Then I was fumbling with the two bolts, easing them back inch by inch, hardly daring to breathe. The front door swung open, creaking as I am sure it had never creaked before. Richard stood silhouetted against the starlight. He was in dark clothes, and his face looked paper-white.

I glimpsed his startled expression as he realized who had let him in. He had expected it to be Sarah. Then he tiptoed past me, whispering, 'Cadi ... thank you, you're wonderful.'

I caught his arm and made him stand still while I carefully bolted the door, then I urged him towards the stairs. My eyes were more accustomed to the dark now, and I could see very faintly. I wanted to guide him to his room for fear that he would blunder into something.

As we crept up the stairs I moved my hand to his shoulder. He flinched, and stifled a gasp. I realized then that he was hurt. I could hear him breathing quickly and a little harshly.

Two minutes later he opened the door of his room and turned as if to speak to me, but I moved forward so that he had to give way, and then I closed the door behind me. 'Light a candle,' I whispered, and heard the rattle of matches and the faint clatter as he found the candlestick.

The flame threw flickering shadows around the room, picking out the strange trophies which hung on the walls. Eyes seemed to gleam behind the empty eye-holes of the African witch-doctor mask, redness tinged the blade of a throwing-spear, the cheeks of an oriental idol seemed to crease in a dreadful smile.

'I'll be all right now, Cadi.' Richard's voice was so low I could scarcely hear the words. 'You . . . you won't tell my father?'

I whispered, 'You're hurt. What happened to you, Richard?' There was a film of perspiration on his white handsome face, and he stood stiffly, awkwardly, as if movement was painful. With an effort he smiled, the candlelight making his violet eyes brilliant. 'It's nothing. Please forget all about it. Go to bed, Cadi.'

'No! You've hurt your shoulder. I felt you wince when I touched it. What happened?'

'Nothing.' He turned, and moved his arms as if to take off his jacket, then froze rigidly and gave a muffled gasp of pain. When I went to him I saw that his eyes were closed and beads of sweat stood on his brow.

Without a word I began to ease the jacket very carefully back over his shoulders. He seemed about to protest, but then his head fell forward wearily, as if in acquiescence. I suppose I should have felt greatly embarrassed at being with

Richard in his room at this hour of the night, but I had no thought to spare for correct behaviour. What filled my mind was that he needed help and I was the only one who could give it.

The back of his white shirt was torn slightly in several places and covered with thin, smudgy dark lines running across it, some overlaying the others. I moved round in front of him to unbutton the shirt, for it seemed to hurt him when he moved his arms. He said weakly, 'No, Cadi,' then turned away and sank on to the bed face down.

'I can't leave you like this!' I whispered fiercely. He neither moved nor answered. As I could not reach the buttons of his shirt I put two fingers of each hand in one of the tears down the back, and jerked my hands apart. The fine linen ripped, and I gasped with shock as I stared down. The white skin of his back was marred by a dozen or more livid red weals, and though the skin was unbroken the flesh was swollen and fiery. It was little wonder that he had been unable to climb the ivy that night.

'You've been . . . flogged!' I breathed incredulously. 'Only a whip could do that!'

'A riding crop.' His voice was muffled against the coverlet. 'I'll be all right, Cadi. Just stiff for a few days.'

My throat seemed to have closed up, and I could not speak. I went to the wash-stand in his room and poured cold water into the bowl, then brought it to the bed. My hands were trembling with indignation as I brought towels and spread one on the bed beside him to protect the coverlet while I bathed the swollen weals. He seemed to understand, for with an effort he eased himself on to the towel, and then lay still.

I found scissors on his dressing table and cut the rest of his shirt away so that I could soak pieces of it in the water. Even when I had swallowed hard half a dozen times it was still difficult to speak.

'Who did it?' I managed at last as I laid an oblong of the cool damp linen gently on his whipped back. 'Who did it, Richard?' A thought struck me. 'Was it that woman's husband?'

108

'Sarah told you, then? I suppose she had to.' He rested his head on one forearm. 'No, her husband left her long ago. It was nothing to do with that.'

'Then *who*, Richard?'

He did not answer for long moments, then slowly turned his head and opened his eyes so that he was looking at me over one shoulder. There was something of surprise in his gaze, and I saw bitterness in the painful smile that twisted his lips.

'Who?' he whispered. 'Why Lucian, of course. Who else?'

My heart pounded with new shock, yet I knew he was telling the truth.

'But why?' I breathed. '*Why*, Richard?'

He made to shrug, then winced and let his head fall forward again, so that I could not see his face.

'Sometimes . . .' he said slowly, then hesitated. 'Sometimes Lucian does strange things. Dangerous things.'

'He must be mad! You'll have to tell your father.'

'I can't, Cadi. Ahhh . . . that's good.' A long sigh of relief escaped him as I replaced the linen with a fresh piece, cold from the water. 'I can't tell Father without telling him that I was out tonight. Lucian was waiting for me as I came home through the woods.'

I gave a little start. For a moment I had forgotten Richard's behaviour, and why he was out, but remembering it now took second place to the hot indignation I felt against Lucian. 'Then I'll speak to Lucian myself,' I said fiercely. 'He can't do things like this!'

Richard lifted himself on an elbow, flinching a little, and turned to take my hand and hold it. The candlelight glinted on his golden hair. 'Don't, Cadi,' he said with gentle patience. 'Promise me you won't speak to Lucian of this. It would do no good. You see, he won't remember.'

'Won't *remember*?'

'He never does.' Richard's smile was the smile of a sad angel. 'There's a . . . weakness in his mind, Cadi, a blemish. Usually the strange things he does from time to time cause no harm. Tonight was a little different, that's all.'

As if from a long way off I heard my own voice say, 'Lie

down again, Richard.' With automatic movements I wrung out another piece of linen. Tiny cold fingers of horror were awakening suspicions in my mind that left me numb.

'The things he does. . . .' Richard had said. What things? I thought of a broken rudder pintle, and a bridle ring that had snapped. Lucian had been there on both occasions. He had even shown his suspicions clearly, and been almost frightening in his anger. But was that because some twist in his mind had made him forget what he himself had done?

Chapter Six

I CAME TO MYSELF, and realized that for a minute or two I had been simply staring down at the torn piece of linen covering Richard's back, staring but not seeing anything except a confusion of half-formed pictures which sprang from my imagination.

Impatiently I pulled myself together and stood up. 'Wait there and don't move,' I whispered. 'I'll be back in a few moments.'

On tiptoe I crept to my room and returned with a bottle of witch hazel. In Cornwall we had always used it for bruises and sprains, and Mrs. Mansel, who made up her own special potions from herbs, was a great believer in it. I spread a new piece of linen on Richard's back, and soaked it in the witch hazel. After a little while, as the lotion took the fire from his hurts, he whispered gratefully, 'Oh, that's wonderful . . . bless you, Cadi.'

He closed his eyes, and I think he must soon have fallen into a half-sleep, for we did not talk any more, but for the next two hours I sat by him on the edge of the bed, moistening the linen afresh when it began to dry. My mind was busy with the turmoil of thoughts about Lucian, but in a little while I grew too tired to think and had difficulty in keeping my own eyes open. At last the bottle was empty, and when

I peeled back the linen I saw with relief that the weals were far less swollen and angry.

'I can't do any more, Richard,' I whispered.

He gave a little start, and lifted his head slowly. I waited until his eyes focused, then went on, 'Tomorrow you'd better pretend to have a feverish cold for a day or two, so you can stay in bed until you're able to move easily again.'

'You're . . . not going to tell Father?'

I hesitated, realizing that I must have made up my mind without being aware of it, but I still felt very unhappy, for helping to deceive Mr. Morton seemed like betraying his trust in me; yet to tell him about Richard would be the act of a tattle-tale, and cause a dreadful upheaval at *Meadhaven*.

'I suppose not,' I answered reluctantly. 'But for goodness' sake stop going to see this woman, Richard. It's bound to bring trouble in the end.'

He eased himself up on one elbow and put his hand on mine. I was glad to see that he did not wince as he moved.

'I wish . . .' he said, then stopped. Whatever he wished, he did not complete the sentence but gave a little shake of his head, then went on, 'Thank you, Cadi. You're the most wonderful girl in the world. I love you so much.'

'Don't talk foolishness,' I said, and stood up. 'I'll leave the candle for you to undress by. Don't forget to blow it out.' I moved to the door, and when I looked back he was gazing at me intently, with a kind of wonder in his violet eyes. 'There's another thing,' I whispered. 'I'm going to tell Sarah never to let you in by her window again.'

He seemed to take no notice of my words, but as I closed the door I heard him say softly, 'I'll make it up to you one day, Cadi.'

I went thankfully back to my room, and felt I could well have slept the day through, but Sarah came bouncing on my bed at half-past seven, round-eyed and wanting to know what had happened. I told her that Richard had been unable to climb the ivy because he felt ill, and that I let him in, but thought he had a fever and would not be surprised if he had to stay in bed for a day or two.

'I'm not going to tell your father this time, Sarah,' I said, looking as stern and determined as possible, 'but if I ever catch you helping Richard in something like this again, I'll tell!'

She lost colour at the threat. 'I didn't mean any harm, Cadi. It was just . . . well, Richard asked me, and it seemed . . . exciting in a way. You know?'

I did know what she meant. Although I behaved as if greatly shocked, there was much pretence in this, for I too felt that there was something rather wickedly exciting about Richard's escapade. What truly shocked me was that Lucian had beaten Richard so cruelly. In the light of day I found it hard to believe that Lucian's mind was disturbed, that he could do such things and be unaware of them later. It occurred to me that his action might have been one of jealousy. Perhaps he also made visits to the woman in the village, and had attacked Richard as a rival.

I still had not decided whether or not to speak to Lucian of what he had done, but when I went down to breakfast I found that there was no decision to make, for Lucian had gone from *Meadhaven*.

'He left last night,' said Mr. Morton, helping himself to kidneys and bacon at the sideboard. 'A sudden decision, but characteristic of Lucian. He asked me to say goodbye to you girls on his behalf.'

Sarah sighed and looked tearful. She had expected Lucian to be with us for another day at least. I felt relieved, for I had not looked forward to confronting Lucian, with his cool gaze and mocking tongue. It might be six months or a year before we saw him again, and I knew that by then it would seem absurd to speak of what had happened last night.

During breakfast I found it difficult to meet Mr. Morton's gaze or respond to his amiable conversation, for I was miserably conscious of failing him in not telling what I knew. I tried to comfort myself by thinking that it would be worse to tell than to remain silent, but still felt horribly uncomfortable. It was a relief when Mrs. Morton swept in, fluttering with alarm and saying that poor Richard was abed with a chill. 'He simply refuses to have the doctor,' she said, sinking into her chair. 'You must speak to him, Edward, and insist.'

'I will certainly have a word with him, my dear. But one usually recovers from a chill just as quickly without the aid of medicine, I fancy. To stay in bed is the surest cure.'

'But he could be sickening for something!'

'In that case it would be better to leave calling the doctor until the symptoms have developed sufficiently to permit a firm diagnosis.'

I missed the next minute or two of the conversation, for I had suddenly felt chilled myself by the thought of how awful it would have been if anybody had discovered me last night when I was tending Richard's back.

'Would you like that, Cadi?' Mr. Morton said.

I gave a start, and blinked at him in confusion, for I did not know what he was talking about.

'Bless me, you haven't been listening,' he chuckled. 'Shall I offer a penny for your thoughts? No, I'm sure if they were worth no more than that you would give them for nothing. I was just saying that we shall be having a guest from one of the foreign embassies to dine with us tonight, and suggesting that you and Sarah might like to join us on this occasion.'

Since my coming to *Meadhaven*, Mr. Morton had several times brought home a guest to dine and stay the night. They were usually foreign gentlemen, diplomats, with whom he wished to have some quiet and unofficial talks away from the Foreign Office. On these occasions Sarah and I would have an early dinner alone. Afterwards, in the drawing room, we would be introduced to the guest, and then would discreetly make ourselves scarce for the rest of the evening.

'You are both growing up,' Mr. Morton went on, 'and I feel that a family atmosphere at dinner, with you young ladies present, might have a pleasantly relaxing effect on our guest. Well now, would you like that, Cadi?'

'Yes, it would be very nice, Mr. Morton. Thank you.'

'I hope he speaks English,' Sarah said with a giggle.

'He understands English very well, but is not fluent in

speaking it,' Mr. Morton answered. 'However, I'm sure we shall manage.'

I knew that Mr. Morton spoke French and German, and felt rather glad that we would probably not have much to do in the way of conversation, but would simply be there for decoration. He made as if to speak to Sarah, then gave a little sigh and turned to me with a smile. 'I'm sure that if I tell Sarah not to giggle it will only make her more likely to do so, willy nilly. But you have great influence with her, Cadi, and a knack for setting the right atmosphere, so I shall rely on you to make sure that she is not in a giggly mood this evening.'

'I'm sure she'll be very grown-up and dignified,' I said. 'We'll practise this afternoon.'

Mrs. Morton roused from her own thoughts. 'I think, Edward,' she said firmly, 'that you should not insist on calling Doctor Bailey to see Richard. Surely it would be wiser to wait a little, and see if any definite symptoms develop?'

Mr. Morton nodded, put down his napkin, rose and moved to the far end of the table, where he patted his wife's shoulder and bent to kiss her cheek. 'A very sensible suggestion, my dear,' he said approvingly. 'What should we do without you?'

That evening Sarah and I came down to the drawing room half an hour after Mr. Morton and his guest had arrived. Somewhat to my shame, I had made sure that she was in a quiet and subdued mood by dwelling on the terrible scandal there would be in the household if Richard's escapade came to be known, and emphasising her own foolishness in the matter. The guest was a tall man of about the same age as Mr. Morton, with thick black hair, grey-flecked, brushed smoothly back. He had a long, pointed nose and a quick warm manner that matched his smiling eyes and reminded me strangely of Granny Caterina.

'These are my daughters, signore,' said Mr. Morton. 'Cadi, Sarah, this is Signor Vecchi.'

I dropped a little curtsy as I shook hands. It was foolish to be surprised that our guest was Italian, but the possibility had not occurred to me.

'Good evening, Cadi,' he said slowly with a pleasant smile. 'Good evening Sarah. I am honoured to meet such charming young ladies.' His English accent was far from good, and he seemed to have to think carefully before each phrase.

By instinct I almost greeted him in Italian, but just stopped myself in time. Would that be rude? I thought of Miss Rigg's many lectures on good manners, but I was still not sure. To answer in Italian might seem like showing off, I felt, and also it could be taken as a criticism of the way Signor Vecchi spoke English. I decided to be safe, and murmured a few polite words in English as a response.

'I think . . . you will be very—ah—very proud of your daughters, Mr. Morton,' Signor Vecchi said, hesitating at every few words. 'They are much attractive, and yet so different. The one dark, the other so blonde.'

'Cadi is not of our family,' Mr. Morton said. 'She is a young friend we have taken under our wing. I speak of her as our daughter because she is that to us in spirit, and I am extremely proud that this should be so.'

'Ah, yes,' Signor Vecchi said, nodding. It was clear that he had no difficulty in understanding English, even though he spoke it poorly, and this was very natural, for it is much easier to understand another language than to speak it. Sarah and I sat quietly while a rather slow and laboured conversation went on between Signor Vecchi and Mr. and Mrs. Morton. At last John the butler entered to announce that dinner was served, and we moved into the dining room.

Mrs. Beale had excelled herself with the dinner, and as time passed I found myself taking a great liking to Signor Vecchi. Perhaps this was partly because, being Italian, he was a link with Granny Caterina and with my mother, but he was also very kindly in his manner, and was careful to see that Sarah and I were included in the general conversation.

It was as we reached the dessert stage that I forgot myself for a moment. Signor Vecchi had been admiring a big vase of chrysanthemums, fresh cut from the garden. 'In Kent is very nice,' he said, 'but still more nice at April. I have passed then in the train. There is much beautiful . . .' He pondered, frowning as he tried to recall the word he wanted, then clicked his fingers impatiently and muttered '*fioritura . . . fioritura . . . ?*'

'Blossom,' I said without thinking.

'Ah, yes——' He stopped short, looking at me in surprise. '*Lei parla l'Italiano?*'

I could scarcely deny that I spoke Italian, and answered, '*Si signore. Lo parlo da sempre. La mia nonna era un'Italiana——*'

I broke off, suddenly conscious that Mr. and Mrs. Morton and Sarah were all staring at me in complete astonishment. I flushed and said, 'Excuse me, I'm so sorry.'

'You . . . you have no need to apologize, Cadi,' Mr. Morton said rather dazedly. 'But where on earth did you learn to speak Italian?'

'I've always spoken it, Mr. Morton,' I explained, still somewhat flustered. 'That's what I was just telling Signor Vecchi. My grandmother was Italian, and I learned it from her when I was first learning to talk. My mother spoke it too, of course.'

'Why didn't you *say*?' Sarah cried, bouncing in her chair with excitement. 'Why didn't you tell us? It's *ever* so clever of you, Cadi!'

'It's not clever, it just happened,' I said, quite unjustly annoyed by her excitement. 'And I didn't say anything because I just never thought about it.'

Mr. Morton sat back in his chair and began to laugh. Signor Vecchi's face was creased with amusement, too. 'It is most funny——' he began, then changed to Italian and went on rapidly. 'Please tell them I find it so amusing that I should discover you speak my language when even the family you live with did not know!'

I translated, and Mr. Morton nodded, still chuckling. 'Most amusing,' he agreed. 'And since I speak no Italian, there may well be occasions when you could help me by translating, Cadi.'

'Why not tonight?' Signor Vecchi said in English. He looked at Mr. Morton and continued, glancing at me inquiringly from time to time when he wanted me to supply a word or two. 'After all, Mr. Morton, we shall not be discussing secrets of State, merely having an unofficial exchange of views on several matters. For me it would be much help to have such a skilled interpreter to call upon. I am sure she is discreet, and will understand that our discussion is confidential.'

Mr. Morton inclined his head. 'I would not have suggested it myself, signore, but since the idea is your own I am happy to accept it. As for discretion, our talk will have little significance for Cadi, and in any event she is to be trusted entirely, I assure you.'

He looked at me with a hint of apology, and sighed, shaking his head. 'I realize now that we have never asked you about your family, Cadi. No doubt we refrained in the first place to avoid distressing you, but I expect the passing of time has healed your grief somewhat by now, and we can repair our omission. Your grandmother was Italian, you say—would you like to tell us how that came about?'

Hesitantly I began to tell the story, but then I became lost in it and my tongue ran on. I told how young Robert Penwarden, who was to be my grandfather, had sailed into the Bay of Naples nearly fifty years ago. His ship lay at anchor there for three days, and because the waterfront was a nest of scoundrels and thieves a guard-boat was set to row round the ship at night.

On the third night, Robert Penwarden was with the crew in the guard-boat when they heard the sound of oars nearby. They could see nothing, for a light sea mist hung over the bay.

As they pulled through the mist to investigate, there came a heavy but muffled splash, followed at once by the sound of oars once again. At that moment a breeze stirred the mist. Robert Penwarden and another seaman glimpsed a small boat with three men pulling hard for the dockside. Then it was gone. The guard-boat crew rested on their oars, drifting, and in the silence they heard the sound of big air-bubbles breaking the surface, close alongside their boat.

It was Robert Penwarden who snatched up the end of a coil of rope and dived into the black water, on an impulse he was never afterwards able to explain, even to himself. As his ears sang under the pressure of the water, his groping hands felt a rough, shapeless object which was sinking slowly as globules of air rose from it. A canvas sack, his hands told him, loosely tied at the neck, weighted, and carrying something soft and yielding.

Fighting the pain in his aching lungs, he somehow contrived to make fast the end of the rope to the neck of the sack. Then he clawed his way to the surface and hung panting to the side of the boat, gasping to the men to haul in. Soon the dripping sack lay in the well of the boat. Robert Penwarden cut open the neck of it with his knife, then carefully slit down one side of the thick canvas.

This was his first sight of Caterina. In the yellow light of the boat's lantern he saw that she wore a white dress which clung to her soaked body. Her long hair was uncoiled, the dark wet tresses plastered about her face. Her hands were bound in front of her, and an ugly bruise showed clearly on one temple. In the bottom of the canvas sack were three heavy pieces of rusting iron.

They brought her aboard the ship believing her to be dead. It was Robert Penwarden who felt the feeble flutter of her heart and knew that she might yet be saved. While the other seamen gathered to stare and chatter, he laid her on rough blankets and worked for half an hour to force the water from her lungs. Captain Dowding was called, a dour man with little sympathy in his nature, who swore with rage because the ship was to sail at dawn and this affair might cause long delays if the Naples authorities were called in. He went away and drank some rum, and decided that the whole affair was none of his business.

'Now hear me, Bob Penwarden,' he said when he returned, a little unsteady on his feet. 'Alive or dead, that wench is not to be reported to me until after we've sailed. I've no fancy to rot here in Naples for a week or so, with cargoes waiting in Falmouth.'

Robert Penwarden felt strangely glad. There were men not far away who had tried to kill this young girl, and he had no wish for her to be taken back ashore in Naples.

'She's alive, Cap'n,' he said, pulling a blanket over her and rising from his knees. 'She'll live, given care. But if she's to have care, she'll need a cabin.'

'Cabin!' cried the Captain. 'D'ye think I'll turn the Second Mate out into the foc'sle for a drowned foreign wench?'

'Better so, Cap'n,' Robert Penwarden answered stubbornly. 'If not, she'll die maybe, and you'll carry the blame, for I'll not perjure myself by saying she was dead when we took her aboard.'

The Captain raged at the young Penwarden, threatening him with the lash for his insolence, but his wrath was mostly bluster, and he yielded in the end. Caterina was carried to the tiny cabin of the Second Mate, to his anger and to the amusement of the seamen, though there were some who were superstitious and muttered against having a woman on board.

There was no doctor on the ship. Robert Penwarden himself was in charge of the few bandages, splints and medicines that were carried. As a boy he had worked as an apothecary's assistant for two years, and so he was called upon for any doctoring needed on board. His skill was small enough, but in eight years at sea he had gained some experience in splinting broken bones, sewing up wounds, and brewing draughts for fever or stomach pains. The crew considered themselves better served than they would have been on most other ships.

So it was that Robert Penwarden nursed Caterina on the voyage home. It was two days after she recovered her senses before she was able to make him understand that her memory was gone. Her fear was very great, but gradually Robert Penwarden's patience and gentleness brought home to her that she was safe in his care. She had a quick ear, and within ten days had learned enough words and phrases of English to be able to hold a laboured conversation with him.

They fell in love. He knew by instinct, and by the clothes she had been wearing, that she was of gentle birth. Caterina knew it too, but this did not touch her love for the young lower deck seaman who had saved her life and was nursing her with such tenderness.

When Captain Dowding was told that his unwanted passenger had lost her memory it put him in a happier mood. 'It's no task of mine to go ferreting around to find who she is and send her home,' he said with surly satisfaction. 'That's for you to fret about, Penwarden. And you can do as you please, for all I care, so long as you say we picked her up *after* we'd sailed. Take her to the Eye-talian Ambassador when we reach home, and let him do what's needed. But let no blame fall to me, or I'll see you starve before you get a new berth.'

My grandfather brought Caterina from Falmouth, where they landed, to his home in Mawstone. There his parents took her in, and after their first surprise and doubts came to love her. Robert Penwarden gave up the sea and took work in the mines. Reluctantly he tried to persuade Caterina to go to London with him and try to discover who she was, but she would have none of this. He spoke of the grief and distress her family must be enduring, but still she would not be moved. She said, in her careful English: 'No, Robert. If there was anybody close to me, anybody to feel sorrow, I would try to find them. But there is not. I know. I do not remember, but I know. And I do not want to remember, for I believe that what I have forgotten is better left forgotten. I do not wish to find out why some person wanted me dead . . . and who it was.'

Six months later Caterina married the young Cornishman who had saved her. And now, so many years later, I, Cadi Tregaron, her grand-daughter, sat in the big dining room at *Meadhaven,* telling the story as Robert Penwarden had told it to his wife, and as she had many times afterwards told it to me.

The room was very quiet as I ended my tale. Dessert and coffee had been neglected. Sarah's eyes were swimming, and Signor Vecchi was leaning forward, listening with great concentration. Mr. Morton had his head a little to one side, curiosity strong in his eyes as he gazed upon me. Even Mrs. Morton had forgotten herself for the moment and sat with chin resting on her clasped hands, her eyes half-closed as if following my story in her imagination.

'I never knew my grandfather,' I ended. 'But Granny Caterina used to tell me that it was like an English fairy-tale—they lived happily ever after.'

'I th-think it's a beautiful story,' Sarah said in a shaky voice. 'Oh, I'd love it to happen to *me*.'

'There are disadvantages to being put in a sack and thrown in the sea, my dear child,' Mr. Morton pointed out with a touch of impatience, then looked at me. 'It can't have been easy for Caterina to begin a new life in a strange land. Both she and your grandfather were people of courage, I think.' He smiled. 'But that hardly surprises me, Cadi.'

Signor Vecchi looked from one to the other of us with raised eyebrows, as if about to ask a question, but before he could do so I began to speak again. One thing I had left untold, and I told it now, the way in which Granny Caterina and my mother had died together. It was in one of the bad years, when food was short and we had to tighten our belts. They had gone out along the cliff tops to gather samphire for pickling. Rain had made the grass slippery.

Young David Moulton had seen the tragedy, had seen my mother lose her footing on the sloping edge of the cliff, seen my Granny snatch at her arm to save her . . . and lose her own balance. They had slid over the edge together, down to the brutal rocks below.

When I had finished speaking there was another little silence until Mr. Morton looked along the huge dining table with its gleaming cutlery and linen, sighed, and said quietly, 'We have never known hunger. It almost makes me ashamed.'

I shook my head, surprised. 'You shouldn't feel that, Mr. Morton. It wouldn't have helped to bring the pilch-ards into our waters if you'd gone hungry too. And there were more good years than bad. We were very happy most of the time.'

Mrs. Morton roused from a reverie. 'Did you never find out who your Granny was, Cadi?' she asked wonderingly.

'Did she have nothing about her person to help identify her?'

'Nothing, Mrs. Morton. She was wearing a locket, and I still have that, but the picture inside was spoiled by salt water.'

'A locket? What is that, please?' Signor Vecchi asked.

'*Un medaglione, signore.*'

'Ah, thank you.' He changed to Italian, and went on. 'A souvenir of a very strange and moving story. Would you mind letting us see it, Cadi?'

'Not at all, signore.'

I translated for Mr. Morton, who said, 'I'm sure we would all be fascinated. Run and get it now, Cadi, if you're sure you don't mind.'

I went up to my bedroom and returned with the locket. Everybody was talking at once when I re-entered the dining room, but they fell silent as Signor Vecchi took the locket and studied it. '*Bellissimo lavoro,*' he murmured. 'Beautiful work. Your grandmother was not of poor family, that is sure.'

He opened the locket carefully, studied the ruined daguerreotype inside, then passed it to Mr. Morton.

'Fascinating . . . fascinating,' Mr. Morton said as he examined it. 'But there is no engraving, nothing to help solve the mystery. Were the would-be murderers just thieves? I think not. Common robbers do not go to such lengths to dispose of a victim, certainly not in Naples half a century ago. Ah, if only this locket could speak, no doubt it could tell a strange tale. Here, Sarah, take this and pass it to your Mamma.'

As Sarah skipped eagerly round the table Mr. Morton looked at me in a way I remembered from several past occasions, smiling but with a touch of bewilderment. 'Well, Cadi . . . will you never cease to surprise us? Certainly you have provided rare entertainment for us and for our guest at table tonight.'

There came a little squeak of dismay from Sarah. Between them, she and her mother had managed to drop the locket as Sarah handed it to her. It bounced on the table, slithered off and fell to the floor, and as it fell it seemed to break into two parts. Mrs. Morton cried out, and her husband half rose, uttering a sharp, indignant protest. Sarah began to cry. I felt I could have pulled her hair till she squealed, but gritted my teeth and managed to smile as I said, 'Don't be upset, Sarah. I'm sure it can be mended.'

'But it's so *special*,' she wailed, picking up the two pieces. 'Oh, Cadi, I'm sorry——' She broke off, her tearful face brightening. 'Wait a minute, I think it's just that the photograph has come out.' She ran to her father. 'Look, Papa.'

He took the pieces, peering at them, then gave a little sigh of relief. 'Yes. The copper plate of the daguerrotype was tightly fixed, and it has simply sprung out. There's no damage, Cadi. We can——' He stopped short with a little exclamation, staring more closely into the locket, and there was such a look of excitement on his face that I came to my feet. He raised his eyes and said softly, 'Great heavens above. Come here, Cadi, your sight is keener than mine.' I almost ran to his side. He was pointing to the inside of the locket, the back of it, against which the daguerrotype had rested. 'Look, child. Surely that is a name engraved there!'

The engraving was fine but quite clear, and my own voice sounded strange to me as I read out the name, 'Caterina Chiavelli.'

The writing blurred before my gaze as it struck home to me that now, by pure chance, I knew what Granny Caterina had not known throughout almost forty years of married life—her true name. Yet the secret had lain under her hand all that time.

Caterina Chiavelli. The name did not seem strange to me, but almost familiar. Why? I heard Signor Vecchi murmur as if to himself, 'Chiavelli of Venice, perhaps . . . ?'

Venice! I looked up with a start, and saw that Mr. Morton was gazing at me as if thunderstruck. I could read the thought in his mind, and knew now why the name of Chiavelli was familiar to me—and familiar to him. It was the name he had been given by the art dealer when he had inquired about the picture that hung in the hall. The palace that for years I had seen clearly in my dream, the palazzo in that painting—it was called *Palazzo Chiavelli*!

Dazedly I realized that this must have been the young Caterina's home—until the day when she had been left for dead in a weighted sack dropped into the Bay of Naples. A shiver ran through me. What had happened between Venice and Naples? And why . . . ?

It seemed to me that a door was opening slowly before me, opening on dark strange secrets which had remained hidden for two generations. One part of me wanted to throw the door wide and let light shine into the darkness, but another part of me was afraid.

Chapter Seven

I FELT THE COLOUR begin to ebb from my face with the shock of knowing that my dream was based on reality, on a fragment of hidden memory inherited by some whim of nature from my Granny Caterina. There was no doubt of it now, and I could see that Mr. Morton knew it too.

I tried to recall what he had told me about the *Palazzo Chiavelli*. Part of it was still occupied by descendants of Count Chiavelli, who had built it in the sixteenth century. Granny Caterina was one of his descendants . . . and so was I. Now, in this moment, I had relatives of high birth who lived in a Venetian palace and who did not know that I existed. The thought was strange, exciting, yet in some ways frightening, though I would have found it hard to say why.

I was afraid Mr. Morton would begin to speak of the picture, and of my dream. I did not want him to do so, for I had an almost desperate feeling that I needed time to think, to absorb this startling discovery. He put his hand on my arm, and with relief I saw him give me a tiny shake of his head in warning, as if telling me that this was not the time to speak. I realized that he also wanted a breathing space in which to reflect on all that had been revealed, for if I was truly a descendant of the Chiavelli family through my grandmother, then this might be a momentous discovery.

'Sit down, child,' he said, guiding me to my chair. 'Here, take a little wine. This is all rather overwhelming for you.' He poured me a half glass of wine and waited while I sipped it, hushing Mrs. Morton and Sarah sternly when they tried to ask questions. In a few moments I felt steady again. Mr. Morton still stood beside me, a comforting hand resting on my shoulder.

He said, 'Do you know the family of Chiavelli, Signor Vecchi?'

'I know but very little of them,' came the slow reply. 'A Venetian family of much wealth, I believe. I can tell no more, but if you wish an Italian . . . *avvocato*, how do you say that, Cadi? Ah, a lawyer. Thank you. If you wish an Italian lawyer to look at this affair for you, I gladly recommend my own. Avvocato Bonello, of Rome.'

'That is very kind. Perhaps we could speak of this privately later. For the moment I think we should let the matter rest.' A wail of protest came from Sarah and I saw Mrs. Morton draw breath to speak, but Mr. Morton lifted his hand sharply. 'We have had enough excitement for one evening. To go further at this stage will simply mean a great deal of feverish speculation, which will do nobody any good. Do you agree, Cadi?'

I nodded, too full to speak, and grateful for his words. Something very wonderful had happened, but it was all too huge and vague for me to want it gossiped about unendingly by Mrs. Morton and Sarah.

'Then that closes the subject for now, Mr. Morton said. 'Since Signor Vecchi does not smoke, I shall forgo my own after-dinner cigar and we shall go straight to my study for our talks. Under the circumstances, Cadi, I think that it would be an imposition for us to claim your services as an interpreter this evening. Perhaps you would like to retire to bed?'

I knew he had suggested this so that I would not be left

alone with Mrs. Morton and Sarah, who would be quite unable to avoid the 'feverish speculation' he had spoken of. But I knew that if I went to bed early I would lie awake for hours in speculation myself. 'I would really prefer to help with translation if you and Signor Vecchi still wish it, Mr. Morton,' I said hopefully. 'It will be more useful than for me to do nothing and have this going round and round in my mind.' I touched the locket.

He laughed and squeezed my shoulder. 'My ever practical Cadi.'

'For me, I thank you,' said Signor Vecchi with a smile. 'It will be much more easy.'

For the next hour and a half I sat in the study with the two men. Sometimes Signor Vecchi spoke in his laborious English, looking to me for any words or phrases that he did not know, but mostly he spoke quickly in Italian, pausing for me to translate. In this way, as he said, the shades of meaning were better conveyed. There was nothing exciting in the various subjects of their talk. Most of it was beyond my understanding, for although I still read *The Times* regularly, from force of habit instilled by Miss Rigg, I had never bothered my head very much with politics. But although my understanding was vague, I found it easy enough to translate whatever was said, and they both seemed to be highly satisfied with my help.

At last Mr. Morton said, 'I think that concludes our chat, signore. May we now spend a moment on a personal matter? You suggested I might use your lawyer in Rome to make investigations for me on Cadi's behalf.'

'*Ah, si.*' Signor Vecchi looked at me and spoke rapidly in Italian.

When he had finished I translated to Mr. Morton: 'He says he will give you his lawyer's name and address in Rome, and will write a letter of introduction to him. If you will give him the name of your own lawyer here, the two legal gentlemen can proceed with the matter together.'

Signor Vecchi spoke again, and when he had finished I continued, 'Since there may be some question of proving my identity, and since there are differences between English

Law and Roman Law, he suggests that it is better to have the matter in qualified hands in each country.'

Mr. Morton considered for a moment, then said, 'Splendid. An excellent suggestion, signore.' He turned to me, 'Tomorrow I shall see old Caldwell in Lincoln's Inn, and explain the matter to him. Then all we can do is wait. No doubt it will take time, and I think we shall have several weeks to wait before we hear any news.' He stood up and took my hand. 'Cadi, child, you look a little tired, and no wonder. Thank you for all the excellent translating. I could wish that some of our official interpreters at the Ministry were as good.'

When I wished Signor Vecchi goodnight, he bowed over my hand in a way which made me feel very grown up. 'In a few weeks I am to leave the Embassy and return to Rome,' he said in Italian. 'But I hope Mr. Morton will keep me informed of this matter.' He smiled. 'I have a personal interest because you have been so kind, and we are friends now, I hope. If ever I can be of help, you have only to ask.'

I thanked him sincerely, and translated for Mr. Morton, who added his own thanks before taking my hands and looking at me with his head on one side. 'Are you thrilled, Cadi?'

'Yes. I feel a little strange . . . but it's exciting to know I have a family.'

'Of course.' He gave me that familiar, half sorrowful smile. 'You may even be a titled lady. Had you thought of that? But no, we must avoid speculation.' He gave a little sigh. 'I hope we're not going to lose you, Cadi. I would find life very . . . different without you.'

The fear I had felt earlier grew suddenly sharp. 'Lose me? But surely that can't happen, Mr. Morton! I mean, nobody could *make* me leave you?'

'No, no, no, child, he said quickly, patting my shoulder. 'I will allow nobody to make you do anything unless you wish it.'

I let out a long breath of relief, and smiled. 'Then you won't lose me. I'll go on being a trial to you, please.'

'A trial?' Signor Vecchi said, puzzled.

Mr. Morton laughed contentedly. 'Just a little joke of ours. I will explain in a moment, signore. But first we must allow this young lady to retire.' He kissed me goodnight, tucked my arm under his, and escorted me to the door.

The next two days were miserable for me. Mrs. Morton and Sarah would talk of nothing else but the marvel of discovering who my Granny Caterina had been, and the coincidence of the picture in the hall, for Mr. Morton and I had felt bound to tell them that this was of the *Palazzo Chiavelli*, though we had said nothing about my strange dreams.

Fortunately, neither Sarah nor her mother could remain interested in anything outside everyday life for very long, unless their interest was fed anew, and as Mr. Morton and I did not speak of the matter they quickly reverted to their own favourite preoccupations, Sarah to her romantic daydreams and Mrs. Morton to her paying and receiving calls.

Richard remained in bed for three days and then recovered from his supposed feverish cold. I was supervising Young Kemp's work in the stables when I saw Richard going to his little workshop. I knew that our first meeting since that night of his escapade would be embarrassing, and wanted to get it over as soon as possible, so after a little while I made my way to the workshop.

Richard was fiddling idly with some gadget on the bench, and looked up as I came in. Then he looked quickly down again.

I said softly, 'Is your back all right now?'

He nodded. 'Yes. I can hardly feel it. Thank you again, Cadi.'

'No need to thank me.'

'There's every need. You didn't tell my father, I know that. And you didn't speak to Lucian?'

'No. But I've told Sarah she'll be sorry if she helps you again.'

'You needn't worry. I go back to Oxford soon, anyway.' There was an awkward pause, then he went on, 'Mother told me about discovering who your Granny was, and that perhaps you're really a titled lady.'

'She hopes so, I expect, but it's very unlikely. I don't want to think about it, much less talk about it.'

He raised his eyes and looked at me. I was taken by surprise when he said simply, 'You're so pretty, Cadi.'

'I can't look very pretty in a grubby old jersey and breeches.'

He smiled. 'You do. I like you that way, and with your pigtails.' The smile faded and he said soberly, 'I meant what I said that night, Cadi. I love you.'

'Well, I hope you do,' I said quickly, trying to keep my voice light. 'I'm one of the family now.'

'I meant more than that. Much more. No, you needn't say anything. I know you don't feel the same. But I'm glad if you just like me, that's more than anyone can say of the others.'

He spoke the last words without any hint of self pity or resentment, just as a simple statement of truth.

'Richard, don't be so foolish!' I said sharply.

'It's not foolish, you know.' His voice was gentle. 'Mother and Father, even Sarah, they're never quite at ease with me. If you listen when they speak to me you'll find they're always a little stiff and awkward, as if I was a stranger. They can't help it. I think I *am* a stranger to them. But not to you, Cadi. You're warm and loving, and you're completely natural with me.' He smiled again. 'Even when you tell me not to be foolish.'

'And that's what you are,' I said firmly. 'I don't agree with what you say, but if there *is* anything in it, then you're as much to blame as they are. If you were warm and natural with them, they'd be the same towards you.'

'If . . .' he echoed, his smile sweet but sad. 'Some of us haven't the gift, Cadi.'

'Then some of us ought to try harder.'

He laughed and said, 'Oh, Cadi.' Then he looked down again at the little board of wires and terminals he held, turning it slowly in his hands. Light from the small window shone on his golden head. 'I do love you,' he said in a matter-of-fact voice. 'You'll see, one day.'

I was silent, for I could think of nothing to say, and after a moment he went on, 'Don't ever trust Lucian Farrel, will you?'

It came so much out of the blue that I was completely taken aback. 'What on earth do you mean, Richard?'

'Only what I say. You remember what I told you that night. For your own sake, don't ever put your trust in him.'

'Because he beat you? Because you say he does bad things and then forgets them?'

'Not just that.' He seemed to reflect for a moment. 'Because he's a master of deceit.'

'Deceit?'

'Yes. That's not my own description. It's my father's.'

'Your *father's*?' I was becoming more and more bewildered. 'But your father likes him!'

'Perhaps. But I've heard him say that Lucian is a master of deceit. Whether he likes him because of that or in spite of it, I don't know.'

'Well, I don't think you should say bad things about Lucian, and I'm not going to listen. I like to make up my own mind about people.' I turned away and went back to the stables with strangely mixed feelings. I had no wish to defend Lucian Farrel, even in my own mind, but whatever his faults and weaknesses might be, instinct told me that he did not dissemble. If my instinct was right, what Richard had said must be untrue, and therefore it was a wicked thing to say. If my instinct was right. . . .

Four days later, to my surprise, I received a letter from Lucian. It was just a short note which read:

Dear Cadi,

Uncle Edward had lunch with me today, and told me your startling news. I hope that whatever you may discover about your family will bring you much happiness.

Yours,

Lucian.

I took the letter to show Mr. Morton, who looked mildly surprised. 'Yes, I told Lucian at lunch yesterday,' he said. 'You should be flattered that he has written to you, Cadi.

It's rare that our Lucian can be troubled to put pen to paper.'

'It was kind of him, but I don't feel especially flattered, Mr. Morton. More puzzled. I find it hard to make Lucian out.'

He smiled. 'So do most people. I seem to manage rather well, but I confess to being puzzled in this. I don't mean his writing the letter, but when we lunched together he asked many questions about you and the Chiavelli discovery.'

'Why do you think he did that?'

Mr. Morton shrugged. 'Who knows? Lucian keeps his own counsel, and turns questions aside by solemn mockery. You've heard him, my dear.'

'What did he say about me?'

'Oh, let me see. I asked why he was so interested and he said, "But my dear Uncle. Suppose our little Cadi proves to be a wealthy heiress. Then naturally I would want to court and marry her with all speed."'

I almost stamped my foot. 'Oh, how dare he say that! It's ridiculous, anyway!'

Mr. Morton spread his hands, eyes twinkling. 'But that is Lucian. A most shocking young man in some ways, I agree. But very amusing.'

On a sudden impulse I said, 'Would you call him a master of deceit?'

He stared, then said slowly, 'Wherever did you hear that phrase?'

I stood silent, wishing now that I had held my tongue, and after a moment he went on. 'Never mind. It was young Sarah, I suppose, but you don't want to tell tales.' He sat with hands linked across his stomach, gazing down at his desk for long seconds, then began to chuckle softly to himself. 'It's my own phrase, of course. A master of deceit. Yes, I think it well applies to Lucian.'

So Richard had spoken the truth. I felt all at sea for a moment, then stammered. 'But—but you *like* him, Mr. Morton!'

'Oh, very much.' He gave me a little smile. 'You see, it depends upon who is being deceived, and why.'

At that moment there came a tap on the door and Sarah entered with a piece of embroidery she had come to show her father. I was glad of the interruption, for I did not want to talk about Lucian Farrel any more. If he was a master of deceit, then so be it, but I did not want to know any more about it, and I felt a little sad to hear Mr. Morton trying to defend him by suggesting that it mattered who was the victim of Lucian's deceit and why. When Sarah left I went with her, and I suppose Mr. Morton forgot the subject, for it was not raised again.

Three weeks passed by, and it was during this time that I became steadily more aware of the person I came to think of as the grey-eyed stranger who seemed to haunt *Meadhaven*. I first saw him two days after Signor Vecchi's visit, as I rode Pompey along the bridle-path that ran through the woods on the western flank of *Meadhaven*.

He was sitting at ease on a dry grassy bank, doing nothing in particular. I judged him to be from the city, for he wore a grey suit and a grey bowler hat. As I approached at a trot he rose to his feet, raised his hat and gave me a polite good morning. His hair was light brown and well trimmed, his dress neat, his voice pleasant. I found him difficult to place by what he wore. He was not from the gentry, but neither was he a villager or a working man, and his manner was too self-possessed for him to be a shop assistant. His face was nondescript except for the rather cool grey eyes, which were strangely alert in contrast to his easy manner. In age he might have been anything between twenty-five and thirty-five, for though his face was youthful it held a deep maturity.

I returned his greeting and rode on. When I looked back I saw that he still stood with his hat in his hand, gazing after me.

After that it seemed that I rarely went out without seeing the grey-eyed stranger. Sometimes he would be strolling on the hill where I galloped Pompey, sometimes walking or taking his ease on one of the bridle-paths. And sometimes I had the strong impression that he was watching me unseen. When we passed, he always gave me the same polite greeting but made no attempt to converse. I began to feel irritated by his constant appearance. Strictly speaking he was on Mr. Morton's land, but there were several much-used footpaths with right-of-way, and Mr. Morton made no objection to anyone strolling in the woods or pasture.

One day, meeting the stranger at the foot of the hill where I had been exercising Adam, I reined to a halt as he wished me good afternoon.

'Good afternoon,' I replied a little coolly. 'You seem to spend much of your time strolling in these parts.'

'I hope it's causing you no annoyance, Miss,' he said. I caught the faint lilt of Irish in his voice now, and thought I detected a note of insolent mockery, but I could not be sure of that.

'No, it's causing me no annoyance,' I said shortly. 'There's freedom for anyone to walk here. You're not from Wealdhurst, are you?'

'I'm from parts greener than Kent,' he said casually. 'But I'm staying at *The Three Tuns* in Wealdhurst for a while,' As he spoke he reached out a hand to caress Adam's nose. I started to utter a warning, for I knew that Adam had a strong dislike of being fondled by strangers. but to my astonishment he snickered with pleasure and moved forward slightly to nuzzle the man's shoulder.

'Why, he likes you!' I said in surprise. 'Are you experienced with horses?'

He smiled, a brief smile that vanished almost at once. 'I've had a little to do with them now and then. This one's a fair mount, but not as fine as the other.'

'You've a good eye for them,' I said, warming to him a little.

He nodded. 'You've harness and saddlery that are well cared for, I see. That's good. Would you believe it now, but I've known accidents come from poor harness.'

I stiffened. That was a strange remark, too strange for it to be completely casual, or so it seemed to me. But how could this man know of the fall I had taken that day because of the broken ring on the cheek-bar? It was impossible, unless he had watched the incident unseen, or unless—but no, that thought was ridiculous, it could not have been this man himself who had filed down the ring to breaking point. There would have been no difficulty for him or anyone else in gaining access to the harness room by night, but what reason could he have for such a wicked act?

'I've had an accident myself from poor harness, and not long ago,' I said, watching him carefully.

He raised his eyebrows, and the cool grey eyes looked at me without surprise. 'Have you now, Miss? Well then, you'd best take care in future.'

'I'll do that. Will you be staying in Wealdhurst long, Mr. . . . ?'

He ignored my invitation to introduce himself, and said, 'It depends. I'm a travelling man, as you might say, but I've no fixed plans.'

'I see. And you don't grow bored with strolling about the countryside?'

'Bored? Why, never for a minute. A student of nature is what you might call me.'

I was sure I heard mockery in his voice now, and felt a quick flash of temper, but did not show it. I said, 'You surprise me. You haven't the look of a nature-lover.'

'It's a surprising world altogether, Miss, d'you not think? But there, I mustn't keep you from your ride.' He stepped back and raised the grey bowler hat. 'I'll wish you good afternoon.'

I responded, but felt annoyed as Adam cantered away, for it seemed that the stranger had dismissed me, whereas I felt that I should have been the one to end the conversation when I chose. Then I began to laugh at myself for having such a thought. 'You're getting to be a snob, Cadi Tregaron,' I said. 'So be careful.' But by the time I reached the stables I was in a thoughtful mood. The grey-eyed man had left me puzzled and uneasy, for I felt there had been undercurrents beneath the surface of his conversation. He knew far more of me than I of him, I was sure of that, and I also felt certain that he was in Wealdhurst for a purpose.

Strangely, I found myself almost trying to believe that it was he who had come close to causing my death when Pompey threw me, though for what reason I could not

134

imagine. But until now I had believed Lucian was responsible, or at least half-believed it, and to have suspicion lifted from him by this new possibility brought me a sense of relief that surprised me. After that meeting with the stranger I saw him more seldom, but often I had a powerful impression that he was close at hand, watching me. On the few occasions that we passed within speaking distance we only gave each other good day, as before. Since he was staying at *The Three Tuns* it would have been easy for me to discover his name, simply by talking to any of the villagers or to Young Kemp, but I would not allow myself to satisfy pointless curiosity.

The night before Richard went back to University, the dream came to me again. The events were the same, but the reality was more intense than ever before. This time I knew that the boat in which I rode was a gondola moving on a canal, and that the magnificent house was a palace in Venice, with the striped mooring poles outside. It was the Bad Dream, and as joy turned to terror and I fled from the man with Lucian's face, I woke to find myself choking and groaning in an effort to scream from a throat which seemed paralysed.

Shaking a little, my face wet and my breath shuddering, yet thankful to be awake, I got out of bed and moved to the window. The room seemed like a prison, and I wanted to look out on the open sky. I drew back one curtain and stood for a while gazing at the stars, a sense of peace gradually soothing my taut nerves. In the light of a thin bright moon, the trees threw long shadows across the lawns.

For five minutes I stood there, and was about to turn away when from the corner of my eye I thought I saw movement in the dark shape of a shrub, even though there was no wind. I stared hard, and had just made up my mind that my eyes had played a trick, when a figure moved out from the shadows of the shrub and stood for a moment or two gazing towards the house. Though I could not see his face I could clearly make out the shape of the neat grey bowler hat, tilted a little to one side, and I knew that this was the grey-eyed stranger. Oddly enough I felt no alarm, only indignation. My first thought was to open the window and call to him, asking what he was doing there at this time of night, but that might have alarmed the household, especially Sarah and Mrs. Morton.

I started towards the door, thinking to rouse Mr. Morton and tell of the intruder in the grounds, but then hesitated. Would it be stupid to make a fuss in the middle of the night? The house was bolted and barred, and I felt sure that the intruder was not seeking to break in. He was simply watching, as he had watched me for three weeks or more past, though for what reason I could not fathom.

I went back to the window, and the figure was gone. Nothing stirred on the lawns, though I waited for a full ten minutes. Thoughtfully I went back to bed. I would speak to Mr. Morton of it in the morning, and he could have the stranger questioned if he thought fit. But I decided that I would examine all the harness and saddlery with great care before I rode out next day.

I followed neither of the decisions I had made, for they were driven out of my head as I came down for breakfast. The front door stood open and Mr. Morton held a telegram in his hands, reading it. The telegraph boy was riding off down the drive on his bicycle. The arrival of telegrams caused no alarm at *Meadhaven,* for they came quite frequently, but this was not one of the usual messages from Mr. Morton's office. He looked up, saw me on the stairs, and said, 'Cadi, my dear, as soon as we have finished breakfast I want you to go and dress for a trip to London. We're going to see Mr. Caldwell.'

'Mr. Caldwell?' I echoed, unable to place the name.

'Yes. My solicitor. It seems he has important news.' Although Mr. Morton spoke quite calmly, I could see that he was restraining his eagerness. Since that night when the locket had yielded its secret I had tried resolutely not to think about the *Palazzo Chiavelli* and the family there of which I was a part, but now it seemed that I was soon to learn what Signor Vecchi's lawyer in Italy had done, and I was torn between excitement and apprehension.

I tried to imagine how the Chiavelli family would feel on learning of my existence. Would they be glad or indifferent?

If we met, how would they look upon me, with affection or as an intruder? I could not finish my breakfast, and hardly tasted what I ate. Sarah was bubbling and Mrs. Morton was in a state of agitation. 'The title must have continued, must it not, Edward?' she asked. 'In that case Cadi must actually be related to an Italian nobleman! I imagine *that* will put dear Mrs. Carpenter's nose out of joint when I tell her.'

Mrs. Carpenter was one of the few people in the Mortons' circle of acquaintances who had not accepted me as one of the family, but instead referred to me as, 'your little fisher-girl orphan, dear Mrs. Morton'. For all her affected ways, Mrs. Morton had long since come to treat me as a child of the family, no less than Sarah or Richard, and it angered her to hear anyone sneer at me.

'I share your opinion of Mrs. Carpenter, my dear,' Mr. Morton said, setting down his cup, 'but I must ask you to wait until we know precisely how matters stand before you attend to her nose—then do it with a will! Have you finished, Cadi? Then run along and change. If we catch a train before half-past nine we shall be in good time for our appointment. You will find old Caldwell rather formidable, perhaps, but don't let that worry you. He's a good lawyer, which is the main thing.'

It was a relief to get away from Sarah and Mrs. Morton. Young Kemp drove us to the station, and on the train journey Mr. Morton read his daily newspaper, sometimes turning to give me an encouraging smile. He knew how I felt, and that I did not want to chatter about what we might be told but would rather wait to learn what had really happened.

It was a crisp and beautiful morning, and as we were in plenty of time we did not take a hansom from Charing Cross, but walked along the Strand and up Kingsway to reach Lincoln's Inn Fields. Mr. Morton had offered me his arm, and as we walked along together he told me how nice I looked in my lilac coat and little round hat in pale grey with a matching lilac ribbon. Nervousness must have made me more sensitive than usual, for I was very conscious of his affection for me. He had repaid me a hundred times over for what I had done during his terrible ordeal in Mogg Race Bay, but his affection was no part of that. Such as I was, he loved me for what I was, and my awareness of this almost brought tears to my eyes. He was not a handsome man, with his rather gnomish face and funny little beard, but I could not have been more proud and glad if I had been walking with my hand on the arm of King Edward himself.

Mr. Caldwell was a plump man with mutton-chop whiskers that were becoming quite old-fashioned now. A young gentleman showed us into his office and then withdrew. I was introduced, and Mr. Caldwell puffed around, getting us comfortably settled in big leather armchairs, then sat down behind his big desk and opened a folder which lay on the blotter in front of him. Fixing pince-nez on his nose, he peered at Mr. Morton over the top of them.

'Well now, things have moved much more quickly than we could have expected, Mr. Morton. Haven't bothered you with interim reports. You didn't want 'em. Told me to get matters sorted out and then let you know.' He thumped the papers in front of him. 'Well, here it is. Your friend, this Italian chap, Signor Vecchi, he hurried things along by having government couriers carry some of the letters from Avvocato Bonello in Rome. That's the Italian lawyer. Sound chap. Pleasure to deal with.' He paused and glanced at me, frowning rather ferociously. 'I gather you want the young gel here while I tell you about it?'

It was clear that Mr. Caldwell did not approve of my presence on this weighty occasion, but Mr. Morton waved a hand and said coolly, 'Pray tell Miss Tregaron what you have to say, Caldwell. It's her affair, and I'm simply here to watch her interests.'

Mr. Caldwell looked taken aback, grunted, and muttered under his breath something about 'modern ideas . . .' and 'young women these days. . . .' But he suddenly seemed to me much less forbidding since Mr. Morton had spoken. At last he cleared his throat and turned his swivel chair a little to look at me.

'Very well then, Miss Tregaron. Mr. Morton gave me all

details about you and this locket affair, and put me in touch with my colleague in Rome. First thing I did was to secure an affidavit from Signor Vecchi, as witness to the incident of the locket, when the engraving inside was discovered.' He turned to Mr. Morton. 'Does she know what an affidavit is?'

Mr. Morton looked at the ceiling and sighed. 'She is an intelligent girl, Caldwell,' he said patiently. 'If there's anything she doesn't understand, she will tell you.'

Mr. Caldwell sniffed and cocked an inquiring eye at me. I said gravely, 'I've read about such things, Mr. Caldwell. I believe an affidavit is a sworn statement.'

'Good enough, good enough,' he grunted, and seemed to mellow a little. 'Well, young lady, then I sent a man down to Mawstone. He saw your Vicar there, a woman called Miss Rigg, and several others. Got affidavits from them, declaring that it was common knowledge that your grandfather, Robert Penwarden, saved an Italian girl from drowning in Naples Bay, brought her home and married her. She'd lost her memory and only knew her name was Caterina. They had issue, a child called Jennifer, who grew up and married Donald Tregaron. And you, Caterina Tregaron, are the issue of that marriage. Understand me so far?'

He had learned his lesson, and asked the question direct this time, instead of through Mr. Morton. I said, 'Yes, thank you, that's very clear, Mr. Caldwell.'

'Good. Now the next step. Sent all this to Avvocato Bonello. Question of whether it was sufficient under Roman Law to establish that Caterina, your grandmother, was in fact Caterina Chiavelli. He's a good chap. Said that before, didn't I? Never mind. Anyway, he had inquiries made in Venice, where the present Count Chiavelli and his family still live. Dug up an amazing story, though there was no secret about it. Whole thing reported in the journals of the day.'

He turned some pages in the folder. 'Here it is. You could read it yourself if you knew Italian. Newspaper cutting of some sort.'

'She both speaks and reads Italian fluently,' Mr. Morton said gently, looking out of the window.

Mr. Caldwell sighed. 'I see . . . well, you can read it later. I'll explain the gist of it in a moment, but I'd better give you the background first. Caterina, born in 1841, was the only child of the then Count Chiavelli of Venice. Her mother, the Countess, died ten years later, and the Count did not remarry. In fact he became something of a recluse, and the young Caterina was brought up by his sister, Marguerita, and her husband, who was a penniless Hungarian Baron. He doesn't affect the situation, so we won't bother with his name.'

Mr. Caldwell peered down at what seemed to be a drawing of a family tree among the papers, sniffed contemptuously and added, 'Wouldn't know how to pronounce it anyway. However, their issue has some importance, but we'll come to that later. Let's concentrate on Caterina for the moment. When she was in her twentieth year, her Aunt Marguerita took her on a trip to Rome and Naples. They were three weeks in Rome, and then posted by carriage down to Naples, where they stayed at the house of a wealthy friend of the family. And there, during the second week, Caterina disappeared.'

Mr. Caldwell paused, offered a huge snuff-box to Mr. Morton, who declined, and took a pinch himself.

'Disappeared,' he repeated impressively. 'One evening she quite simply could not be found. The last that anyone saw of her, she was walking in the grounds just before dusk, wearing a white dress. Bonello managed to dig up the police reports of the time, heaven knows how, and Marguerita is reported as saying that Caterina was a somewhat headstrong young woman, difficult to control, and that she, Marguerita, had felt increasingly suspicious that Caterina had a romantic attachment to some unknown man. When she disappeared, the first theory was that she had been kidnapped, the next that she had run away with her—ahem—her lover. Nobody ever discovered the truth, for she was never seen or heard of again.'

'Except by Robert Penwarden that same night?' Mr.

Morton suggested. 'And later by all those who knew her in Mawstone?'

'Exactly, sir!' Mr. Caldwell banged his hand on the table triumphantly. 'The dates coincide. I have inquired at Lloyds, and at the shipping company, which still exists, and also among several folk in Mawstone who well remember Robert Penwarden and his wife. The night on which he found Caterina in Naples Bay was the same night that she disappeared. So we know now that she didn't run away with a man. She was taken by force, to be brutally murdered. What we don't know is *why*. And I suppose we never shall. . . .'

There was silence in the room, and I think we were all wondering why anyone should have wanted to take the young Caterina's life. But this was something I had often brooded upon before, and I knew it was useless to wonder.

Mr. Caldwell cleared his throat again. 'Now,' he said, 'let's go back for a moment to the family situation at that time. Marguerita had a son and a daughter. The boy died while in childhood. The daughter was a few years older than Caterina. After his daughter's disappearance, the Count became even more of a recluse. He lived to be seventy-six, and his title was such that it could continue through the heirs-female of his body issuing, and collaterally through blood kinship. Understand that piece of legal jargon, young lady?'

'I'm not very sure, Mr. Caldwell. Does it mean the title could pass to a daughter if there was no son, and to a brother or sister if there were no children at all?'

To my surprise Mr. Caldwell smiled, looking suddenly like a plump and friendly frog. 'Pity you can't rewrite some of our law-books, Miss Tregaron. Make it all much simpler. Very well then, the title passed to the Count's sister, Marguerita, who became the Countess. She'd long been a widow. The Hungarian chap drank himself to an early death. But she only survived her brother for a year, so the title passed down to her daughter, who was married to another husband who doesn't concern us. They're both dead now, but they produced a son and a daughter. The daughter became a nun. The son is now forty-nine, and is the present Count Chiavelli. He married the daughter of a minor Italian nobleman when he was in his twenties, and now has a son of twenty-five. The Count, his wife and his son all live in the *Palazzo Chiavelli*.'

Mr. Caldwell leaned back in his chair, took off his pince-nez and polished them with the corner of his handkerchief. 'Any questions to ask on Miss Tregaron's behalf at this stage, Mr. Morton?' he asked. 'These family trees are rather complicated for anybody.'

'The present Count and his wife would be of Cadi's mother's generation?' said Mr. Morton. 'And the son would be of Cadi's generation, is that right?'

The solicitor nodded assent. Mr. Morton gave me an inquiring look. 'All clear, Cadi?'

'Yes, thank you, Mr. Morton.'

'Good.' He looked at Mr. Caldwell again. 'Does all this have any material effect on Cadi, except to know that she is second or third cousin, once or twice removed, to the son of the present Count Chiavelli?'

'I'm coming to that, sir. I'm coming to the nub of the matter now,' Mr. Caldwell said with a rather smug and tantalizing air. 'The old Count always clung to the belief that his lost daughter was alive and would one day be found. Reading between the lines, I rather think he was ashamed of having neglected her. Hard to tell at this distance, but I don't much like the sound of this Marguerita woman, and perhaps young Caterina felt the same way.'

I thought it likely that Mr. Caldwell had made a shrewd guess, for if my Granny Caterina had felt neglected by her father and had disliked her aunt, this would explain why she had instinctively made no attempt to find out where she came from or who she was.

'Be that as it may,' Mr. Caldwell went on, 'the Count made a strange provision in his will. Couldn't do anything about his title of course, that's a matter for the courts, but he was a wealthy man, and he entailed his whole estate.'

I leaned forward and said, 'I'm not sure what that means, Mr. Caldwell. Would you very kindly explain?'

'Happy to, Miss Tregaron. In simple terms it means that when he died his estate did not pass on to his heir—his sister in this case. All she got was the revenue from the estate, the money earned from the lands, property and investments he owned. But the capital of the fortune couldn't be touched. That clear now?'

'Yes. Thank you very much.'

'At the time he died, your grandmother, Caterina, would have been forty years old. So the Count entailed his estate for a limited period of thirty years, which would have brought your grandmother to three-score and ten. After that time, the entailment was to cease and the estate would go free of all encumbrance to the then beneficiary. That means to the descendant of his sister Marguerita, the legal heir in the absence of your grandmother or *her* descendants. In other words, the present Count Chiavelli.'

'Do you mean that if my grandmother was alive today she would inherit the estate?' I asked, a little dazed by the thought of Granny Caterina being rich.

'Quite right,' nodded Mr. Caldwell. 'Can't speak as to the title. Whether or not the present Count would have to give that up in her favour would be a complicated matter for the Italian courts to decide. But she would certainly inherit the estate.' He took off his pince-nez and put them down on the documents in front of him, looking at me with his bewhiskered head a little on one side. 'But as she is no longer alive, and neither is your mother, the inheritance will pass to you, Miss Tregaron, when you reach the age of twenty-one.'

I jumped with shock, and felt my eyes growing round with astonishment. Lucian had joked about this with Mr. Morton, and Sarah had built wild daydreams, but I had never for a moment imagined that anything like this could happen.

'You say, when she is twenty-one.' There was a query in Mr. Morton's voice.

'That is correct, sir. The will is quite explicit. The entailment is for thirty years, which would bring us to the year 1911. Until that time, the estate is held in trust by two

143

Italian banks for Caterina Chiavelli, daughter of the old Count, if she should be found alive, or otherwise for her closest living descendant on attaining the age of twenty-one years. My colleague, Bonello, is also of opinion that the courts may eventually declare in her favour as regards the title, but that remains to be seen.'

Mr. Morton looked at me, smiling, waiting for me to speak, but I could not. All my careful composure for Mr. Caldwell's benefit had disappeared. In the shock of what I had just been told, I did not feel thrilled or happy. It was all too huge for me to grasp, and if anything I felt afraid. I pressed my hands to my hot cheeks, and when at last I could speak I only managed to blurt out, 'I—I don't think I want to be a Countess! Please, Mr. Morton!'

Chapter Eight

HE CAME TO ME QUICKLY and held my hand. His eyes were bright with laughter and delight, but his voice was sympathetic as he said, 'There now, Cadi, I know this is all rather overwhelming, but don't be frightened, my dear.'

'I'm sorry—I feel so confused. What will happen now, and what shall I have to do? You will help me, won't you, Mr. Morton?'

'Always, Cadi. I stand as a father to you for as long as you may need me. You know that, child.' He turned to Mr. Caldwell. 'Let us forget the title for the present. Is the fortune a large one?'

'Very substantial.' Mr. Caldwell rummaged through his papers and put on his pince-nez again. 'Until Miss Tregaron's identity as a direct descendant of the old Count is legally proved, we have no right to information from the banks responsible for administering the Trust. But Bonello has been able to make a rough assessment. He suggests that a quarter of a million sterling would be a conservative figure.'

I gasped and clutched Mr. Morton's hand tightly. It was only by becoming furious with myself for my own weakness that I was able to avoid bursting into tears. But Mr. Morton gave a great peal of exuberant laughter.

'A quarter of a million?' he echoed. 'Oh, my little Cadi. Can you imagine what my wife will do to Mrs. Carpenter's nose, armed with that information!'

The thought was so funny to me that I joined in his laughter, a little hysterically I fear, but at least it served as an outlet for my pent-up feelings. Mr. Caldwell watched us in bewilderment, then shrugged and took another pinch of snuff.

said at last. 'Will this be difficult in law?'

When we had recovered, Mr. Morton paced thoughtfully across the room, his hands linked behind his back. 'You mentioned the matter of proving Cadi's identity, Caldwell,' he

'Not in Bonello's opinion,' came the reply. 'And it's his opinion that counts, since we shall be dealing with the laws of Italy. But the evidence is overwhelming. The girl Robert Penwarden saved from death and brought home to Cornwall was undoubtedly Caterina Chiavelli. The sequence of events alone makes that almost sure, and the locket she was wearing clinches it beyond any doubt. There's also no doubt that this young lady is her granddaughter. Half Mawstone can vouch for that, and the parish records prove it.'

Mr. Morton nodded. His manner was serious now. 'The present Count may lose his title then, and when Cadi becomes twenty-one he will certainly lose the fortune he otherwise expected to inherit in a few years' time, when the entailment ends in 1911. I imagine he will fight the case in the Italian courts.'

'I thought the same,' said Mr. Caldwell, 'and so did Bonello. We'd win, of course, but we thought the Count would fight. However, we've misjudged the man.' He gave a self-satisfied smile and paused expectantly, like a conjurer who has produced a rabbit from a hat.

Mr. Morton's eyebrows shot up. 'You mean he already knows about this? The Count *knows* of Cadi's existence?'

'Yes, sir. He does. You gave me wide discretion, and I gave

the same to Bonello. Once we had the whole story, Bonello felt it could do no harm, and indeed might save time, if he visited the Count and placed the facts before him. Had to be done some time, and Bonello wanted to judge the fellow's reaction, so he could advise as to whether or not there was going to be a legal battle.'

Mr. Morton fingered his beard, then nodded. 'I think he did right. And you say the Count doesn't propose to fight?'

'On the contrary, it seems that after the first surprise of it he was quite delighted to learn that the great family mystery of Caterina's disappearance had been cleared up at last, and that a grand-child of hers existed. Warmhearted sort of chap, apparently, and with a strong family feeling. Anyway, the fact is, he's accepted Cadi as being who she claims to be without the slightest quibble. No question of fighting the claim.'

I said slowly, 'It seems unfair, somehow . . . I mean, for me suddenly to appear after all this time and—and take his fortune.'

'My dear child, it is *not* his fortune,' Mr. Morton said gently. 'It is your great-grandfather's fortune, which he left to your Granny Caterina, and through her to you. I agree the present Count may well have been disappointed in his expectations, but that is another matter entirely. Neither you nor he have any justification for criticizing the manner in which the old Count disposed of his estate. And the present Count seems to be a gentleman of sufficient wisdom and character to realize this, I'm happy to say.'

'Very rare,' Mr. Caldwell grunted. 'Very rare indeed. I'm a lawyer and I've handled wills by the hundred. Seen families fight like wild-cats over a piano, let alone a quarter of a million.'

Mr. Morton smiled. 'I'm sure you lawyers see the worst aspects of human nature, Caldwell, but we appear to be fortunate with Count Chiavelli.'

'So it seems, so it seems,' Mr. Caldwell agreed grudgingly. 'You may well get a letter from him in a few days, Miss Tregaron. He decided that he'd allow time for Bonello to inform me, and for me to give you the news, and then he would write to you direct. Speaks English quite well, I understand.'

'Then we shall wait upon events,' said Mr. Morton. 'Oddly enough, we had half planned to visit Venice next year. We shall certainly have to do so now. Cadi must meet her new-found relatives, and also the banker Trustees of the estate which is to be hers. Well, thank you very much, Caldwell. You carry on the good work and let us know when the Trustees have accepted the new position legally.'

'Shouldn't take very long now, Mr. Morton, since the Count himself has accepted it.' Mr. Caldwell got up and waddled round his desk to see us out. At the door of his office he said, 'By the way, Bonello's visit to the palazzo gave us another bit of proof. Remember I asked you to provide me with some good photographs of Miss Tregaron? Well, I sent a couple to Bonello. It appears there are quite a few portraits in the palazzo, and one of them is of Caterina, painted only six months before she disappeared. Bonello says she's the very image of her granddaughter. Staggering likeness between 'em. And she was wearing the locket when she sat for this portrait. It's there on canvas.'

As we walked through Lincoln's Inn I was in a dream. That first sensation of fright had passed now, and it seemed I ought to feel thrilled and overjoyed at the thought that in little over a year I would be rich, with more money than I had ever dreamt of, but somehow the feeling eluded me. My stupid mind was vaguely trying to think of presents I could buy for Sarah, for Mrs. Morton, and for all the family. I suppose they might have amounted to a few pounds in all. Beyond that my mind was blank. I lived in a beautiful home, I had pretty clothes, I was well fed, and under the fatherly care of a man who was kindness itself. I could think of nothing I wanted that money could buy. In sudden exasperation I turned to Mr. Morton as we walked together and cried almost plaintively, 'Whatever am I going to *do* with the money?'

He looked down sideways at me with that funny half mournful smile. 'Have you come to the truth of it so quickly then, Cadi? Ah, but you were always a wise child. Well ... forget the money for now. And when it comes to you, use the wisdom you've been blessed with. To have sufficient

money for your needs is very pleasant. To have a great deal
more than sufficient can be a burden, if you allow it to
be. So rich or poor, just be yourself, Cadi, and don't change.
Give yourself to what is important, as you've always done—
to people, not to things.' His smile lost its touch of sadness,
and he chuckled. 'Rescue silly old gentlemen who go out
sailing in boats. Dance with outcast young men when everybody else leaves the floor——' he broke off as if struck by a
thought, then said, 'Speaking of Lucian has given me an excellent idea. I have to go to my office for an hour or two, and
I've been rather wondering what to do with you. But if we
take a cab to Lucian's flat first, I can leave you with him, pro-
viding we find him at home. How would you like that?'

I was caught a little off balance, but tried not to show it
and smilingly agreed. Yet Mr. Morton must have seen my
hesitation, for when we were sitting in the cab he glanced
at me and said, 'Don't you wish to visit Lucian, Cadi?'

I was not at all sure of my feelings about visiting Lucian
and being left with him for an hour or two. It would be the
first time I had seen him since the night he had beaten
Richard so cruelly, and I did not know how I would feel
when I saw him, or if I would speak about that night. But I
could not tell Mr. Morton this, so I gave another reason for
the reluctance I must have shown, but still a true one.

'I was wondering if it would displease Mrs. Morton,' I
said. 'I know Lucian is of the family, but . . . well, I'm sure
she wouldn't approve.'

'So am I,' agreed Mr. Morton. 'She is rather more concerned about socially correct behaviour than I am myself.
However, Lucian has a housekeeper, who lives out but will
be at the flat by this hour, so you will be sufficiently chaper-
oned. Does that relieve your anxiety?'

I smiled. 'I wasn't anxious for myself, it's just that I
wouldn't like to upset Mrs. Morton.'

'You're quite right, my dear, and it's very thoughtful of
you.' He shrugged a little ruefully. 'Although I rather think
it will be impossible to prevent all anxiety for her as time
goes on. She is not very flexible in her ideas of propriety, and
she will find it hard to accept that the days of the chaperon

are fast passing.' He nodded as though to himself. 'Yes, in London now, and in many big cities, we have young women working as clerks, typists, private secretaries, and in the retail trade, quite apart from the professions of medicine, journalism and the like. I believe that there is one female clerk for every three male clerks today, and the proportion is growing.'

He glanced out of the cab window at the busy street as we clattered along High Holborn. 'You can see for yourself how the old order is changing. These ladies travel unescorted, and work side by side with men. I believe it to be a good thing, myself, a healthy and natural development. Your sex has been too much dominated by mine over the last thousand years or so, I fear.'

I was always interested when Mr. Morton talked in this manner, giving his thoughts on the way of the world. I knew that most men of his generation fumed at what they considered the lack of propriety and dangerous freedom of modern young women, but Mr. Morton was above all a fair and just man, without prejudices. I had once overheard him say to Colonel Rodsley, 'Certainly I agree with you that women are not the equals of men, Colonel. But neither are men the equals of women. They are quite simply entirely different creatures, thank God, and not to be compared. But that one should be subordinate to the other in the eyes of the law is an injustice I hope to see rectified before I die.'

I think he enjoyed talking in this way with me because I was interested in what he said, and on this occasion his reflections lasted until the cab came to a halt in Half Moon Street, where Lucian's flat lay. There he told the cabbie to wait, and we climbed two flights of stairs to the front door of Lucian's flat.

I felt very nervous, but in a way I was glad because this left no room in my mind to think of all that I had learned in Mr. Caldwell's office.

A grey-haired lady with a fresh complexion and wearing an apron answered the door-bell.

'Good morning, Mrs. Redman. Is Mr. Farrel in?'

'Why, it's you Mr. Morton, sir. Come in, please. Mr.

Farrel's in the studio. I'll call him at once. A lovely morning, isn't it?'

She led us through to the drawing room, then excused herself, leaving the door open as she went out. I looked about me curiously. After *Meadhaven* and the other big country houses I knew, this room seemed to be very sparsely furnished, and the walls were painted pale blue, in strange contrast to the dark colours and heavy florid wall-papers that so many people favoured. Yet I liked the room, for though it was not large it seemed spacious and uncluttered. The pale walls reflected sunlight from the window and made all seem light and airy.

Then we heard Lucian's voice calling. 'Hallo there, my aged Uncle. Will you come through? I'm up to my elbows in clay.'

Mr. Morton smiled, moving to the open door and calling, 'So Adam was created, I understand. And I have with me a most charming specimen of Adam's rib. May we both come?'

'Aunt Helen?' came Lucian's voice, a little doubtfully.

'No, it's Cadi.'

'Ah, come along then. Aunt Helen would disapprove of my work, I'm afraid.'

We went a few paces along the passage, passing Mrs. Redman on the way, then turned through an open door into Lucian's studio. It was a big room, very long, with a huge window in one wall and a fanlight half as big set in the ceiling.

There were two heavy round tables, rather above normal height, two rather worn armchairs, a couch, and a bench on which lay several mallets and an assortment of chisels and gouges. Around the walls stood roughly cut blocks of wood, some large, some small. I recognized mahogany and oak, but there were woods of other colours and graining which I could not name. On shelves and on plain side-tables stood a number of wood-carvings. There was a life-sized head of an old man with the lined face of a peasant; a miniature carving, in relief on a flat oval of wood, showed a naked goddess with arms lifted as if to the sun; the head and fore-part of a horse rose from a base of rough-hewn wood as if from the sea; the twelve-inch figure of an Asiatic in rags leaned on a crude plough. There were two smooth hands, clasped with fingers interlocked; a man's sinewy arm lying half-sunk in the rough block from which it had been carved; a bare ankle and foot, shapely, feminine.

A bust near the window caught my eye, and I knew that this was the carving Sarah had spoken of. The woman was young, yet her face seemed to hold the experience of all the ages, and the careless fall of the low-cut fabric, the tilt of the head, the curve of the mouth, all gave the effect of wicked feminine assurance and insolence. Yet though I had never known such a woman, I had the overpowering conviction that there was truth in this sculpture of her, that what she was, what Lucian saw and knew, had been faithfully captured. This essence lay in all the carvings. Their impact was immediate, yet they did not tell all at a single glance. There was a depth to them that held the mind and eye, and what I had first thought of as the fragments of sculpture were entire in themselves—the clasped hands, the negligent foot, required no more substance than Lucian had given them.

He stood by one of the tables, scooping handfuls of grey clay from a huge jar and building it round a thick rod which rose from a heavy base, squeezing and moulding. After Sarah had told me that Lucian's hobby was wood carving, I had read about it in one of Mr. Morton's encyclopaedias. I knew that the rod was called an armature, and that it was to support the mass of clay while Lucian moulded it into the shape he wanted. The clay could be altered, remoulded, trimmed and shaped until at last he had the model to his satisfaction. Only then would he take up his chisels and begin to carve from a block of wood, using the clay model to guide him, and calipers to measure and confirm the proportions.

Lucian wore a shirt open at the neck and with sleeves rolled up. Both this and the rather shabby old trousers he wore were smudged with clay. His dark face with the flaring eyebrows was very intent. We stood in silence for perhaps thirty seconds, watching him. Then he lifted his head and smiled.

'How are you, Uncle Edward? How are you, Cadi? Please

take a seat. I don't think the chairs will collapse. Forgive my rudeness but I just wanted to finish that little job.' He moved to a bowl of water and began to wash his hands. 'What brings you here this morning?'

'Necessity, my dear nephew, necessity,' said Uncle Edward regretfully. 'We would hardly seek the company of a shabby, clay-smeared reprobate for pleasure, would we?'

'A fanciful thought indeed, uncle mine,' Lucian agreed, drying his hands on a towel. 'What necessity drove you to it?'

'As a matter of fact,' said Mr. Morton, dropping his bantering manner, 'we've just come from old Caldwell. He had considerable news for Cadi.' Lucian looked at me, and I felt myself flushing, for though we had met so few times and had talked together hardly at all, his look was not that of a near stranger but of one who was confident that he knew me completely. He twitched an eyebrow upwards and said, 'Considerable news? That sounds exciting. And yet our Cadi doesn't appear to be excited.'

'I haven't had time to think about it yet,' I said rather sharply.

'It's more a matter of her being level-headed, thank God,' said Mr. Morton, leaning back warily in his creaking armchair. 'The thought of trying to restrain Sarah and your Aunt Helen in their emotions makes my mind boggle, Lucian.'

'Can you stop boggling long enough to tell me what the news is, Uncle? Is Cadi to be a great heiress, as I suggested?' He threw the towel aside, smiling, and settled himself on the corner of the bench.

'We have discovered,' Mr. Morton said, 'that Cadi is indeed a direct descendant of Count Chiavelli, who was her great-grandfather. The estate he left was entailed, and she will inherit it when she reaches the age of twenty-one. She may also inherit the title, and become a Countess.'

There was a long silence. Lucian had stopped smiling. 'A large fortune?' he said at last, softly.

'In the region of a quarter of a million sterling.'

An even longer silence.

Then, 'I see . . .' said Lucian, and sat with folded arms,

gazing through me rather than at me, broodingly. I felt uncomfortable and resentful.

'You don't appear very excited yourself, Lucian,' I said.

He came out of his reverie with a little start, and gave a quick smile. 'I'm sorry. Of course I'm delighted for you. It's tremendous news.' He looked at Mr. Morton. 'How does the present Count feel about losing his money and his title?'

'The latter is not yet certain, Lucian. But in any event he seems to feel no resentment. We're told he's deeply moved to hear that the old Count's great grand-daughter has been found.'

'Well . . . that's wonderful,' Lucian said vaguely, thrusting his hands in his pockets and getting up to move rather aimlessly about the studio. 'I suppose you'll be taking her to Venice as soon as you can arrange it?'

'There's no haste, I feel. The matter is in the hands of lawyers. But no doubt Cadi will be wanting to meet her relatives, so I imagine we shall go out there not later than the spring.' He looked at me. 'Or does that seem too long a delay for you, my dear?'

I shook my head. 'I'd like to meet them, but they don't really feel like my own family, Mr. Morton. That sounds unkind, but I don't mean it so. It's just that . . . well, we're complete strangers, we've been apart for three generations, and—and Granny Caterina didn't want to go back to her family anyway. I think of *Meadhaven* as where I belong. I'll be glad to go to Venice just whenever it's convenient for you.'

Mr. Morton got to his feet and patted my shoulder. 'So be it, then.' He turned to Lucian. 'I'm inviting you to lunch, dear boy, little though you deserve it. I have to spend what's left of the morning in Whitehall, and I'd like to leave Cadi in your care. I'm not asking if you mind, it was a matter of asking Cadi if *she* minded, and to my astonishment she agreed to suffer your company for an hour or so.'

'She has a kind heart,' Lucian said absently, 'there's no doubt of it.' He was prowling now, looking at me intently, first from one side and then the other, but as if I was an object rather than a person. 'I suggest you make it the Café

Royal for lunch, Uncle Edward. And I'll have champagne, to celebrate Cadi's good fortune. It will be expensive for you, but parsimony is bad for the liver at your age.'

Mr. Morton laughed and picked up his hat and cane. 'Cadi shall have a glass, and we'll split the rest of the bottle between us, my boy. At one-thirty, then.'

When he had gone I felt suddenly very embarrassed. Lucian said nothing, but continued to move about, gazing at me in that strange way.

'I like your sculptures, Lucian,' I said at last, rather desperately. 'I like them very much.'

'H'mm? Yes . . . good. But never mind that. Take your hat and coat off, Cadi.' He seemed to be seized with sudden excitement, and took my hand. 'Be quick. Here, let me help. Good. Now come and sit on this upright chair, here under the fanlight.' He lifted his voice and shouted. 'Mrs. Redman!'

She came bustling into the studio, and Lucian said, 'Take Miss Tregaron's coat and hat, will you? She's going to sit for me. Do you want anything, Cadi? A cup of tea? A biscuit?'

'No—no, thank you. Do you mean you want to sculpt *me*?'

'Yes, of course. Now sit down. That's right. Where's something . . . ?' He looked about the studio, running a hand through his hair. 'Ah, this will do.' He picked up a piece of rope that lay on top of a small crate. 'All right, Mrs. Redman, there's nothing we need. You go on with your work. Now then, Cadi . . .' he paused as he bent to double the rope and tie the ends round a leg of the table, then he moved towards me and put the loop of rope in my hands. 'Draw it tight—no, not like that! You're supposed to be holding *reins*, Cadi. Ah, that's better.'

With quick, energetic movements he turned to the shapeless clay on the armature and tore handfuls of it away. 'Keep still, there's a good girl. No, dammit, that won't do.' He came to me again and made to touch the sleeves of my dress, but I jerked my hands away.

'You'll make it all dirty with clay!' I exclaimed.

'All right, all right,' he said impatiently. 'Unbutton the sleeves and roll them back to leave your wrists bare.' Somewhat in a daze I obeyed, all thought of protest smothered by his almost feverish energy. This was a Lucian I had not seen before. The aloofness and the mockery had vanished. Excitement ran deep in him, the excitement of the artist, and for the present he wore no armour and was without pretence.

'Now, hold the reins again. A little tauter . . . so! That's good. Talk if you want to, tell me all about old Caldwell if you like, and how you're going to be rich. Sing if you like, anything, but don't move your hands.'

'My . . . hands? *Just* my hands?' I could feel myself going hot with indignation again. During the hectic moments when he was posing me I had imagined that he intended to start modelling for a sculpture of me, a bust perhaps, and I had felt quite flustered with delight at such a compliment. He was working on the clay now, and did not respond to my question, so I spoke again, loudly.

'Lucian!' I said. 'Are you just going to do my hands?'

'What? Yes, of course!' He did not look up from his work.

Of course, indeed! There was a fine compliment. My temper was slipping when the humour struck me. I had been a vain little idiot to think he would want to sculpt my head, and well deserved to be brought down to earth with a bump. All Lucian wanted was a pair of hands, anonymous hands, and I happened to be there. My only consolation was that it seemed slightly better than being an anonymous foot. I almost started to giggle at the thought, but then froze for fear of moving.

'Why do you want to carve my hands?' I asked.

'Because they're beautiful,' he said brusquely. 'Pull harder on the rope, I want to see the effort in them.'

'Beautiful?' My voice was incredulous, for I truly could not believe that he meant what he had said. 'Oh, not mine, Lucian. Those others that you've carved, the clasped hands —they're beautiful.'

He made a sound of comtempt. 'Good for making daisy chains, that's all. Chocolate-box hands.' Tight-lipped and intent, he worked with vigorous fingers on the clay, so absorbed that he seemed to be speaking his thoughts aloud to himself rather than to me. 'Hands aren't just ornaments, they have purpose as well. Can't be beautiful without that element. Yours are beautiful. I knew it that first day, after Mogg Race, when you'd worn them raw on the looms of the oars. They're more elegant now, but they haven't lost their character. They're hands for trusting in.'

He stopped speaking abruptly, and I sat gazing down at my own hands as if seeing them for the first time, trying in vain to understand what Lucian found in them. At least there was some pleasure in realizing that it was not just any pair of hands he wanted to sculpt, but mine.

For a while I talked, telling Lucian all that had passed in Mr. Caldwell's office, but it seemed to me that he was hardly listening, for he asked no questions and made no comment. At last I stopped, but he seemed unaware of the silence. My hands and arms were beginning to ache, but I set my teeth, determined not to ask if I could rest. Instead I did what I had sometimes done in Mawstone whenever I was very tired or in pain from some hurt. I tried to separate my mind from my body, and to think without feeling.

I was alone in this studio with the man who had flogged Richard, the man Richard had warned me was perhaps dangerously unbalanced, yet I felt no alarm. Now, with Lucian present, I simply could not believe Richard's warning. If it was true, Mr. Morton would surely know, and he would not have been content to entrust me to Lucian. So it could not be true. But then, why had Richard lied? And who had played that dangerous prank with the harness, almost killing me? There was the grey-eyed stranger. I had seen him prowling at night. Or . . .

The thought came unbidden to my mind, astonishing me. Could it have been Richard himself? What had Mr. Morton once said? 'He is not a *sincere* young man . . . it is difficult to know his true feelings.' But Mr. Morton had also said of Lucian that he was a master of deceit. And Richard had no cause to harm me, on the contrary, he seemed to think that he loved me. But then, neither Lucian nor anyone else had reason to harm me, as far as I knew.

My thoughts went round and round in circles, finding no solution. Perhaps there was none to find. Perhaps all that had occurred was due to coincidence, and I was reading too much into what Richard had said and into Mr. Morton's casual words.

I watched Lucian, keeping my mind fixed on him, for I was distantly aware that my hands were on fire with the strain now, and I did not dare to think about them. He had brought out from the clay the rough shape of two hands, down-curving and with the knuckles resting on clay for support.

The fingers were not yet clearly defined, but with a wooden spatula he was now beginning to pick out the sinews of the wrists.

There came a tap on the door and Mrs. Redman entered carrying two letters. 'Here's the mid-day post, sir—oh!' She stared indignantly. 'Have you had the young lady sitting for you all this time? Heavens above, Mr. Lucian, what are you thinking of? She'll be tired out!'

'Eh? All what time?' Lucian straightened up, almost glaring at her and looking more satanic than ever. But Mrs. Redman did not retreat. 'All this last hour and more!' she said firmly.

'Hour?' He blinked, then relaxed suddenly and threw down the spatula. 'Sorry, Cadi. I didn't realize. Why the devil didn't you say?'

'And that's no way to speak in front of Miss Tregaron,' Mrs. Redman said severely, putting the letters on a table. 'It's late for a cup of tea, but I'm going to make one anyway. And I'll thank you to change your clothes and take tea with your guest in the drawing room, Mr. Lucian, as any respectable gentleman would.'

She stumped out. My hands were resting on my lap now, but I could not straighten my fingers. The muscles were locked after the long tension. Lucian was washing his hands. As he dried them he said, smiling, 'You're a stubborn little creature still. Hate to give in, don't you?'

'I just didn't want to disturb you,' I said, and winced as pain shot up my arms when I tried to move my fingers.

'What's the matter?' Lucian dropped the towel and moved towards me. 'Cramp?'

'My fingers are . . . stuck!' I said helplessly.

Frowning, he knelt by the chair, took my right hand, and started to massage it, gently at first but then kneading and squeezing more firmly to ease the stiff sinews. Almost at once the pain began to lessen.

'Are you pleased with what you've done so far?' I asked.

He turned to look at the half-finished clay model. 'I think so, but it's too early to be sure. You must give me another sitting so I can finish it, Cadi.'

'Well, I—I can't say when. You'll have to ask Mr. Morton.'

'I'll ask him. Now tell me what's been happening at *Meadhaven*.'

'What sort of things?'

'Oh, whether Pompey's behaving himself. The latest village gossip. Who Sarah's in love with this week. The state of Old Kemp's rheumatics. How Aunt Helen's feud with the Hattons is going.'

My mind still felt oddly far away. I ought to have felt flustered and embarrassed to be sitting there while Lucian kneaded the pain from my hands, but somehow it seemed quite natural. I began to talk about *Meadhaven*, a little dreamily I think, and as I talked I watched Lucian, sometimes his hands and sometimes his face. His head was turned a little, for he kept his eyes on the clay model, as if he were trying to see in it the hands that he could feel under his own.

As I talked, idly, absently, I felt a strange warm feeling steal over me. One hand was easy now and Lucian was massaging the other. I did not want him to stop. Even when the pain had quite gone I wanted him to continue. I knew that he was unaware of me, absorbed in his study of the model once again, but I was aware of every shade of expression on his face, from the slight lift of an eyebrow to the movement of a lock of hair which had fallen over his brow.

Within me I felt a great yearning and softening, a sweet warmth that I had known before only in the aftermath of the

158

Good Dream. Not suddenly, but slowly and irresistibly, like a rising tide, I knew that I loved Lucian Farrel.

I had never believed that love came like a stroke of lightning, and to the extent that my dazed mind could think at all, I did not believe so now. This feeling towards Lucian must have been growing within me since . . . when? I could not tell. Perhaps it had begun from the moment when he snatched me up on to his horse in Mawstone, or when I knew it was he who had chosen the blue linen dress for me to replace the one I had ruined in Mogg Race Bay. Whenever it had been seeded within me, I knew now that it was not new and sudden. It had been growing stealthily, and the suddenness lay only in my realization of the fact.

For as long as his hands gripped mine, my mind was a prisoner of my body through which the blood raced and churned with tingling warmth, otherwise I would have struggled against believing that I loved him. As it was, my poor feeble mind put up no resistance at all, and I gave myself up to the joy of the moment with no tremor of doubt or apprehension. Here was Lucian Farrel, and I loved him, and the feeling was wonderful beyond all imagination.

When he turned his head at last and said, 'Is that better, Cadi?' I nearly jumped out of my skin, and snatched my hand quickly away. The dreaming sensation vanished. The world was real again, the spell of wonder was broken, and I felt only panic. It was madness to love such a man. He was almost unknown to me, and what little I knew was more alarming than reassuring. He was an outcast, cashiered from the army, perhaps unbalanced, a master of deceit. He was an artist, and surely very bohemian, all artists were notoriously bohemian, so I understood. And only an hour ago Mr. Morton had called him a reprobate. The insolent, languorous face of the actress he had sculpted seemed to mock me.

I tried to pull myself together. Very well. I loved Lucian Farrel, but it was puppy love, stemming from youth and quick blood rather than from heart and mind. Not something for me to feel ashamed of, to be sure, but something to be very wary of with a man like Lucian Farrel.

'Cadi?' he said, and I was terrified that he might read in my face the thing that had happened to me.

'Oh, my hands are quite better now, thank you!' I said too loudly, jumping to my feet. 'They were just a little stiff.' I began to move about the studio, pretending to look at his work. 'You'll have to have two or three shorter sittings next time, Lucian. I mean, if it can be arranged at all,' I added hastily. 'I'm not sure that it will be convenient for Mr. Morton to bring me up to town. Hadn't you better go and change? Mrs. Redman must have the tea almost ready now.'

He gave me a puzzled look. 'Yes, all right. Come along, you can wait in the drawing room and I'll be with you in five minutes.'

In the next half hour or so, as we took tea, I seemed to do nothing but make a fool of myself. Sometimes I chattered feverishly and quite as stupidly as Sarah at her worst. Sometimes my mind went blank and I could only sit and stare miserably, without a word.

'You're not yourself, Cadi,' Lucian said at last. 'It must be the delayed shock of discovering that you're an heiress.'

'Yes, I expect so,' I said numbly, glad of any excuse as long as he did not hit upon the truth.

He stood looking out of the window, hands in his pockets. 'You'll have the fortune hunters after you as soon as everything is confirmed. Be careful, Cadi. You'll find many a young man eager to fall madly in love with your money.'

I almost burst into tears. 'But not with *me*, I suppose!'

He turned, the black eyebrows flaring in surprise, then moved towards me and put out a hand to touch my cheek, but I moved back. He dropped his hand and shrugged. 'You know that's not what I meant.'

'I don't know *what* you mean—I never do!' I caught myself hastily. If I went on in this absurd way he would surely guess the truth, and that was not to be thought of. It was bad enough to know that I had fallen in love with Lucian Farrel, but for him to know it would be more than I could bear. 'I'm sorry, Lucian,' I said quickly. 'It's just the excitement, as you said.'

He looked at me consideringly for a few moments, and

I wondered what was going on behind the mask of his face. At last he gave a brief smile, and picked up his hat and gloves which Mrs. Redman had put on the table. 'We mustn't keep Uncle Edward waiting,' he said. 'Nor the champagne. Will you take my arm, Miss Tregaron?'

That lunch at the Café Royal should have been a wonderful experience for me, but I was hardly aware of it. Our cab was held up in such a jam at Piccadilly Circus that at last we alighted and walked the short distance to the Café Royal. Inside, all seemed red plush, gilt, and mirrors. Mr. Morton was waiting for us at a table, a bottle of champagne standing in a silver ice-bucket at his elbow.

There were very few ladies present. Many of the men seemed to know each other and exchanged greetings as they passed between the tables. Mr. Morton rose as we approached. 'Cadi, my dear. Come and sit here, with your back to the wall, so that you can watch the human zoo at feeding time. How are you, Lucian? I doubted that they would allow you in, but I suppose Cadi's presence casts a pleasant aspect over even the most ruffianly of escorts. How have you spent the morning?'

'I've been modelling Cadi's hands,' Lucian said as the waiter handed us each a menu. 'I want to sculpt them. Can you bring her up to town one day next week for another sitting, Uncle Edward? Wednesday or Friday for preference, I'm supposed to be down at the Epsom stables the other days, but I can change that if need be.'

'It's entirely up to Cadi,' Mr. Morton answered blandly. 'Well, my dear?'

I wanted to refuse, but my benumbed mind could find no excuse to offer, and so I nodded. 'If it's convenient for you, Mr. Morton.'

He looked at me sharply. 'You seem tired, child. Are you all right?' His gaze moved to Lucian.

'Cadi's having a reaction to all this business with old Caldwell, I think. It's hardly to be wondered at,' Lucian said.

'Ah, a glass of champagne right away, then. Did she tell you the whole story, Lucian?'

'Most of it, I think . . .'

I only half listened to their conversation, but I was vaguely conscious of the fact that Lucian had dropped his usual manner of light-hearted raillery, and that he was asking question after question in a way which made it clear that he had heard every word I had told him, in spite of his concentration on the work of modelling. Point by point he was going through the whole story with Mr. Morton, to make sure he knew exactly how matters stood.

I sipped the champagne. At first it tasted like lemonade without enough sweetening, but gradually the taste seemed to improve as the glass emptied. Soon my spirits lifted and I felt quite carefree. The meal was excellent, and I began to join in the conversation a little. I had the strange sensation of being two persons. One was sitting at the table, chatting rather gaily, and perhaps even wittily, though I could never afterwards recall what I said. I only know that Mr. Morton was smiling and amused. When more champagne was poured I looked hopefully at my empty glass, but he said, 'I think perhaps one glass is sufficient for this occasion, my dear.'

The other Cadi Tregaron was curled up deep inside me, furtively watching Lucian Farrel and wondering why I should so dread that he might guess I loved him. I tried to persuade myself that this was natural modesty; that since he did not love me it would be humiliating for me if he discovered my feelings. But this was not the real truth. Deep within me I knew that I was afraid of what I felt for Lucian Farrel because I mistrusted him, and feared that if he knew that I loved him he would in some way, with deceit and calculation, use me to his advantage.

When we left the Café Royal I realized that it was only the champagne that had given me a brief uplift of spirits. Now the two Cadi Tregarons had merged, I felt very tired and my heart ached. It was a great effort to be bright and cheerful, and to pretend that I had enjoyed the treat Mr. Morton had provided. All I wanted now was to go home and to be alone with my tangled thoughts.

'Can we give you a lift, Lucian?' Mr. Morton said as he hailed a hansom. 'Since we shall be going to Charing Cross, it will only increase rather than diminish the length of your journey to Half Moon Street, but I like to be polite.'

'I'm touched, Uncle mine,' Lucian responded, rather absently. 'Don't think me ungrateful, but after that splendid lunch I shall enjoy a walk. Give my love to Aunt Helen and Sarah, please. And I hope to see Cadi next week.'

'Possibly,' said Mr. Morton. 'Goodbye, dear boy.'

We climbed into the cab. Halfway round Piccadilly Circus Mr. Morton muttered to himself and tapped on the trap. The cabbie opened it and looked down. 'Yes, sir?'

'Go round the Circus and up Regent Street again, will you? I have a package to collect from my tobacconist.' He turned to me. 'A box of cigars. He'll have them wrapped ready for me, so it will only take two or three minutes, and we have plenty of time to catch our train.'

There was less traffic now, and the hansom rattled round Piccadilly Circus at a good clip. We turned up Regent Street, and after about forty yards Mr. Morton called to the cabbie to stop.

Excusing himself, he got out and then went into a tobacconist's shop. I was deep in my thoughts, though I scarcely knew what I was thinking about, for all was confusion. Perhaps a minute passed before I realized that I was gazing across the broad street at the façade of the Café Royal, which we had just left. Lucian stood on the steps there, his hat tilted slightly back on his head, cane under his arm, smoking a cigarette and watching the passers-by. I had the impression that he was waiting for somebody.

Traffic kept passing between us, and he did not see me in the hansom on the far side of the road. The ache in my heart was a pain and a pleasure at the same time. I wondered almost angrily why I should have fallen in love with a man who was an enigma to me. I prided myself that my head was not full of romantic nonsense, like Sarah's. I would not be attracted to a man simply because he was a mystery to me.

An omnibus stopped on the far side of the road, and Lucian was hidden from me for a few moments. Then it moved noisily away, and as I saw him again I went stiff with shock. A man was approaching him, a man in a grey suit

163

and with a small, curly-brimmed bowler hat. I knew him instantly. It was the grey-eyed stranger who had haunted the woods and fields around *Meadhaven* for several weeks past. Lucian was looking the other way along Regent Street. The stranger stopped and spoke. Lucian turned, gave a smile of welcome and dropped a hand on the stranger's shoulder in a gesture which spoke of close friendship. They conversed for a moment, and I saw Lucian laugh. Then they turned together and began to stroll slowly up Regent Street, deep in conversation.

Chapter Nine

'THAT DIDN'T TAKE LONG,' said Mr. Morton's voice, and I turned to see him climb into the cab, holding a package. 'All right, cabbie. Charing Cross now, please.'

I looked across the road again, but a line of traffic was trailing behind a slow-moving dray, and I could no longer see Lucian and the stranger. The cabbie whipped up his horse and we turned across the road to head towards Piccadilly Circus again.

'My dear, you look so pale,' Mr. Morton said with concern. 'Quite unlike your usual self.'

I hesitated. That morning I had been going to speak about the grey-eyed stranger, but the arrival of the solicitor's telegram had driven everything else out of my head. Now I shrank from speaking, though why I could hardly tell. There was no reason why Lucian should not know a man who happened to be staying in Wealdhurst, but I was inwardly certain that this was not coincidence but something more sinister. If so, I did not want to speak of it, I wanted to forget it, however unwise that might be.

'I'll soon look better when we're in the fresh country air again, Mr. Morton,' I said, managing to smile. 'I expect the excitement and rich food and champagne have made me feel a little wobbly inside.' I slipped my arm through his.

'Anyway, Mrs. Morton is always saying I look too brown and healthy.'

That made him laugh, as I knew it would, and we fell into one of our usual easy conversations. At Charing Cross we had ten minutes to spare, so he took me into a chemist's shop and asked them to mix up a draught to settle my stomach. It tasted horrid, but by the time we were on the train I felt more my usual self. I dreaded all the excitement and questions to be faced on our return to *Meadhaven*, but I think Mr. Morton sensed this, for he dealt with the matter very firmly. Mrs. Morton and Sarah were in the drawing room for tea when we arrived, and Mr. Morton quickly stopped the eager babble of questions by raising his hand for silence.

'This affair may take many months to settle,' he said, 'and I will not have it continually discussed in the meantime. That would be disturbing for us all. Now I will give you a short account of what we have learned today, and that must be the end of it until further developments arise. I am thinking particularly of you, Helen my dear. Your health will suffer if Sarah and Cadi are continually pestering you with questions and speculation.' He looked sternly at Sarah, then at me, but with a flicker of one eyelid as he said, 'Have I made that quite clear to you young ladies?'

'Yes Papa,' from Sarah, much disappointed.

'Yes, Mr. Morton,' meekly, from me.

He told the facts briefly, allowed a few minutes for a very natural renewed outburst of excitement, then declared the subject closed. I was greatly relieved, and from then on, as the weeks went by, we only spoke of the matter when he and I were alone together in his study, though it was difficult to deter Sarah for the first few days, when she came to my bedroom for her usual gossip before going to bed.

On that first night I got rid of her quickly, and fell at once into a kind of sleep I had so far known only in utter weariness after a long full day in the boat with my father. I woke with the dawn and lay thinking. Yesterday seemed like a dream. How could I ever have imagined that I had fallen in love with Lucian Farrel? It was absurd. I did not trust him and was very doubtful that I even liked him. I decided that the visit to Mr. Caldwell had affected me much more deeply than I had thought at the time. I must have been thrown quite off balance, and so had been a prey to sudden and foolish imaginings when I was in Lucian's studio.

It was a comfort to put the incident behind me, but the next night, and the one after that, the Good Dream came to me, and Lucian with it, and in the dream my heart seemed close to bursting with love for him. I was torn between my sleeping and waking emotions, ashamed of my longing for the Good Dream to come yet again, and almost wishing for the Bad Dream. I felt it would be safer to fear Lucian than to love him.

Four days after our visit to Mr. Caldwell a letter arrived for me by the first post, with a crest embossed on the envelope. I had only just risen when Betty brought it to me. Something of the news had filtered to the servants' quarters, causing much excitement there, and Betty hovered for a while, but I would not open the letter until she had gone. It was in a beautiful hand, and written in excellent English with scarcely a wrong turn of phrase.

My dear Caterina,

My family and myself are overjoyed. As you will know by now, Avvocato Bonello has visited us with the news that you, the great-grandchild of the seventh Count Chiavelli, are alive and in good health.

Your great-grandfather died only twenty-three years ago, and I remember him well. He never ceased to mourn the strange loss of his daughter, Caterina, and we mourned with him, for we are a united and affectionate family.

My wife, my son and I look forward most eagerly to embracing you and to receiving you among us as soon as you are able to make the journey to Venice. It will be like a miracle that we are rejoined again. I look at the portrait of your grandmother as I write, and my heart is very full.

You will know that the legal gentlemen in England

166

and Italy are discussing what is the correct position. I think that this may cause you to feel embarrassed, and so I beg you with all sincerity not so to feel. What is yours must be yours, and we yield it to you with gladness in our hearts.

Dear Caterina, please write to us so that we may learn to know you before we have the great pleasure of reunion. We send to the English gentleman, Mr. Morton, who has shown you such kindness, our respects and gratitude, and we hope that he and his family will come with you to Venice.

To you we send our family love and affection.

Guido
Count Chiavelli (pro tem.)

I took the letter down with me to breakfast, and gave it to Mr. Morton to read out. When he had finished, Mrs. Morton dabbed her eyes with a tiny lace handkerchief and said, 'How very heart-warming, Edward, how very sensitive. I'm sure that the Count and his family are of true quality, as one would expect.'

'We can certainly be glad that there is to be no legal battle,' said Mr. Morton. 'The lawyers have no doubt about the outcome, but it would all be very distasteful. However, the Count evidently accepts the situation with the utmost grace, and I am thankful. I see he has even added *pro tem.* to his title, since this will be in doubt, and that is a very proper attitude.'

Sarah said in sudden alarm, 'You won't be *leaving* us, Cadi? You won't go away to live there, will you?'

'Of course not, silly,' I said impatiently.

'But you might have to!' Her voice took on a tearful note. 'You can't be a Venetian Countess in *Meadhaven*.'

'Don't distress yourself over problems which have not yet arisen, Sarah,' Mr. Morton said mildly. 'And Cadi, please don't call Sarah silly, even when she is.'

'I'm sorry. Sarah, I'm sorry.'

'Oh, there's no need for that, silly.'

Mr. Morton started to speak, then gave a resigned sigh

and handed me back the letter. 'You must answer it today, of course,' he said. 'Please give the Count our respects, and say that we plan to visit Venice in the spring. From the very warm way in which he has written, I'm sure it will please him to know we are making definite plans.' He looked down the table at his wife. 'A trip to Venice would make a very pleasant holiday for you, my dear. If we arrange it while Richard is on vacation we can all go together.'

Mrs. Morton put a hand on her breast and closed her magnificent eyes. 'I should adore it, Edward,' she breathed, enraptured. Her eyes opened. 'I know you do not wish us to speak of Cadi's affairs until all is settled, but may I tell Mrs. Carpenter that we shall be going to Venice next year by invitation of Count Chiavelli? I am visiting her this afternoon.'

'By all means,' said Mr. Morton, rising from the table. 'I'm sure it will make your visit most enjoyable, my dear.'

That night when Sarah came to my room she was agog with excitement, for she had accompanied her mother for the afternoon call on Mrs. Carpenter. 'It was *wonderful*, Cadi!' she squeaked, trying to keep her voice down. 'When Mamma told her, Mrs. Carpenter tried to take the wind out of her sails by asking if we would be taking our poor little fisher-girl with us, and Mamma said, "Do you mean our daughter Cadi, Mrs. Carpenter? Then I must tell you that there are matters concerning her which will be of *great* surprise to you in time to come. In fact it is *through* Cadi that the Count has invited us! But my lips are sealed, Mrs. Carpenter, I can say no more at present."' Sarah buried her head in a pillow to stifle her giggles. When she could speak again she said, 'And Mrs. Carpenter was *crimson* with curiosity all the time we were there. I think she'll burst when she learns that you're really a Countess!'

'For goodness' sake stop saying that, Sarah. The idea of being a Countess makes me feel—I don't know—silly.'

She stopped her giggling and gave a long sigh. 'I know how you feel. It must be an awful responsibility. I don't suppose Countesses are allowed to gallop about on horses, or do any of the things *you* like, Cadi. And then there's all that money when you're twenty-one. I was trying to think what I'd do if it was mine, and all I could think of was that I'd eat more chocolates, but Mamma wouldn't let me do that anyway, though I suppose it's all right if you're twenty-one. What you really need is somebody to worry about everything for you, Cadi.'

She gave a little gasp and clasped her hands together. '*I* know! I've just thought! You should marry Lucian, and then *he* can look after all the money and estate and everything.'

The only light was from my bedside candle and I was thankful for this, for my face felt like fire and I knew that I was blushing deeply. I pretended to yawn, and said, 'I thought you were madly in love with Lucian yourself.'

'Oh, I was, Cadi. But not any longer. It's somebody else now.' She did not sigh and flutter her eyes in her usual way, but sat on the bed gazing thoughtfully at the candle flame.

'Somebody else?' I asked.

'Yes. I'm really and truly in love this time.'

'Who is it, Sarah?'

She shook her head and glanced sideways at me. 'It's a secret. I can't tell you.'

'All right.' I was not very curious. No doubt Sarah's ready heart had been captured by another man who was completely unaware of her passion for him, but I could not help admiring her for the way she could keep a secret when she wished, even if in this case it was a foolish, romantic secret.

'So you could marry Lucian, and everything would be lovely,' Sarah said. 'I'm sure he's madly in love with you. He must be, if he wants to sculpt your hands.'

I would have smiled at her strange logic, but her words reminded me of something I was dreading. 'Oh, go to bed now, Sarah,' I begged. 'I've spent hours writing to the Count today, trying to find just the right words, and I'm tired out.'

'All right.' She slipped from the bed, and giggled. 'Goodnight, Countess.'

Alone with my thoughts, I wondered about my next meeting with Lucian. Mr. Morton had arranged it for the Friday, and I could find no good excuse for refusing to go. Sarah was

169

to go with me for the outing. Mr. Morton would leave us with Lucian for the day, and come to collect us in the afternoon, to take us home. It helped to know that Sarah would be there. She was thrilled at the prospect, but I did not share her eagerness. I was clinging to the belief that my sudden feeling for Lucian had been a thing of the moment, when I was not myself, and that there was no reality in it. How could there be? I was a practical Cornish girl, and I could not fall in love with a man unless I saw in him those qualities that are lovable, the kind of qualities Granny Caterina had found in Robert Penwarden, and my mother in my father. All that I knew of Lucian as yet was obscured by mystery and suspicion, and it was against all reason that I could love him. Yet deep within me I was afraid to test myself, afraid that when I saw him next I would again feel that sweet and terrible heartache in spite of everything.

'Little fool!' I muttered to myself aloud. 'You're as bad as Sarah with all her romantic nonsense.' But when I woke in the morning I felt strangely disappointed because Lucian had not come to me in the Good Dream. For the first time, I had dreamt about Richard, an ordinary dream, rather muddled, but it reminded me that Richard had told me he loved me. I felt a sudden affection for him as I remembered the quiet yet insistent way he had spoken, and a kind of sadness for him at the same time.

Friday came, and I made the journey to London with Mr. Morton as before, except that this time, because Sarah was with us, we took a cab from Charing Cross instead of walking. When we reached Half Moon Street, Mr. Morton kept the cab waiting while he handed us over to Mrs. Redman, then went off to his office in Whitehall straight away.

My first sight of Lucian brought me a sense of relief, for I felt nothing of the emotions I had feared. My heart did not beat faster and the colour did not rush to my cheeks. His manner was brisk and businesslike. As he posed me he told Sarah to chatter as much as she liked, but not to expect any answers from him. She was to watch the clock he had placed on a side table, and tell him each time twenty minutes had passed, so that I could rest for ten minutes.

He worked very rapidly once he had started, and by lunch-time the clay model was finished to his satisfaction. But by lunch-time I was in despair, for as I watched Lucian at work, intent, absorbed in what he was doing, that same feeling I had known before grew steadily within me, a yearning towards him, an awareness of him that was so powerful it almost hurt. I tried hard to resist, tried to concentrate on Sarah's chatter and to gossip lightly with her, but to my anger and self-contempt it was hopeless. Lucian held me, fascinated, as I had sometimes seen a rabbit held powerless by a weasel, except that Lucian was unaware. I felt my heart jump absurdly at the tiniest things, the moving sinew of a forearm as he worked the clay, the tightening of his mouth as he carefully shaped a curve or plane with the spatula.

When the morning's sitting ended, Mrs. Redman showed us to the bathroom, so that we could wash our hands before sitting down to the light lunch she had prepared. There, alone for a few minutes, I stood looking at myself in the mirror. 'All right, Cadi Tregaron,' I whispered to myself grimly. 'You've fallen in love with Lucian, you stupid creature, but it's just puppy love, the kind of thing that's happened to Sarah half a dozen times. It will pass, so don't you dare let it show, or I'll never forgive you!'

Now that I had faced the truth and accepted it, I felt a little better. Over lunch Lucian talked amiably, but always with that touch of self-mockery lying behind his words. I was truly thankful for Sarah's presence, for her frivolous chatter helped to hide my own lack of conversation.

'When can we come to Epsom and see your stables?' she asked eagerly. 'Cadi would love that. She loves anything to do with horses. I don't, though. But I'd like to come to Epsom. Cadi, you ask Papa. You can always get round him.'

'I *don't* get round him!' I said indignantly. 'I never do that.'

'Well, it comes to the same thing. You know he adores you, so he does anything you ask without your having to get round him.'

Once again Sarah had surprised me by the occasional insight which lay beneath her muddled thoughts. What she said was true, in a sense. Mr. Morton did not love me more than his own child, but we were closer in some ways and our minds were more in harmony. Yet Sarah accepted this quite without resentment when she might very easily have disliked me for it. I was touched, and made up my mind that in future I would act more kindly towards her and ignore the occasions when she irritated me.

'I'm sure a visit to the stables can be arranged,' Lucian said. 'Would you like that, Cadi?'

'It's very kind of you.' I wanted to avoid his eyes, but made myself look at him squarely. 'But I really don't know when I'll be free. It takes a great deal of my time to look after the stables at home, and to carry on with teaching at the orphanage.'

'Well, you do surprise me!' Sarah said. 'I thought you'd love to go.'

I did not answer. Sarah was right, of course, but I had decided that the less I saw of Lucian the more quickly I should be free of this ridiculous but painful puppy-love that afflicted me.

'As your father says, Cadi never ceases to surprise one,' Lucian remarked with an ironic smile. 'I hear that she is in correspondence with the Count, and that you're all going to Venice in the spring.'

'Yes! Isn't it wonderful?' Sarah bubbled. 'Oh, perhaps you could come too, Lucian!'

'I might well be in Italy about that time,' he said thoughtfully. 'Perhaps I could sell some horses to the Count.'

'That's a lovely idea! I'm sure he has stables and would be glad to buy your bloodstock or whatever it is.'

I looked at Lucian and said tartly, 'Horses in Venice? Surely you'd do better to breed gondolas.'

'You don't breed gondolas, silly——' Sarah began, then clapped a hand to her mouth and gave a smothered laugh. 'Oh, you were *joking*! She was joking, Lucian.'

'I'm glad you pointed it out,' he said politely, then looked at me. 'Count Chiavelli owns land near Padua, about fifty miles inland from Venice, and he has a small racing stable there. So the idea of selling him horses isn't really absurd.'

I looked down at the plate in front of me, knowing I had made a fool of myself again. 'I'm sorry, Lucian. It was very rude of me to be sarcastic.'

'Cadi's ever so good at apologizing,' Sarah said proudly. 'As soon as she's snapped at you she says she's sorry. I thought horse-racing was only in England.'

'No. You'll find it all over the Continent, as well as in America. The French have been at it for seventy years. They started with English blood, but they've since bred in American and other strains, and today their horses are as good as any in the world. Italy isn't quite up to the same standard, but there's growing interest in the sport.'

'How do you know about the Count's stables, Lucian?' I asked, and was amazed to hear my own voice sounding so calm. I wanted to touch his hand, to push back the lock of hair that drooped over his forehead, helpless little idiot that I was.

He shrugged, but I saw that his eyes were suddenly narrowed, as if he were thinking quickly. 'It's part of my business to know who's interested in buying or selling horses. I've made inquiries about Count Chiavelli.'

'You mean before you knew that I was related to him?' I tried to make my manner artless.

Lucian hesitated for a fraction of a second before saying, 'No. Since then.' He smiled suddenly and with a return of the old mockery. 'It was an impulse of curiosity, and I'm glad now. After all, perhaps you'll own that land of his in Padua when you're twenty-one, then we can do business together.'

Somehow I knew that he had not made those inquiries on impulse or from idle curiosity. For a moment I wondered what the truth of it was. Perhaps for his own secret reasons Lucian wanted to discover how large a fortune I would inherit—I hastily turned away from that line of thought, for it was too distressing.

After lunch we returned to the studio. Lucian set a block of dark golden wood on the bigger table. It had been cut very roughly to an outline of the shape he wanted with a saw. From the slope of the base projected a solid piece from which he would carve my wrists and hands.

'I can work from the model now,' he said, picking up a mallet and a broad-bladed chisel, 'but I may ask you to pose for a little while now and again, Cadi. There's more life in flesh and muscle than in clay.'

He began to carve the wood, and at once became absorbed. Sarah was interested at first, but after a little while she became bored and said she would go into the drawing room and watch the traffic and the passers-by from the window there.

Sometimes, at a brusque word from Lucian, I took up the pose for a few minutes, but mostly his attention moved from the clay to the wood as he worked, with occasional pauses when he took measurements with the calipers.

It was silent in the studio but for the tapping of mallet on chisel and the sound of his breathing as he worked with intense concentration. The longer I watched, the more that unwanted yearning grew within me, and I suppose it was in desperation that at last I tried to break the spell.

'May I ask you a question, Lucian?'

'H'mm? Yes, if you want to.' He spoke vaguely.

'Why did you beat Richard with a riding crop last time you were at *Meadhaven*?'

He straightened up slowly, and there was nothing vague in his manner now. His eyes were hard and watchful—or were they simply puzzled? It was difficult to tell how much my imagination was at work. 'Beat Richard with a riding crop?' he echoed. 'Did he tell you that?'

'Yes.'

'He must have been dreaming.'

'But *I* wasn't dreaming. I had to let him into the house. that night, because he couldn't climb to Sarah's window. I realized he was hurt, and made him let me attend to his back. What I saw wasn't imagination.'

'So young Richard took a thrashing?' Lucian murmured. 'And he told you I did it?'

'Yes.'

'Did he say why?'

I hesitated, suddenly realizing the trap I had laid for myself. I could not say to Lucian's face that he was capable of doing wild, dangerous things and then forgetting them. I

174

could not tell him that Richard had said his mind was blemished.

'Richard gave no reason,' I answered. 'He didn't even tell me he was hurt at first. I had to find that out for myself.'

'And how did you find out?'

'I . . . well, I tore his shirt off.'

Lucian gave a quick explosion of laughter. 'Trust you, Cadi!'

'It's nothing to laugh at!'

'Perhaps not. What was Richard doing out at night? Why was he coming in through Sarah's window?'

'Because . . .' I faltered again, but there was no help for it. 'Because he'd been down in the village.'

'With one of his lady-loves who can't resist that angelic face?'

'You *know*?' I gasped.

'Of course,' he said impatiently. 'The boy's young, and he was tied to his mother's apron strings for too long. It's only natural for him to break out.' He looked down at the carving, where the curve of my wrists was beginning to emerge. 'Perhaps Richard was caught by an angry husband. Did that occur to you?'

'Yes. But it wasn't so. The woman he was . . . visiting, she didn't have a husband. He'd left her.'

'Ah, that will be Meg Dawson, the dressmaker.'

'So you know her?'

He set the chisel to the wood and tapped gently. 'Yes, I know her, Cadi.'

'Then perhaps you didn't like having Richard as a rival? Perhaps you objected to the attentions he was paying to a woman you were interested in yourself—and so you beat him?'

Very thoughtfully he chiselled away a tiny shaving of wood, then straightened up again, rubbing his chin with the handle of the chisel. 'That's right,' he said unexpectedly. 'I gave Richard a thrashing because I didn't like the attentions he was paying to a woman. I remember now.'

'You remember *now*?' I think those last words startled me more than his admission.

'Yes,' he said. 'But it's all over and best forgotten—unless you intend to raise the subject with Mr. Morton.'

I shook my head dumbly.

'Good. Then that's settled.' Lucian's eyes moved from the model to the wood. 'Take the pose again, Cadi. I want to see how the light falls on your wrist.'

I obeyed, and sat there with my thoughts whirling. There seemed to be nothing more I could say. Lucian had quite simply dismissed the subject. Ten minutes later Sarah rejoined us and spent the next hour chattering about the people she had seen from the window. At four o'clock Mrs. Redman called us to tea, and soon afterwards Mr. Morton arrived to collect us.

'Will you want any more sittings, Lucian?' he asked.

'They'd be a help, Uncle Edward, but they're not really necessary. I'm well pleased with the model. It's up to Cadi.'

'I think I find it rather tiring,' I said awkwardly, keeping my eyes on Mr. Morton. 'I mean, I get more tired just sitting still than doing something active.'

'There you are then, my boy,' Mr. Morton said cheerfully. 'If you can run alongside Cadi while she's actually riding, and sculpt her hands, then you're quite welcome. Otherwise you'll have to manage without. Personally I sympathize with her attitude, I should find it most distasteful to have to sit still and watch you mangling wood.'

We said our goodbyes and took a cab to Charing Cross. There we found that we had just missed a train and would have to wait for half an hour or more, so we walked down to Trafalgar Square and passed the time feeding some of the thousands of pigeons which flocked there. When we returned to the station the train was waiting, and we took our seats in one of the first-class compartments. It was still early, and most of the business gentlemen had not yet left their offices, so there were few people on the train.

Mr. Morton opened a small case he carried and took out some papers. 'I've work to do,' he said, settling himself in a corner. 'You two young ladies can take those seats by the other window and talk quietly, if you please.'

'Very well, Papa,' said Sarah. 'Cadi, you sit with your back to the engine, that's supposed to be nicer, though I always like to see where we're going. Papa, did you know Lucian plans to sell horses to Count Chiavelli? He said so today, didn't he, Cadi?'

Mr. Morton sighed and looked up from his papers. 'I'd be surprised, if I could be surprised by anything Lucian did,' he remarked. 'Horses?'

I said, 'It's just that he's learned that the Count has some stables in Padua. He only spoke of it idly.'

Mr. Morton smiled. 'Few of Lucian's words are idle. However, I shall once again try to get on with my work now, if Sarah will allow it.'

A few minutes later the train pulled out from the station and across Hungerford Bridge. 'I know,' Sarah said eagerly. 'You tell me about your Granny Caterina.'

'But you know all about her, Sarah.'

'Of course I do, but I want you to tell it again. Please, Cadi.' Her eyes grew moist. 'It's such a lovely story.'

I did not feel much like talking, but I preferred it to sitting and thinking about Lucian, so I collected my thoughts and launched into the story, speaking quietly, while Sarah listened with all the breathless rapture of a child being told a fairy-tale. When another train passed us, or when we went through a tunnel, I had to pause because of the noise. There were no lights on in the compartment, for it was still broad daylight, and at each tunnel Sarah squeaked with pretended alarm as we were suddenly engulfed in darkness. She would not let me miss out a single detail, and often broke in to ask questions. Some I could answer and some I could not, but in one way and another the telling spread out to occupy most of our journey.

We were pulling out from Sevenoaks as I finished my story at last and Sarah was still sighing over it as we reached the tunnel that lay between Sevenoaks and Hildenborough. This was the longest tunnel in the south, I had been told, more than a mile and a half. The noise of the wheels echoed and re-echoed as we roared into the darkness, and I could smell the smoke from the engine as it came creeping through the crack of the window. Sarah called to me above the noise.

'Isn't it ghostly, Cadi? I've got my hand in front of my nose and I can't see anything!'

I was about to reply when I felt a sudden draught and the musty smell of smoke in my nostrils. Although I could see nothing I sensed movement just in front of me, and could only think that Sarah must have stood up and opened the window, which was an astonishing thing for her to have done. I drew breath to speak to her sharply, but in the same moment a hand touched my arm, gripped for a second, then darted up and seized me by the throat with brutal strength. Terror exploded within me, but no sound could reach my lips. I clawed madly at the hand, but next instant the man had leaned his body on me, smothering me under his weight as I was pressed back in the corner, his hand still gripping my throat.

Through the drumming in my ears as I fought in frightful silence against the attacker I could hear Sarah's voice running on. 'I always like this long tunnel, it's so nice and frightening. Oh, there's so much smoke coming in! We didn't leave the window open, did we, Cadi?'

Beneath the panic that consumed me a tiny shred of logic remained. I could still just breathe, and in another half minute or so we would be in daylight again, which would surely bring an end to my ordeal.

'Oh, I'm sure it's not just the window that's open!' Sarah cried in sudden amazement. 'It must be the *door* that's come unlatched! It's like a *wind* blowing in!'

As if from a long distance I heard Mr. Morton say sharply, 'Stay quite still, you girls. Don't attempt to touch the door. I'll attend to it as soon as we're in daylight again.'

It was doubly horrible to hear them speaking so naturally, quite unaware of my silent and desperate struggle. My attacker's weight came off me suddenly, and I was jerked to my feet. I lunged for the unseen face with my nails, but in a flash he had twisted me round and clamped an arm across my throat from behind, his free hand gripping my wrist.

Then I was thrust towards the open door.

It seemed that an age had passed since we entered the tunnel, but still no gleam of light penetrated from the far end. Perhaps all this frantic struggle had lasted only for a few endless seconds, and the man would yet have ample time to achieve his terrible purpose. Sudden enormous fury broke within me, almost swamping fear. I would not die like some petrified sheep under this creature's hands. I would *not*! I let myself sag so that he had to hold me up, and then, when he had taken my weight, I suddenly lifted my legs as he thrust me forward again. My feet found the frame at one side of the open door. With tortured effort of will I let him push forward until my knees were bent, then suddenly I straightened my legs and lunged back against him with all my strength.

He was taken by surprise, and staggered back off balance. We lurched along the compartment, half falling, and I heard Mr. Morton give a sudden exclamation of alarm as we cannoned into his legs. My assailant's grip slackened for a moment and I tore free, throwing myself sideways on to the seat opposite Mr. Morton and turning with clawed hands ready to fight off any new attack. I was trying to scream, but could not drag enough air down my bruised throat.

Then in the darkness I heard the scuffling of feet as the man moved quickly away. Mr. Morton called out, 'What's happening? Sarah, Cadi, are you all right?'

A scrambling sound from the door, then silence. My voice came out at last, shrill to breaking point. '*Man . . . tried to kill me! Sarah, come here—away from the door!*'

A squeal from Sarah, then she bumped against me as she threw herself along the seat. A hand touched me. I cringed for a moment, but then came Mr. Morton's voice again, close to me, bewildered, sharp with alarm. 'Cadi? All right, it's me.' He was standing, leaning over us as we huddled in the corner. I could see him dimly now, head turned a little, arms spread to ward off any attempt to approach us. I saw him grope with one hand, and next moment there came a shuddering squeal as the train began to slow quickly to a halt. I realized then that he had pulled the communication cord.

The light grew stronger, and we emerged from the tunnel. The three of us were alone in the compartment, which was full of smoke. The far door was wide open. Sarah found my hand and clutched it. With a final jerk the train stopped at last. Mr. Morton looked down at me. His face was pale, his eyes frightening in their anger, but his voice was steady and soothing as he spoke. 'Don't break down, Cadi dear. Try to hold on. A man, you say?'

'Yes . . .' My voice went up and down as I struggled to control it. 'As soon as we were in the tunnel. He—he must have climbed along from the next compartment. He caught my throat. I couldn't cry out. Then he tried to push me out . . .'

'Tried to push you out?' Mr. Morton stared incredulously, then gently pulled down the collar of my dress a little and tilted my head to look at my neck. I saw his eyes show horror, and then he said bleakly, 'There's a madman at large on the train.'

With surprising speed he darted to the open door and looked out. I could hear voices as people leaned out from the windows of other compartments and called to one another asking why we had stopped so abruptly.

'My daughter has been attacked,' I heard Mr. Morton call in a harsh voice. 'Have any of you gentlemen seen a man running from the train?'

I got slowly to my feet and joined Mr. Morton by the door. Three or four men had jumped down on to the track and were gathering outside our compartment now. 'Girl attacked in the tunnel?' said one. 'Good God, the fellow must be out of his mind. Is she badly hurt?' Before Mr. Morton could reply another man cried suddenly, 'I say, look there! At the top of the slope!'

Through the window I could see a running figure, a man neatly dressed but hatless, thick chestnut hair cut rather long, a familiar build. I caught no more than a glimpse of him as he plunged into the line of trees at the top of the slope. but I knew beyond all doubt that it was Lucian Farrel.

Chapter Ten

MY WHOLE BODY began to shake, and my teeth to chatter. Mr. Morton took my arm. 'Sit down, Cadi. Breathe deeply. Sarah, open the other window and try to fan some of this smoke out.'

Sarah obeyed, then called. 'There's the guard walking along the track. He must be coming to see who pulled the cord.'

'Then wave to him.'

'I *am*!' Sarah retorted, and I had never before heard her speak so sharply. 'Ah, here he comes.' She turned from the window and moved across to us. 'Oh, come away, Papa. I'll see to Cadi,' she said impatiently. 'You talk to the guard.'

Mr. Morton blinked in surprise, but made way for her. She sat beside me and began chafing my hands, talking softly. 'There Cadi, you're all right now. We won't let anyone hurt you. Have a good cry, dear. You'll feel much better.'

I could feel tears on my cheeks but at the same time I had an hysterical urge to laugh, for I had never thought to find myself being mothered by Sarah. Yet I was truly grateful for her comfort. Now that the first shock was past she was very calm and had taken over from her father with astonishing firmness. When I thought of this moment later, with a clear mind, I realized that Sarah was growing up, and was far less feather-headed than she sometimes seemed.

The guard opened the door and climbed up into the compartment. Mr. Morton told him briefly what had happened. 'My daughter isn't fit to be questioned yet,' he ended, 'but I shall call the police as soon as we reach Hildenborough.'

The guard scratched his head, looking somewhat out of his depth. 'That'll be best, sir. And begging your pardon, but I'll need your name and address for my report, please.'

Mr. Morton had just finished giving this when there came a sudden buzz of talk from the men still on the track, and somebody called out, 'He's coming back! That man's coming back!' Mr. Morton turned to the open door, and

I stood up with Sarah beside me, looking through the window.

'Why, *that's* not him!' she exclaimed. 'That's Lucian!'

He came trudging down the grassy slope, paused to pick up his hat from behind a hummock where it had fallen, then continued down to the track, made his way through the staring men and swung himself up through the open door.

'Lucian,' Mr. Morton said dazedly. 'How on earth . . . ?'

'I lost him,' Lucian said abruptly. 'He got away after we reached the woods.' He looked at me. 'Cadi. Thank God it was no worse.'

'But how———?' Mr. Morton began again, when Lucian broke in. 'Let's sit down in private, Uncle Edward. The train can go on now, I take it?'

'Yes . . . of course.'

A few moments later we had shut ourselves in the compartment and the other gentlemen had returned to their places, no doubt disappointed at being unable to satisfy their curiosity. Sarah sat beside me. She had taken a tiny bottle of lavender water from her handbag and was dabbing it on my bruised neck with a handkerchief. Lucian and Mr. Morton sat opposite. Lucian seemed not to realize our complete bewilderment at his appearance on the train so soon after we had left him at his flat. He sat gazing at me with sombre eyes.

'What happened?' Mr. Morton asked abruptly.

'I was alone in the next compartment,' Lucian said, still looking at me. 'I didn't know you were here, I thought you'd caught an earlier train. I was on this one because I had a telegram just after you'd left, about a horse I'm thinking of buying in Tonbridge. I was on my way to look at it.'

'Never mind that,' Mr. Morton said testily. 'What did you see of this man?'

'Not much, I'm afraid. We were almost through the tunnel when I heard a banging sound, like an open door swinging back and hitting the side of the carriage. That's what it was, of course. Your door. I opened the window to look out, but it was still very dark. That was the moment when I heard Cadi cry out that a man had tried to kill her. I didn't recognize her voice, but she called Sarah's name, telling her to come away from the door, so I knew who it was. Then I made out this fellow hanging on between your compartment and mine. He must have climbed along from the other direction to reach you. As we came out of the tunnel the train started to make an emergency stop, so I knew you must have pulled the cord. I leaned out to grab the man's arm, but he broke free, dropped to the ground, fell down, picked himself up, and took to his heels. I opened my door as we stopped, and went after him.'

'Did you see his face?' Mr. Morton asked.

'Yes, briefly. Just before he dropped to the ground. A coarse, heavy face. A man about forty. He wore a decent suit—I suppose he'd have to, in case somebody saw him getting into a first-class compartment and challenged him. But he didn't go with the suit, he looked the kind of bruiser you'd expect to find in a dockside alley or a thieves' kitchen.' Lucian gave a little shrug. 'I gained a few yards during the chase up the slope, but he had a good start, and when he reached the cover of the trees I lost him.'

'A pity . . .' Mr. Morton shook his head slowly. 'A great pity, Lucian. This has been a dreadful affair, disturbing beyond words.'

I thought so, too. Disturbing that Lucian should have been on the train unknown to us. Disturbing that he alone had seen the mysterious attacker. And there was something else.

'Your hand's bleeding, Lucian,' I said, trying to keep my voice steady. 'You have a bad scratch.'

He glanced down, then took out a handkerchief and dabbed at the trickle of blood that came from a long scratch down the back of his hand. 'It must have happened when I caught his arm and he tore free,' Lucian said casually.

I closed my eyes, wondering if this was a nightmare and I should soon wake up. All that Lucian had said was possible. Each part of his story was plausible. But when it was all put together the whole thing was too much of a coincidence. At that moment I found it hard to doubt that the nails which had drawn blood from Lucian's hand were my own. Yet in spite of myself there was something within me that fought desperately against what my reason told me. More than anything in the world, I did not want to believe that Lucian had tried to kill me, and I scoured my mind to find cause for disbelieving.

He had no reason to wish me ill, I told myself. True, he had never shown any great warmth towards me, but he had been pleasant enough in his rather sardonic way, and certainly I had never seen any hint of hatred or menace in his face. No, the attacker must have been . . . somebody else. But who? Once again I swung round to the opinion that my narrow escape when riding Pompey had not been a natural accident—and if not, then it seemed to me that whoever my enemy was he must have been responsible for that as well as for the attack today. Could it be the grey-eyed stranger? That would not do either, for he had no more reason to harm me than Lucian had, as far as I knew. And besides, he did not in any way tally with Lucian's description of the man he claimed to have pursued from the train. They knew each other, of course, for I had seen them together outside the Café Royal, but that might mean anything or nothing.

One thought brought me wry relief. For a time I had half wondered if Richard had been responsible for causing my fall from Pompey that day, but now I knew such suspicion was false, for at this moment Richard was in Oxford, a hundred miles away, and he did not have half the strength of my unseen attacker.

Sarah broke in on my thoughts, voicing the question to which I could find no answer. 'It doesn't make sense. Why should anyone want to hurt Cadi?' she said.

Mr. Morton frowned. 'Don't be foolish, Sarah. There's no reason to be found. The man was clearly unbalanced. He might just as readily have made an assault upon you as on Cadi. Such men exist, I'm afraid, though you are hardly old enough to be aware of it.'

Sarah dabbed the last of the lavender water on my neck.

'I'm sorry to contradict you, Papa,' she said politely, 'but I do know such things can happen. I know there are bad men with twisted minds. But I don't believe that kind of man would climb along a moving train and try to kill the first girl he came across.'

Mr. Morton stared at his daughter with mingled surprise and respect. 'That's a remarkably sound thought,' he acknowledged. 'I apologize for calling you foolish, my dear. However, lunacy takes strange forms, and there is no other possible explanation for this dreadful affair.'

Lucian said nothing. His gaze rested on me but his expression was withdrawn. Absently he dabbed at the scratch on his hand with the handkerchief.

There was a telephone in the office at Hildenborough Station, and from it Mr. Morton made a call to the police and to Dr. Bailey. Then Young Kemp, who had been waiting with the carriage to meet us, drove us all home, for Lucian had said he would postpone the visit he was supposed to make to Tonbridge.

At *Meadhaven* Mrs. Morton was given a watered-down account of what had occurred, and became distraught. Dr. Bailey arrived, came to my bedroom to examine me, and quickly pronounced me unhurt physically except for a bruised neck. He wanted me to go to bed and take a sedative, but I refused, and he then turned his attention to Mrs. Morton, who seemed to need it more than I.

A sergeant came from the police station, and I had to tell him what had happened while he wrote it all down. Then it was Lucian's turn, and finally Mr. Morton and Sarah added what little they could tell. All this took a great deal of time, and when at last it was all over I felt very weary. I found myself unable to talk naturally to Lucian, and was glad when he left. Mrs. Morton remained in her room, so there were only three of us sitting down to dinner, and we were very subdued. I began to wish I had taken Dr. Bailey's advice, and after I had managed to eat a little food I said, 'If you'll excuse me, I think I'll go to bed early.'

'Yes, of course you must, my dear,' Mr. Morton said, rising and coming round the table as I got to my feet.

'Today was a horrible experience for you, but thank God you have a rare resilience.' He managed a little smile. 'Somewhat outside Dr. Bailey's normal expectation, I fancy. However, you must rest well and get plenty of sleep for a day or so. Try not to re-live what occurred. I know it will be hard, but try to put the whole thing behind you, and just think of the future.'

'Yes, I will, Mr. Morton,' I said. But I wanted only one thing of the future, and that was to be free of the helpless, love-sick longing that Lucian Farrel had awakened in me. I wished that he had never existed, and that I did not love him, and suspect him, and fear him.

That night Mrs. Morton walked again in her sleep, and I woke to find her standing over me with a candle, her eyes open but strange and distant as she spoke to me, calling me John and chiding me gently for being late for tea.

I must have been still in a rather tense state, for at the first moment of awakening I almost wept with the unexpected shock. But then I pulled myself together and began to coax her soothingly back to her room. On the big landing she began to grow agitated, and Mr. Morton must have heard her voice, for he came hastening from his room, pulling on a dressing-gown.

He was able to get her back to bed without too much difficulty, but when he closed the door of her room and turned to me his face seemed tinged with grey in the candlelight. 'Oh, my dear, I'm sorry,' he whispered wearily. 'As if you hadn't suffered enough distress for one day.'

'It's all right, please don't worry, Mr. Morton. I'd have managed without waking you if she hadn't become difficult.'

'I believe you would,' he said, and put his hand against my cheek for a moment as he added in a voice I could barely hear, 'How John would have loved you, child.' Then he pulled himself together and said, 'Go back to bed quickly, before you catch cold. And thank you, Cadi.'

Within a little while the memory of that day began to lose some of its sharpness. All was normal at *Meadhaven*, and daily life went on its accustomed way, so that soon it was almost as if my experience in the train had been a bad dream rather than a reality. During the next month the police sergeant called twice, but only to report that no progress had been made in finding the man Lucian had described. The story caused great excitement locally when it first spread round Wealdhurst, but since Mr. Morton had told us all to avoid discussing it when people wanted to indulge their curiosity, the interest soon died from lack of fuel to feed it.

No mention was made of a further trip to Lucian's flat, and for this I was very glad. I nursed the hope that the less I saw of him the quicker my infatuation for him would pass. I had sometimes mocked Sarah for her absurd affairs of the heart, and it was humiliating to think that I cut no better figure myself.

I kept myself busy with the stables and with teaching at the orphanage. To my surprise, Sarah took to riding out with me. I was puzzled, for I felt sure she did not enjoy it, but she seemed to have made up her mind on the matter, whether she found it pleasurable or not. Even when the days grew short and the cold of winter shrivelled the last late roses, Sarah rode out with me, squeaking and clutching at the reins, sitting to watch when I galloped, and dismounting thankfully when we returned. She had also taken to going for walks by herself, in the woods adjoining *Meadhaven* or across the fields. This was something new, for she had never been one to seek the open air very much, but together with the riding it began to put colour in her cheeks and make her look much healthier, somewhat to Mrs. Morton's distress.

'You have had a remarkable effect on Sarah,' Mr. Morton said to me one day. 'It's quite astonishing. She seems much less empty-headed than she used to be.'

'I'm sure it's not my doing, Mr. Morton. She's just growing up, that's all.' I thought for a moment, then added, 'Even when I first came here she sometimes surprised me. I mean, I found she had much more insight than anyone might expect.'

He nodded, a little ruefully. 'I'm sure you're right. I've always felt at something of a loss with Sarah, and I don't doubt she's felt the same with me. Perhaps she needed more understanding than I've been capable of, and you've supplied that now. I really must try harder.'

I felt guilty, for to be truthful I had rarely gone out of my way to encourage Sarah by praise and understanding. If she showed me a piece of her embroidery I would tend to be rather patronizing in my approval—no doubt because I could not have done half as well myself. Now I decided that I must try to mend my ways in future.

The grey-eyed stranger had gone from the district, or so I thought, and it came as a shock to me one day when Sarah and I were trotting through the woods, the dead leaves crunching beneath us under a scattering of snow, to see him walking towards us. He wore a top coat against the cold, and stopped short on seeing us. I had the impression that he was as surprised as I. Then he moved aside to make way for us, and politely raised his hat.

I drew Pompey to a halt and said, 'Good morning. You're back in Wealdhurst, then?'

'I've not been away, Miss Tregaron,' he said, the Irish brogue touching his cool voice.

'Really? I haven't seen you for several weeks.'

'Well now, I'm not a noticeable man, maybe. I just go about here and there, minding my own business as you might say.'

I went a little pink, not quite sure whether he was being rude, and said, 'Then I'd better mind *my* own business, I suppose. Good morning.'

'The very best of it to you, Miss Tregaron. And to you too, Miss Morton.' He inclined his head to Sarah.

I put Pompey to a canter, and then had to wait while Sarah caught up. By then we were out of sight of the stranger. 'You were very sharp with him, Cadi,' she said, tugging on Adam's reins.

'I used to see him about here a lot,' I answered, frowning. 'Every time I rode out, I'd see him. I had a funny feeling he was watching me.' I was about to add that I had seen him in London, talking to Lucian, but stopped myself at the last moment, mainly because I did not even want to speak Lucian's name To my anger, I still felt my blood grow warm whenever he forced himself into my thoughts, and I still longed for him to come to me in the Good Dream, even though I tried hard not to.

'I thought he seemed very nice,' Sarah said, grunting with effort as she tried to stop Adam walking round in a circle. 'Don't you like him, Cadi?'

'I've no reason to like or dislike him. Have *you* seen him lurking about before, Sarah?'

'Me?' She gave a wide-eyed stare. 'Gracious, I haven't time to notice *anyone* when I'm riding. And you know what Mamma tells us to do when we're out walking. Just look straight ahead and don't speak to strangers.'

I had the curious feeling that behind her innocent stare Sarah was gently mocking me, and I felt a flash of annoyance. 'Oh, for goodness' sake stop talking like a schoolgirl, Sarah. And stop dragging on the reins like that, you'll ruin poor Adam's mouth.' I turned and galloped away, then quickly reined to a halt, turned again, and cantered back to where Sarah was labouring after me at an uneasy trot.

As I opened my mouth to speak she said, grinning, 'Now you're going to apologize for snapping at me.' She was right, of course, but that only made me angry again, and instead of apologizing I glared at her speechlessly. She sighed and said, 'All right, don't then. Oh dear, I wish I could get angry like you, so my eyes would flash the way yours do, Cadi. You really look like a Countess when you're in a temper.'

My annoyance dissolved in laughter, which was the usual end to my moments of irritation with Sarah. From then on I used to watch for the grey-eyed stranger whenever we rode out, and although I did not see him again in Weald-hurst I never quite forgot him, for in a strange way I was always half expecting to encounter him. Yet when at last that encounter came, it was to be in a far place, completely unexpected, and truly terrifying.

The weeks passed. Christmas came and there was all the joy and bustle of preparation, of buying presents and sending cards. Sarah and I saved regularly from our pocket money for this, but we also took over part of one of the greenhouses and grew pot-plants there, which we later sold to a florist in Sevenoaks, aided by Young Kemp. Sarah had green fingers and seemed to have a knack of making the plants grow beautifully by talking to them and coaxing them. I was the one who sold them when they were ready.

We kept this a secret until after Christmas, and when Mrs. Morton learned of it she was overcome with shame at our 'being in trade' as she called it. But Mr. Morton only laughed until the tears came to his eyes.

Lucian stayed with us for two days at Christmas, and I was depressed to find that my feelings for him had not faded. Instead of being natural with him I was either surly or over-gay. He brought with him the finished wood-carving of my hands, as a present for Mr. Morton. It seemed to me that they looked much too strong and capable for the hands of a young lady, and I wished he had cheated a little to make them more elegant, but Mr. Morton was delighted and made a place for the carving in his study. 'A reminder,' he said to me when we were alone there. 'A reminder that but for those hands I would not be here today, Cadi, my dear. Not that I shall ever need to be reminded.'

It should have been a wonderful Christmas, but for me it was something of an ordeal, partly because of my awkwardness with Lucian and partly because my thoughts often turned to Mawstone and my father, which I suppose was only natural at this time, the first Christmas since his death.

Richard was with us for the vacation, and I wondered with some alarm how he and Lucian would behave towards one another, but my fears were groundless. Even knowing what had happened at their last meeting, I would never have guessed from their manner that anything was amiss. They talked naturally with each other, and seemed as friendly as they had ever been. If there was any undercurrent, Richard's usual reserve with all members of the family served to disguise this.

For a few moments only I felt my heart in my mouth, and that was when we gave out our presents. Richard's present for Lucian was a brand new riding crop. When Lucian unwrapped it and I saw what it was, I held my breath, watching them both. But their two faces, so different, like angel and demon, gave no hint of what they might be thinking. 'I don't know if you need a new one,' Richard said with a smile, 'but I thought that even a riding crop must wear out if it's used too much, Lucian.'

'I'm rarely heavy-handed with a crop,' Lucian responded pleasantly, 'but my old one is rather worn, and I'll be glad to throw it away.' He examined the crop. 'This is splendid. Thank you very much, Richard.'

The moment of tension passed, and I heaved a silent sigh of relief.

With Christmas over I settled down once again to put Lucian out of my mind. In Mawstone, January and February had always been bleak and cheerless months, but at *Meadhaven* it was different. There was a warm house, a comfortable bed, no anxiety about the next day's meals, and plenty of ways for me to keep myself occupied. Sarah's birthday came in January, and my own, my twentieth birthday, five weeks later. We each had a birthday party, with many young people from the district as guests. Lucian sent his greetings and a present on each occasion, a fob watch for Sarah, and for me a pair of earrings brought back from one of his trips abroad. They were of silver set with green peridots, and made to fasten without need for the ears to be pierced. The first time I put them on, Sarah gave a little awed gasp.

'Cadi! With your black hair and nice long neck they make you look . . . *queenly*!'

'They are certainly very dramatic on you, Cadi,' Mrs. Morton said doubtfully. 'But a little old, perhaps?'

It was foolish of me, but wearing those earrings from Lucian gave me a strange impression of intimacy, and brought him so close that I felt thoroughly uneasy. It was as if once again his hands were kneading my own numbed hands as they had done that day in the studio. 'Yes,' I said quickly, staring at myself in the looking-glass. 'I'll keep them till I'm older, I think, Mrs. Morton.'

About twice in each month I received a letter from Count Chiavelli. The manner of his writing was affectionate, and he told me little pieces of news about his family and about whatever was going on in Venice at the time. I always answered promptly, and tried to respond in the same vein. On only one occasion did his letter contain anything concerning the matter of my inheritance, and that was when he wrote:

And now forgive me for touching upon a matter which I am well pleased to leave to the legal gentlemen, but I wish to reassure you. Please do not think that the passing of your great-grandfather's fortune into your hands will be an embarrassment to me or to my family. Because my parents and grandparents used the income from the Trust wisely, I am a person of considerable substance in my own right, and we shall not be in any way deprived by the happy circumstance that brings you to your birthright, dear Caterina . . .

I felt very much easier in my mind after this, for it was something which had troubled me, in spite of the Count's generous and open-hearted acceptance of me in his first letter.

In the middle of February, Mr. Morton called me to his study.

He had received a lengthy report from Mr. Caldwell, and the gist of it was that I had been legally acknowledged under Italian law as being the true descendant in direct line from Granny Caterina, and that I had been declared the sole contingent beneficiary of the old Count's estate.

'The word contingent is used,' Mr. Morton said, 'because your inheritance is contingent upon your reaching the age of twenty-one. However, under the terms of the will you are entitled to the income from the estate until that time. A problem arose from this, because you are still a minor, and a trustee is required to be responsible for your financial affairs until you come of age.'

'But aren't those Italian banks the trustees?'

'For the estate, yes. But the income they will transfer to you, and you need a trustee here in England for that.'

'I don't see any problem, Mr. Morton. Couldn't you be my trustee, if it isn't too much trouble?'

'I shall never find anything I can do for you too much trouble, Cadi. The problem arose because you have no parents or guardian, or at least no official guardian because I have never adopted you legally.' He gave a wry smile. 'It scarcely seemed necessary. But the fact is that the Count himself could have claimed legal guardianship of you, as your nearest blood relation.'

'Oh!' I was taken aback by the thought that somebody I had never seen could claim any rights over me, however nice he might seem from his letters.

'But as it happens,' Mr. Morton went on, 'the Count has waived any such claim. He thinks it right that I should be your trustee for this income over the next year until you come of age. It only remains for you to agree, should you so wish.'

'Me?'

'Yes, my dear. Our laws allow you some rights in the matter, I'm happy to say.'

'Then that's what I'd like, please.'

'Very well. I think you should draw a reasonable allowance from the income, but we can discuss that later.' His eyes twinkled suddenly. 'At least you will no longer have to sell pot-plants to augment your pocket money.' He looked at Mr. Caldwell's report again. 'I don't think there's anything else on that matter at the moment, but it means we should press ahead with arrangements for our trip to Venice, I feel. Since the Count has been so kind and helpful it's only right that we should take you to visit him as soon as possible now. April seems a good time. I'll give thought to the matter.'

He put down the report, got to his feet, and paced slowly about the study, his hands behind his back. I sat waiting, wondering what was pressing on his mind, for I could see what I thought was puzzlement and uncertainty in him. At last he said, 'There is another matter which I've hesitated to speak about, though really I have no choice.' He halted in front of me, frowning, then went on abruptly, 'I spoke with Lucian a few days ago. In fact, he sought me out, asking if he might pay his attentions to you.'

'His . . . attentions?' I said incredulously, and felt flame in my cheeks.

'Yes, Cadi. It seems he wishes you to be his wife.'

'His *wife*?'

Mr. Morton smiled mournfully. 'Dear child, try to do more than simply echo my last words. Perhaps out of respect for his aged uncle, Lucian has followed a custom which is falling out of fashion now, and asked my permission before speaking to you. He wishes to marry you.'

'Marry me?' I repeated, and caught myself. 'Oh, I'm sorry, Mr. Morton. But——' A hundred questions whirled in my head, and of course I chose to speak the most stupid of them all. 'But how can he pay his attentions to me when we hardly ever meet?'

Mr. Morton stared and rubbed his pate. 'Why, he had in mind to stay here at *Meadhaven*—but my dear Cadi, that is hardly the point. I want to know how you *feel* about this.'

'But—it's absurd, Mr. Morton,' I stammered. 'Lucian has never treated me as anything but . . . well, a child. Why does he suddenly talk about marrying me?'

'Presumably because he has realized you are no longer a child and has fallen in love with you, my dear.'

I shook my head. Pangs of longing stabbed through me, painful yet strangely sweet, making it difficult to collect my tumbled thoughts. Mr. Morton was saying, 'I know it is still the custom for parents to arrange marriages for their daughters, and you are a daughter to me, Cadi. But I am strongly opposed to this custom, and no man shall pay court to you, or to Sarah in due time, unless by your own wishes.'

It was so tempting to forget all else and to drift in a rosy dream of believing what a part of me so desperately wanted to believe. But I would not yield to that sort of self-deception. If Lucian loved me, he had never shown it by so much as a word or a gesture.

'I don't believe Lucian has fallen in love with me,' I said in a strange-sounding voice. 'Do you, Mr. Morton?'

He made a troubled gesture. 'I wish I knew, Cadi. I've

194

always been very close to Lucian, always fancied that we had a good understanding of one another, but I must confess he has puzzled me of late. I find him less frank, less communicative.'

There was a long silence. 'Do you think,' I said at last, reluctant to utter the words, 'do you think that it's because I'm an heiress now?'

Mr. Morton paced away, then looked over his shoulder. His face had a set expression, but with weariness behind it. 'If you had asked me that a few months ago, even a few weeks ago, I would have laughed at the suggestion. I believe I still ought to laugh at it . . . but I'm unable to do so, Cadi. I am uneasy.'

I thought of all that I suspected of Lucian, all those things I had shut away deep in my mind and refused to look at because they made me afraid. Mr. Morton came to me and put his arm about me for a moment. 'There now, don't be troubled. Do you know, I once had a little secret dream. It was after the night of that first ball, when you defied them all and danced with Lucian. That was when I first truly realized that you were no longer a child, Cadi. I had, I still have, a great regard for Lucian, and it stole into my mind that one day you and he might be drawn to one another. That was my little dream.'

Mr. Morton wrinkled his brow and sighed. 'Yet when Lucian spoke to me the other day,' he went on, 'I felt anxiety rather than pleasure. I'm not sure why. Perhaps because we have ceased to be at ease with each other as we once were. He no longer teases me as his aged uncle. There is something very much on his mind. Lucian is a strange young man. When he has a purpose, he keeps it to himself and follows it through to the end. I sense a purpose in him now, not simply to marry you, but a purpose behind that. And I cannot decipher what it is.' He gave a shrug and spread his hands. 'But we need not be concerned with his purpose, Cadi. You have only to tell me whether or not you wish Lucian to pay court to you.'

My heart was a leaden weight within me as I formed in my mind the words I would speak. There was not even bitter

195

satisfaction in knowing that I was being sensible and crushing down infatuation, for I felt there could be no greater pain if I had been denying love itself. 'I want Lucian to leave me alone, Mr. Morton,' I said tiredly.

'Very well.' It was as if he did not know whether to be glad or sorry. 'I shall inform Lucian.'

'Does he know that you were going to speak to me?'

'No. He asked my permission in the matter and I told him I would reflect on it. I'm sure he will guess that I have asked what your wishes are, but I won't mention that when I speak to him. It will soften any blow to his pride somewhat if I present the decision as my own, even if he knows otherwise. I may well suggest that I consider the time is not yet ripe.'

'Yes . . . whatever you think best, Mr. Morton.'

That night, and three times in the next month, I had the Bad Dream, and it was worse than ever before, a grotesque nightmare. In the quiet of the *Palazzo Chiavelli* I moved along the broad passage eagerly, with glad anticipation, to find the man who was waiting for me. The door opened and Lucian's faced looked upon me, the eyes warm and loving as I had never seen them in my waking hours. But then, as joy rose within me, he turned, and horror choked me, for instead of seeing the back of his head I saw another face, like the two heads of Janus. It was still Lucian's face, but this was a satanic caricature that struck terror into me and woke me from my sleep writhing and whimpering.

Towards the end of March, when preparations for our trip to Venice were well advanced, Mrs. Morton was taken ill with influenza. The rest of us escaped, but it was three weeks before she could leave her bed, and even then she was still very weak. Strangely, she made far less fuss when she was genuinely ill than she made about trivialities when she was in good health.

Dr. Bailey prescribed a sea-voyage to help her throw off the aftermath of the illness, and so Mr. Morton made a change of plan. He arranged for Mrs. Morton, Richard, and a nurse-companion to go to Venice at the end of April by a passenger ship which stopped at several ports in the Mediterranean. The trip would take three weeks, and would make an excellent convalescence. The delay meant that Richard would be absent from University for part of the term, but this did not seem to disturb him. On the other hand, Mr. Morton could not be away from his office for too long, so Sarah and I would leave with him only two days before the ship was due in Venice, crossing to Calais by the Channel ferry and travelling through France and Switzerland to Italy by train. We could have completed the whole journey in only thirty-six hours by taking sleeping compartments on the train, but Mr. Morton felt that such a nonstop journey might be too tiring for Sarah, so he arranged for us to spend the first night at an hotel in Chalons and continue on another train next day. This would bring us to Venice only a few hours after the ship was due to arrive there.

At first Mr. Morton had planned to make the train journey alone, while Sarah and I made the sea voyage with the rest of the family, but Mrs. Morton did not like to think of him being left on his own in the house with only the servants to look after him, and besides, Sarah was a bad sailor who dreaded the thought of a voyage, so together we persuaded him to let us stay at *Meadhaven* and accompany him on the rail journey later.

One thing troubled me. Mr. Morton had decided that we could not impose the whole family upon Count Chiavelli as guests for the month that we would be in Venice, partly because he felt it would be a burden to the Count's household and partly because it might spoil my reunion with the family to which I belonged. He had booked rooms at a comfortable hotel in Venice, and the Mortons would stay there while I stayed at the palazzo.

I felt uneasy about this arrangement, for I knew that I would be very nervous. I wished that Mr. Morton could have been with me at the palazzo, or even Sarah, but when I spoke to him about it he said gently, 'I know it will be something of an ordeal for you at first, Cadi, but I'm sure the Count would wish it this way. He has even hinted as much in the letters you've shown me. And since he has been so very kind in making no difficulties whatsoever, I feel we are bound to respond. Besides, we shall be seeing you very frequently, no doubt.'

Reluctantly I confessed to myself that what he said was right, but it did nothing to make me less nervous.

The day Mrs. Morton departed with Richard and her nurse-companion, Miss Tetchley, there was great excitement, for Mr. Morton had hired a motor-car and chauffeur to take them to Southampton, where they would board the ship. An hour before they left I found myself alone in the garden with Richard. He looked very handsome in the dark blazer he wore, and his violet eyes were almost startling against the gold of his hair. It struck me that he seemed to have grown from a boy to a man since the turn of the year.

'You'll take good care of your mother, won't you?' I said. 'She really has been ill, Richard, so don't do anything to . . . well, don't get into any mischief, or she might be dreadfully upset.'

He smiled. 'I won't get into any mischief. I'm taking some books with me and I'm going to study hard. I want to do well in my examinations.'

'That's a change,' I said, teasing him a little. 'You usually waste your vacations fiddling around in that workshop.'

'I know, but it's different now. I want to do well.' He took my hand and halted, turning to face me. Shrubbery hid us from the house. 'Will you kiss me goodbye, Cadi?' he asked.

I pretended to misunderstand, and said, 'Of course I'll kiss you goodbye, I always do when you go away.'

His eyes were brilliant as they dwelt on my face, his expression intent. 'I didn't mean in front of the family, Cadi,' he said with gentle persistence, and took my other hand. 'I mean now.'

I did not know how to refuse without being unkind, and it would have been coy to pretend again that I did not realize his meaning, so I tried to take the matter lightly, and smiled as I said, 'All right, if you want me to, Richard.' I put my arms up round his neck, and went up on my toes a little to touch my lips to his. I meant it to be no more than that, but he drew me close to him, holding me and kissing me hard.

Without wishing to be, I was stirred, and could feel my heart beating a little faster when he let me go. 'You're not my sister, Cadi,' he said. 'I love you.'

I was troubled. 'But——' I began, then stopped, not knowing how to go on. I had been moved by his kiss and had responded, but that was all. I wanted to say that nothing had changed, that I did not feel love for him in the way he wanted, but could not bring myself to utter the words.

'But you don't feel the same?' he prompted, and smiled. 'I know, Cadi. And perhaps you never will. But perhaps . . . well, it's a strange thing and it can come without warning, as it came to me that night you helped me. I'm content to wait and hope.'

Without waiting for an answer he took my arm and we strolled on past the shrubbery and across the lawn towards the house, while he talked of the coming journey as if nothing had taken place between us.

For the next two weeks and more I found myself acting as mistress of *Meadhaven*. I felt this was Sarah's place, and told her so after a few days, but she pulled a face and shook her head firmly. 'I abdicate,' she said, and smiled. She giggled much less these days, and yet had more humour. 'You're much better at handling Mrs. Beale and John the butler than I am. We'd be having her beastly currant pudding for dessert every day if it wasn't for you.'

That was true. I usually got on well with Mrs. Beale, but only yesterday I had done battle with her in the kitchen about the frequency of currant pudding. 'However did you know about that?' I asked Sarah. 'You weren't there.'

'Papa and I were listening at the top of the stairs.' Sarah gave a small eruption of laughter at the memory. 'We nearly *died*, Cadi, especially when she said she'd speak to the master about you, and you told her that if she served currant pudding again she'd better not go *near* the master or he'd throw it at her. We simply *ached* trying not to make a sound.'

I felt sudden pleasure at the thought of Sarah and her father at the top of the stairs to the kitchen, listening and giggling together like children. They were much closer to each other than when I had first come to *Meadhaven*.

Soon the day arrived when our trunks were packed, mostly with new clothes for the holiday, and we caught the boat train. The Channel seemed smooth to me, but poor Sarah quickly felt sea-sick. I made her lie down in a deck chair in the open air, with her eyes closed, and chatted to her to keep her mind occupied. When she was sick I attended to her, and then made her eat some bread so that her stomach was not empty. She clung to my hand and was so grateful that I immediately began to remember all the times I had been sharp with her, and felt guilty.

As soon as we were on land again she recovered, and we were both fascinated by the strangeness all about us, the Frenchmen in their blue working clothes, the signs and advertisements in a strange language, the cries of the porters, and the chatter of the French passengers as we moved through the train to our reserved compartment.

Then we settled down to the long journey ahead. Sometimes we read books we had brought with us, sometimes I played bezique with Mr. Morton, for he had taught me this card game during the winter evenings, and sometimes we watched the unfamiliar countryside flash by, first the flat plains of northern France, with their immense fields of newly sown grain, then more undulating country where woods and green hills jostled together and were cut by little rivers.

It was about six o'clock in the evening when we reached Chalons. The town stood on the River Marne and was threaded by canals and small streams. Our trunks were left for safe-keeping at the station, a big smoky place full of clanking and whistling as long lines of carriages were shunted. We took only a small case each for our overnight stop.

Mr. Morton chatted in French with the driver of the hotel trap which had been sent for us, telling him that we would be continuing our journey at the same time the next evening.

Our hotel was in a pleasant square off Avenue Jean Jaurés. The room I shared with Sarah looked out over the square. I thought the furnishing seemed very heavy and ornate, but the room itself was light and airy.

Mr. Morton had told us to join him in the lounge when we had washed and tidied ourselves, and then we would have dinner. Since we left the train, Sarah had seemed rather nervous and flustered, and as soon as she was ready she went downstairs without waiting for me. I was a little puzzled by her manner, but put it down to the fact that this was a foreign country and all very new to her. It was the same for me, of course, but by now I was more used to being in new surroundings than Sarah.

Five minutes later I found Mr. Morton in the lounge, reading a French newspaper. He smiled and said, 'Well, what do you think of Chalons, my dear?'

'I've only seen a little of it so far, Mr. Morton. On the drive from the station I thought it looked an interesting town to explore. It seems very old.'

'It is indeed. Attila the Hun fought the Romans here. That was fifteen centuries ago.'

'Did they beat him?'

'Yes, as a matter of fact they did. Why do you ask?'

'I'm not sure. Yes I am. The Huns destroyed things, and I don't like that, so I'm glad the Romans won.'

'So am I,' Mr. Morton agreed. 'I don't think there can be much left from that day, but we shall have time to look at some beautiful things tomorrow. There is the cathedral of St. Etienne, which has some notable stained glass windows, I understand. And there's Notre Dame, which goes back to the twelfth century. It's a pity we shan't be able to visit the caves in the limestone hills, where they store champagne.' He looked at me mischievously. 'I seem to remember it was a subject you enjoyed when we were at the Café Royal with Lucian.'

I did not want to talk or think about Lucian, so I just smiled and made a little grimace at the memory of the way the champagne had affected me, then looked round the lounge and said, 'Where's Sarah?'

His eyebrows shot up. 'I thought she was following you down.'

'No, she came down before me.'

He stood up, frowning. 'Then where has she got to?' We went out of the lounge and into the reception hall, but there was no sign of Sarah. Mr. Morton marched up to the desk and began to question the clerk there, but at that moment Sarah came in through the open doors which led to the street.

'Sarah!' her father said in astonishment. 'What on earth are you doing outside?'

Sarah looked blank. 'It's such a warm, close evening, Papa. I walked up and down for a few minutes to get a breath of air.'

'But my dear child, it's almost dark!'

'Not really, Papa. It only seems so when you're inside, in the light.'

Mr. Morton let out a gusty sigh of exasperation. 'Well don't go wandering out on your own again, even when it only *seems* dark, Sarah! Now come along and let's have dinner.'

He strode off towards the restaurant, and we followed. I whispered to Sarah, 'Whatever's come over you?'

'Over me? Nothing, Cadi. *You'd* take a little stroll up and down outside if you wanted a breath of air.'

'Yes, but—that's different. I mean, you don't do that sort of thing.'

She thought it over for a moment, then said solemnly, 'I didn't *used* to. I expect I've caught it from you, Cadi.'

It took me several seconds to realize that she was teasing me, and I was so surprised that I could think of nothing else to say.

We dined well, perhaps too well, for next morning both Mr. Morton and Sarah were pale and drawn with upset stomachs. I felt well enough myself, and ate a good breakfast while they watched with a touch of envy.

'I should have remembered,' Mr. Morton said sadly, 'that though French cuisine is excellent, the English stomach needs to adjust to such differences gradually.'

'They cook everything in oil,' I said. 'Miss Rigg told me. I expect it makes the food rather rich. But I did like that oyster sauce they served with the fish last night. It had a delicious flavour.'

Sarah turned her head away and said faintly, 'Please, Cadi.'

'I was referring to the normal and average English stomach, of course,' said Mr. Morton. 'Not to Cadi's. Sarah, my dear, you and I will have to rest and take only a light diet today, or we shall be in a poor state to continue our journey this evening.' He gave me a look of apology. 'I'm sorry, Cadi, but we shall have to cancel our exploration of Chalons.'

So it was a dull day for me, even though the weather was brilliant and the sun almost freakishly hot for so early in the year. I spent the morning in our bedroom with Sarah, reading to her, playing pencil-and-paper games with her, and making sure she took some unpleasant medicine Mr. Morton had asked to have made up by the chemist in the main road near the hotel. I asked Mr. Morton to let me go out to collect the medicine myself, just so that I could walk in the open air for a few minutes, but though it was interesting to see the French people going about their business and the carriages driving on the right-hand side of the road, I saw very little of the town.

I had a good lunch in the hotel restaurant, all by myself, and an hour later I went to see Mr. Morton in his room. He was sitting up in bed reading a book, and looked a little better now.

'May I go out just for an hour, Mr. Morton?' I asked. 'I've been looking at the map in the reception hall, and I thought I could just walk to the market, spend a little while there, and come straight back.'

He hesitated. 'Do you think you should, Cadi? On your own?'

'Well, it's only three o'clock, and it doesn't even *seem* dark outside,' I said hopefully. 'I've seen several girls of my age unescorted. You wouldn't mind if I walked round the market in Sevenoaks on my own, and the only difference here is the language, but I wouldn't talk to anybody, so that doesn't matter, and I promise I won't get lost.'

'There's an inexorable logic about your arguments, Cadi,' he mused. 'I can usually find the flaw in them afterwards, but not at the time.'

I was about to say reluctantly, 'If you don't think it's quite proper . . .' for I knew that would persuade him. He had a great dislike of many things which other people considered proper but were really only meaningless customs which had endured long past the time when there was a reason for them. But I did not say the words, because it suddenly seemed to me a sly way of getting what I wanted, and I couldn't be sly with him.

'Well . . .' he said slowly, 'I don't see that any harm can come to you. But don't be more than an hour, Cadi. Keep to the main streets, and just go to the market and back. Write down the address of this hotel before you go, and if you have any difficulty just show it to a gendarme.' He took my hand and looked at me with his head a little to one side. 'Now, what was it you were going to say just now but managed not to?'

I went very red as I told him what I had been about to say, and why, and also why I had stopped myself, but he only laughed and said, 'My faithful Cadi,' and put my fingers to his cheek for a moment. When I left him he was still chuckling and shaking his head. He often laughed and was kind to me when I thought he had reason to be angry, and though I didn't understand I was very glad.

When I told Sarah I was going out she looked at me round-eyed, sitting up on the bed in her petticoat. 'Oh Cadi, do you think you should? I mean, it's a *foreign* place! You might get lost—or be run over by a carriage. They drive on the wrong side of the road here.'

'Stop fretting,' I said gently. 'We're not in the middle of Darkest Africa. I'm only going to walk to the market and back, so there's no need to worry.'

Sarah stared at me uneasily for a moment, then suddenly pouted. 'You didn't snap at me,' she said almost indignantly. 'I like you to sometimes, then it's just like having a real sister.'

I couldn't prevent myself laughing, but I saw what she

meant. After the rather stiff politeness of my first week or two at *Meadhaven*, Sarah and I had become very much like real sisters. I gave her hair a tweak and said, 'All right, I'll bite your head off next time.' Then I put on my hat, wrote out the hotel address on a piece of paper, picked up my handbag and went down into the street.

I had the map fixed firmly in my mind, and it took me only ten minutes to reach the market. There must have been fifty stalls in the square, but the scene was disappointing for me, for they were all closed. Their wooden doors, flaked with weathered paint, were fast secured by padlocks and hasps. An old woman sat on the ground in the shade of one of the stalls, leaning her back against the wheel, fast asleep. Beside her, four small live chickens with their feet tied together lay unmoving except for the blink of their bright black eyes.

The stalls were set at one end of the square. At the other end was a strip of sandy ground edged by a line of plane trees, and here in the shade four old men in overalls were playing a game similar to bowls, in which they tossed heavy wooden balls towards a jack. I had hoped to find all the bustle of a market, with the sellers of meat and fish, vegetables and groceries, candles and cloth and trinkets, all plying their trade. I had hoped to listen to the chatter of bargaining in a strange tongue, to watch the people, and to see how like or unlike they were to those who went to market in Sevenoaks or Mawstone. But there was only the almost empty square lying silent under a sun that pretended it was mid-summer rather than early spring.

I realized that the morning must be the busy time for this market, and perhaps the evening as well, but evidently the afternoon was a time for resting. Unwilling to return to my hotel yet, I walked slowly round the square, looked at the row of pigeons sitting like ornaments along the porch of the church, then sat down on a wooden bench under the shade of a tree and watched the bowls-like game going on a short stone's throw away. I suppose it was a very peaceful scene, but I wanted to be moving about and seeing new things here in this strange land, not to be sitting alone in a drowsy square with only the distant thud of the wooden balls and the occasional voice of a sleepy pigeon to disturb me.

But two minutes later I had no cause to complain about the quietness. From one of the roads leading off the square there came the sound of marching feet, faint at first but growing steadily louder. There must have been forty soldiers marching in the column, all wearing smart blue uniforms with stripes down their trousers, and carrying drums, horns, flutes, cornets, bassoons, trombones, and every variety of wind and reed instrument.

It was a band, a military band, and I remembered Mr. Morton had said last night at dinner that there had been a large training centre for troops to the north of the town since the days of Napoleon III. The band was under the command of a very splendid individual with a huge moustache. He stood in the middle of the square and barked orders which brought the soldiers round in a well-spaced formation in front of him, then from under his arm he took a baton and prepared to conduct. There was a minute or two of tuning up or blowing the dust out of their instruments, then the music crashed forth in a great blare, the pigeons took wing, and the bowls players shrugged hugely, shook their heads, lifted their eyes to heaven, and went on dourly with their game. Here and there round the square, some windows and shutters banged to.

I was laughing to myself and wishing so much that Mr. Morton had been with me, for he would have thoroughly enjoyed the comedy. It was clear that the band had been ordered to play in the square, and it was equally clear that the good people of Chalons did not want their peace disturbed, certainly not at this time of day when they were resting. But orders are orders, and the bandsmen soldiers were determined to do their duty. The bowls players ignored them. Even the pigeons had gone to seek a quieter place. The band was playing for an audience of one, Cadi Tregaron, and I was sitting fifty yards away behind them, so I think hardly any of them knew I was there.

Their opening tune was a march with a fine rhythm. Later

I hummed it to Mr. Morton, and he told me it was a famous French marching song called *Madelon*. It was a tune I did not quickly forget, because what happened soon afterwards, while they were still playing it, burned the powerful melody so deeply into my mind that even weeks later I would sometimes wake at night with the sound of *Madelon* running round and round in my head.

Within two minutes I decided that if I sat there any longer I would have a splitting headache, and I wondered how the bandsmen themselves could stand it. Not wishing to cross the square and draw their eyes, I got up and moved quietly away to the west side, intending to walk round the edge of the big square and on back to the hotel.

It was as I made my way past the church that I saw a man coming towards me, moving quickly, his head turning from side to side as if looking for somebody. He wore a grey suit and bowler hat, with a short cloak thrown over his shoulders, and I saw his face clearly as he stared about him. It was the grey-eyed stranger from Wealdhurst. He had not seen me, even though I was in full view, perhaps because the sun was slanting down into his eyes and I was in the strip of shadow thrown by the church. But I knew that in another second or two he must see me, and I was seized by a chill of alarm.

This could be no coincidence. He was here, hundreds of miles deep into a foreign country, because I was here. He must have known our plans, which were common knowledge in the village, and he had taken the same journey, been on the same train, no doubt. I could not have said what I feared, for there were forty soldiers in the square, but in some way the blaring music which smothered all other sound made me feel alone, isolated, and I only knew that I dreaded the stranger finding me. In his face was a hard grimness and purpose I had never seen there before, and I had a keen sense of imminent danger.

My instinct was faster than my thoughts, for in the first moment of seeing him I turned aside into a narrow street which ran down beside the church, quickening my pace until I was almost running. At least he could never hear my footsteps over that music. Glancing back, I saw him pass across the end of the shadowed side-street, and out of my view.

I let out a sigh of relief and stood still, waiting for my heart to stop beating so quickly. Within a few seconds I began to feel rather foolish for giving way to such unreasonable fears. But all the same they were still with me, and I did not intend to let the grey-eyed stranger find me. Conjuring up the map in my mind, I decided that if I walked on to the end of this little side street, then turned right and right again, I would come out in the main road which lay between the square and the hotel.

I set off, but after I had turned right for the second time I was not so sure of my route, for I found myself in an alley rather than a street, with high windowless walls on each side.

The alley curved round ahead of me, and I was afraid it led back to the square, for even here the sound of the band filled the air. As I started to turn back, a tall man wearing the white jacket of a hotel porter entered the alley by the way I had come. He was a big, slouch-shouldered man, and to my surprise he lifted a hand as he approached and made a gesture as if urging me to go back. I said, stupidly, 'I beg your pardon?'

He stopped, seemed to search for words, then pointed along the alley towards the square and said, 'M'sieu Morton.' He shaped the name as if it was difficult for his tongue. For a moment I forgot the grey-eyed stranger. 'What is it?' I asked. 'What about Mr. Morton?'

He shrugged his shoulders, uncomprehending, pointed again, moved past me, and said, 'M'sieu Morton! Come!' He beckoned urgently, and set off along the alley. After a moment's hesitation I followed, full of anxiety as I tried to think what could have happened to make the hotel send out a porter to find me. We passed round the crooked curve of the alley and the noise of the music grew louder. Then the man ahead of me stopped and turned. Beyond him a blank wall stretched across the alley. The music seemed very close, and I think that only a small, high-walled garden separated us from the square. But there was no exit. The alley was blind.

The man put a hand under his jacket, and when he withdrew it I saw that he was gripping a piece of iron bar almost a foot long. He darted one sharp glance beyond me, then lunged towards me quickly. There was no doubting his intention, and terror exploded within me as I turned to run, struggling to lift the skirt that hampered my legs. I was trying to scream, but shock seemed to have driven all the air from my lungs and I could only utter the faintest whinny of sound.

I came to the bend of the alley, running with all my strength, praying that I could reach the street at the back of the church before he caught me, for there at least I had the hope of help from a chance passer-by. It was a slender hope indeed, for I felt that all Chalons was asleep or resting, and even if I found breath to scream I would never be heard above the noise of the military band, for the music was rising to a final crescendo now. But I thrust on desperately. There was no other hope.

Then, twenty paces ahead of me, at the entrance to the alley, the grey-eyed stranger stepped into view, and those grey eyes were as cold as the bitter sea-fog of winter that eats into the very bone.

The man with the iron bar was close behind. I could not hear him but I knew it. I was trapped between the two of them, and my terror gave way before a crushing despair that seemed to drain all strength from my body.

Chapter Eleven

WITH SHOULDERS HUNCHED, expecting at any instant to be struck down from behind, I threw myself to one side and turned with my back against the wall of the building, lifting my handbag in futile readiness to strike as my assailants came at me from each side.

Then I saw that the man with the iron bar had stopped. He hesitated, as if startled, his glance darting past me to the grey-eyed stranger, who was moving quickly forward. As he moved he spoke, and in that very instant the music stopped, leaving only the echoes of a final crashing chord to reverberate through the hot still air. I heard again that soft voice with its underlying Irish brogue. 'It's all right, Miss Tregaron, don't you be worrying now.'

Next moment he had passed in front of me and was standing between me and the big, sallow-faced Frenchman. As he passed, without looking at me, he took off his hat as I had seen him do many times when we met near *Meadhaven*. Bewilderment addled my senses, but I heard myself utter a sob of relief as I realized that he was not attacking me but guarding me from attack. Then came new alarm as I saw the Frenchman take a firmer grip on the iron bar and lunge forward at the smaller man who stood between us.

Calmly the grey-eyed stranger spun his hat into the Frenchman's face, so that the hard brim struck him across the bridge of the nose. What happened next was too quick for me to follow, but I saw the iron bar miss its intended mark by inches. For a moment the men were at close quarters. I heard two soft-sounding blows, a whistling gasp, a sharper blow as of bone on bone, then the big man lurched against the far wall and slithered to the ground, the iron bar clattering as it fell from his limp hand.

The grey-eyed stranger picked up his hat, brushed the dust from it, and turned to me. His eyes were bright and his smile so full of mischief that the last threads of fear fell away from me.

'That was closer than I'd wish for you,' he said almost apologetically, 'but all's well that ends well. Go back to the hotel, Miss Tregaron, and be easy in your mind, for I'll not be far behind you.'

'Thank you,' I stammered. 'I—I don't know what to say. . . .' My voice trailed away. I clenched my fists and drew a long breath to stop myself breaking into tears. He watched me curiously, and gave a little nod of approval, as if something only half-believed until now had been confirmed for him. 'My respects to you, Miss Tregaron,' he said, 'you're a fine steady girl.'

He squatted down and began to go quickly through the pockets of the unconscious man. I saw now that the porter's jacket was far too small and the only item of uniform the man wore. He must have stolen it for his purpose. With an effort I tried to gather my scattered wits. I was still shivering, but no longer felt close to tears. 'I . . . I don't understand,' I said helplessly. 'Did you *know* this would happen?'

'If I'd known, I'd not have let things run so damn close, Miss Tregaron,' he said a little grimly.

'But who is this man? Why did he try to harm me?'

'Ah, now. If we could answer that we'd be much wiser than we are.' He stood up empty-handed, with a grimace of disappointment. 'There's nothing in his pockets to tell us.'

'But . . . who *are* you? And how did you come to be here?'

'Didn't I once tell you I'm a travelling man? I just happened to be passing, let's say.' Again he gave me that quick, mischievous smile. 'Will you hurry now please, Miss Tregaron? We want to be away from here.'

I nodded, too confused to press any further questions. As I reached the entrance of the narrow alley, with my legs feeling as if they did not belong to me, I turned and looked back. He had put on his hat and was about to follow me. The Frenchman moaned but did not stir. 'Please come and meet my family,' I said. 'Mr. Morton will want to thank you.'

He shook his head. 'Best not trouble him with this. He'll feel bound to call in the police, and the wheels turn slowly in France. You'll find yourselves having to spend a week or more in Chalons before you know where you are. Besides, you have Miss Morton with you and she might be much alarmed, d'you not think?' There was a hint of the mockery in his manner that had once annoyed me, but now it seemed friendly and without any bite to it.

I said, 'Then won't you at least tell me your name, please? I'm so much in your debt.'

For a moment he hesitated. Then, 'Call me Flynn. But away with you now, Miss Tregaron, and a pleasant journey to you.'

'Thank you, Mr. Flynn. Thank you again.' I hardly knew what I was saying, but it came from a full heart.

I walked back into the square, where the band had begun to play another piece of music, then along the road to the hotel. Once I looked round. There was no sign of Flynn, but I felt strangely sure that he was not far away. I could feel my hands trembling again, and I felt sick. Luckily I had been away from the hotel for only half an hour, even though it seemed like a lifetime, and so I was able to sit quietly in the little courtyard garden at the back of the hotel for a while and recover from the shock. Gradually my body stopped shivering and I felt the blood coming back to my cheeks. I had managed to order a cup of tea from a waiter as I passed through the lounge, and though it was very weak and scarcely tasted like tea it was comforting.

As I sat drinking it I tried to decide whether I should tell Mr. Morton what had happened. It seemed the right and sensible thing to do, but I found myself shrinking from it. As Flynn had said, if the matter was taken up it would cause a long delay in our journey no doubt. It would also put Mr. Morton in a great state of distress, not only for me but for Mrs. Morton, who would disembark at Venice tomorrow and would be frantically worried if we failed to arrive as planned. Then again, Sarah would have to be told the story, and that would cause more distress.

I don't know which of these reasons weighed most with me, or whether I acted for some reason obscure even to myself, but in the end I decided to say nothing now. In two or three hours we would be leaving Chalons. I would tell Mr. Morton later, when he and I were alone, and when I felt calmer.

I finished my tea, pulled myself together, practised a cheerful smile once or twice, then went upstairs to make Sarah laugh with the story of the military band.

We left the hotel at half past five, and within an hour we were on the train for Venice once again. Mr. Morton and Sarah looked a little worn, but said they felt much better now. That night, in the sleeping compartment I shared with Sarah, I lay awake for a long time as the train rattled rhythmically across France and into Switzerland, my sleepy mind plodding round and round, seeking answers to unanswerable questions. Over the past year I had been close to death three times, once when Pompey bolted, once in the tunnel near Sevenoaks, and again behind the square at Chalons. Somebody wished me ill, but I could not guess who it might be. At different times I had vaguely suspected Richard, Lucian, and the mysterious stranger I now knew as Flynn. I could no longer suspect Flynn, for he had saved me today. Richard had been far away on the day of the attack in the tunnel, and both he and Lucian were far away from Chalons at this moment. But that did not eliminate all suspicion. The man who had tried to strike me down with an iron bar was surely a hireling of somebody, for he was French and I had never seen him before. Who was his master? I could not believe it was Richard, but just possibly it might be Lucian, who travelled much abroad.

Yet . . . why?

Richard said he loved me. Lucian had spoken to Mr. Morton of marrying me. Could there be somebody else, an unknown enemy? For a moment my imagination ran wild, and I wondered if Count Chiavelli wished me dead because I was a claimant to his inheritance, but that made no sense. He could have fought the claim vigorously, but had not attempted to. Instead he had acknowledged my rights with gladness and affection. Besides, he was a wealthy man in his own right. Above all, he had not known of my existence at the time when Pompey threw me, and had barely learned of it at the time when I was attacked in the tunnel.

I found no answers to the questions that danced in my head, or to the mystery of Flynn. I felt sure that he had travelled from England with us, and this gave me a sense of comfort, for I knew now that he at least was not my enemy.

My thoughts turned suddenly. Did I really have an enemy at all? It seemed so, and yet I did not want to believe it, for such a belief cast frightening shadows upon the future. I looked back again on all that had happened. The broken harness could easily have been an accident. Mr. Morton had taken for granted that the man who attacked me in the tunnel had simply been a poor deranged creature who might as readily have attacked any girl. Could the same be said for the man at Chalons?

No, I thought reluctantly. He had actually spoken Mr. Morton's name, to lure me right into the blind alley. For one frightful and shocking moment my brain staggered under the unbelievable thought that Mr. Morton himself might have known what was to happen. I twisted in the narrow bed and put my hands over my ears as if to shut out the whispering thought. It was madness. I could as well have suspected my own father if he had been alive.

I closed my mind, setting my teeth and starting to recite in my head all the Shakespeare speeches that Miss Rigg had set me to learn over the years. If I could even begin to think such a thing of Mr. Morton, then it meant that my weary brain had gone beyond all reason and entered the world of fantasy. I must stop thinking, and wait until time and rest had steadied my mind and given me a true perspective.

I slept at last, and my dreams were fevered. When morning came, my imaginings of the night seemed foolish beyond words. But I did not speak to Mr. Morton of what had happened to me in the alley behind the market square.

Once again a familiar pattern was about to repeat itself. I had passed through danger, and my mind was full of questions, doubts and fears, but almost at once I was to be caught up in new events which occupied all my thoughts, blunting the sharp edge of anxiety as immediate memory grew blurred.

At dawn next day we passed through the wonderful St. Gotthard Tunnel, over nine miles long. I was still asleep, and did not regret having missed the experience, for I had no love of tunnels now. At Chiasso the Customs men came aboard, and when they had finished their examination the train sped on its way to Como and then to Milan, where we had to change to another train for the trip across the Lombardy Plain to Venice. In the evening came journey's end, when we crossed the great causeway linking Vicenza to Venice, supported above the sea by two hundred and twenty-two arches, so Mr. Morton told us.

Porters with trolleys were everywhere, and there was a great bustle and shouting as luggage was unloaded from the train and trundled away to waiting gondolas and big rowing-boats. I felt tears come to my eyes, for the Italian accent I could hear all around me was not that of Signor Vecchi, who was a Roman, but the same accent I had learned from my mother and Granny Caterina. The Italian spoken in Venice was the Italian I spoke myself. Even without any other proof, I would have known in this minute that Granny Caterina had come from Venice.

I wondered if Flynn had been on the train when we left Chalons. I had not seen him during the journey, even when we changed at Milan, and there was no sign of him now, but that meant very little. While I was wondering about him, Richard appeared. He was edging his way through the throng, his usually pale face lightly tanned now from the sea voyage and his violet-blue eyes seeming brighter than ever. We greeted him excitedly and with a flurry of questions.

'Mother's very well,' he said, smiling. 'The trip was a splendid tonic for her. We arrived this morning and the Count himself was there to meet us——'

'What is he like?' Sarah broke in excitedly. 'Is he nice?'

'Very nice indeed. Mother's quite overwhelmed. He took us to our hotel, to make sure we were comfortably established there, and an hour ago he called for me in one of his private gondolas so that we could come to meet you.'

'Oh! He's here now?' I asked, suddenly conscious that I must look travel-weary and far from my best after the long journey.

'Yes, of course. Don't worry, Cadi, you look splendid.' Richard gave me a warm, encouraging glance, then turned to his father. 'There's a gondola waiting to take us to the hotel, with a rowing boat for the luggage. Cadi will go with the Count, straight to the *Palazzo Chiavelli*.'

'Oh!' I said again, for everything seemed to be happening too quickly for me. 'Must I go there at once, Mr. Morton? I mean, couldn't they find room for me at the hotel with you just for tonight?'

He slipped his hand through my arm. 'I can understand how you feel, Cadi, but after all you are the Count's guest and you are of his family. I think it would be discourteous to delay your arrival at his home.'

I felt very lonely, as if everybody was suddenly deserting me. This was stupid, of course. I had long known that I would be staying at the palazzo, but somehow I had not prepared myself for being separated from Mr. Morton and Sarah as soon as we reached Venice.

Sarah giggled and said, 'I do believe Cadi's nervous.'

'Nonsense!' I snapped quickly, pride coming to my aid. 'Just because *you'd* be nervous——'

'Quite so,' Mr. Morton broke in. 'Please don't make silly remarks, Sarah. Now Richard, where is the Count?'

'Waiting by the jetty, Father. It's only a few steps. He sent me on to meet you so that I could explain what had been arranged.'

'He's very thoughtful, as we might expect,' said Mr. Morton. 'Lead the way, Richard.'

My first sight of Count Chiavelli did much to ease the nervousness I had denied feeling. He wore a dark suit and white silk cravat, a hip-length tiered cloak of black velvet thrown back from his shoulders. Hat in hand, he stood waiting for us close to where two beautiful gondolas painted in red and gold were moored. Four gondoliers in matching uniform waited on the steps. The Count's hair was thick and dark, the eyes wide-set. His features were strong, sharply defined, hinting at a powerful character, but his smile went straight to my heart, for it softened his face as sunlight softens the harsh peaks of snow-capped mountains, and it was so like Granny Caterina's smile that my heart jumped as if in recognition.

'Caterina!' he said softly, and came forward, dropping his hat carelessly as he reached out to take both my hands in his. He kissed me on each cheek, then looked at me and shook his head in smiling wonder. 'How very much like her you are,' he said in English.

'I'm very happy to make your acquaintance, sir,' I said clumsily. He laughed and gripped my hands. 'No formalities, please, Caterina. We are some sort of cousins, but in view of my age perhaps you will call me Uncle Guido.' He turned to Mr. Morton and made a laughing gesture of apology. 'Forgive me, sir. I have not waited for introductions, for I am carried away with pleasure. You will be Mr. Edward Morton, and this is your daughter Sarah. Yes? Caterina has told me much about you in her letters.'

There was hand-shaking and an exchange of greetings. The Count's manner was so friendly and informal that even Sarah was immediately at ease and did not look embarrassed when he raised her hand to touch it to his lips.

'Ah, you should all stay with me,' said the Count a little regretfully. 'We could have opened other rooms in the palazzo without great difficulty.'

'We would not dream of it,' said Mr. Morton. 'I'm sure we shall be very comfortable at the hotel you so kindly recommended, and we should have felt ourselves to be a burden if we had imposed on you.'

'Nothing would be too much trouble for the family which has restored Caterina to us.' The Count picked up his hat, grimaced humorously as he noted the patch of grime on it, and tossed it to one of his gondoliers. 'You will be tired now,' he went on, 'and so will Caterina. I shall see you safely on your way to the hotel, and I hope that tomorrow you will bring your family to dine with us, Mr. Morton. I will send a gondola for you at seven o'clock, if that will be convenient?'

'We shall look forward to it, sir.'

At a word from the Count my luggage was taken from the trolley and put in one of the red-and-gold gondolas, while Mr. Morton's luggage and Sarah's was put in the rowing-boat which hovered by the other gondola.

'Well . . . goodnight, Cadi, my dear.' Mr. Morton put his hands on my shoulders and kissed my cheek. 'Sleep well, and we shall see you tomorrow.' His hands tightened for a moment in a little squeeze of encouragement. I said good-night to Sarah and Richard, and two minutes later all three were moving away from the steps in their gondola, with the rowing-boat following. I waved, feeling a little lost.

When I turned, the Count was looking at me. 'Poor Caterina,' he said sympathetically. 'Of course you feel strange to be separated from those you know so well. But we are your family and we shall make you happy.' He gave the familiar smile that brought Granny Caterina back to me so strongly, and waved one arm in a wide gesture. 'Venice has a warm heart for all travellers, but especially for her own children. She will remember you, Caterina, for though she is very old, she has a long memory.'

He took my arm and guided me down into the gondola. One of the two gondoliers took up his position in the stern, holding the single long oar, and then we were moving quietly over water that gleamed with the rose tints reflected from the glowing bank of mackerel cloud left by the setting sun. 'This is your first sight of Venice,' said the Count in a voice so soft it was almost a whisper. 'I will not spoil it by talking. There is time for that later. Just look, Caterina, with your eyes and with your heart.'

We were in the Grand Canal, and at this moment of twilight it was like fairyland. Already the lamps along the banks of Venice's liquid high-road were being lit. The water shimmered, pink and gold. All about us were moving craft, gondolas, cargo barges, the little rowing boats called *sandolo*, as I learned later, a fishing boat under sail, a *bragozzo*.

Venice wore her great age with dignity. The weathered stone of her houses and palazzos bore the marks of time, yet this in itself was an enhancement, for the façades carried a regal maturity that newly quarried stone could never achieve. I saw that the tide was falling, for a ribbon of damp green an arm's length deep showed at water-level along the base of the buildings. It was a very little tide compared with the tides of the English Channel.

On either side of us, small canals wound away from the Grand Canal and I could see the figures of people crossing the arched bridges which spanned them. Lights shone from windows and from mountings on the outer walls. A water-bus chugged slowly past us, a *vaporetto*. We rode easily over its wake, and passed on.

I felt in a dream. Everything seemed so strange as to be

unreal, yet it was a wonderful strangeness, for to me it was as if hundreds of years of history were all gathered together here, passing before my eyes. What little I knew of architecture came from studying Mr. Morton's books, but I knew that within less than a mile we passed buildings whose style placed them in periods ranging from a hundred years to many centuries past.

The shadows hung strangely, tricking my eyes, so that at one moment the great façade of a church or a palace would seem to be without depth, like a huge structure of painted cardboard; then a change of our position would give sudden depth and permanence to the same building. Everywhere were carvings, on walls, pillars and balustrades. I saw stone lions supporting windows and doorways, a winged horse above the porch of a mansion, and two mythical creatures with talons perched each end of a broad cornice.

As we passed under the Rialto Bridge, a man in a small rowing-boat pulled up to the steps. A dog waited there, a big, slow-moving old dog. With the ease of long practice it jumped lazily into the boat and settled down. Its master turned and began rowing back the way he had come. I laughed aloud in delight, realizing that every creature in Venice was born to the canals. They had narrow roadways and alleys to walk, and bridges to offer crossings, but when anything had to be moved there were only the canals, for nothing bigger than a hand-trolley or small cart could move in the tiny streets I could see winding off from the canal banks. A barge passed, carrying a pile of furniture, chairs and couches, beds, tables and pictures. Somebody was moving to another home, and the waterways gave the only route.

I fell in love with Venice in that short half-hour as we glided slowly down the Grand Canal, even though I had seen almost nothing of her treasures yet. There was an atmosphere that gripped and held me. It came from many things, the soft quality of the light, the sense of slow dreamy movement, the very texture of the ancient stone. At some deep level of my being I had inherited fragments of Granny Caterina's memories. I knew this, from my dreams in which I had seen the palazzo. Now it seemed that time slipped backwards, and I was in another age, seeing with my granny's eyes and feeling with her heart. My own life seemed far distant. Mawstone was a vague blur, *Meadhaven* scarcely seemed to exist. The Mortons were no longer real, but like characters I had read of in a play or story, and . . . yes, even Lucian held no part of me.

I was so deep in the spell that I had forgotten I was not alone, and it came almost as a shock when the Count said quietly, 'We have arrived, Caterina.'

'Oh! I'm sorry, you must think me so ill-mannered.'

'Not at all. It would have been rudeness on my part to intrude upon your first meeting with the Queen of the Adriatic. That is what we call Venice.'

'It's a true name for her. Thank you for being so understanding.' I hesitated, then added, 'Uncle Guido.' I had to accustom myself to calling him by that name. He looked pleased, then pointed as the gondola slid into a canal leading off the Grand Canal. 'There is your home, Caterina.'

The dusk had deepened almost to night during our journey from the station, and when I turned to look at the *Palazzo Chiavelli* I saw it exactly as I had always seen it in my dreams, exactly as it had been painted in the picture which hung in the hall at *Meadhaven*. There were the broad stone steps rising between the two great pillars and leading up from the water to the splendid portico. There were the tall railings which extended from each pillar to hem the grounds, and there were the striped poles rising from the water, which I now knew to be typical Venetian mooring poles.

With a deft touch of the oar, the gondolier brought his craft alongside the steps. His companion sprang out and held the gondola with a boat-hook while Uncle Guido put a hand on my arm to steady me as I stepped ashore. Together we walked up the long flight to the portico, and as we arrived the double doors were swung open from within.

A dark-suited servant stood on each side of the doorway, and beyond them waited a lady in a long green dress with her mahogany hair piled high on her head. Beside her was a young man in a grey suit and a deep red velvet waistcoat.

'Here is our little Caterina,' said Uncle Guido. 'Dear child, I present you to my wife, your Aunt Isola as I hope you will call her, and my son, Bernardino.'

After the long journey and the overwhelming impact of the brief voyage in the gondola, I was too tired and too spellbound to gain any very definite impression of Uncle Guido's wife and son at this moment. They greeted me in Italian, and I responded in the same tongue as we embraced. Their manner was a little less spontaneous than Uncle Guido's had been, but their words were warm and welcoming. I think the only thing I noticed at the time was that the Countess, Aunt Isola, was plump and soft, and that Bernardino's cheek, when it touched mine, felt as soft as his mother's.

We began to move down a long hall. At the end I saw a majestic stairway rising to the next floor. On either side of the hall hung great portraits.

'Now you shall see something,' said Uncle Guido happily. 'Now you shall see why we had no doubts that you were Caterina's grand-daughter when we saw your photograph.' He touched my arm and halted, pointing. The picture was in a beautifully carved golden frame, and it was as if I was looking at myself. This was Granny Caterina at my age, or a little younger. She wore a white dress, delicately pleated, and the gold locket hung about her neck. The horror of what had happened to her came suddenly upon me, and I felt close to tears as I whispered, 'Poor Granny . . .'

I turned to Uncle Guido. 'Do you remember her?'

'Quite well,' he answered. 'I was only a child of five when she disappeared, but I have a clear memory of her in my mind. She was very beautiful.'

We moved on past other portraits, and Uncle Guido recited their names to me, but they meant nothing. I saw the old Count, Granny's father, a man with sombre, hooded eyes, but it was another picture that suddenly caught and held my attention.

'Who is she?' I asked, staring up.

'That is Marguerita, the old Count's sister and my own grandmother,' Uncle Guido replied. 'This was painted when she inherited the title from her brother and became Countess briefly, a year before she died. I remember her well. A formidable old lady.'

So this was the woman who had taken the young Caterina to Naples, where she had disappeared. The face was strong-featured, like Uncle Guido's, but in contrast to his it was proud and haughty. The eyes held a hard, penetrating stare. I did not quite know what had seized my attention, for there was nothing startling about the face, but as I gazed I felt a shiver run through me. Again, as it had been in the gondola, my own mind grew still, as if in some strange trance, and I seemed to be gazing not with my own eyes but with the eyes of Granny Caterina.

Shapeless fears flickered through me, like bats fluttering unseen in the night. Without cause or reason, unless it was the nameless traces of memory which had been born with me from my grandmother's blood, I felt such dread of this woman who stared down upon me that my body shook and I flinched.

I had known fear before—in Mogg Race Bay, in the long dark tunnel, and only a day ago behind the square at Chalons. On those occasions I had had good cause to be afraid. The fear I felt now was quite groundless and unreal, yet in a peculiar way it was more intense and horrifying than any I had known, for I felt that I could not breathe, that I was suffocating . . . drowning. The painted eyes looked down. They seemed to know what was happening to me, and were glad.

Chapter Twelve

I HEARD UNCLE GUIDO'S VOICE saying with quick concern, 'Are you all right, Caterina?'

His words broke the suffocating spell. Air rushed into my lungs, and I dragged my gaze from the portrait. 'Yes . . . I was only thinking.'

His perception was very quick. 'Thinking that Marguerita was the last of our family to see your grandmother before she disappeared?' He looked at the painting and nodded. 'Yes. It was the great tragedy of her life. She was never quite the same again.'

I nodded, saying nothing, and moved on. The moment of intense fear had passed, but had left me feeling drained of energy. I remember little else of that evening. I was shown to my room, which was large and handsomely furnished, decorated in pale blue and gold, and my luggage was brought up.

After I had washed and changed I joined Uncle Guido and his family for dinner. I was making such an effort to hide my weariness that I hardly tasted the food, but simply ate whatever was put before me. We spoke partly in Italian and partly in English, for Uncle Guido insisted that Aunt Isola and Bernardino should practise their English as much as possible now that I was here.

He must have realized how tired I was, for as soon as we rose from dinner he suggested that I might like to retire to bed, and I gratefully accepted. Five minutes later I pulled on my nightdress and sank into the softness of a big four-poster, leaving the hovering maidservant to put out the lamps.

Looking back, I realize that I must surely have been an incurable optimist or very stupid, for it always seemed that no matter what happened to me a night's sleep and the coming of a new day wiped away my anxieties. I forgot, or ignored, whatever danger I had known and whatever mysteries hung unsolved about me. When I woke the next morning I felt refreshed and excited, and I must have stood by my window, looking out upon the magic of Venice, for almost a quarter of an hour before the maid knocked and brought water for my bath.

From the haze that hung over the city I could guess that at dawn the mist had been heavy, but now the sun was dissolving the last cobwebs of it, clothing the spires and turrets of Venice in robes of gold. I longed to explore, and looked forward eagerly to the coming day.

At breakfast I had my first chance to gain an impression of Aunt Isola and Bernardino, but I still found little substance from which to form any opinion. Aunt Isola was soft and plump, I knew, but she seemed also to have a soft plump mind. She continually smiled at me, but did not appear to have any thoughts of her own, and simply repeated whatever Uncle Guido said but in different words. Bernardino seemed to take after his mother, except that he kept paying me compliments and then glancing at his father as if for approval. 'You are much more beautiful than your photograph, Caterina,' he would say. Or, 'It is such a great pleasure to have you with us.' Or he would comment flatteringly on my hair, my eyes, my hands, my dress.

At first I was embarrassed, but after a while I wanted to laugh, particularly when he praised my 'pretty little feet'. That was too much. They were quite well-shaped in a practical sort of way, but they were not little, and to call them pretty was ridiculous. Both Bernardino and his mother struck me as empty characters, but Uncle Guido made up for them both. He talked well and amusingly, and was always interesting. It soon became clear that he was a man of many activities, quite apart from running the stables in Padua which Lucian had told me about.

After breakfast on that first morning I was shown round the palazzo. Uncle Guido acted as guide, and Bernardino trailed along with us. He did not speak very often, and when he did it was only to echo something his father had just said. There were forty rooms in the palazzo, but over half of them had been closed, and the family and servants occupied only fifteen rooms. 'We are a small family now, compared with the old days,' said Uncle Guido. 'I would like to see the palazzo as it was when I was a boy. There were three times as many servants then, and the whole place was in use.'

'I suppose times were different then,' I said. 'It would be a terrible expense today.'

Uncle Guido nodded and rubbed his chin. 'It is still an ambition of mine, Caterina. As for the expense, well, I am not an idle man and I have many business interests that are prospering. So in a year or two we shall see what can be done.'

I remembered what he had said in his letter, that he was a man of substance in his own right and that I must not feel badly about inheriting the fortune which lay in trust for me when the time came. If he could hope to open up the whole palazzo, then he must certainly be very prosperous.

We made our way through two salons and a great ball-room, a library, a study and a sewing room. Sunlight gleamed through tall windows upon walls of gold brocade which rose to marvellous painted ceilings. I had always thought the rooms at *Meadhaven* large, but they could never have contained the massive furniture of the *Palazzo Chiavelli*. Vast couches and chairs, intricately carved and often in gilded wood, were set spaciously about. Immense Persian and Chinese carpets lay beneath glittering chandeliers. I was awed by the thought that over years and even centuries past, all this had been brought to the palazzo by the water-ways of Venice.

Later that morning, as I went to my room to tidy myself for lunch, I stopped to look again at the portrait of Mar-guerita, bracing myself a little, determined not to be so foolishly affected as when I had looked upon the picture last night. Then slowly I relaxed. An old lady gazed down at me, a formidable old lady, as Uncle Guido had said, with arrogant eyes and haughty stare, but she inspired no fear in me. I felt none of that drowning sensation which had so frightened me before, when I had seen her as if through Granny Caterina's eyes. After a while I made a very unladylike face at her and turned my back.

We lunched on a broad terrace of stone flags, from which we could look out upon the canal which ran at the back of the palazzo. 'I expect you would like to rest a little this afternoon, Caterina,' said Uncle Guido. 'You don't want to be over-tired when your friends come to dine with us this evening.' He must have seen the disappointment on my face, for he went on, 'Is there something else you would prefer to do?'

'I'm not at all tired, Uncle Guido, and I'm longing to

see something of Venice by day. I was hoping it would be convenient to make a little tour this afternoon.'

'Why certainly!' He looked pleased. 'I am delighted at such energy. Bernardino, you can take Ugo as gondolier and show Caterina something of our city this afternoon.'

My heart sank a little at the thought of Bernardino being my escort, and I was not wrong to have misgivings, for I found that to drag answers from him to any of the hundreds of questions I wanted to ask during our trip was like drawing a tooth.

For the first ten minutes, if I asked what the history of any particular building was, or tried to find out about any of the sights that interested me, he would gaze with blank uneasiness for a while, and then give some vague, uncertain answer. Soon I gave up, and encouraged Ugo, the gondolier, to tell me all he could as we made our way along the network of canals.

Ugo was hesitant at first, but when he saw that Bernardino was relieved rather than put out, he became quite talkative and proved an excellent guide. The magic of Venice by day was different from her magic by night, yet just as wonderful. Sunlight shimmered over the water and turned to silver under the bridges. Arcaded shops stood shoulder to shoulder with great mansions whose walls still bore the faded traces of frescoes which had once glowed in brilliant crimson, blue and gold. The movement of the people as they strolled was as smooth and unhurried as the gliding of our gondola through the tremulous water.

We passed under the Bridge of Sighs, and there we left the gondola, mounting steps from the canal to make our way into the very heart of Venice, the Piazza San Marco. The vast square was thronged with strolling people and fluttering pigeons, and it seemed to me that there must be hundreds of gaily painted chairs and tables set outside the cafés. We drank coffee at Florians, which Ugo told me was almost two hundred years old, and I found myself breathless with wonder as I looked about me at the great cathedral, at the superb bronze horses on the basilica's façade, and the statues of the tetrarchs carved in red porphyry.

Ugo, standing beside us as we sat with our coffee, told me of the day only a few years ago when the great bell-tower of St. Mark had tumbled down after standing for almost a thousand years. It had been expected, he said, for the structure was failing, and he had been on the perimeter of the square himself, watching with thousands of Venetians on that July morning. The tower, over three hundred feet high, had trembled and then collapsed slowly, gracefully, into a huge mound of brick and rubble. But wonder of wonders, the great bell, the marangona as it was called, which had tolled for six centuries, was unbroken by its fall. Now the bell-tower was being rebuilt, and in another four or five years perhaps it would be finished.

I came to like Ugo, with his wrinkled face and slow manner, for whatever I asked he always produced some fascinating story to go with the answer. Our coffee finished, we strolled round the square. All about us was the work of sculptors and masons for a thousand years past, lions and angels, golden spires and domes, the great Gothic arches which held the pink and white Palace of the Doges as if suspended upon air.

We explored the narrow surrounding streets for a little way, then returned to the gondola. I felt almost glutted with impressions, and realized with awe that anyone could spend years in Venice without exhausting the treasures she had to offer.

Soon we were in the Grand Canal again, but instead of following its winding course Ugo turned where a smaller canal edged a glorious palazzo that seemed of an older style than any I had yet seen.

'Which palace is that Bernardino?' I asked, trying once more to engage him in conversation.

'That?' He gazed at it with his mouth slightly open, then said, 'Contrarini-Fasan.' He looked at me and seemed to be searching his mind for something to say. Finally he added, in English, 'Your eyes are so bright. I think you are the most lovely girl in England, Caterina.'

'Thank you,' I said, and managed to suppress a sigh. 'Ugo, is it a very old palace?'

'Quite old, signorina. It was built before Columbus sailed to America.'

I had seen older buildings in England, of course, but they did not stand upon wooden piles driven down through a hundred feet of mud to a bed of clay, and again I marvelled at the achievements of those ancient craftsmen.

Suddenly, and to my astonishment, Bernardino spoke of his own accord. 'Beyond the next bridge, that hotel on the corner is where Mr. Morton and his family are staying.'

At once an enormous longing rose within me, and I said quickly, 'Let's call on them, Bernardino! Oh, we can't just pass by!'

'But—but it may not be convenient,' he said, disconcerted.

'It's four o'clock and they'll be having tea. At least we can try.' I felt Bernardino longed for his father to be there, for he even cast a harassed glance at Ugo as if for guidance. 'Well . . . I expect it will be all right,' he said feebly at last. I saw Ugo turn his head away to hide a grin as he sent the gondola gliding towards the hotel.

To my joy they were all on the terrace, waiting for tea to be brought, and we greeted one another as if we had not met for years. Mrs. Morton looked very well and embraced me with great affection. She no longer needed the nurse-companion, Miss Tetchley, who had remained on the ship for the return journey to England. The whole family had made a tour by gondola that afternoon, and were full of it. We chattered furiously for half an hour, while Bernardino sat sipping his tea and looking mournfully uneasy. Sarah could not remember the names of anything they had visited, but kept asking if I had seen 'that place with the horses on it in the big square', or 'that huge statue which hammers the bell on the clock tower'.

I was sorry when the time came for us to leave, but I looked forward to the evening, when they would come to dine with us. When we reached the *Palazzo Chiavelli*, I thought Bernardino seemed quite nervous as he told his father we had called upon the Mortons. It was as if he was afraid Uncle Guido would be displeased, but instead he smiled and nodded approval. 'Excellent, my boy. It is good for them to know as soon as possible that our little Caterina is happy with us.'

That evening was wonderful. We all sat round the magnificent table in the great dining room of the palazzo, and the conversation had no awkward pauses. Both Mr. Morton and Uncle Guido were excellent talkers, and more than made up for the lack in Bernardino and Aunt Isola. Sarah bubbled with excitement, and made everybody laugh by mixing up the places she had seen that day and by the way she pronounced one or two names she had tried to learn.

What struck me most of all was that both Richard and Mrs. Morton were clearly enthralled by Uncle Guido. When he told tales of his youth, of masked balls, romantic escapades, and even of a duel fought by one of his friends, Richard sat drinking in every word, his eyes shining, and though Mrs. Morton may have been a little startled she was also enraptured.

'I hope I do not shock you with such stories, Mrs. Morton,' Uncle Guido said, smiling. 'They are all a part of the historic fabric of Venice. Among the noble families here there have always existed strange, fierce undercurrents, and a kind of secret wildness.'

'The history books alone reveal that,' Mr. Morton agreed. 'But is it the same today, my dear Count?'

Uncle Guido shrugged. 'Venetians have changed with the rest of the world, of course. But not quite so much, perhaps. Less than three years ago, in a palazzo I will not name, I saw a young fellow from a noble but impoverished family stake everything he possessed on the turn of a card.'

Mrs. Morton gasped. 'But . . . what did he possess if he was impoverished?'

'The family palazzo. But he was unable to maintain it. And rather than sell, he gambled it against a sum of . . . let me see, now . . . forty thousand of your English pounds.' Uncle Guido paused to drink from a vermilion and blue wine-glass while we all gazed round-eyed.

'And what happened, sir?' Richard asked for us all.

'He won,' said Uncle Guido, and smiled. 'With the turn of a card, he re-established his fortune.' He looked at Mrs.

Morton and raised a reassuring hand. 'I am not commending his action. We Chiavellis stand aside from such headstrong wildness as remains in the Venetians, dear lady. I still think that young man was foolish.'

He lifted his glass and looked at it. 'The Chiavellis are more practical people. These glasses we are using, they were made in my own glass foundry. Beautiful, are they not?' We all murmured admiringly, but for myself I thought the glasses much too ornate and colourful. I guessed that Mr. Morton felt the same, for instead of commenting on the glasses he said, 'Your glass foundry is on the island of Murano?'

'Not quite. On a small islet a short distance from Murano. I bought the islet and the foundry some few years ago.'

'Can we go there?' Sarah asked eagerly. 'I'd love to see glass being made. They blow it, don't they?'

'Yes,' Uncle Guido smiled, 'they blow it, Sarah, and they colour it with chemicals, and mould it with a paddle of charred wood, just as their forefathers have done for centuries. I have seen it a hundred times, but I still find it a small miracle to watch.'

I took some little part in the conversation myself, for Mr. Morton and I were eager to compare notes on the different boats we had seen in Venice, especially the gondolas. 'I'm told they are made from several different woods,' said Mr. Morton. 'Oak and walnut, cherry and elm. Their constructions are quite marvellous, but I cannot fathom how they can be steered on a straight course when they have no rudder and the gondolier uses a single oar on one side only!'

'Ah, I asked Ugo that,' I said, very pleased with myself. 'They're built thirty-six feet long, but the right side is ten inches shorter than the left, and that makes up for the sweep of the oar on one side only.'

Mr. Morton slapped his hand on the table in delight. 'Lop-sided!' he exclaimed. 'Where else in the world but Venice would they have the imagination to make a lop-sided boat?'

The evening passed all too quickly, and at last I stood on the steps with Uncle Guido as his own gondola carried the Mortons away to their hotel. Two days passed before I saw them again, and then we met for the visit to the glass foundry. It lay only a mile away across the lagoon, and consisted of a sprawl of buildings in the centre of the little islet.

The heat of the furnaces was too much for Mrs. Morton, but the rest of us watched with fascination as the men drew their long blow-pipes from the furnace pot, each with a blob of molten glass glowing on its end, then blew, rolled and swung the blow-pipe, blew again, re-heated, shaped with a charred wooden paddle, and finally cut the excess glass away with shears. There was much more to it than this, for the decoration had to be applied and the stems shaped and fitted, but I lost track of all the intricate operations. What left me amazed was that a man could produce goblet after goblet all of identical size and shape.

'It is a matter of experience,' Uncle Guido said when I asked him about this. 'They begin as little boys, and their craft is a mystery handed down from father to son.'

Every day I was taken out, either to see some new part of Venice or to visit Uncle Guido's friends. In this way I came to see the inside of several palazzos and mansions, and each night when I fell asleep my head was buzzing with fresh impressions. Uncle Guido took great pride in presenting me to all his friends, and I was very kindly received. They knew the story of Granny Caterina's disappearance, and how I, her grand-daughter, had been discovered. He also insisted that Mr. Morton should take me to meet the banker Trustees of the fortune I was to inherit. Since I knew nothing of business matters, I asked Mr. Morton to speak for me, and simply acted as interpreter. He asked many questions, and later assured me that he was well-satisfied with the whole situation.

Friends of Uncle Guido twice gave a party in my honour, and on these occasions Mr. Morton and his family were invited. Though they were all enjoying their visit thoroughly, they told me that they missed having me with them, for we only met for somewhat special events. I was deeply glad to know that they felt incomplete without me, for I found more and more that I missed seeing them daily. It was the little things which affected me most. I missed Sarah tiptoeing to my bedroom to gossip when we went to bed; Mr. Morton's little dry jokes, and our easy conversations; Richard's quick affectionate smile; and even Mrs. Morton's breathless fluttering.

I enjoyed Uncle Guido's company, but Bernardino and Aunt Isola seemed to have no spirit of their own. I found that the evenings in particular grew irksome, for though I saw much of Uncle Guido during the day he was usually abroad in the evenings and did not return until long after the rest of us had gone to bed, which left me with only the Countess and Bernardino for company.

It was towards the beginning of the third week that I realized with a shock that Uncle Guido expected me to stay on at the *Palazzo Chiavelli* when Mr. Morton and his family went home. The subject had never been discussed, but various remarks of Uncle Guido's made it clear to me that he thought I now looked upon Venice as my home, and that having returned to my true family I would stay.

Though I had lost none of my first delight in Venice, I did not want to stay. Soon, I knew, I would begin to long for the green lawns of *Meadhaven*, the tall trees and the beaten paths through the woods, the pink clouds of flowering cherry in the spring, the riot of summer roses, the golden fall of leaves in autumn, and the delicate winter tracery of snow-clad branches. Venice had cast her spell on me, but I did not want to live always under that spell, and England had her own strong magic, a magic I had taken for granted until now.

Above all I realized that, for me at least, the ties of blood could not compare in strength with the ties of heart and mind. For half a century or more the two lines of the Chiavellis had been separated, and though Uncle Guido was kindness itself I felt no real kinship with the family. My love and my sense of family-belonging lay with the Mortons now. I did not feel there was any betrayal in this, for I knew that my father himself would have had far more in common with the Mortons than with the Chiavellis.

The situation was awkward for me, for I did not wish to hurt Uncle Guido, and so from time to time I began to make little observations to indicate that I had always expected to return to England with the Mortons. Uncle Guido was quick to notice, and two days later, when I was choosing a book from his library with which to pass the evening, he came in and closed the door behind him, saying, 'There is something I wish to speak to you about before I go out, Caterina.' He was dressed in a fine suit, and wore a light cape against the coolness that came upon Venice at night. I said, 'Yes, Uncle Guido,' and waited, knowing what he wished to discuss and feeling nervous. He put his gold-topped cane on the table and smiled at me a little wistfully. 'I thought you were happy here, Caterina. We have done our best to make you feel so.'

'Oh, but I am,' I said quickly. 'You couldn't have given me a happier time.'

He looked puzzled. 'But it seems you wish to leave us. I have only recently realized that you are thinking of returning with Mr. Morton and his family. Surely Venice is your true home and we are your true family?'

I felt myself going red, for there was no way of saying what I had to say without seeming ungrateful to this man who had shown me such warmth and generosity.

'I've only ever thought of this as a visit,' I said, stumbling over the words. 'It's hard to explain, but I've lived all my life in England, and I think of that as my country.' I managed to force a smile. 'I suppose it's because I'm only one quarter Venetian and three-quarters English. Oh please don't be hurt, Uncle Guido. You've been wonderfully kind and nobody could have done more for me, but when my father died I was alone, and then I was able to make a new home and find a new family with the Mortons, and . . . and it's not very easy, however kind people are, so I don't want to have to do it once again. Please understand.'

He did not look angry, only regretful, and nodded his head slowly. 'I understand. Do not distress yourself, Caterina. But . . .' He was silent for a long while, as if not quite knowing what to say, then he hitched himself on the corner of the library table and began to toy with his cane, frowning at the gold knob.

'I have to tell you something,' he said at last. 'My son, Bernardino, is in love with you. Did you know that, Caterina?'

'Bernardino?' I exclaimed, startled.

'Yes.' Uncle Guido sighed and lifted his eyes to look at me with a rueful smile. 'Deeply in love. But he is a very gentle, very timid boy, and finds it difficult to speak to you of this. In fact, he has not even spoken to *me*. I first learned of it from my wife.'

'I'm . . . I'm very honoured,' I faltered. 'And I think very highly of him, naturally.' It was a lie, but the truth would have been insulting. 'Bernardino has my—my affection, of course, but I'm afraid I don't . . .' My voice trailed away.

'You do not reciprocate his feelings?' Uncle Guido said, and gave a wry shrug. 'I know. But shyness makes him tongue-tied in your presence, and for that reason you do not really know him yet, Caterina. There has been no time for you to learn his real qualities, and I assure you he has many.' He sat brooding for a few seconds, then went on softly, as if to himself, 'When I heard how he felt towards you I was delighted. It seemed to me a wonderful happening that the two lines of our family should be united again, and I felt sure that in time Bernardino would overcome his shyness and awaken a response in you. I would do anything to help make that possible.'

He paused and looked at me.

'I'm sorry,' I said helplessly. 'Really, Uncle Guido, I'm very sorry.'

'Could you not give him a little time, Caterina?' he said almost pleadingly. 'That is all I ask. Stay with us here for a while, just until the end of the year, perhaps. I do not ask you to fall in love with my son, I only ask you to give him time, to give yourself time to know him better.'

I was twisting a handkerchief in my fingers, and had torn the lace edging in my agitation. For a moment I was tempted to agree, if only to be freed from the dreadful embarrassment I felt, but somehow I restrained the impulse.

The thought of spending the rest of the year being wooed by Bernardino was more than I could bear.

'I can't!' I said desperately, and felt tears begin to trickle down my cheeks. 'I'm sorry, but I can't!'

He stood up and came to me quickly, with no hint of anger. 'There now, do not cry, my little Caterina.' He took my hands and held them gently. 'And do not be sorry. It is for me to apologize for upsetting you so.' He gave that rueful smile again. 'But a father is bound to do all he can to help his son. Now dry your eyes and we will say no more. I simply ask that you will think of what I have said, and tell me if you change your mind.'

I knew I would not change my mind, particularly when I sat throughout the evening with Bernardino and his mother, struggling to keep some kind of conversation going so that we should not sit in silence. But although I felt tired and empty when I went to bed, I also felt immense relief, for at least it was settled that I should return to England with the Mortons, and the ordeal of telling Uncle Guido was past.

Two days later Mr. Morton and his family came to tea—*my* family. I was so overjoyed to have them about me again that I kept feeling my eyes grow moist, and when I greeted Sarah I hugged her until she squeaked in surprise. Except for Richard they all looked very fit and well, and it was clear that the holiday had refreshed them, but Richard seemed tense and on edge, as if his nerves were raw. There was an almost feverish look in his eyes.

For a few minutes Sarah and I were alone together, walking through the little rock-garden that lay beyond the terrace. 'Cadi,' she whispered, and glanced furtively over her shoulder, 'I don't know whether to tell you.'

It was wonderful to be called Cadi again. I laughed and linked arms with her. 'Who have you fallen in love with now?' I asked.

'Oh, it's not that!' She looked quite hurt. 'I wouldn't think of falling in love with anybody else.'

'Is it the same man, then? And is it still a secret?'

'Yes.' She nodded impatiently. 'Stop teasing and listen, Cadi. Richard has been going out at night again.'

I turned to look at her. 'Here? In Venice?'

'Of course, silly! He creeps out after we've all gone to bed. I don't know where he goes, but I couldn't sleep the other night, and I was standing at my window, looking out on the canal, when I saw him come back in a gondola. The side door of the hotel is always left unlocked, so he must come in that way.'

I felt very troubled. 'You're sure it was Richard?'

'Yes. I saw his face in the moonlight. What shall I do, Cadi? I daren't tell Papa!'

I thought quickly. 'I must get Richard alone for a few minutes and speak to him.'

'But it's so *difficult* here, Cadi. There's always somebody nearby. I thought I was never even going to be able to tell you.' She gave a little wail. 'Oh, look. Here come Mamma and the Count now.'

'Tell Richard that you know and you've told me,' I said quickly. 'Tell him that if he . . . if he cares what I think of him he'll stop these escapades at once. Tell him I'm very, very angry.'

She looked at me curiously for a moment, rather wide-eyed, and said, 'All right. I'll do that, Cadi.' Then, in a louder voice, 'Aren't these little flowers pretty? Oh, do come and look, Mamma. Perhaps the Count can tell us what they are.'

That evening I did not trouble to make conversation with Bernardino and his mother. I sat pretending to read a book, while Aunt Isola busied herself with embroidery and Bernardino spent two hours writing a letter and wasting most of his time gazing sheepishly at me as if he would say much if only he could think what to say. He seemed to have run out of compliments at last.

I found it hard to believe that Richard was behaving here as he had done in Wealdhurst. He had said that he loved me, and said it with all sincerity as far as I could tell, which made it strange that he should go out secretly of nights, no doubt to some Venetian equivalent of Meg Dawson, the Wealdhurst dressmaker. But perhaps I was being un-worldly. After all, I had not returned the kind of love

Richard felt for me. Perhaps he was seeking the company of other women because I had not responded to him. With a flash of anger it came to me that I could not respond to any man while Lucian Farrel still gripped the fibres of my being——

And there my thoughts took an abrupt turn, for I realized that something very strange had happened. For weeks past I had set a barrier in my mind against thinking of Lucian. He was always a shadowy figure, hovering on the fringes of my awareness, but I would never let him enter my thoughts, and would never allow myself to dwell on any memories of him, for I had resentfully known that even to remember the touch of his hand could still send the blood to my foolish head. But now something had changed.

Cautiously I let myself picture Lucian. The image was blurred and indistinct, not sharp and clear as it had always been before. I put my hands to my cheeks, and they felt cool.

More boldly then, I recalled the moments in the studio when he had kneaded life back into my numbed fingers. My heart remained steady. I called up a dozen memories, and it was as if they were not my own memories but another's. No painful longing stirred within me and no fire touched my blood.

I was free, and in my joy I could have taken the book that lay in my lap and tossed it into the air. I had won the battle, and my infatuation was dead now. I had suffered the puppy-love that was a common torment of the young, and now it was over. I felt older and wiser. I also felt a great pang of emptiness, but I knew that this would quickly pass. Confidently, almost disdainfully, I dismissed Lucian from my thoughts and returned to Richard.

It was surprising that he had managed to strike up acquaintance with a woman so soon, and in a strange land, not knowing the language, and in the company of his family at least throughout the day. However, we should be going home in only a few days now, and he would soon be back at Oxford. For the first time I was struck by the thought that there must be women to be found in Oxford, as well as

Wealdhurst and Venice, and that Richard might very well be indulging his fancies there, unknown to me.

I was not particularly shocked by the thought, for in one way and another I had gathered the impression that many young men of Richard's class would have affairs before settling down. Miss Rigg had once lectured me somewhat bitterly on this subject, and I guessed later that she had been speaking from an unhappy experience in her own youth. I did not think it was very fair, but if that was the way the world wagged then there was no point in being shocked at the thought of young men sowing their wild oats before they married. Better then than afterwards, it seemed to me. However, I knew that Mr. and Mrs. Morton would take a very different view, and my main concern was that they should not learn of Richard's escapades. I felt they were much less likely to do so when he was away in Oxford than when he was here with them in Venice or under their roof at *Meadhaven*. It was with this thought that I eased my anxiety.

Now that I knew I would soon be going home, I made the most of my remaining time in Venice, and spent many hours exploring the city with Bernardino as an almost silent companion and Ugo as my guide. I had hoped that during my visit I might be taken on the train to the stables in Padua, and had even packed my riding breeches in my luggage when we left England, but Uncle Guido made no suggestion about such a trip and I did not like to ask.

It was two days before our departure, and we had just finished dinner, when Uncle Guido said, 'Isola, my dear, I should like you and Bernardino to withdraw for a short while. There is a matter I wish to discuss with Caterina.'

'Of course, Guido,' Aunt Isola said, looking quite nervous as she rose quickly from her chair. 'Come, Bernardino. Take me to the small salon, my dear.'

When they had left, Uncle Guido sat frowning down at his half empty wine-glass for a moment or two. Then he took a slip of paper from his pocket and passed it to me. 'Will you look at that please, Caterina?'

A few words were scribbled on it in Richard's handwriting, and I felt myself go white as I read them. 'It . . . it says he owes seven thousand *pounds*!' I whispered. 'But he can't! It's not possible!'

Uncle Guido took the paper back and looked at it, pursing his lips. 'I'm afraid it's true,' he said, and shook his head regretfully. 'It is a note of hand from Richard Morton, what you would call an I.O.U. in English, I believe.'

'But I can't believe it! How could he owe anybody so much money?'

Uncle Guido looked surprised. 'It is a gambling debt, my dear. And there is no doubt about it, I assure you. I saw him write this note out at the card-table myself.'

My head whirled. '*You* saw? But how?'

'Because I was present. Richard and I have been to several card parties. I gamble a little myself.' Uncle Guido smiled and filled his glass. 'But only for amusement. I fear Richard has been very headstrong. He would take no warning.'

'Then . . . *you* took him gambling? At night? And without his parents knowing?' I was trembling with shock as I spoke. 'Oh, how could you do such a thing?'

He looked puzzled. 'What are you saying, Caterina? Perhaps things are different in England. Here, we expect our young men to indulge in the excitements which attract all young men. But by custom it is not for the father to encourage the son. It happens that my son is of a quiet nature, and for this I am glad, but if it were otherwise then it would not be for me to act as his guide in the matter of worldly amusements. It would be for one of my friends, a man of my own age, to be his companion and preceptor.' He shrugged. 'In showing Richard the more hidden entertainments of Venice, discreetly and without reference to his parents, I have only followed our customs.'

'But it's *not* like that in England!' I cried. 'And even so, surely you should have protected him from himself?'

Uncle Guido sighed. 'In that I have some responsibility,' he said. 'But it is not easy to protect Richard from himself. He is very susceptible to wine, and when he has drunk a few glasses he will hear no advice. Until last night he had won a little money at our *chemin-de-fer* parties, but last night he lost, and plunged, and lost again. You have no knowledge of gambling, perhaps, but I assure you that when a rash and confident young man, slightly befuddled, keeps doubling the stakes to regain what he has lost, he can very soon achieve a debt of seven thousand pounds.'

I sat stunned with horror, staring down at the white lace of my table napkin. 'You should have stopped him,' I whispered. 'You should have stopped him!'

For a moment Uncle Guido's voice held a note of anger as he said brusquely, 'You speak without knowledge, Caterina. When gentlemen play cards, there is a limit to the advice that one gentleman may give to another without it becoming a serious insult. I assure you, I went so far in trying to restrain Richard that in the old days, and between Venetian gentlemen, the matter could well have ended in a duel.'

I could only stare at him, for what he had just said put the whole matter beyond my understanding. His voice lost its edge and became sympathetic as he went on, 'It is hard for you to comprehend, Caterina, I know that. But believe me, dear child, I risked my reputation in front of my friends, and still I could not stop Richard. The fever was upon him.'

In the long silence that followed I could hear only the ticking of the great ormolu clock and the thudding of my own heart. Whatever Uncle Guido said, I still thought the blame was his, but there was nothing to be gained by argument, for his way of thinking in this matter was completely foreign to mine.

Seven thousand pounds! It was a huge sum. All *Meadhaven* could not have cost so much. I knew Mr. Morton was well-to-do, but I had long since ceased to think of him as rich, and for him even to hear of this affair would be appalling. Something flickered in my mind. In less than a year I would be rich, so rich that I had wondered whatever I could find to do with the money. Seven thousand pounds would mean nothing.

I looked at Uncle Guido with sudden hope. 'Was the money lost to one of your friends?'

'To an acquaintance, rather. A gentleman, but one who lives by gambling.'

'Would he wait to be paid? I mean, would he wait for a year if he was paid extra money?'

Uncle Guido shook his head. 'The note of hand promised repayment within one month. Very generous for a man like Lazoni. But he will certainly not consider letting the money earn a year's interest. That is not the way of a gambler.'

My hopes slumped, then rose dizzily again as Uncle Guido said slowly, 'But Lazoni is no longer the creditor. I paid the debt myself, this morning.'

I gasped. 'You *paid* it? Then—then it's all right!' I ran round the table to him, full of gratitude and relief. 'Oh, thank heavens. I thought . . . I was so afraid . . . I mean, about Mr. Morton finding out and having to pay Richard's debt.' I blinked back tears. 'I'll repay you myself, Uncle Guido, I promise I will, as soon as I'm twenty-one, and with the interest or whatever it is.'

He sat twisting the note in his fingers for a moment or two, then slowly tore it to pieces. 'It is done with. I do not want you to pay the debt, Caterina.'

'But I must! I must give you back the money. How else can I repay you for saving Richard?'

He pushed the scraps of paper away and turned to look at me, a rather sad and whimsical smile on his lips. 'I will be truthful with you, Caterina,' he said. 'The Mortons are pleasant people, but I have no ties with them and I would never pay the boy's debt simply from kindness of heart. A gentleman should know how to drink and gamble within his capacity, or suffer the consequences. I paid his debt because I thought it might help me in striving for my son's happiness.' He raised a hand reassuringly. 'Have no fear that I would compel you in any way, Caterina. To convince you of that I have destroyed the note. I can only ask, and hope, that if you truly wish to repay me then you will stay here with us until the end of the year.'

Elation drained from me, and I struggled to hide my feelings. My thoughts ran round and round like little caged creatures as I sought some way of escape, some excuse for refusing, but beneath my confusion I knew with sinking heart that there was only one answer I could give.

Uncle Guido had risked that huge sum of money on the hope that I would stay, and the even more slender hope that by staying I would come to love his son, Bernardino. As he had said, I was under no compulsion. Whatever I chose to do, Richard had been saved from disgrace and Mr. Morton from a shocking revelation as well as from a crippling financial blow. Uncle Guido had wrung no promise from me before paying the debt, and for this I respected him.

I managed to smile, and said, 'I'll stay, Uncle Guido. And thank you, with all my heart.'

His answering smile almost made me feel guilty, for I knew that his dreams were hopeless. I would never even like Bernardino, much less fall in love with him. He stood up and put a hand on my shoulder. 'Thank you, dear Caterina. I am sure that one day you will be glad.' He made a wry grimace. 'I am afraid we cannot tell Mr. Morton the reason that you are staying on with us. That would never do.'

'No,' I said hastily, and then it came home to me that another ordeal lay ahead. Slowly the full realization dawned, and the sadness that pierced me was like a physical pain. 'No . . . I can't tell him the truth,' I went on heavily, 'and there's no excuse I can make. I can only say . . . that I *want* to stay. That I don't want to go home.'

I was glad to retire early that evening. Even the distress I felt at having to stay on in Venice for so many months was nothing compared with the distress that came from knowing how much I should hurt Mr. Morton. On the day before their return to England, the Mortons were coming to dine at the palazzo, a farewell dinner. They would expect me to join them at the station the next day, to catch the train. I had found throughout my life that any expected ordeal was usually far worse in the anticipation of it than in the reality, and I tried to comfort myself with this thought during the next two days, as I waited in dread for the moment to arrive. But this was one ordeal which proved even worse than I had imagined it would be.

At table, Mr. Morton and Uncle Guido were in a very happy mood and created an atmosphere of gaiety. Mrs. Morton had become far less fluttery, far less concerned with

herself than I had ever known her, and she joined in the
conversation without seeming to be wrapped in thoughts of
her own as she usually was. Aunt Isola and Bernardino were
as dull as ever, but we were all used to that by now. Sarah
was ecstatic about the holiday, but seemed excited to be
returning home. Richard was withdrawn, not saying very
much, but watching Uncle Guido with a curious, wondering
look. I could understand that, for I knew Uncle Guido had
taken him aside on some pretext before dinner and told him
that the debt had been cleared, that he had paid it himself.
No doubt Richard was dazed by his good fortune and
wondering at Uncle Guido's generosity.

I had planned what I would do, and throughout dinner I
made a great effort to appear natural and happy. It was
when we were all together in the drawing room later that I
summoned up my courage to speak, but Uncle Guido fore-
stalled me.

'I hope you will have a very comfortable journey home,'
he said, smiling round upon the Mortons. 'Please do not
worry about Caterina. She will be cared for in every possible
way, and she will write to you frequently, of course.'

A startled silence fell on the room. Then Mr. Morton said,
'I don't quite understand. We've always assumed that Cadi
would return with us after her visit here.'

Uncle Guido looked startled and a little embarrassed.
'Oh!' he exclaimed. 'Please forgive me if there has been
some misunderstanding. I hoped—but no matter what I
hoped. It is for Caterina to decide what she wishes to do, as
I am sure you will agree.' He looked at me inquiringly.

I saw Mr. Morton relax, and his eyes twinkled as he turned
his head to gaze across the room at me. 'Well, Cadi?' he
asked.

My hands rested in my lap, and it was only with a struggle
that I could keep them still. I had to look at Mr. Morton as
I spoke, and I think this was the most difficult thing I had
ever had to make myself do.

'I'd like to stay for a while, Mr. Morton,' I said, and was
amazed that even to me my voice sounded quite calm. 'Perhaps until the end of the year.'

Chapter Thirteen

ALL EYES WERE ON ME NOW, and there was that intensity of silence which follows a thunderclap.

'You . . . wish to stay?' Mr. Morton said at last. I knew that he was trying to speak naturally, but the shock was too much for him. He blinked and rubbed his brow, as I had seen him do before when he was agitated. I felt a liar and a traitress as I answered, 'Please don't be offended, Mr. Morton, but I've only just discovered my real family, and I want to be with them for a while. I'm sure you can understand.'

I had expected squeals of protest from Sarah, but none came. She simply sat watching me from the couch with a shrewd, thoughtful look as if trying to solve a puzzle, a look I had noticed in her occasionally of late and which had surprised me.

After one startled glance, Richard gripped his knees with his hands and stared down at the floor. His face was very pale. Mrs. Morton waved her hands in vague distress and murmured, 'She will be in good hands with the Count, of course, but . . .' Her voice faded to silence.

'Yes,' Mr. Morton said at last in an uncertain voice. 'Of course we understand.' He pinched the bridge of his nose, rubbing his eyes with finger and thumb. 'The decision is entirely yours, Cadi, my dear. I have been foolish to think . . .' He broke off and drew in a long breath, pulling himself together and forcing a smile as he looked at me. 'But we must not be selfish . . . that would never do.' Beyond the smile I saw such sadness that I could have wished for the palazzo walls to fall in upon me. I wanted to run to him and hug him, as I had many times done before, but I knew that if I weakened for a moment my resolution would fail. All that gave me strength now was the thought that at the end of the year I would go home, home to *Meadhaven* and the family I loved. I would never be able to explain why I had deserted them for a time, for I would have to keep Richard's secret, but if they took me back I would somehow make up for the hurt I had inflicted.

'So it is settled,' Uncle Guido said pleasantly, and Mr. Morton nodded. The next half-hour was horrible. Everybody tried to continue chatting as before, as if nothing had happened, but the atmosphere was strained to breaking point. It was a relief to me when at last Mr. Morton rose, looked at his watch, and said quietly, 'I think we must take our leave. We have to rise early tomorrow.'

As we stood at the top of the steps, with the gondola waiting below to take the guests back to their hotel, Uncle Guido said, 'I shall bring Caterina to see you off at the station tomorrow, of course.'

'If you will forgive me,' Mr. Morton said politely, 'I should prefer to say our goodbyes now.' Again he forced a smile. 'I have a great dislike of partings, particularly at railway stations.'

He kissed me, then held me tightly for a moment, and though he said nothing I knew he was telling me that his affection was as strong as ever, that I would always be welcome to return. I was so shaken by distress and weary from effort that I scarcely remember saying goodbye to the others. When the gondola was swallowed up in darkness, Uncle Guido said, 'Well . . . that was not as bad as you feared, eh, little Caterina?'

I could not respond. I could only mutter an apology before turning and running into the palazzo, down the long hall where the line of portraits gazed upon me with their painted eyes, and up the great staircase to my room, where I threw myself on the bed and wept as I had not wept since the day Mr. Morton had come to me after my father's death.

Pride made me present myself at breakfast next morning. I was paying the price, of my own free will, for what Uncle Guido had done to save Richard, and it would have shamed me to pay grudgingly. In any event, it was not for Cadi Tregaron that my heart ached, but for the way I had hurt Mr. Morton. Six or seven months in Venice was no hardship, I told myself. At the end of the year my debt would be paid and I could go home to *Meadhaven*. During the night I had made up my mind that in the long months ahead I would show no signs of moping but would try to be cheerful, and even try to bring Bernardino out a little, to please Uncle Guido. In this way the time would pass more quickly for me.

My resolution was firm, but I found it very hard to keep, for even in the next few days it seemed to me that a different atmosphere pervaded the palazzo. Slowly I began to feel that the quietness of Aunt Isola and Bernardino, their lack of conversation and their anxiety to please Uncle Guido, arose not from timidity but from fear. There was nothing I could put my finger on, but from the glances they darted at Uncle Guido before speaking, or after they had spoken, I felt that they were almost terrified of saying something out of place.

It was ridiculous, of course, for they were the last people to say anything amiss, and in any event I had never seen Uncle Guido show anger or even annoyance with them. The impression must lie in my own imagination, I decided, yet I could not throw it off. Even worse, I began to imagine that I was being watched all the time now. It seemed that except when I went to bed I was never left alone, and if I walked out into the gardens I would find Bernardino strolling behind me, or Aunt Isola, or one of the servants.

Naturally I could not leave the grounds of the palazzo unescorted, and one day when Bernardino was kept abed by a slight chill and could not accompany me on my explorations in Venice, I asked if Ugo could serve as my guide. Regretfully Uncle Guido said that this would be a breach of convention, and not at all the proper thing to do. I found this surprising, but could not very well argue with him about it. Two days later Ugo was dismissed from the palazzo, for impertinence I was told, and so I lost the one person, apart from Uncle Guido himself, with whom I felt reasonably at home and who seemed to have taken a liking to me.

I knew that this was just a coincidence, but it added to my feeling of being fettered, of being a prisoner. Even outside the palazzo, Venice herself seemed to be changing for me, and showing a hidden face I had not seen before. When I walked the narrow streets with Bernardino, or drifted along the beautiful network of small canals, I began to see that Venice's nature held much that was menacing and grotesque.

Among the thousands of carved animals that adorned the city's piazzas and buildings there were many that seemed the work of men with twisted minds. In the arcade of the Doges' Palace a carved column showed nothing but beasts devouring their prey; a gryphon devouring a rat, a wolf with a mutilated bird, a whole tangle of entwined beasts gorging in horrid gluttony. On the wall of Santa Maria Formosa was a hideous head, neither man nor beast, with bolting eyes and lolling tongue. In a dark archway not far from the Rialto Bridge was a creature called the crab-lion, a bestial monstrosity in plumage. This was not all. The torture scenes shown in some of the great religious paintings were as horrifying as the macabre sculptures. I shuddered at the head of Goliath in the church of San Rocco, and at the writhing souls of Titian's *Last Judgement*.

This was a city with a bright and glorious past, but intertwined with that past were all kinds of cruelty and evil. In a book I borrowed from Uncle Guido's library I read of events that chilled my blood, and these were not all ancient stories but told of times not long past, when in England the young Victoria sat on the throne. I read of the fearsome and secret Council of Ten and Council of Three, who ruled by terror. I read of spies, assassins and torturers. I saw for myself the ancient dungeons of the Doges' Palace, and it seemed to me that the dank stones still echoed the groans of the victims they had held. Though I stopped reading the histories, and tried to ignore the grim sculptures and paintings, all this worked upon my mind. Those days were past, I kept telling myself. This was the twentieth century. It was absurd to feel that I was being watched, that I was in any way a prisoner.

And then, on a night when the dream that had been with me half my life was finally broken, I came to know that I was not a victim of my own imagination but of a dreadful truth.

It was two weeks after Mr. Morton and his family had left. Uncle Guido was away in Padua for two days and was to return late that evening. I had gone to bed early, and when the dream came it was in a curiously muddled way. I approached the steps of the palazzo in a gondola. I passed along the dark hall and up the staircase. Then there seemed to be a time of confusion and half-waking before I found myself walking along the broad corridor.

There was the door ahead of me, with the crack of light showing beneath, but on this occasion there was also a wider strip of light down the edge of the door, for it stood an inch ajar. I had never compared my dream with what I now knew as the reality of the palazzo's interior, but I was dimly aware that this was one of the spare bedrooms. I touched the door, and it opened a few inches, silently. Confusion swept me, for now all familiarity ended. I saw no man confronting me, I felt neither joy nor fear, only a strange and remote bewilderment. I could see, as I looked obliquely through the doorway, a dressing table with an ornate mirror. Something moved, and a reflection appeared in the mirror . . . a man, wearing slim dark trousers, pulling on a white shirt over his head. I could see part of a bed, with discarded clothes scattered on it. Hair-brushes and razors were set out on the dressing table.

In that moment I knew I was awake. My dream had merged with reality. I had walked in my sleep from my bedroom, to stand before this door wearing only my night-dress. Shock ran through me as if I had been touched by lightning. For a moment I could not move, I could only stare through the slightly open door at the mirror which showed part of the lighted bedroom and the man who occupied it.

Then his head emerged from the neck of the shirt as he pulled it on, and I saw that it was Lucian. If I could have drawn breath to cry out I would not have been able to prevent myself, but every muscle seemed frozen. That the man in the room was Lucian gave sufficient cause to be startled, for I had thought him to be in England, but I was more than startled. I was shocked and terrified by the expression on his face. The eyes were narrowed, the lips set. The long black eyebows flared like those of a demon. There

248

was none of the mockery in his expression that I knew so well, none of the cool humour. I had never in my life seen a face so cold, so hard, so merciless. He was fixing links in the cuffs of his shirt, and had not noticed yet that the door had swung open a little. I did not dare to pull it to, in case the movement caught his eye.

With an effort I forced my legs to obey me, and backed slowly away, five paces . . . six. Then I turned and fled on bare soundless feet, down the long corridor and across the upper gallery to my own room.

I cannot tell how long I lay on the bed with my mind in chaos. I know that after a while I found my teeth were chattering, and I crawled under the covers for warmth. Slowly the shivering passed. I was able to think again, and as always I began to seek sensible reasons for what seemed incredible.

Lucian was here. Then it must be because he had come to do business with Uncle Guido. Perhaps he had been in Padua with him, at the stables, for the last day or two. They had come here to complete their business. But why hadn't Uncle Guido mentioned Lucian's coming? Perhaps he had not known at the time he left for Padua. That was quite possible. Or perhaps Uncle Guido felt it would make a happy surprise for me to find Lucian here in the morning. But though my head found reassuring reasons, my heart would not accept them. With the instinct that goes beyond reason, I *knew* that Lucian had come secretly to the palazzo, arriving after I had gone to bed, I *knew* that something dark and sinister was growing up around me, and that Lucian was a part of it. I remembered the look on his face as I glimpsed it in the mirror, and shivered again.

I lit the candle by my bedside and looked at the little watch that lay on the table. It was well past midnight, and perhaps twenty minutes since I had walked in my sleep along the corridor. Lucian had been changing his clothes then, so it seemed likely that he had been getting ready to go downstairs to join Uncle Guido. There was nothing strange in this, for I knew that Uncle Guido rarely went to bed until the early hours.

I got out of bed, pulled on my dressing gown, and cautiously opened the door of my room. I had to steal along the corridor as far as the gallery before I could see Lucian's door. No light shone from beneath it. He must have gone downstairs. I went back to my room and lay there for a long time, the same thoughts and questions churning round and round in my head.

Quite suddenly I knew what I was going to do. All that it needed was enough courage. I was going to creep downstairs and listen to what Lucian and Uncle Guido were saying.

No twinge of shame touched me. Here in this ancient palazzo, with its centuries of strange secrets, I felt completely alone. There was nobody to help me, nobody I could trust. I did not know what might lie ahead, but all my senses were sounding a warning now, and I was afraid.

I would have given anything to stay in bed and pull the covers over my head, but I got up and stood for a while kindling anger at myself for such cowardice. Gradually the anger began to glow within me, and it was not only towards myself but towards Lucian and Uncle Guido and all the mysteries that seemed to entrap me. With pounding heart I snuffed out the candle, went silently out of my room and along the passage, and crept down the stairs.

They were in the library. The big doors were closed, but I could hear the faint sound of their voices. Quietly I opened the door of the small adjoining room, which had once been used by a librarian. The voices were suddenly louder, for there was a small hatch set in the wall with only two thin wooden doors between the rooms. I crouched in the darkness with my back to the wall, so that my head was close to the hatch. There came the sound of clinking glass as wine was poured.

'A good wine,' said Uncle Guido's voice. 'A damn good wine, Farrel. And we're doing it justice, by God. I like a man who can drink deep and still keep a clear head.' I could detect a very faint slurring in the words, and knew that there must indeed have been heavy drinking over the last hour to produce such an effect on Uncle Guido.

Lucian laughed lazily. 'Did you think me a namby-pamby young fool like Richard?'

'I may have done.' There was a note of regret in Uncle Guido's voice. 'Yes. I may well have done, for I have let you out-bargain me over the horses.' He laughed and uttered a curse in Italian.

'Ah, come now. It's a good bargain for you, Chiavelli. You need my stock for those stables of yours, and I'm giving you a year to pay. God knows why I'm being so generous.'

'Generous?' Uncle Guido chuckled again. 'At that price and that rate of interest? You are a rogue, Farrel. But then I like a thorough-going rogue.'

'We're two of a kind, my friend. Two of a kind.' Lucian's voice sounded heavy from the wine also. 'Look at the risk I'm taking. You're mortgaged to the hilt, and I might never get paid.'

'You will be paid,' Uncle Guido said good-humouredly 'Never fear.'

'I'd have less fear if my dear little adopted cousin wasn't going to collect the Chiavelli fortune you've been counting on.'

There was a silence. I stood up and put my eye to the crack where the doors of the panel met. It was only a small crack, but the two men were on the far side of the library and I could see something of them both. Uncle Guido lolled in an armchair, his back half turned towards me, a glass in his hand. All I could see of Lucian was his legs, sprawled out towards the great fireplace.

Lucian broke the silence. 'If it was my fortune,' he said with a tinge of contempt, 'I'd not let some girl from nowhere take it from me.'

Uncle Guido shrugged, but sat up a little in his chair. 'The law is on her side, so how would you prevent her?'

'Damn the law.' Lucian laughed brusquely. 'I'd deal with her the same way somebody dealt with her grandmother fifty years ago—but I'd make a better job of it.'

A chill of horror, sharp as a knife, reached into the marrow of my bones, and my heart seemed to contract within me. I had once suspected Lucian of trying to injure me, not deliberately perhaps, but because his mind was unsound. This cold-blooded suggestion, casually made, was something quite different. He was saying that if he had been in Uncle Guido's place he would seek my death.

Uncle Guido did not seem to be shocked. He sat forward with his elbows on his knees, the glass cradled in his hands, looking down into it, and said slowly, 'I will tell you something, Farrel. A secret that my grandmother, Marguerita, told me on her deathbed.' He gave an admiring chuckle. 'Ah, she was a real Venetian, that one. Dark and dangerous. Not like her brother, the old Count. He was a fool.'

'What secret?' Lucian did not sound much interested. I saw his face for a moment or two as he leaned forward and helped himself to more wine. He looked utterly different from the man I had once known, for now his face held cunning, slumbrous cruelty, and a gleam of avarice.

'It was Marguerita who got rid of her, Uncle Guido said dreamily, the slurring of his words very marked now. 'Took her to Naples and hired footpads to kill her and drop her in the bay. Caterina would have had the title and the fortune when her father died . . . but Marguerita wanted them for herself and for her own child . . . and by God, she got what she wanted.'

Lucian sat back, and his face was hidden from me again, but I heard him laugh. 'Not the fortune, Chiavelli. Only the income from it. And there's the rub, my friend. But it was a good try, and I'm not greatly surprised. It's all there in her face, in that portrait, if you know how to look, and I can always spot my own kind.'

Uncle Guido wiped his face with a handkerchief. 'I have told you between these four walls,' he said with a touch of unease.

Lucian crossed his legs. 'You needn't fear I'll give away your secret,' he said scornfully. 'It's too long ago to matter, too long ago for *me* to make any profit out of knowing it. Besides, I admire her, Chiavelli. She had a bit of fire in her belly, that old woman. She knew damn well that if you don't help yourself in this world, nobody else is going to help you.'

They fell silent, drinking occasionally, each man busy with his own thoughts. I remembered the fear that had come upon me when I first looked up and saw the face of Marguerita staring down from the wall, and I knew now that this must have been a remembered fear of Granny Caterina's. She had sensed, or perhaps even known, that Marguerita wished her ill.

When Uncle Guido spoke again it was as if something in Lucian's contemptuous manner had goaded him. 'You think I lack Marguerita's courage?' he said in a low voice. 'You think I will let that child snatch a fortune from me when I am in debt up to my ears? You are wrong, Farrel. From the day I learned she was alive, I knew something had to be done——' He broke off, looked furtively about the room, then shook his head and muttered, 'I am talking too much.'

'Too much or too little,' Lucian grunted. 'And I don't give a tinker's curse either way. But if you're afraid to talk, I'm not—so between these walls I'll say this. She means nothing to me, that girl. When I heard she was going to be rich, I tried to marry her, but my dear Uncle Edward put a stop to that before I could even begin. So I've nothing to gain from her . . .' He paused before adding significantly, 'Except through you, perhaps.'

'What do you mean?'

'I'll tell you when I know your own plans.'

'How do you know I have any plans?'

'If you haven't, you're a fool,' Lucian said with scornful impatience. 'Let's forget about it and talk of horses.'

'No, wait.' Uncle Guido sat in thought for a few moments. At last he said, 'I will tell you this. I hope to marry her to Bernardino. That will give him control of the fortune, and that in turn will mean that *I* have control of it.'

Lucian laughed, softly but at length, and I heard him splutter at last as if he had choked on the wine. 'Dear God, she'll never marry *him*,' he said. 'I don't know the boy, but you've told me yourself that he's an empty fool. Cadi won't marry that kind.'

'They are thrown together a great deal,' Uncle Guido said as if trying to convince himself, 'and I have schooled

Bernardino in what he must do. He has six months to make himself acceptable to her.'

'He could have six years and he'd not succeed,' Lucian said bluntly. 'She's a brat with a mind of her own.'

'But her feelings are easy to play upon,' Uncle Guido said, and as he turned his head I saw the smile of cunning on his lips. 'She wanted to go home, but agreed to stay. Do you know why?'

'No. It puzzled me.'

'I worked through Richard. Took the boy out gambling and wenching—and put him seven thousand pounds in debt.'

'Seven thousand!'

'Ah, I thought that might surprise you. Then I bought his note of hand, to save him from disgrace, and told Caterina. That is why she agreed to stay. It was from gratitude towards me.'

'Where the devil did you raise seven thousand to buy the note of hand? You told me you'd spent every penny and more in keeping up appearances.'

'I have. The note cost me only one hundred. Lazino, who won the money, is a professional card-sharper. I hired him for the task.'

Lucian laughed again, but this time there was a note of respect in it. 'Yes . . . I can see that would touch Cadi's loyal little heart. She's a fool in some ways. But all the same, she won't marry Bernardino, take my word for it. Staying on here for a time is one thing, but marriage is something different, no matter how you play on her feelings. In six months she'll come home, and soon after that she'll be twenty-one. Then you'll lose everything.'

'No,' Uncle Guido said very quietly. 'If you are right, Farrel, if I can see in a month or two that Bernardino has no chance, then . . .' He did not complete the sentence.

'Then what? The only thing left is to do what Marguerita did to the old Caterina—get rid of her.'

Uncle Guido rubbed his chin. 'You were going to suggest something after I had told you my plans, Farrel. Well?'

Lucian leaned forward and came into my view. He set

his wine-glass down on the low table, and the two men stared at each other. To me it seemed that all the worst and darkest traditions of Venice lay in that tableau, all the malignance of those writhing, distorted beast-carvings I had seen throughout the city.

'I'll do it for one fifth of the fortune,' Lucian said in a whispering voice. 'If she has an accident while she's in your care, there'll be suspicion.'

'I have provided against that.' Uncle Guido's voice was as soft as Lucian's, and I had to turn my ear to the panel to catch his next words. 'Why do you think I wrote those letters, full of affection and welcome? Why do you think I made no attempt to fight her claim legally? I *knew* I would lose, so I accepted without even a quibble. Morton and the lawyers and the Trustees know that, and it has made the impression I wished to make. They believe I am the most generous of men. And here in Venice, everyone who matters knows that I have lavished affection on the girl.'

As I put my eye to the crack again I saw him touch a finger to the side of his nose in a sickening gesture of cunning. 'I would have preferred to see her disposed of before ever she came to Venice. But if it has to be done here, I have made sure that nobody is likely to accuse me.'

'There'll still be suspicion.' Lucian's voice was positive. 'Not accusation, you've prepared the ground too well. But don't deceive yourself. If anything happens to her while she's in your charge, there's bound to be suspicion. You stand to gain too much.'

My mouth was dry and there was sickness in my throat as I crouched against the wall, dazed by the hideous knowledge that I was listening to these two men discussing my death.

'A little suspicion will not trouble me,' Uncle Guido said, but I could hear doubt in his voice. 'It will quickly pass, I think. And there will be no proof, you can rest assured of that. I have men I can trust.'

'All the same . . . it will be the second time in three generations. You don't want to have a shadow hanging over your family, Chiavelli—not when you're going to be rich enough to avoid it.'

Another long silence, then Uncle Guido said, 'There may be something in what you say. Well . . . the cards are on the table now. What is in your mind, Farrel?'

'Cadi doesn't know we've met.' Lucian's voice was soft and persuasive. 'You arranged for us to arrive late tonight, and I know why. You don't want her to have contact with her family, or with anybody outside the palazzo. That's very wise, and so be it. I'll be gone early, before she's awake, just as you wanted. But I'll come back openly—in a month's time, let's say. By then you'll know, if you're not a blind fool, that Bernardino has no hope in the world of marrying her.'

'And when you come back openly?'

'Why, Cadi will be delighted to see me. I'm one of the family, and we've always got on tolerably well. I can take her out and about, sailing perhaps, or we might go to your stables in Padua for some riding. It's little more than an hour on the train. But whatever happens, she'll be under *my* care, and my care alone, when the accident happens.'

'The . . . accident?'

'Yes. We don't want another mysterious disappearance. An accident, Chiavelli. A fatal fall from a horse or under a train, a boat overturned while sailing. I'll have ample time to arrange something convincing. But above all, it will happen while she's in *my* care, not yours. Then you'll have a quarter of a million pounds, Chiavelli, and there'll be no breath of suspicion.'

Uncle Guido said in a thick voice, 'By God, you're a cold-blooded rogue, Farrel.' There was grudging admiration in his manner. 'You'd have done well in Venice in the old days.'

'I hope to do well in the present,' Lucian said, and through the crack in the hatch doors I saw him lean back in his chair. 'One fifth of the fortune. That leaves plenty for you.'

'I have not made up my mind yet,' Uncle Guido said. I noticed that his hand wavered as he set down his glass, and guessed that he knew the wine was affecting him. He wanted to have a clear head when it came to making a decision. 'But in any case,' he went on, 'your price is too high. One tenth is enough. Twenty-five thousand sovereigns.'

'Forty thousand. I'm the only man in the world who can do this for you without causing a breath of suspicion.'

'Thirty thousand, or you can go to the devil, Farrel. That is my last word.'

I could bear no more. Strange though it may seem, this dreadful bargaining sickened me more horribly than all that had gone before. My hands were pressed over my ears as I turned blindly away. It was hard to restrain myself from blundering across the room and out of the door regardless of noise, but somehow I kept a rein on my feelings. Very slowly and quietly I crept out into the passage and up the stairs.

Two minutes later I lay in bed in the darkness, hugging the covers about me to warm the chill from my bones, my mind reeling as fragments of thought danced wildly in my head.

I was in danger. I was in danger of my life. From Uncle Guido. From Lucian. I must escape. But I was always watched. I must seek help from one of the servants. But the servants were Uncle Guido's, and went in fear of him. With Ugo gone, there was not one I could even begin to trust. I must escape alone. But how? And where to? I had no friends in Venice. I could run away from Bernardino one day while we were out, but what then? If I ran to a policeman in the streets or squares, and told him my uncle was planning to kill me, he would think me mad or suffering from nervous collapse. A doctor would be called, I would be taken back to the palazzo, put to bed, given strong sedatives. . . .

I shuddered at the thought of being so deeply drugged that I would lose even the will to escape.

A month, Lucian had said. That gave me a little time. *I could write to Mr. Morton——!* The hope died as it was born. Uncle Guido always took my letters to post them. I could be sure he opened them carefully and read them first. But I would write, anyway, and hope for a chance to post the letter myself. How could I get the stamps without asking Uncle Guido? I writhed at the shocking absurdity that my life might hang upon so small a thing as a stamp.

I would write, and have the letter ready in case any opportunity arose, but that was not nearly enough. I must plan to escape. A boat. There was a dinghy moored with the gondolas, and it carried a sail for use out in the lagoon. I could sail that to the mainland, only a mile or two. No, that was not far enough, for I would be hunted as soon as my escape was discovered. Down the coast then, twenty miles, thirty—as far as the wind would take me by night. And then? Go ashore and find a town—no, not a town, for who would take in a girl on her own, babbling a wild story? Townsfolk were wary and suspicious. Find a fishing village, then.

Yes, I was a fisherman's daughter and I could talk with my own kind. They would listen, and somebody would take me in. Like Mawstone folk, they would gossip among themselves but not outside the village. There I could stay hidden and write to Mr. Morton, telling him everything, and he would come for me.

I clung to my plan as if to a life-line, and indeed it was no less. In my mind, as I went over the plan again and again, all things happened as I wished, and there were no problems which did not dissolve at a touch of my imagination.

At some time towards dawn I must have dozed for a while, for I opened my eyes to bright sunshine as Maria, the maid, drew back my curtains. When she saw that I was awake, she smiled and said good morning. For a moment I was tempted to confide my terrible plight to her and ask her help, but caution prevailed. If she believed me she would be terrified, far too terrified to help me against her master. But it was much more likely that she would think I had suffered a nightmare. She would gossip, and the gossip would reach Uncle Guido. . . .

I said, 'I think I have a chill, Maria. Will you tell the Countess, please, and ask her if I may stay in bed today?'

I had spoken on impulse, and then realized that there was good reason behind it. Today, and in the days to come, I would have to act a part very carefully, otherwise Uncle Guido would suspect something. I needed time to prepare myself for that part, so that when I faced Uncle Guido and his family I would appear as friendly and at ease with them as they had come to expect. I was no actress, but my life depended on this, and I was determined to play out the grim game of cunning with all the skill I could muster.

It was two hours before Aunt Isola appeared. By then I had taken a light breakfast in bed and held a dozen conversations with her in my mind. Since whatever she said was always predictable, this was not a difficult task. She seemed more nervous than I, and avoided meeting my eyes. After talking for a minute or two she took her leave and seemed glad to do so. She must have known that Lucian had stayed the night, and I wondered bitterly how much she knew or suspected of Uncle Guido's plans. I realized now why both she and Bernardino feared him so greatly, for I had just been made cruelly aware that behind the amiable mask was a sly, devious and completely unscrupulous mind, the mind of a man very much to be feared.

After dinner that evening, and before he went out as usual, Uncle Guido called to see me in my room with Aunt Isola. I believe I did very well in my manner with him, for I smiled, and apologized for being a nuisance, and kept gazing straight at his face. I had decided that this was the best way to avoid giving the impression that I was hiding something, and in the end it was Uncle Guido who averted his eyes and walked about the room as he chatted, so that he had an excuse for not looking directly at me.

As I had expected, nothing was said of Lucian's brief visit. Later that evening, very casually, I tested Maria, saying I thought I had heard somebody about during the night, but she only gave me a blank, rather alarmed look, and shook her head. I knew that the servants who had attended to Lucian's room had been warned to silence.

The next morning I got up, saying that my chill had passed, and began to prepare for my escape. For several days I hoarded food in my room, bread and biscuits and sweetmeats. This was not difficult, for I simply pretended once or twice that I would like to take afternoon tea in my room, as I was sketching the view from my window there, and Aunt Isola made no objection. I studied the atlas in Uncle Guido's library, trying to plan where I would land on the Italian coast. This was not very satisfactory, for the map in the atlas was very small-scale, and I did not dare to ask for a larger map.

Above all, I spent much time testing how well the palazzo was guarded, and it was this that gradually brought me to the beginnings of despair. By day I was never left alone except in my bedroom, but I had been very conscious of this even before that dreadful night when Lucian came. I knew from the beginning that my escape would have to be made after dark, and so I spent an hour or two each night, when the rest of the household had gone to bed, studying the grounds from the windows of different downstairs rooms. To my dismay I found that from nightfall to sunrise there was always a man patrolling the grounds with a big mastiff. No dog was kept at the palazzo, and when I saw the man's face in the moonlight he was a stranger. I could only guess that he and his dog had been hired by Uncle Guido on the pretext of guarding the palazzo against thieves. But I knew the true reason. Even though Uncle Guido could have no idea that I was aware of his plans for me, he was taking no risks.

I also discovered that at night the great iron gates at the front of the palazzo were closed and locked. This meant I could not slip straight from the house and into the small boat that was moored with the gondolas. Somehow I would have to open the gate or climb the tall railings which towered to twice my height all round the grounds of the palazzo.

I hid a bottle of water in my room, and threw away the bread, which had gone stale, deciding that I would replace it only just before I escaped. In Uncle Guido's library was a paperweight in Venetian glass, a novelty with a small compass set in it. I planned to steal that on the night I escaped. I had no money of my own, so I also intended to steal anything small but of some value when the time came, so that I would not be completely penniless.

I felt no shame at such plans, for I would be stealing not for gain but for my life. In the past, when danger seemed to threaten, I had always brushed it aside after a night's sleep, telling myself that what had happened was a coincidence, or an accident, and that I was simply imagining things. Now I had no such illusions. Each day I woke with the same sure and dreadful knowledge that I stood between Uncle Guido and a fortune he was determined to have; that if I did not marry his son, Bernardino, he would kill me to get it, as his grandmother had tried to kill my own Granny Caterina. There was surely a black and evil strain in Uncle Guido's side of the family.

I even considered pretending to fall in love with Bernardino, in the hope that the watch on me would be relaxed, but knew that I could never have acted well enough to convince Uncle Guido, particularly after what Lucian had said to him about me. He would have seen through my pretence, and quickly guessed that in some way I had discovered what was afoot.

I did not allow myself to think of Lucian. I knew him now for what he was, and that was bad enough, but if I let myself remember the past, the day of Mogg Race, the day of the summer ball when I had danced with him, the day in the studio when I had been shaken by the sweet agony of first love, then the contrast now would have been too horrible to bear.

Sometimes I sat gazing at my face reflected in the looking-glass on my dressing table, and could scarcely believe that it showed so little of the fear and turmoil within me. I wondered how long this outward calm could last, for I was completely alone and very frightened. Every day it became more and more difficult to hide my fear, for although I worked steadily at my preparations I could still see no way to escape from the palazzo.

Ten days went by, and I sat one afternoon by the rock garden at the rear of the palazzo, sketching the houses on the far side of the narrow canal. I had little skill for this, but it kept Bernardino from bothering me and served as an excuse to spend time in the grounds and at different windows of the palazzo, pretending to concentrate on my sketching while I studied the canals which hemmed us like a moat.

A wrought iron door, far smaller than the front gates, was set in the tall railings at the back of the palazzo, and today I was studying it as I sketched. It was kept locked at night with a big padlock and heavy chain. I could think of no way to get the key, for presumably it was carried by the night guard. The chain could be filed through, but I had no file and I guessed that such a task would take an hour or more, besides being very noisy. From spying on the guard and his mastiff as they patrolled at night, I knew that I would have no more than five minutes to get past the railings. Even then I would be poised on the narrow ledge of wall which skirted the railings and dropped straight to the canal waters. I would have to edge slowly round the perimeter until I reached the front of the palazzo before I could get to the little dinghy moored there, and the dog would surely find me while I was doing that.

I was in a mood of black despair, and gazed almost unseeingly at a small boat moving towards me as it made its way along the canal. It carried a mast, but the sail was not raised, for it was impossible to use sail in the small canals, they were far too narrow for any manoeuvres. A man was at the oars, pulling slowly. He wore a shabby black hat with a floppy brim, and a worn jacket of dark blue, with a scarf twisted about his neck. Without thinking consciously about it, I assumed he had been out in the lagoon, where the wind was sometimes cool.

My fingers froze on my pencil as a thought struck me. My letter to Mr. Morton was ready, though still unstamped. I kept it hidden in my bodice. If I could give it to a passing boatman and beg him to stamp and post it for me, even to post it unstamped . . . it might still be delivered . . . it might. . . .

I turned my head. Alfredo, the gardener, was only thirty paces away, working on part of the rock garden. I knew he would not go until somebody arrived to keep an eye on me in his stead. Bernardino, perhaps, or Aunt Isola, or another of the servants. They might not know why they were watching me, but the Count had given his orders and they would be obeyed. I bent to my sketch again with tears of frustration in my eyes. I would never be left unobserved for long enough to persuade a passer-by on the canal to post my letter for me.

A small pebble fell close to my feet and I looked up in surprise. Through the railings I saw that the boatman had rested for a moment to wipe his face with a handkerchief. He was only ten yards away from me, and it seemed there was nobody else who could have thrown the pebble. He lifted his head, taking the handkerchief from his face. Every fibre of my body went taut as I saw those brilliant violet eyes set in a pale face, staring at me from under the brim of the hat.

It was Richard. He put a finger quickly to his lips and darted a glance beyond me. From his position on the water he could not see Alfredo, for the grounds stood several feet above water level, but it was clear that he knew somebody was there. Next moment he made a small circular movement with his hand, then held it up with the fingers widely splayed. His head dropped so that the floppy brim hid his face again, and he rowed slowly on along the canal.

Chapter Fourteen

HOPE AND EXCITEMENT raced through me like fire, even though my mind almost seemed to have splintered with amazement. Richard was here! And he must know I was in danger, for his disguise and his furtive manner made that very clear. How he knew, I could not guess, nor how he came to be here. I struggled to thrust aside the questions that tumbled about in my head. What had his signal meant—a circular movement of the hand, then splayed fingers?

I gathered my wits. He did not dare to approach and speak to me openly, yet we *must* communicate. So he would come back after circling round the palazzo. The splayed fingers meant . . . at five o'clock? No, that was two hours away. Five minutes, then. That must be it. In five minutes I had to be ready to pass a message to him. Or receive one? No, for he could have tossed a message with the pebble.

My pad lay on my knees, and I tore a strip from one page. Pointless to ask for him to suggest a way of escape, for he did not know the exact situation in the palazzo, or how much freedom of movement I had. It was for me to take the initiative.

I made up my mind that it must be tonight, for I could not endure the thought of delay. Somehow I would get past those massive railings which now made the palazzo so much a prison for me. I scribbled: *At this spot tonight, two a.m. Have sail ready to hoist, and two spare oars. Take care. Very dangerous. My love to you. Cadi.*

I might have written a better note if there had been more time, but I was frantic with the fear of being unready, and for Richard to circle the palazzo yet again might rouse suspicions if he had been seen passing the front gates. I wrapped the scrap of paper round the pebble, and waited, terrified that Bernardino might come into the garden to join me. Two unending minutes passed, and then I saw Richard's muffled figure again, pulling slowly down the canal as before. I did not dare stand up and move closer to the railings, for if I drew Alfredo's eye he would see me throw the message.

Richard brought the boat close to my side of the canal. He did not look up. As he came level with me I threw the wrapped pebble between two of the railings. It fell just short of the boat's side, and hit the water. I caught my breath, but though the pebble sank the paper floated clear, and in a flash Richard had reached over and scooped it up. Then he was pulling steadily along the canal once more, hunched over the oars, head bowed. He turned into a little waterway off the far bank and vanished from my sight.

My hands were shaking and my body felt weak with relief. I was no longer alone, and that was something so wonderful that no words could describe it. Now the questions flooded into my mind again. How had Richard known I was in danger? Had he come back to Venice on his own? Had he never left Venice? He should have been at Oxford for the past two weeks at least. Was Mr. Morton in Venice? My heart jumped with the thought, but after a moment I reluctantly decided that this could not be so. If Mr. Morton were here, if he knew the truth, he would have marched into the palazzo and confronted Uncle Guido. But . . . could he do so? He could have no proof of Uncle Guido's intentions, and to accuse a Venetian nobleman of planning to kill me would sound like madness. In sudden fright I realized that Uncle Guido had a stronger claim to be my guardian until I was twenty-one than Mr. Morton, who had never legally adopted me. I was deeply glad that it had not occurred to me simply to give Richard my letter to post. That would have meant days of anxious waiting and an uncertain outcome.

The only sure way to safety for me was to escape, and only one thing was important at this moment—I had to find a way past those high stout railings, whether through them or over them. It was half an hour before I found what I thought was a solution to that problem, then I packed up my sketch-pad and pencils and went into the palazzo.

For the rest of that day I was in dread that I would fail in the part I was acting, and that Uncle Guido would detect something suspicious in my manner. I set myself out to appear happy and at ease, and spoke of trips and explorations I would like to make during the summer. I must have been convincing, for after dinner Uncle Guido patted me on the shoulder and said how glad he was that I had settled down happily. He glanced at Bernardino, then back at me with a rather questioning smile. I returned the smile, then looked quickly down as if embarrassed, which was the best I could do in the way of response to his unspoken question. I hoped it would seem to be neither a denial nor a confirmation of his hopes, for to pretend a sudden attraction for Bernardino would have been foolish.

At one o'clock in the morning I was fully dressed in warm clothes and a topcoat, wearing my riding breeches and with woollen socks pulled on over my shoes to muffle any sound. My hair was down and plaited in pigtails. My little hoard of food and water, together with the compass and a silver snuff-box I had stolen from the mantelpiece in the library, were all tied in a blanket.

From one of the spare rooms which looked out over the front of the palazzo I saw Uncle Guido return from his evening pleasures. The night guard, dog at heel, locked the big gates after him. I stole back to my room and lay in bed, still fully clothed, just in case he might peer stealthily in to make sure I was there, but it was a wasted precaution. I heard him pass by on the way to his bedroom, then nothing more.

The next three-quarters of an hour crawled painfully by. I think I must have looked at my watch a hundred times before the moment came at last when I could gather up my bundle and creep down the great staircase. Every stair seemed to creak and groan, as if trying to cry out a warning to its master. By the time I reached the kitchen, perspiration was running down my face. I fumbled with the bolts of the small door which opened on to the grounds at the rear of the palazzo, and drew them slowly. Opening the door an inch or two, I peered out. Swirling ribbons of mist hung in the night air, writhing and drifting in the gentle breeze.

I bit my lip, not knowing if this was good or bad. The mist over the lagoon might be thick. Ugo had told me of the way it could suddenly descend upon the lagoon at night, rolling and shifting with the wind, so that at one moment a boat might sail easily in the moonlight, and the next moment would be blanketed so heavily that the bow could not be seen from the stern. I might be glad of the mist to hide me, but not if it became so thick that I lost myself.

I strained my eyes, watching for the night guard and his mastiff to pass along the railings on their rounds, and praying that if Richard came early he would lie off a little and only approach when he saw me at the wrought iron door. I knew now that I should have told him this in my note. Ten minutes crept by, second by leaden second. Then, through the coiling shreds of mist, I saw the figure of the night guard with his dog on a leash, moving slowly past the rock gardens. I eased the door to, afraid that the dog might scent me, and waited two minutes. When I opened it again, they had gone.

I drew a shaky breath and went out, closing the door behind me, then ran for the wrought iron gate, my muffled shoes making no sound.

I set down my bundle and peered through the iron curlicues of the gate. The canal was empty. Despair rose like sickness in my throat, and I gripped the cold damp iron feverishly. A shadow moved. A boat took shape as it slid from the misty darkness of the far bank. I almost sobbed with relief. The boat touched the wall below me, and Richard's face looked up.

'An oar,' I whispered urgently. 'Pass me an oar.'

He looked startled, but obeyed, passing up the oar between the bars of the iron gate. I had decided that I could not climb the high railings for they curved inwards at the top. I would have to open the iron gate. There was no way to break the chain or force the padlock, but as I sat there that afternoon I had noticed the way the gate was hinged. Two short thick butts of iron, jutting upwards, protruded from the upright on which the gate was hung. Each hinge, and there were two on the gate, consisted of a strip of iron which curled round at the end to form a sleeve two inches deep, and these two sleeves fitted loosely over the iron butts of the jamb. If I could lift the gate bodily two or three inches, and then ease it forwards or back, the hinges would come clear of the butts on which they turned.

I slid the oar beneath the bottom of the gate and levered upwards with all my strength. The hinges groaned faintly as iron rubbed on iron, but I could see the gate lifting. An inch . . . two inches. The hinges *must* be clear of their butts. Gasping, I thrust forward. The gate wavered. Then, with its hinges free, it fell away from me, but the chain held it on the padlock side so that the gate twisted on one corner, lurched, then swung round and away to hit the tall railings with a great clangour that seemed to echo over all Venice.

Fool that I was, I had expected the gate to stay upright as I forced it open, even though it was held only by a looped chain on one side. For a frightful second I was petrified, and then, even as the sound still rang through the darkness, I threw the oar down to Richard, snatched up my bundle, and slithered down the steep wet slope of the canal wall to fall in a heap in the boat.

I heard the deep bark of the mastiff, and a man's voice shouting. In an instant I was up again. 'Oars!' I croaked desperately, and threw myself on to the bow thwart. The oars hung in the rowlocks there, and Richard was slipping the spare oars into the midships rowlocks.

'Just pull!' I whispered fiercely. 'I'll steer.' That was why I had taken the bow position myself, for I would have to keep looking over my shoulder to steer, and I had far more experience of boats than Richard. I saw him now as he settled down with his back to me, gripping the oars. I said, 'Give way now,' and next moment we were gliding into the darkness and shifting mist. I was looking for the turn into a branch canal close by, and as we made it I heard furious barking, glimpsed the watery gleam of a lantern veiled by mist, and heard a man's voice raised in an urgent cry which held a note of fear. '*Chiama il Conte!*' Call the Count.

I knew my route, for I had gone over it in my mind many times, but the mist hid the moon and I could see little more than three boat-lengths ahead of us. This meant that I had to row with my head twisted round all the time, for fear that I might steer us into a bank and damage the boat. When one side of my body ached with cramp, I turned and looked over the other shoulder. Then at last we emerged from the network of minor canals I had chosen for our escape route, to strike the Grand Canal well above the Rialto Bridge. On the far side lay the *Ca' d'Oro Museum*, and beside it ran a canal which would take us into the lagoon north of Venice.

I had planned two ways of escape, one to the south and one to the north, for I wanted to be sure of a following wind for our journey. Tonight the breeze was blowing gently from the south-west, and so I had chosen to head north-east, out past the islands of Murano, Mazorbo and Torcello, to strike the mainland near Porte Grandi and to seek a fishing village there. Suddenly despair had gone and my heart was bursting with hope, for I had Richard with me now, and all I had planned would be so much easier.

We slid out from the canal into open water, and after another two minutes of rowing I said, 'Oars, Richard.' We shipped our oars and hoisted the sail. It flapped, then caught the faint breeze. I sat at the tiller with Richard in front of me, his hand on the mainsheet. He turned to peer at me through the gloom, speaking for the first time. 'Are we moving, Cadi? It feels very slow.'

'It's a little quicker than it feels. Better to save our strength for the oars in case the wind drops. Besides, they don't know where to look for us. They'll probably think we headed down the Grand Canal and turned west past *La Giudecca*. My heart went out to him suddenly, and I was close to tears, voice shaking a little as I said, 'Oh, thank God you came, Richard. I'd almost lost hope.'

He smiled, taking off the broad-brimmed hat, and even in the grey darkness I could see a whole world of happiness in his face. I rummaged in my blanket bundle for the paperweight compass and passed it to him. 'We have to head north-east. Can you see the needle?'

He nodded. 'Just, if I hold it close.'

'Keep me on course. Richard, are you on your own here? Did nobody come with you?'

'I'm on my own, Cadi. I've been staying at a little back-street hotel for the last three days, and rowing past the palazzo half a dozen times a day, trying to see you.'

'But . . . how did you know I was in danger?'

He turned his head sharply. 'I was right, then?'

'Yes.' I shivered a little. 'Uncle Guido wants me dead before I'm twenty-one, so he can have all the money.' My throat seemed to close up and I had to force the next words out. 'Lucian was going to . . . to see to it for him.'

'Lucian?' Richard almost dropped the paperweight compass, and his eyes were glistening round pools in the darkness. 'But that *can't* be so, Cadi. I mean, Lucian . . .'

'I heard him say it. I heard him offer to make sure I had an accident.' The remembrance was an aching lump in my chest. 'You were right, Richard,' I went on wearily. 'You once told me his mind was blemished. It's worse than that. This wasn't some wild act that he did without knowing it, like the time when he beat you with a crop. This was something he offered to do for money.' My voice broke. 'I heard them . . . bargaining.'

Richard sat hunched, staring down at the compass. After a while he said, 'Port a little, Cadi.'

'Port,' I repeated dully. My ecstasy at winning free had passed, corroded by bitter memories of that night when I had discovered Lucian's true nature. 'How did you know, Richard?' I asked at last.

'I didn't know about Lucian,' he said in a low voice. 'It was Sarah who opened my eyes to the Count.'

'Sarah?'

'Yes. We all thought you meant it when you said you wanted to stay here instead of coming home with us. We were hurt . . . troubled. But we believed it. Only Sarah had the sense to guess there was something wrong. She knew you thought of us as your family. She knew something or somebody was *making* you stay.'

Sarah. Dear, wonderful Sarah, the silly one of the family, whose simple belief in me had proved more wise than all the puzzled wonderings and vain heart-searchings of the others.

'She said as much on the train home,' Richard went on, his head still bowed over the compass. 'But we all shushed her. We didn't want to talk about it. Then, just over a week ago, she wrote me a letter in Oxford. She said she *knew* you wanted to be with us, and that you must be breaking your heart in Venice, so there had to be some reason why you pretended. She'd been thinking about it a lot, and wanted to know if I'd got into any scrapes there, because perhaps you were doing this for *my* sake.'

He raised his head and looked at me squarely. 'Then I knew, Cadi. Everything fell into place. It was all so clear.' His face was stony with self-contempt. It must have been hard for him not to turn his head away, but he continued to look at me steadily as he spoke. This was a new Richard I had not seen before, perhaps a Richard nobody had seen before, not even himself. The soft speech and the withdrawn manner had gone. There was strength and purpose in him,

270

and the courage to meet my gaze while he made his confession.

'Seven thousand pounds,' he said slowly. 'I must have been mad as well as drunk. But I thought if I made a lot of money like that, I could buy a practice when I qualified as a solicitor, instead of having to turn to my father for the money. And I'd have been in a position to marry, too . . .' he smiled briefly, without bitterness, 'if you ever came to love me, Cadi. But I lost. It was a stupid dream. I know that now. And then, on our last day in Venice, the Count took me aside and said he'd paid the note of hand for me, to save me from disgrace.' He shrugged, and again I saw self-contempt in the twist of his lips. 'I was so grateful, so desperately grateful. It makes me sick to remember it.'

'He cheated you,' I said. 'He hired a card-sharper to cheat you.'

'Yes. I guessed the swine had done something like that,' Richard said with harsh savagery. 'When I read Sarah's letter I guessed everything. I knew that man wasn't generous. I'd seen him at the card tables. He's greedy and he's ruthless, and he'd never have lifted a finger to help me for my own sake. That meant somebody else had persuaded him to do it—at a price. And it could only be you, Cadi. That's how he made you stay, isn't it?'

'Yes, except that I didn't have to persuade him. It was all planned. I heard him tell Lucian. He tricked me too, Richard. I stayed out of gratitude to him for paying your debt, but it was all a trick.'

Richard muttered an oath. 'That's the way he works. Well, then I asked myself *why* he'd made you stay. And as soon as I'd asked the question I knew the answer, Cadi. I couldn't prove it, but I knew. I can't think why I didn't see it before. He wanted the estate, the fortune. He'd expeced it all his life. Now *you* stood in his way, and to have what he wanted he had to get rid of you.' I saw his mouth set in a hard line, and he gave a sudden violent shake of his head. 'I was frightened to death for you, Cadi,' he said in a low fierce voice. 'I wanted to kill the man. I knew he'd arranged everything so that he could keep you under his hand, and there could be only one reason for that.' He looked about him at the grey swirling darkness. 'There's old blood in Venice,' he went on more quietly. 'It runs dark and deadly. I remembered what had happened to your grandmother . . .' His violet eyes flared at the memory.

'So you came?'

'I came.' He nodded grimly. 'It was no good speaking to Father. We've never been able to talk very easily, and I couldn't have made him see things as I saw them, as I knew them to be. He doesn't know the Count as I do, and he wouldn't have believed me. So I borrowed some money in Oxford, and came here to take you away. Nobody knows yet.' He shrugged. 'Well, I suppose Mother and Father know I'm missing from Oxford by now, but they don't know where I am.' He looked at me. 'I didn't realize you knew of your own danger. There was a note wrapped round that pebble I threw to you, but it came off and fell in the canal.' His lips thinned in a humourless smile. 'I'm afraid I'm not very good at this sort of thing yet, but I'll improve as we go along. At least you're not alone now, and that's something.'

'Oh, Richard . . .' My whole heart was in my voice, but though I groped for words to thank him they all seemed too small and clumsy. Then the boat shuddered faintly, and a jar ran through her timbers. Richard stared at me. 'What was that?'

'We're aground. It's only a mudbank, I think. The lagoon's full of shallows. See if you can push her off with an oar.'

I was too optimistic. It was ten minutes later, and we were knee deep in mud, before we managed to heave the bow free and drag ourselves into the boat again. That was only the first of our disasters. I had thought myself able to handle a boat in any waters, but I had not realized the true nature of the Venetian lagoon. It was a trap for all who did not know it, and only the men of Venice were familiar with its ways. The lagoon was neither one thing nor the other, for its waters were a mixture of salt and fresh, while its shallows, mudbanks and reedy patches made it half land rather than true water.

If I could have seen the *bricole,* the tall stakes driven into the mud and marking out the channels which criss-crossed the great lagoon, I might have navigated with more success, but the darkness and mist were my enemies now. Three times in an hour we found ourselves stranded on a mudbank, and on the third occasion Richard let slip the compass as we struggled to thrust the boat free. It sank into the watery mud and was lost. We were soaked to the thighs, and coated in mud to our knees. The sail had long since been lowered, and we had taken to the oars, yet we dared move only at a snail's pace, for the mist had grown heavier and we dreaded driving so deeply into one of the mudbanks that we should never get free.

I could have wept with anger. Above the mist I knew there was a full bright moon. It might have shown our sail to any who were seeking us, but in its light I could have followed the *bricole* and found a way through the channels. As things were, it seemed likely that we would grope our weary way from mudbank to mudbank until the dawn sucked up the mist and left us in full view.

I did not know if the night guard had seen our boat as we pulled away from the palazzo for my head had been turned to look forward, but I knew that Uncle Guido would have every boat and every man he could muster out searching for us.

Richard was pulling gently while I stood in the bow and probed ahead of us with an oar, hoping to get a second's warning of the next mudbank. I was comforting myself with the thought that the lagoon was large and that Uncle Guido had no idea which direction we had taken, when a thought so shattering struck me that I gave a cry of alarm.

Richard backed with both oars to hold the boat and said, 'More mud?'

'No.' I sank down in the bow. 'Oh, I've done an awful thing, Richard.' My voice had a wailing note, like Sarah at her most plaintive, but I was too miserable to care. 'I drew maps of the canals and traced two routes. Because of the wind I decided we'd strike out north from Venice across the lagoon, and I had the map beside my bed tonight, studying it while I was waiting . . . *and I left it there, Richard!* Uncle Guido's bound to find it!'

Richard wiped his face on the sleeve of his jacket, leaving a smear of mud. 'Well . . . perhaps he won't. Let's just carry on, Cadi. If we could find one of the little islands we might be able to hide there during the day in a patch of reeds, as long as we unstepped the mast so it didn't show. Then we could make for the mainland tomorrow night.'

My hopes rose again, for Richard's idea was sound. We blundered on slowly for a while, and then I felt a new coldness on my cheek. An hour ago the wind had died completely, but now a breeze was beginning to blow. It might blow steadily, or it might be no more than a gentle gust lasting only a few minutes, but with luck it would help us.

'Get the sail up, Richard,' I said quickly. 'There's a breeze started, and if it rolls this mist back long enough for us to spot one of the islands, we'll make the most of it.'

I moved to the tiller, and as soon as the sail was up I turned the boat into the wind while we waited. The mist seemed as thick as ever, but I could see it rolling across us under the thrust of the breeze. Quite suddenly we were bathed in moonlight, and I saw the solid wall of mist rolling away from us to starboard. Eighty yards away I glimpsed a line of *bricole,* curving away to our starboard quarter, and to one side of the line, still partly hidden by mist, I caught the shadowy outline of land rising from the water.

'Starboard oar, Richard,' I jerked out. 'Bring her round.'

He heaved on the oar, and the bow came round to point towards the *bricole.* I held the mainsheet myself, and felt the wind take the sail. As the dinghy came alive I heard Richard say huskily, 'Boats, Cadi! Astern now!'

I threw a glance over my shoulder, and felt cold with shock. Three gondolas and two big rowing boats, each with several men aboard, were strung out in a line. The nearest rowing boat was no more than forty paces from us. The gondolas were Chiavelli craft, and I knew that Uncle Guido had found the map I had so stupidly left.

I looked quickly ahead, saw that we were on course for the line of *bricole,* and looked back again. 'They're stuck,'

Richard said, and I saw that the rowing boat nearest to us was on a mudbank, for two of the men were knee deep in the water, trying to push her off. Somebody shouted, and a man in the boat stood up, staring towards us. In the clear bright moonlight I recognized the figure of Uncle Guido. And then I saw something else, something which brought me new hope. Beyond the line of boats which were spread out like beaters on a hunt, a tall grey cliff of mist was rolling towards us. Already it hid the last gondola in the line. The freak breeze had cut a great swathe through the mist, but now the clear space was being filled again.

As I turned I heard a sound as if someone had snapped an oar in trying to lever the big rowing boat free. The gust of wind was dying now, but we were still moving at a good five knots and I could see the shape of the *bricole* jutting from the water close ahead of us. I brought the dinghy round to starboard and headed for the next of the tall poles.

A glance to my right showed only the wall of mist, very close now, its tendrils already writhing about us. Uncle Guido's boats and men had been engulfed. I stared ahead, trying to burn into my mind a picture of the line taken by the *bricole*, knowing that in another few seconds the rolling mist would hide them from my sight, leaving me to steer by memory alone.

'There's an island close by,' I said, keeping my voice to a whisper even though I knew the mist would help to deaden any sound. 'I think I can hold the course for it, Richard. We still have a chance.'

He muttered something I could not catch, but I was too busy now to ask what he had said. Still the dying breeze held, and by luck or by instinct I kept to the curving line of poles as we crept along. One by one they loomed up, barely visible in the blanket of mist, and we passed them by. When I had counted five of them I put the tiller over and came round to port, for if my judgment was right it was here that I had glimpsed land. The sail flapped and hung loosely, but still we had enough way on us to keep the dinghy drifting on. Then, with a faint rustling sound, the bow drove into tall reeds.

'Sail down!' I whispered urgently, but Richard seemed to be in a daze. He sat unmoving as we swished slowly through the reeds and slithered to a halt on mud. Impatiently I left the tiller and ran the sail down. 'It's one of the little islands!' I said, leaning to speak close to his ear. 'I saw it when the mist cleared for those few moments just now. Come *on*, Richard, don't just sit there!'

He lifted his head, and the whiteness of his mud-smeared face in the darkness frightened me. 'You go on, Cadi,' he whispered hoarsely. 'I'm hurt.'

'Hurt?' I could not think what he meant.

'When the Count fired. He missed you . . . but hit me.'

I sank to the thwart beside him, and could feel shock draining the blood from my face. He was still hunched, one forearm pressed awkwardly across his chest. Now I remembered the sound I had thought to be the snapping of an oar. It had been a pistol shot, and I knew whose hand had fired it. But Uncle Guido's aim had been amiss. The bullet must have passed wide of me as I sat in the stern, and struck Richard.

'Where did it hit you?' I whispered. He moved his head in a downward nod. 'Somewhere in the side of my chest . . . the ribs.'

'Richard . . .' I took his face between my hands, almost afraid to touch him for fear of hurting him, and I felt tears pouring down my cheeks.

'Don't cry, Cadi. Don't cry.'

With a huge effort I pulled myself together. 'Can you move, Richard? Can you get ashore if I help? You can't stay here, or you'll die in this cold and damp. I've got to find shelter for you, and fetch help.'

He nodded, his teeth chattering. 'See if you can find shelter, Cadi. But—but don't call out for help. If the Count finds us he'll kill us both. He'll have to now. He's gone too far to draw back.'

With sick despair I realized that Richard spoke nothing but the truth. My instinct had been to surrender, anything so that Richard could be taken to a doctor as quickly as possible, but it was too late to surrender. Uncle Guido was desperate now and had shown his hand. If he caught us, we would die.

I said, 'I'll be as quick as I can. Will you be all right?'

It was a stupid question, but Richard nodded and I saw him smile faintly. 'I think so. I don't seem to be bleeding badly. During the war Lucian had a bullet in his side for three days before they got him to a surgeon, and he survived.'

I did not care what had happened to Lucian, but those words kindled a flicker of hope in me. If we could stay out of Uncle Guido's hands we might yet live through this nightmare. I climbed out of the boat and plodded through soft mud which gradually became more solid as the reeds thinned out. Then the ground sloped up sharply and I found dry ground beneath my feet. It seemed that the slight lift of the land created an up-draught which dispersed the mist a little, for I could see for a good thirty paces all about me.

I took off the mud-caked socks I wore over my shoes and put them down to mark the point where I would have to re-enter the reeds to find Richard again, then I moved on slowly through a straggle of low bushes, looking back every few seconds to mark the way I had come.

The mist grew thinner still, and suddenly I knew why. Ahead of me I could see a huddle of stone buildings, and from the largest of them rose a chimney from which a wisp of smoke coiled up. We were on the tiny island near Murano which held Uncle Guido's glass foundry. Nobody lived here, for the glass-workers came daily by boat, but always one man stayed the night in the foundry to keep the furnaces stoked. There was a constant pall of warm air over the islet, and it was this which was lifting the mist.

I drew back a little. The man in the foundry would be Uncle Guido's man, and loyal to him from fear if from nothing else. As soon as he heard that we were sought, he would hand us over to Uncle Guido with all speed. I dared not risk even being seen by him if I hoped to escape with Richard another night, when our scent was cold. Standing there with my sodden breeches clinging to my legs I searched my memories of that day I had spent on the islet. After watching the glass-workers I had strolled round the shore with Sarah, and it had taken us only ten minutes. On the eastern side, to my right now, there was an old landing stage, I recalled, and near it a stone hut which had long since fallen into disuse.

Five minutes later I had found the hut. The ancient wooden door was unlocked. Groping about inside, I found only bare earth and a pile of old canvas which had once been sails.

Richard had not stirred when I waded through the reeds to the boat. I took my blanket bundle in one hand and put my free arm about his waist so that he could lean on me as we moved slowly up the mud-bank to the shore. Twice we had to stop and rest while he gathered his failing strength, but at last we reached the hut.

'There's some canvas somewhere,' I whispered, feeling for it with my foot. 'Yes, here. Lie down and I'll put the blanket over you.' As I felt him lie down in the blackness a new feeling of helplessness swept me. I had thought to look at his wound, and to do what I could to bandage it, but with the door closed against the soaking mist there was not even a gleam of light in the hut, and I might as well have been blind.

'Cadi . . .' His voice was husky. 'There's a little lantern and matches from the boat's locker. I put them in your bundle while you were gone.' Even as he spoke I felt them under my hands as I untied the blanket. When I had found a match dry enough to strike I saw that the lantern was of the unspillable kind. I lit the wick and that yellow glow of light was like a blessing. It brought the comfort of sight and even seemed to warm the air.

There were no windows, but I wedged a strip of canvas into the crack of the door for as high as I could reach, to stop any gleam showing through. And then, for the second time in my life, I eased Richard's clothes from his body to examine his hurt. I had to force myself to look as I drew off his shirt, for I was afraid of what I might see, but the wound was much less frightening than some I had seen among the fishermen of Mawstone when they came to Mrs. Mansel with gashes for her to tend. There I had often helped her by boiling water or rolling bandages.

The wound in Richard's side was small and not bleeding heavily, but all around it was a huge black-and-red bruise spreading over the ribs. I guessed that the bullet had struck a rib and been deflected. It had not come out, for there was no sign of its exit, and though the wound looked less alarming than some I had seen I was very much aware that it might be more serious.

'I can only put on a dressing, Richard,' I whispered, my voice shaking. 'I'm sorry. Does it hurt very much?'

He managed a small smile. 'Not much, Cadi. It's all right as long as I don't breathe too deeply.'

I pulled my petticoat out from the waist of my breeches and tore off some wide strips, then made a bulky pad of the cambric and placed it gently over the wound. The next part was more difficult, for I had to help Richard sit up while I bound strips of the petticoat round his chest to hold the pad in place. Before he lay back again I spread my topcoat beneath him to stop the cold striking up, then covered him with the blanket and put his jacket on top.

It was hard to think clearly, for a sense of unreality kept stealing over me. The escape, the struggle through the mudbanks, the confusion of being lost in that cold mist, the chase and the danger, and above all the shock of Richard's wounding—these things seemed part of another world in which I was a stranger. I would gladly have squatted by the lamp, my mind vacant, thinking no thoughts, making no more efforts, but somehow I forced that temptation away and drove my weary brain to consider our situation. I was not sure whether it would be a good thing for Richard to eat or drink, but felt that he must try to keep up his strength if we were to have any hope at all, so I fed him with some of the biscuits and sweetmeats, and gave him small sips of water from the bottle.

For myself, I did not want to eat, but he insisted gently, and in the end I obeyed. 'Are you cold, Cadi?' he asked. I was, but I shook my head. 'No, I'm all right. Try to rest, and don't worry about me, Richard.' I put all the confidence

279

I could muster into my voice. 'If we can stay hidden here tomorrow, Uncle Guido will think we've got away. Then tomorrow night we'll escape without any trouble. It's not far to Porte Grandi and we'll never have a mist like this two nights running.' I was far from sure of that, but I tried to sound convincing.

Richard lay looking at the lamp for a while as I knelt beside him, then he turned his head towards me and said slowly, 'Hold my hand while I tell you something, Cadi.'

I felt under the blanket and gripped his cold hand. 'I'll hold your hand, but don't talk, Richard dear. Try to sleep.'

'I have to tell you, Cadi. I have to tell you why Lucian whipped me that night. It was because . . . because I tampered with your bridle, and when the ring snapped you were almost killed.'

I sat stunned, unable to find words. Still without taking his eyes from my face he went on. 'Don't hate me, Cadi. I hate myself so much.'

'I'll never hate you,' I managed to say at last. 'But *why*, Richard? Why did you do it?'

He moved his shoulders slightly and closed his eyes. 'I don't know. I've done things like that before. My brother John, he died long before you came to us. It was my doing, Cadi. I took his gun to my workshop, and I did something to the safety-catch, so that when the catch was on it didn't really work.' Tears squeezed from beneath his eyelids. 'I didn't mean to hurt him, Cadi. It was just . . . an experiment. He tripped, and when the gun went off it killed him, even though the safety-catch was on.'

I could not utter a reproach, for it was useless, and his need now was for comfort. 'I know you didn't mean it,' I said, and pressed his hand. 'Did your father find out?'

He opened his eyes again, and I saw pain and bewilderment in them. 'Yes. When he and Lucian examined the gun they found out what had been done to it, and they knew it must be me. I think my mother knows, but she would never let herself believe it. And then . . . then I did another thing when we were on holiday in Bosney. The rudder pintle . . .'

I had known it even before he told me. I remembered the way Lucian and Mr. Morton had looked at each other. They too had known who had sawn halfway through the broken pintle.

'It always goes wrong,' Richard said suddenly, his voice anguished. 'I couldn't know John would trip and fall, or that the pintle would break in Mogg Race Bay.' He turned his head to look at me despairingly. 'Or that Pompey would be going at a gallop when the ring snapped, and that he'd bolt with you.'

'Of course you couldn't know,' I said, fighting to keep the horror from my eyes. 'Don't talk about it any more, Richard. You were just playing a joke.'

'Oh no, Cadi,' he said earnestly. 'I wouldn't play jokes like that. All those things . . . they were experiments, really.' He shook his head slightly, and his voice became slow and sad. 'Sometimes a strange thing comes over me, and I'm tempted. It's like gambling, Cadi, to see what will happen. Gambling is an awful temptation. Like a hunger gnawing inside. I have to do these things to see . . . well, to see how they turn out. Like testing a mousetrap. An experiment. Can you understand? I don't mean to harm anyone, but sometimes I feel strange, and then it's as if there's somebody else inside me, using my hands.' He gave a little sigh. 'I think it comes to me from my other side of the family. Her father was . . . strange.'

I knew now why Mr. Morton had been so anxious when I told him the cause of my fall from Pompey. He had suspected Richard, and been relieved when I told him that the broken ring had simply been an accident. But Lucian had examined the ring closely. He had known the truth.

'That's why Lucian beat me,' Richard said, as if he had been following my thoughts. 'Father had talked to me before about . . . about doing things that might harm somebody. That was after John's accident. Dear God, how he talked to me. He couldn't understand that it wasn't my fault, that I hadn't really meant anything terrible to happen. But when . . . his voice faltered, 'when that thing happened to *you*, Cadi, then Lucian must have decided talking was no use. He flogged me, and threatened worse if I ever made any more . . . experiments.'

'He must have been afraid for himself, then,' I said bitterly. 'Not for me. He's the man I heard offer to kill me for money.'

Richard closed his eyes again, and I felt he was so wrapped in his own misery that he had hardly noticed what I said. He whispered. 'Will you forgive me, Cadi? I love you so much.'

'Of course I forgive you,' I said quickly, and bent to kiss his muddy cheek. 'When this is all over, if you ever feel that horrible temptation again you'll tell me, and we'll remember everything together, and you won't make any more experiments.'

He nodded feebly, and a smile touched his pallid lips. 'I'm glad I've told you, Cadi. Everything will be all right now. I'll rest, and tomorrow night we'll take the boat and—'

He broke off, startled by the sudden clutch of my hand on his, and the gasp of dismay that broke from me. 'The boat!' I said desperately. 'We didn't unstep the mast, Richard. It's sticking up from among the reeds for anyone to see as soon as there's enough light. I've got to go back and hide it.'

'You can't unstep the mast alone,' he said slowly, and moved as if to sit up, but I put out my hand to stop him.

'No! You mustn't move, Richard. And I've just thought, there's another way to hide the boat. She's lying canted over a little, so if I scramble a few feet up the mast my weight will turn the boat on her side, so the mast lies flat.'

I got to my feet.

Richard gazed up at me anxiously. 'But will you be able to right the boat again tomorrow night, and get her afloat?'

'Yes, I'll manage somehow. She's only in a foot of water and she's very light. I can use some of the rigging to haul on for leverage.'

He smiled faintly. 'All right, Cadi. You know about these things.'

I put the box of matches in his hand, blew out the lamp so that no light would show when I opened the door, and told him that I would be back within a quarter of an hour. His answer was a mumble, and I knew that weariness and exhaustion were pushing him down into sleep. That was a good thing. The more he could rest, the better.

Once outside the hut I waited for a few minutes for my eyes to grow accustomed to the darkness, then made my way through the thin swirling mist towards the shore where the patch of reeds lay. It seemed to me that even by the shore the mist was thinner than before. When I reached the beginning of the muddy slope I stopped and peered ahead with sudden unease. I could see a good forty paces through the milky moonlight which now penetrated the mist, and I felt certain that I should have been able to see the mast sticking up from where I stood, but there was no sign of it showing above the reeds.

I turned slowly round to make sure I had come to the right spot, then froze as if every nerve had suddenly turned to ice. A crouched figure, only a few paces away, was moving towards me, a nightmare creature befouled with mud from shoulders to feet, a man with soaked trousers clinging about his legs, and streaks of bare chest showing through the mud that coated his body.

My eyes found his face, and it was Lucian.

For an age-long instant we stared at each other. His brows were a straight line above fierce, urgent eyes, and suddenly I saw his teeth show white against the grime on his face. I could not help myself, and breath rushed into my lungs for a shriek, even though I knew that there was nobody but my enemies in earshot.

Lucian sprang, and I was thrown down under his weight as he seized me, with hands whose strength I so well remembered from that first day when he had lifted me up behind him on the saddle as if I had been a bundle of straw. The breath was knocked from my body as I hit the ground. I knew an instant of pain, bright lights flashed before my eyes, and then darkness struck down upon me like a hammer-blow.

Chapter Fifteen

I WAS WARM. The air about me was dry and heated. Slowly, with dull bewilderment, my mind tried to read the messages of my senses.

Warmth. A faint smell of burning. Something soft beneath me, not a bed, but perhaps a table with blankets spread on it. An aching bruise at the back of my head, which was resting on a pillow or cushion. Dried mud on my face and arms. A voice, quite close though it seemed distant to my numbed brain. A voice tantalizingly familiar, with a lilt, a touch of brogue, a hint of amusement in it. The words took on a pattern . . .

'. . . and Lord help us all but she'll give us the edge of her tongue when she wakes. Did you have to knock the senses from her?'

Flynn! The grey-eyed stranger who had saved me in Chalons. My weary mind struggled with the impossibility. I tried to open my eyes, but they would not respond yet.

'She must have bumped her head when she fell.' Lucian's voice, calm and rather thoughtful. 'I had to stop her screaming out, and there was no time to be polite. Chiavelli and his cut-throats might have heard her.' A pause. 'How's the boy, Paddy?'

'Hard to tell. He's sleeping again now. But he'll be better here than in that hut.'

A confusion of thoughts stirred sluggishly in my mind. I felt no fear now, for I had known the terror of dying as I went down under Lucian, and had passed beyond all fear.

Chiavelli's *cut-throats*? Why would Lucian speak of them in such a way when he himself had bargained with Uncle Guido for the price of killing me? And Richard was here. They had carried him from the hut and were anxious for him. It was all beyond my understanding.

'How the devil did the boy know what was happening?' said Flynn wonderingly. 'It put a year on my life when I saw her break through that gate and jump in the boat with him. Never dreamt it was young Morton.'

I could hear a faint rubbing sound, and when Lucian spoke his voice sounded uneven with exertion. I tried again to open my eyes, and this time the lids moved a fraction. As if through a tiny slit I saw that we were in semi-darkness and that a bright glow came from the three small open doors of a furnace. We were in the glass foundry, not the main part but one of the smaller buildings where special orders were carried out. I realized that I was lying on a bench there. I could see Lucian without turning my head. He was scrubbing vigorously at his body with a strip of blanket, trying to clean off the mud, and in the red glow from the furnace I saw a puzzled frown on his face.

'Richard must have guessed somehow that Cadi was in danger,' he said. 'He came out to rescue her.'

I could not see Flynn, but heard him sigh. 'Fools rush in,' he said. 'Your way was better.'

'Perhaps.' Lucian's bare shoulders shrugged. 'But only as long as Cadi didn't know what Chiavelli planned for her, only as long as she wasn't frightened—and she *must* have known, Paddy. That's why she escaped. My way, she'd have had to wait another two weeks or more, knowing Chiavelli was out to get rid of her but not knowing there was any chance of help.'

For a moment his face showed the frightening savagery I had glimpsed in the looking-glass on the night when my dream had broken. 'Enough to send a girl out of her mind,' he added in a tight voice.

'Not this one,' said Flynn. 'She's a heart inside her as big as Venice, Cadi Tregaron has.'

'I know that, Paddy,' Lucian said very quietly. 'I've known that since the first day. I told you.' He threw the strip of blanket aside and came towards me. 'Thank God we were on hand tonight, though.' I had barely to move my lids to close my eyes. His hand touched my cheek, then moved to brush the hair gently from my brow.

'Poor little Cadi,' Lucian said in the same quiet voice. 'Poor, rich little Cadi.'

I wanted to lie there for ever with his hand on my brow and with this great warm joy spreading through every fibre of me. I did not yet understand what had happened, but I knew now that all I had ever suspected of Lucian was wrong, and for the moment nothing else mattered. This was the most wonderful, the most glorious gift I had ever known, for it changed my world.

Perhaps what I first felt for Lucian on that day in the studio had been puppy-love, as I had convinced myself, and perhaps this had indeed died in the struggle I fought against it, for I knew now that real love, in all its infinite range and richness, can spring only from full trust and knowledge of the one who is loved. But it was from the ashes of first love that something much greater had risen in shining rebirth, like the new day's sun over the sea. I could feel it living and pulsing within me, a thing of the heart and mind as well as of the blood, a rich and glowing longing to give and to receive, but a longing that was now rooted in sure and perfect trust. I was thankful that my eyes were closed, for Lucian would surely have read my whole heart in them at this moment.

'Your jersey's dry,' said Flynn. As I heard Lucian turn away from me I half-opened my eyes and saw him lift his hands to catch a thick dark jersey Flynn had tossed to him. I felt no wish to say anything, for there was a strange but deep happiness in simply watching the man I loved and hearing him speak. I did not deceive myself about his feelings for me. That he was true and loyal in friendship I no longer doubted, for I knew now that even his horrifying conversation with Uncle Guido had been part of a deception to save me. But his manner towards me just now, when he thought me asleep, had been that of a man to a child, no more. Whatever risks he had taken to help me, he would have done the same for Sarah, or Mr. Morton, or anyone he counted as a friend.

He pulled on the jersey and said, 'How's the mist, Paddy?'

'Thinning, damn it. I fancy we'll have company soon. You got them in a tangle with your pranks, but if Chiavelli has any sense he'll bring his bully-boys ashore to reorganize for the search. A rabble's no use for anything.'

'That's sound military sense, but he's not a soldier, Paddy.'

'He's no fool either, Lucian me boy.'

'No, he's not.' Lucian's voice was grim. 'I'll go and watch out for them. You stay here. I don't want Cadi to be frightened when she wakes.'

As he turned towards the door I lifted my head and said, 'Lucian . . . it's all right, I'm not frightened now.' My voice sounded slurred, and the words came slowly from my tongue. He was beside me in a moment, helping me to sit up on the big work-bench.

'Ah, Cadi,' he said, the black brows flaring as he smiled into my eyes. 'That's my girl.'

In the glowing red light from the open furnace doors I saw Flynn standing by one of the shuttered windows. He wore a jersey like Lucian's, and his fair hair was tousled. He inclined his head in that polite, half-mocking way I knew of old, but there was respect and even affection in it now as he spoke.

'Top of the morning to you, Miss Tregaron.'

I held on to Lucian's arm to steady myself, for sitting up had made me feel dizzy for a moment, then said, 'Good morning to you, Mr. Flynn.'

Richard lay on a palliasse of straw on the floor of the foundry, close to the warmth of the furnace wall, a blanket over him, sleeping.

'I have to go out for a while, little cousin,' Lucian said, and put his hand to my cheek. 'But don't worry. You'll be safe with Paddy to look after you.'

'I know. I know that.' I could hardly get the words out. Lucian's manner to me was so gentle, and somehow different from ever before, without reserve or arrogance, without mockery or enigma, and I was suddenly racked by shame as I recalled all that I had believed of him. I drew a long breath, and words poured from me in a stammering wail. 'Oh Lucian, I'm sorry! I have to tell you. I've thought such *awful* things of you. That night when you were with Uncle Guido, I was in the little room next door and I—I heard everything. I thought you really meant it, that you were willing to—to kill me. And before that, I thought it was you who tried to throw me from the train. . . .'

My voice failed. I put my arms round his neck, laid my head on his chest, and cried silently.

'There now, there,' he said, patting my shoulder as he held me. 'You weren't to know, Cadi.' With enormous relief I heard the note of laughter in his voice, and knew that he was not angry.

Flynn chuckled. 'If you overheard this feller at work, twisting the truth from your dear uncle, and *didn't* believe him the villain he made himself out to be, you'd be a fool, Cadi Tregaron. Dear God, I've watched Lucian at that game a time or two, and he'd take in the devil himself, so he would.'

'Shut up, Paddy, or you'll have her doubting me again,' Lucian said. I lay in his arms, and suddenly remembered Mr. Morton's words when he had agreed that Lucian was a master of deception: 'But it depends upon who is being deceived, and why. . . .' Now, dimly, I began to understand what he had meant.

Lucian put a hand under my chin and tilted my face to look at him.

'I've never been false with you, Cadi. I'd not know how to begin.'

I could only nod, trying to tell him with my eyes that my trust was given now, once and for all. He said again, 'That's my girl,' then gave a little sigh and stepped back. 'There's much you'll want to know, but Paddy can tell you. I have to go now.' He looked at Flynn. 'If nothing happens I'll be back in an hour and you can relieve me.' He gave me a quick, reassuring smile, then moved to the door and went out, closing it silently after him.

I got down stiffly from the table, and a spatter of dried mud fell from me. Kneeling down beside Richard, I put a hand gently on his brow. He felt very feverish and his breathing was a little fast, but he did not seem restless in his sleep.

Flynn stood beside me, and I looked up. 'Is there nothing we can do for him, Mr. Flynn?'

'Not for the moment, I'm afraid. Not until we can get him to a surgeon. And I'll answer to Paddy if you'll be so kind, Miss Tregaron.' The corners of his eyes crinkled. 'After all, we've known each other quite a while now.'

'Yes.' I tucked my legs under me and settled down on the floor so that I sat close to Richard in case he woke. 'And I'll answer to Cadi, please. Will you tell me what's happening?'

He chuckled.

'Never ask an Irishman that. He'll talk for an hour without taking breath.'

'We've nothing else to do, Paddy.'

'That's true enough. Where will I begin?'

'I first saw you at Wealdhurst. Why were you there?'

'Ah, now. That was a job the Captain set me to.'

'The Captain?'

'Captain Farrel. Lucian. We soldiered together.' He looked down at me quizzically. 'We were cashiered together.'

I had forgotten that for the moment, forgotten Lucian was an outcast.

'Never mind that part, Paddy. Why did he send you to Wealdhurst?'

Paddy Flynn looked down at Richard's sleeping form, and shook his head regretfully. 'He was frightened for you, Cadi. The boy here, he's a little sick in the head sometimes, you see. It was him that nearly got you killed on Pompey.'

'I know. Richard himself told me today. Lucian beat him for it. You mean he was still afraid of it happening again?'

'Or something like it. I used to watch you by day whenever you were out, and by night I'd prowl the boy's workroom, seeing what he was up to. I was guarding you, as you might say—as best I could.'

'But . . . day and night, for all that time! Why was Lucian so concerned over me?'

Paddy smiled, but ignored the question. 'It wasn't meant to be so long at first, only till the boy went back to Oxford, but by then there was something else. You'd become an heiress, Cadi. So Lucian asked me to stay on watch for you. He couldn't come and keep guard over you himself, for there'd be too many questions, so it was me that had the job.' Paddy Flynn scratched the lobe of his ear. 'I'm a man he trusts quite a bit, d'you see.'

'Yes. Oh yes, I see that, Paddy. But do you mean Lucian suspected Uncle Guido even then?'

Paddy drew a stubby pipe from his pocket and began to fill it from a worn pouch. 'Lucian suspected his nibs the first moment his name was spoken,' he said. 'It's not so strange. We knew a little about the Count. When you're buying and selling horses, you mix in a tight little world that other folk don't know. We'd heard a few rumours about Chiavelli, in France, Italy, and the Levant. Not the feller we fancied doing business with at all.'

'We?'

'I'm Lucian's partner. He took me in when he set up the stables at Epsom. Well, from what we heard, this feller Chiavelli was up to his ears in money troubles, but he was scraping along on credit because of the fortune that was to come to him in a little while. Then *you* appeared, Cadi. By God, that must have been a shock for his nibs. But he didn't fight, he didn't set the lawyers to challenge your identity. He just smiled, and agreed, and wrote those letters. Mr. Morton told Lucian of them. Full of sweetness and charm they were, remember? Mr. Morton was delighted. But not Lucian.'

Paddy pressed the tobacco down in his pipe, the grey eyes a little bleak. 'Lucian was mighty glad then that he'd set me to guard you. "Paddy," he says to me when we met in the woods one day, "can you imagine a Venetian nobleman not caring about losing a fortune unless he was too rich to care? And *we* know that's not so with Chiavelli. I smell a rat, Paddy, and it scares me. I can't say anything to Uncle Edward, for I've no shred of proof. And besides, this is something we're best fitted to handle. I've an idea in my head that might bring me to stay at *Meadhaven* myself to watch over Cadi, but I'm doubtful that it'll work, so she'll be in your hands, Paddy. I want you to stay on here and keep close watch over young Cadi while I make a few inquiries of my own about the Count." '

Paddy struck a match. 'Will it trouble you if I smoke?'

I gave a quick shake of my head. He set the match to his pipe, and went on, 'So I stayed. And the time or two you went to town, I was on the same train with you.'

I gasped. 'The train! The man in the tunnel—you mean Uncle Guido arranged *that*?'

Paddy nodded, with almost comical sadness. 'And I wasn't on the spot for once. Lucian was seeing you safe home that day. He took over while I went down to Epsom for an hour or two for a second opinion on a horse he was thinking of buying.'

'And the man? The man who tried to throw me from the train? Who was he?'

Paddy shrugged. 'A hireling. There's a dozen places in London where you can find a man to cut a throat for twenty pounds.' I shivered, and he went on, 'Chiavelli must have set to work the very moment he knew who you were. Better for him if you died there in England rather than in Venice. We'll never know for sure, but it's a good guess that Chiavelli sent a man to London even before he wrote you that first letter, a man who hired that scum to get rid of you.' He grimaced ruefully. 'And then it was yourself that saved you, not us. That trick of getting to you while the train was on the move took Lucian by surprise. He didn't spot the feller, what with the tunnel and the darkness, and I'd have done no better myself.'

'Then it was true? I mean, what Lucian said about chasing him?'

'Sure and of course it was true! Lucian didn't catch him though, more's the pity.'

'And at Chalons? You travelled with us to guard me?'

Paddy nodded. 'I was on the train, prowling the corridors most of the time. And I got a bed for the night in the little café opposite the hotel.' He gave me an amused glance. 'You're a hard one to guard, Cadi. I never thought you'd be going out from the hotel on your own.'

'Uncle Guido sent that man with the iron bar?'

'Your uncle knew you'd be stopping in Chalons. Mr. Morton had written and told him. So he hired a cut-throat there to watch for a chance at you.' Paddy shook his head.

'I was almost too late myself that time—and would have been but for Sarah rushing across the square in a great fret to tell me you'd gone out.'

'Sarah?' I could not believe my ears. '*She* knew you were watching over me?'

His face softened, and he gazed into the glow of the furnace. 'Sarah knew. We'd met while I was prowling around *Meadhaven*, d'you see.' He shrugged. 'After a while it wasn't by accident we met, and we used to talk quite a bit together. Sarah didn't know just what was afoot, for I didn't tell her, but she has a quick enough mind behind that pretty face, and she'd heard my name as being Lucian's partner. She guessed I was playing guardian angel for you.'

I remembered something—Sarah going out of the hotel almost as soon as we arrived, for a breath of air, so she had said. But she had met Paddy Flynn in the dusk there, to learn where he would be staying. It was just as well, for otherwise I would be dead now. My debt to Sarah was becoming greater than I could ever pay.

'She never breathed a word about it, Paddy,' I said wonderingly.

'She didn't know the whole of it, and I asked her not to speak for it was best so. Why frighten you and the rest of the family without need? Even if we'd told all we suspected, would Mr. Morton have believed a few bits of flimsy suspicion? More important, would you, Cadi? You'd have thought it was some trick Lucian was up to, for your uncle had convinced everyone he was an angel of light with his sweet loving letters. So I told Sarah nothing and she asked nothing, but just trusted me to be doing what was best.'

'She trusted you . . .' I echoed slowly, and a thought slipped suddenly into my mind. 'Paddy, I think she loves you. I know there's somebody, and it must be you. She seemed to become grown-up in such a very short time—as if something *big* had happened to her.'

'I hope so.' Paddy nodded slowly and smiled into the glow of the fire. 'It's on both sides, Cadi.'

'Oh, Paddy. I'm so glad for both of you.' I thought for a moment. 'Now I see why Sarah was worried about me when

I wouldn't come home with the family, she knew already that something was amiss. And that's why she wrote to Richard, of course!'

'Ah, so she wrote to him, did she? And that's what brought him running out to save you. Poor Sarah, she must have been fretting her heart out with neither me nor Lucian there to turn to.'

'Have you been out here in Venice all the time then, Paddy?'

'I have. Pretending to be an artist feller. I rented a top-floor studio in one of the little houses just across the small canal at the back of the palazzo. From the bedroom at the back you can look right out on the palazzo grounds.'

'And Lucian was with you?'

'Not until later. He was moving around between Rome, Venice and Padua, talking to one or two people about your uncle. Important people, especially in Rome.' He drew on his pipe, and frowned. 'We thought you'd be safe enough for a while, once you were in the palazzo, for it wasn't likely your uncle would be fool enough to get rid of you straight away. Too risky. He had to take his time and make everyone believe you were happy with him before he could make a move. But we watched just the same. And then, when the family went home and you stayed behind, Lucian was set to go grey with worry. "I have to get her out, Paddy," he says to me, "but Chiavelli's still a powerful man here in Venice, so we'll need to tread softly. If we try to march in and take her there'll be the devil to pay and she might get hurt, for we've no law on our side." '

Paddy grinned suddenly, his eyes dancing. 'So he played the hand quiet and clever, like I've seen him play it before. He went to the stables in Padua and talked about some fine horses he had for sale. Next day the Count was out there, keen to talk business. Lucian played the rogue for him, sly and sharp, and without a scruple to his name. In two days he had your uncle convinced that Lucian Farrel was as big a scoundrel as you'd find anywhere.'

Paddy's grin faded. 'I wish I could have heard him that night he led your uncle on and twisted the truth out of him,' he said wistfully. 'Better than a play, it must have been.'

I shivered a little. 'It was, Paddy, I can see that now. But it wasn't like a play to me at the time.'

'No. I can imagine.'

We were silent for a few moments before Paddy went on. 'Well, there it was. Lucian tricked the Count into declaring himself. There were no witnesses, of course, or none that Lucian knew of, but it was a great piece of work just the same, for it told us we'd guessed right, and now we knew how things stood. At the same time Lucian set the scene for coming along and taking you away from the Count nice and quietly in a month's time. We decided you'd be safe meanwhile, for your uncle wouldn't hurt you when he was relying on Lucian to do his dirty work for him.' He looked down at Richard and shook his head. 'Then this young feller put a spoke in our wheel.'

'He couldn't know what you were doing, Paddy. He meant well, and it was so brave of him.'

'Sure it was now. But it's made things awkward.'

'You saw us escape?'

'We did. Or I did, rather. I was on watch while Lucian slept.' He scratched his cheek with the pipe-stem. 'It seemed a waste of time to me, watching day and night, but Lucian wouldn't be argued with . . . and he was right. He has a great instinct, our Lucian. It was like that in the war.'

'But how did you keep track of us through all the canals in that mist?'

'We didn't. We followed the Count's string of boats in a little canoe that Lucian bought weeks ago. It's a handy craft, good for night work and faster than a boat. So we were close to the search boats all the time, though they didn't know it. Then the mist cleared just for a minute or so, and we saw you.'

'So did the others. That's when Uncle Guido fired and wounded Richard. I thought they'd catch us then.'

'They might have. But Lucian went over the side and into the water like a fish. Next minute he'd turned over a gondola and a boat without them ever knowing how it happened.

There were better than half a dozen men in the water, and a rare old confusion.'

'They'd have killed him if they'd seen him!'

'He's a hard man to kill,' Paddy said casually, and knocked out his pipe. 'When I picked him up again the mist had rolled down and we'd lost you, or so I thought. But Lucian knew better. "Find that line of *bricole*, Paddy," he says. 'She'll follow the stakes and go to ground on the island, sure as you're alive." So I asked him why. "Because it makes the best sense!" he snaps, edgy-like. "And that's what she'll do—I *know* her, Paddy." '

I saw that Paddy Flynn was looking down at me with a whimsical smile. 'Seems like he was right again. We came ashore, and Lucian sent me on to find the watchman and give him a tap on the head.' He jerked his thumb towards a small door. 'He's safe in the tool-room there, tied up. Meanwhile Lucian was hunting for you. He found your boat, and tipped her over on her side to hide the mast. Then a few minutes later he spotted you as you came out of the hut. What with the darkness, he couldn't tell that it was you at first, so he followed until he could make sure.' Paddy gave a little laugh. 'Lord knows it's no wonder you were set to scream at sight of him. When I saw him carry you in here he was all plastered with mud and weeds like some creature from a swamp.'

There was a long silence in the warm foundry. A kind of sleepiness had come upon me, partly from weariness but partly perhaps from the mental relief of having so many mysteries answered and all my suspicions and doubts wiped away.

'Who are you, Paddy Flynn?' I asked slowly. 'Why have you risked so much to help Lucian keep me safe?'

'I'm a travelling man, Miss Tregaron,' he said, falling into the old manner he had used with me at Wealdhurst. 'Did I never tell you?'

'Ah, don't mock me any more, Paddy. I'm sorry if I was once hoity-toity with you.'

'I nudged you into it,' he said, and grinned.

'So you did. Now tell me who you are. Please?'

'Well then . . . I'm Lucian's friend. We've done many things together, and the bonds are strong.'

'You were an officer with him in the army?'

He chuckled.

'Not an officer. I was his troop sergeant. Did you mistake me for a gentleman?'

'I don't think I made a mistake, Paddy.'

'Maybe not,' he said wryly. 'I've a family in Ireland that's very much out of the top drawer, as they say. But I was the black sheep, d'you see, always in trouble. So my father turned me out, and now I look back I can't say I blame him. I joined up as a trooper. A gentleman ranker, that's what they call my kind.' He smiled. 'But I made a fair enough soldier, and I was lucky to find myself serving under Lucian.'

'You said you were cashiered together. What happened, Paddy?'

His face grew sombre and he gazed with unseeing eyes for a while, as if staring into the past. 'It was a bad war,' he said at last, 'and badly fought, not by the men but by the generals. There's thousands of fine boys lying underground today who died from the stupidity of those who gave the orders, Cadi. We saw it, Lucian and I, for month after month till it was running into years. Then Lucian went home on leave for a while, and he talked with Mr. Morton. They made a plan together.'

'Mr. Morton?' I was bewildered.

'You're forgetting he's an important man in the Foreign Office, Cadi, and he was much involved with the war situation. He knew it was brains would do the trick quicker than guns, especially after Lucian talked to him. So in the next action after Lucian came back to the regiment we let ourselves be captured.'

'You *let* it happen?'

He gave an ironic smile. 'God knows it was easy enough. We had only to obey orders instead of using our heads and turning a blind eye as we'd done before. So after we'd been taken we were questioned by the Boers . . . and we turned against our own side. Little by little we told them our order of battle, the plans for the new attack, and where our lines of communication would lie.'

'And they believed you?'

'It wasn't just as easy as that, now. We let them drag it out of us bit by bit, and we kept bargaining all the while for money after they'd won the war. They despised us for traitors to our own side, but they listened.'

He stretched, and gave a little sigh of satisfaction. 'Lord, how they listened! We both told the same story, the story Lucian had planned with Mr. Morton and some of the military chiefs in London. A good story it was, and false as a wooden leg. They were no fools, the Boers, and I fancy they wondered if I was playing a double game. But Lucian, he had them believing every word. I always thought the Irish knew a trick or two when it comes to blarney, but Lucian's the master at it, so he is.' Paddy laughed with sudden pleasure at the memory, then shook his head with a touch of puzzlement. 'And that's a queer thing to be sure. With his friends, he's straight as a gun-barrel, but when he's dealing with enemies he can play the rogue to perfection, just as he did with the Count that night.'

'And . . . the plan worked?'

'Even better than we'd hoped. You're too young to recall much about the war, Cadi, but because of what we said, the Boer commander in that area, a man called De la Rey, he threw everything into an attack on Lichtenburg—and lost the best part of his army. So there it was. We trailed our coat, he stood on the tail of it, and we snatched his legs from under him. That was the turning point. Oh, the war straggled on a while, but it was the beginning of the end. Lucian and I escaped that night, the night of the battle, and just as well for us. We'd not have lived long once the Boers found how we'd tricked them.'

For long moments I could only stare. Then words tumbled from me in a fury of indignation. 'But Lucian's been an outcast ever since! And you too, I suppose! Why hasn't everything been told? Why can people like old Colonel Rodsley treat Lucian as if he really had been a traitor? It's not fair, Paddy, it's not fair!'

'Easy now,' he said amiably. 'It's no more than we expected. Only a handful of people knew the truth, and we knew it wouldn't be told for a while. We might even have been shot for what we were supposed to have done—betraying secrets to the enemy. The rumours soon crept around. We were arrested and cashiered, and we couldn't defend ourselves with the truth, for it was what they call Most Secret. Oh, there's many an officer and gentleman who'll never shake Lucian's hand again, even though some of them are maybe alive today only because of what Lucian did. But we knew the price, Cadi, so we can't complain.'

'But you can!' I exclaimed. 'Why couldn't you tell the truth at the time? And why hasn't it been told *now*? The war's been over for years!'

'Ah, that's not the way of it,' he said gently. 'It's still too soon. The military intelligence folk hate to have their secrets told, in case they want to use them again. Oh, it'll come out one day. Maybe next year or the year after. But that'll be thanks to Mr. Morton. He's pressing hard, and he'll have his way in the end.'

'I think it's . . . horrible,' I said bitterly, and choked on the last word.

'It's better than war, Cadi. Oh, I'm a soldier myself and with a good liking for a scrimmage, but there's no joy in bloody slaughter against men you respect. Better for a couple of fellers to end up as outcasts than for a few thousand to end up dead.'

Richard groaned in his sleep, and stirred. I put my hand on his hot forehead, and after a few seconds he settled down again without waking.

'You and Lucian must be very great friends,' I said. 'I can understand now why you've helped him take care of me, Paddy. But I still don't understand why Lucian himself should put you both to so much trouble over all these weeks and months for somebody who's very much a newcomer to the family.'

'Do you not, Cadi? Have you really no idea?' His eyes were full of humour.

I looked at him, baffled. 'I know he's very fond of Mr.

298

Morton, and he knows Mr. Morton is very fond of *me*, that's all I can think of.'

He laughed. 'It's a shade more direct than that. I remember . . .' He paused, fingered his chin uncertainly for a moment, then seemed to make up his mind. 'I remember just after the war being worried about Lucian. He was drifting, doing nothing special, not settling down. Then one day nearly three years ago he came to me in London and said he was setting up stables at Epsom and would I come in with him as equal partner. There was something about him . . . he suddenly seemed a different man, and I told him so.'

'Different in what way, Paddy?'

'Well, like a man who's suddenly found something worth living for and working for. And that was just it, for he told me so himself. "Paddy," he says, "the damnedest thing has happened. We've lived hard, you and I, and we're no saints, so you know I'm not some young fool whose head's easily turned. So listen, Paddy. A week ago in Mawstone I met a young girl, a child almost, not much over seventeen and just a slip of a thing, and there's no girl in the world like her." Then he tells me the story of what happened in Mogg Race Bay.'

I found my hands were trembling, and linked them together in my lap. To learn that Lucian had spoken of me in such a way made me glow with joy, yet I was dumbfounded. He had given no hint that he even liked me. He had seemed aloof and arrogant. The beating of my heart sounded so loud to me that I felt sure Paddy would hear it.

He went on. 'When Lucian finished the story he says, kind of pleading with me to agree, "If I wait a year or two until she's grown up a little, I could go to her and court her, couldn't I?" ' Paddy shook his head and made a wry face. 'I had to say it to him, Cadi. "There's only seven years between you, and that's fine," I told him. "But you're a man disgraced, like meself, Lucian. There's that to remember."

' "It's that I'm thinking of," he says. "But if she ever came to like me and believe in me, she wouldn't care what other

299

folk thought. You can see it in her, Paddy. In the eyes. She's a little thing, with little hands, but I swear I'd trust my life in them as I would in yours. Paddy. And by God, that's something I never thought I'd say of any woman, much less a child." '

Paddy looked at me. 'So we started the stables. He wanted to have built up something to offer you when the time came. And we've done well, more than well. I'll tell the truth and say I thought Lucian would forget you in a few months. But no, I was wrong. I hadn't met you then.'

'He . . . he never showed what he felt,' I said. 'I mean, after I'd come to live at *Meadhaven*.'

'Ah, how could he now? You had all the troubles of settling down in a new life and he wanted to give you time, Cadi. But you were quick to settle, and he was just thinking the time was right, that he could begin to visit *Meadhaven* more often and show his feelings, when it came out that you were heiress to a great fortune, and that hit him harder than the bullet he took at Brandwater Basin.'

'Hit him? Why, Paddy?'

He sighed. 'Dear heaven, girl, think now. If he'd begun paying attention to you as soon as you became an heiress, what would you have imagined?'

Looking back on all the suspicions I had felt towards Lucian, I knew that what Paddy suggested was true. 'But it doesn't matter *now*,' I said urgently. 'And anyway, he did ask Mr. Morton if he could court me.'

'Ah, but that was only after we knew you were in danger from Count Chiavelli. Lucian was desperate to be with you at *Meadhaven*. The closer he was, the better he could watch over you.' He shrugged. 'But that came to nothing, for Mr. Morton wouldn't allow it, so we had to manage as best we could.' He pushed his hands into his trouser pockets and stood gazing down at me curiously, as if trying to read my thoughts.

'Lucian loves you. Cadi Tregaron,' he said softly. 'I wonder what you feel for him?'

I did not answer, for even as Paddy spoke I had heard the slight sound of the door opening. Lucian stood there, staring at us with a strange, angry look. He pushed the door shut behind him.

'Damn your wagging tongue, Paddy!' he said, tight-lipped.

Paddy returned the stare, his chin out-thrust a little. 'Damn it as much as you like, but I'm not sorry,' he said stubbornly. Then, with a touch of anger, 'Have you no sense, man? First you keep silent because she's a child, and then because she's an heiress, and you were a fool on both counts, though for good intentions. Has it never dawned on you that if she loves a man she'll love as her grandmother did—because her heart tells her *this* is the man she loves and trusts? And the devil with all else!'

I said, 'Be quiet, Paddy dear,' and got to my feet. I walked towards Lucian and put out my hands for him to take them. Something warm and golden seemed to flow between us. 'The devil with all else, Lucian,' I said. 'And please don't look so fierce.'

He freed one hand, tilted my face and kissed me gently on the lips. Then, with his eyes still upon me, he said, 'They're here, Paddy. Chiavelli and his rogues. They've started searching.'

Chapter Sixteen

MY HEART LURCHED, and I felt the prickle of perspiration on my face. For a few blissful moments I had forgotten the danger that threatened us all, but the tautness in Lucian's face was a grim reminder.

'Chiavelli has brought his men ashore,' he said, holding my hands but looking past me at Paddy Flynn now. 'He must have guessed Cadi's hiding somewhere on the islet.'

'How would he guess?' Paddy asked doubtfully. 'You hid her boat.'

'They may have found it. The mist's gone now, and with no boat in sight on the lagoon perhaps they think this is the only place she could be hiding. Whatever the reason,

Chiavelli must feel certain about it. He's set his men to search the island and the foundry buildings. I heard him giving the orders.'

Paddy nodded slowly, and glanced down at Richard. 'You'd better take Cadi in the canoe and fetch help from Venice, then. I'll stay and guard the boy.'

I was afraid, but something stronger than fear made me say quickly. 'I won't leave Richard. He came to save me, and I won't leave him.' My voice rose a little.

'You have to, Cadi,' Lucian said. He spoke firmly, but his eyes were suddenly anxious. 'You can't help Paddy protect him, so it's foolish for you to risk everything by staying.'

I knew he was right, and for a moment I wavered, but then I knew something else—that if I left Richard now I would always feel tainted, always feel I had committed an act of betrayal. 'I don't care if it's foolish,' I said desperately, 'I've *got* to stay, Lucian. If he wakes up and I'm not with him, he'll be afraid. He'll feel deserted.'

'But Richard himself would want you to be safe,' Lucian began, almost in exasperation, then Paddy laughed shortly and broke in. 'Think back, Lucian. Did *you* leave me wounded that day at Magersfontein because it was the sensible thing to do? Lord knows I've much respect for good sense, and Cadi has that in plenty, but a little heartfelt foolishness makes a fine leaven for it sometimes.'

Lucian's thick brows drew close together. 'All right, I won't argue the point. You take the canoe, Paddy, and I'll stay here with Richard and Cadi. You know what to do when you reach Venice.'

'I know sure enough, but I can't do it. You're known to the people who can best give help, and I'm not. Besides, there's quick talking to be done, and I haven't near as much of the language as you.'

Lucian stood very still. I could see that he was seeking a way round the truth of what Paddy had said. But there was none.

'Don't worry about us,' I said quickly. 'You'll be back before Uncle Guido and his men find us here.'

He shook his head. 'It's not long till dawn. They'll have

searched every cranny within an hour——' He broke off, and from his grimy face the blue eyes shone suddenly bright and hard. 'But not if I give them something else to keep them busy,' he added softly. 'Yes . . . I think I can manage that.' He lifted my hand and kissed it, then led me towards Paddy and put my hand in his. 'For God's sake take good care of her.'

'Be easy in your mind on that. I've had practice.'

'I know.' Lucian turned and went to the door. There he paused and looked back. I knew that in leaving me now he was perhaps doing the hardest thing he had ever done. 'Don't look for trouble, Paddy,' he said roughly. 'But if it finds you, remember Chiavelli has a pistol.'

'And I have me wits, Lucian. Don't be fretting, now. Remember it's yourself that has the worst job, so be careful.'

It was five minutes after we had barred the door behind Lucian that I first saw the flames. I was standing by one of the two windows, peering out through a crack in the heavy shutters. The mist had vanished, and in the semi-darkness I saw a flower of yellow flame suddenly blossom beyond the main foundry building. Dark figures came running, I could see them pointing and gesturing, and though I could hear no sound at this distance I knew that they were shouting.

'A nice distraction, that,' murmured Paddy beside me. 'He said he'd keep 'em busy.'

'There's another fire,' I whispered. 'There, to the right, by that outbuilding.'

Paddy chuckled. 'He was always a devil at the night work. And there's no lack of fuel or fire in a foundry, praise be.'

'Uncle Guido's taking charge. Look, can you see him? He's setting them to form a bucket chain.'

A voice behind us croaked feebly, 'Cadi . . . ?' I turned and ran to Richard. He lay staring up at me with enormous eyes. 'Cadi . . . you're all right? What . . . happened?'

With all my heart I was thankful now that I had stayed. I knelt, and smiled down at him, 'Don't worry, Richard dear. Just try to rest. Lucian's looking after us, and there's a friend of his here.'

'Lucian?' Richard sighed and relaxed. 'That's good . . . oh, that's good, Cadi.' His eyes closed. 'I lied when I said you shouldn't trust him, Cadi. He's a strong man, Lucian . . . like a rock. I was jealous . . .' His voice became a mumble.

Beside me, Paddy said, 'Take a corner of the palliasse and help me pull him round to the back of the furnace, so he can't be seen from the door, Cadi. I don't want to lift him.'

I obeyed, and though Richard stirred a little his eyes remained closed.

Paddy went away and I heard a slight clattering of metal from somewhere in front of the furnace, then he came round to join me again. 'Stay here with him, Cadi. I'm going to keep watch at the windows.'

I sat down on the floor beside Richard, holding his hand with the half-formed hope that it might comfort him as he slept. His breathing was quicker now, more shallow, and I felt a growing fear for him.

That was the beginning of a long vigil. Paddy stood like a statue by one or other of the windows, changing his vantage point from time to time. Now and then, through the slats of the shutters, I could see a red glow from one of the fires Lucian had started, and occasionally I could just catch the faint sound of shouting as Uncle Guido and his men fought to douse the flames. I lost track of time, and seemed to be in a dream. Strangely, despite the danger that threatened so closely, I would have felt full of joy if it had not been for the sharp anxiety that Richard roused in me. Lucian loved me, and my whole being wanted to sing with the knowledge, but it seemed wicked to rejoice with Richard's hot dry hand in mine, and the sound of his troubled breathing in my ears.

My thoughts ebbed and flowed, shifting and changing, moving back and forth in time, as all I had learned that night passed through my mind again. It was a shock when I lifted my head and saw that the grey light of dawn was showing through the shutters.

"Paddy" I whispered. 'What's happening?'

He did not turn as he answered. 'They've doused the fires and they've started searching again.'

'How long has Lucian been gone?'

'An hour and a half. They've wasted most of it.'

'Can he bring help from Venice? Will anybody believe him?'

'It's not just anybody he'll be talking to, Cadi. There's two gentlemen should have arrived last night——' He broke off and I saw him stiffen. 'Ah, now. That's a great pity. They're coming this way at last, his nibs and a few of his cut-throats.'

The dreamlike sensation that held me was brutally shattered and I felt my heart begin to thud. Paddy moved quickly, and the end of the furnace hid him from my view. 'Be easy now,' I heard him say in a low voice. 'We've a trick or two up our sleeves yet.'

I could only think that his words were spoken to give comfort, for the future was suddenly a cold reality to me. Uncle Guido and his men would break down the door in a minute or two, and then we would die. There could be no other outcome. Uncle Guido had gone so far that he could not dare to draw back now. And Paddy Flynn, for all his coolness, his quick wits, and his experience, was only one unarmed man against a dozen or more.

There came a hammering on the door, then a shout. 'It's barred! She is here!' I would not allow myself to crouch like some cowering mouse, and so I stood up. My eyes came just above the shoulder of the furnace, so although the rest of me was hidden I could clearly see the door as it shook under the heavy blows from an axe or a sledge-hammer.

One of the wooden sockets holding the bar gave way, and the door swung open. My heart seemed to turn over within me as I saw a man holding a big hammer. For a moment he was framed in the doorway, then he stepped back and Uncle Guido appeared. His face and clothes were black with smoke. He held a pistol in his hand. Behind him I could see the first pinkness of the rising sun. From the black mask of his face, two eyes glittered feverishly, horribly, as he peered slowly round the gloomy interior of the foundry. I realized that Paddy must be at the end of the furnace housing, hidden by the angle of the ancient brickwork, for evidently Uncle Guido had not seen him yet.

'Caterina!' Uncle Guido cried suddenly in a voice that cracked with long-pent fury. I must have been holding my breath, for now it hissed from my lungs under the shock of that sudden shrill cry. His head jerked up as he peered, seeking me. And then, incredibly, I saw a glowing spear flash through the air towards him, the tip bright red for a full twelve inches of its length.

A blow-pipe! A glass-blower's pipe, its end almost white with heat from having rested in the furnace for the past hour or more. And from the shadows that hid him by the side of the furnace Paddy had thrown it like a javelin. It had neither blade nor point, but the heat made it a frightful weapon, and it would surely have hit Uncle Guido on the chest had he not instinctively thrown up his arms to ward it off. He screamed as the touch of it seared his hand, and I heard the pistol clatter to the floor. A second blow-pipe flashed like some monstrously long fire-fly through the air. Uncle Guido staggered back in panic, falling, and the pipe whistled above him through the doorway as he fell. I heard a new scream as it found a target beyond, and then I saw Paddy leaping across the foundry floor, a thick balk of wood in his hand.

He slammed the door, set the balk of wood at an angle against it, scooped up the pistol and stepped back. A sound broke from his lips, a sound like a triumphant war-whoop.

'Let's have ye, gossoons!' he roared in a great voice, his brogue thicker than I had ever heard it before. 'There's a bullet 'tween the eyes for the first face to show at door or window!'

He turned to me, grinning, his grey eyes alight. 'Tell 'em in Italian, Cadi,' he said, 'for I doubt his nibs will! A bullet for the first man to show—tell 'em quick now.'

I drew a breath, moving out from behind the furnace, and shouted the warning at the top of my voice. Then we stood listening. There came a rapid scuffling of feet moving away from the foundry, and a medley of frantic Italian too muffled for me to follow.

'We have 'em,' Paddy said softly, and weighed the pistol in his hand. 'I fancy they've no other firearm between 'em. Chiavelli's not the kind who'd dare trust his men behind him with guns.'

Hope surged high in me, and by some strange quirk of the mind I thought of the day when I would tell Sarah this story, of how Paddy Flynn, the man she loved, had outwitted our enemies at a single stroke. I moved to one of the windows and peered between the slats. 'There's nobody on this side, Paddy,' I whispered.

'They'll have to break door or shutters to get in,' he said, 'and even your Uncle Guido will find it hard persuading them to face a bullet at point blank range.'

'That was wonderful, what you did just now. I thought we were lost.'

'Ah, well now, I have all me wits, but it was serving under Lucian that sharpened them. When it comes to a scrimmage, he's the master. One day I'll tell you how we escaped the twelve-man guard in De la Rey's camp with just a piece of soap.'

I listened, but there was no sound from outside. 'Tell me now, Paddy.'

'All right. Keep watching the window. How it was, we were in this small cell, d'you see, and never a hope of breaking out. Then Lucian somehow stole this big bar of soap when we were out on exercise. Two days he spent carving it with a spoon-handle, then he rubbed in lamp-black, and by the time he'd finished it looked more like a Luger than the real thing.'

'A Luger?'

'A kind of pistol. Bigger than this one. Even with it stuck under your nose you'd have sworn it would blow your head off.' He gave a little joyous chuckle at the memory. 'More than good enough to persuade the jailer first, and then the rest of the guard. That's Lucian for you. I remember another time, just before Brandwater Basin——'

He stopped short as from some distance beyond the door

there came a shout. Uncle Guido was calling, and there was a trembling wildness in his voice. 'Caterina! Do you hear me?'

I looked at Paddy. He shook his head and I remained silent.

'Caterina!' Uncle Guido shouted again. 'We have bundles of straw and dry wood here, and when we have set them blazing we shall pile them round the walls. If you do not come out, we shall *burn* you out! Do you hear?'

Hope turned to despair, and I felt my shoulders sag. Then Paddy touched my arm, and when I looked up into his face I almost flinched at the cold fury I saw there. 'Burn us out, will they?' he breathed. 'By God, we'll see. Stand by to open the door and shut it fast again, Cadi. I'm going out. And if I can't bring him down with a shot before his pack of wolves reach me, then I'm no soldier. We'll see how fast the pack turns tail when the leader's down.'

I was trembling, and waves of sickness swept me. With an effort I moved to the door and set my hands on the balk of wood jammed against it. I was afraid for Paddy, afraid for Richard and myself, even afraid for Uncle Guido. I did not want him to be killed, but if he lived then the three of us would die. This was the inexorable horror Lucian and Paddy had found in war, and now I could understand why they had sacrificed even their honour and reputations to shorten the span of brutality.

My hands were lifting the balk of wood, and Paddy stood crouched, ready to race forward, when a new sound came from outside—the sudden uproar of shouting, and running feet.

Paddy said, 'Wait!' He darted to one of the windows and stood peering through the slats of the shutter for a moment, then gave a little laugh and turned to lean against the wall, looking at me with humorous eyes from which all the fury and cold purpose had vanished as if they had never been. 'It's sunrise, Miss Tregaron,' he said, his brogue slight again now, his manner as possessed as when I had first met him. 'It's sunrise on a beautiful morning, and Lucian is here—with some friends.'

He came towards me, kicked the balk aside and threw open the door. I saw men running, and being pursued by other men in uniform. Two policemen held Uncle Guido. Lucian was coming towards us, and I gasped as I saw that beside him walked Signor Vecchi, the Italian government official for whom I had acted as interpreter in Mr. Morton's study.

Behind them came a man I had not seen before.

Lucian looked dirtier than ever in the light of day. Even his hair was caked with mud. Signor Vecchi and the stranger looked as if they had been roused from sleep and had dressed hurriedly.

As I came out of the foundry with Paddy beside me, Lucian ran forward. He caught me up in his arms and held me close, murmuring my name over and over again. Then he kissed me, turned his head a little and said, 'Did you have any trouble, Paddy?'

From the corner of my eye I saw that Paddy was watching the capture of Uncle Guido's men. Without looking round he held up the pistol and said, 'A little, but we managed.'

'Good.' Lucian took my arm and turned. 'Cadi, you already know Signor Vecchi. This other gentleman is your Italian lawyer, Dottore Bonello. I've been in touch with them several times over the past week or two, and I managed to persuade them to come to Venice to meet me, so I could tell them exactly what I'd discovered about Count Chiavelli. As it happens, they arrived last night, and I had an appointment with them this morning—which I kept at their hotel rather earlier than they expected.'

Signor Vecchi took my hand and bowed over it. 'It is a great relief to find you safe,' he said in Italian, his distress and agitation very plain. 'We have Mr. Farrel to thank for that. He is very persuasive. At first when he came to me and told me of the bargain he had pretended to strike with Count Chiavelli I could not believe it. But when my friend Bonello urged that we should come to Venice and look into the matter ourselves, I agreed to do so.' His smile was full of apology. 'I am sorry we did not come sooner. After all, I am in your debt, Miss Tregaron, and I once promised that I would always be ready to help you in any way that I could.'

He looked about him, and his face became stern. 'But there is no need for investigation now. Chiavelli is revealed for all to see as a scoundrel who would murder his own kin for gain.'

In the last minute or two, with the knowledge that the long, long night of danger was past, a stupefying weariness had descended upon me. My mind seemed numb and my eyelids were drooping.

'Richard,' I said. Nothing else mattered now. 'Richard is hurt . . . please, please get help to him.' The ground tilted beneath my feet. I clutched at Lucian, felt him pick me up in his arms, and then a great wave of blackness rose to engulf me.

I have only fragmentary memories of the hours that followed, blurred and sometimes grotesque recollections of the moments when I half roused from the stupor into which I had fallen. At one time I was in a boat, and the next thing I remember is sinking into a soft bed while a plump dark penguin drew the covers up about me. It was not until many hours later that I discovered my penguin was one of the two nursing nuns sent by Signor Vecchi to look after me. I was told that as they bathed the mud and grime from my body and put a nightdress on me I had talked continually, about mudbanks and glowing spears, *bricole* and burning straw, sea mist and boats. But always I kept returning to Richard, crying out in anxiety and saying that I must go to him, so that in the end I was made to drink a strong sedative to bring me sleep.

When at last I woke to my proper senses I saw daylight between the drawn curtains of the hotel room where I lay, and felt bewildered until Sister Angelina told me that I had slept the clock round and that this was a new day. She brought broth for me to drink, but before I would obey I asked after Richard.

'A surgeon operated on him at noon yesterday, and we hope all will be well, but it is too early to know yet. Come now, eat your broth, little one.' She spoke in English, for she had spent several years in an English convent, as I learned later. This was how she had so easily understood my ramblings of the day before.

'Where's Lucian—Mr. Farrel?' I asked. 'And Mr. Flynn?'

'They have had much to attend to, and they also needed rest. Signor Vecchi says they will come to you as soon as they can.'

For three hours I fretted, and to my shame even sulked because Sister Angelina would not let me get dressed and go to Richard in the hospital. Then Lucian came, and when I saw his face I felt all hope go out of me. He sat on the side of the bed and took my hand.

'Be a brave girl, Cadi,' he said quietly. 'Richard died half an hour ago. The bullet set up an infection that struck very quickly, and he had no resistance to it after that night on the lagoon and the islet.'

I wept, thinking of Sarah and her mother and father. Lucian sat holding my hand between his own. I was glad he did not try to utter useless words of comfort. When the spasm of weeping had passed sufficiently for me to speak I whispered, 'How will you tell them?'

'I've already sent a long telegram, Cadi. I had to tell them at once. We won't be able to go home for a little while until the authorities have dealt with everything, but I'll write a letter to Mr. Morton today, telling him all the details I couldn't put in the telegram, and Signor Vecchi will send it by courier.'

I gripped his hand. 'How long must we stay? I want to go away from Venice. I want you to take me home, Lucian. Please!'

'I will, just as soon as I can, my darling.' He pushed back the hair from my brow. 'Now lie down and try to sleep a little more. I'll stay with you.'

It might well have been weeks before we were allowed to leave Venice, but to my overwhelming relief we left only ten days later. This was because the powers-that-be wanted as little scandal as possible over the affair. Uncle Guido claimed that he had not intended to shoot Richard, but had meant to fire a warning shot because he believed that I was being kidnapped. It was a hopeless story. Both Paddy and I had heard him threaten to kill us, and he had no answer to that. But a lawyer would be bound to use any defence he could find, and if I had pressed charges against Uncle Guido, or if Mr. Morton had done so because of Richard's death, then the dreadful business might have dragged on indefinitely.

For myself, I did not seek revenge. I did not care what was done about Uncle Guido, if only I could go home. Mr. Morton, for his part, felt the same way. Nothing could bring Richard back, and to prolong the affair would only prolong the distress of us all. He could not come to Venice because Mrs. Morton was in no fit state to be left, but he wrote a long letter to Lucian, who showed it to me. I remember part of it ran:

. . . We mourn Richard, poor boy, and ever shall. There was a strangeness in him, as well you know, Lucian, but I feel that in trying to save Cadi, so rashly, so gallantly, he has redeemed all faults. We grieve, but we can justly temper our grief with pride in what he did.

As for pressing charges against that evil man Chiavelli, I have no heart for it. You say that if Cadi and I agree to take no action against him then he and his family will secretly be banished from the country and forbidden ever to return. Let that suffice. He is penniless, and he will find no place in Europe, for rumours will always dog him there. Let him live with his conscience and his defeat in some far place across the world, and let us forget him.

Above all, bring our Cadi home to us with all speed, Lucian. Her presence will give us comfort as nothing else could . . .

And so, on a day in summer, I came home to *Meadhaven*. Richard's body had been sent by ship, and he was laid to rest in the churchyard at Wealdhurst. By Lucian's wish,

Mrs. Morton was told nothing of the part that he and Paddy Flynn had played in saving me, but was allowed to believe that Richard had succeeded alone, and had given his life in the end for my sake.

Strangely, I found Mrs. Morton more calm and serene than I had ever known her before. After the first dreadful shock of losing Richard, it seemed that some deep and unconscious anxiety within her had been taken away, leaving her a kind of peace beneath the sadness.

Our time of mourning at *Meadhaven* was not long, for Mr. Morton disliked the outward trappings of a family's sorrow. Paddy Flynn and Lucian became constant visitors, and, as the summer wore on, Sarah and I often spent a day at the stables in Epsom.

Sarah's company was a joy to me. I never had the wish to snap at her now, but sometimes remembered to do so because it made her laugh. We were both engaged by summer's end, I to Lucian and Sarah to Paddy Flynn. She still came to my room to chatter before going to bed, and never tired of making me tell once again the story of those terrifying moments in the foundry when Uncle Guido and his men had been breaking down the door.

'I simply can't get Paddy to tell me about it,' she would say indignantly. 'When I ask him he just laughs and puts me up on some brute of a horse so I forget everything else.'

The day of my marriage to Lucian was arranged for early May, three months after my twenty-first birthday. I was very rich, but to my relief and to Sarah's disappointment I had not inherited the title. I took no interest in the reasons for this, but gathered from Mr. Morton that the learned authorities in Rome had decided under all the circumstances that unless I laid claim to the title it should be allowed to lapse.

I did not care to lay claim. I cared about two things. First, that the shadows of disgrace should be lifted from Lucian and Paddy by the truth about their wartime exploit being told, and second, that Lucian should not be troubled by my wealth.

For the first, I had to be patient. 'Another year, no more,

Cadi dear,' Mr. Morton promised. 'I have the Foreign Secretary's firm undertaking on that.'

'But will he *keep* his promise?'

Mr. Morton chuckled. 'So cynical about politicians at such an early age? Well, I have told him plainly that if he fails I shall resign from the Foreign Office, stand for Parliament myself, and raise the matter in the House as a scandal.' His eyes were grim for a moment. 'Believe me, child, they will give way rather than allow that.'

My second care was resolved simply by speaking about it instead of avoiding the subject. We were at the stables one day soon after my twenty-first birthday, waiting for a mare to foal. I put my hand through Lucian's arm as we sat on a pile of straw, and said, 'Tell me what to do about the money, Lucian. I don't want it to spoil things. I love you so much, and nothing else matters. We don't need my money, because the stables are really flourishing now. You know I've arranged with Signor Vecchi to put some of the money in trust, for the *palazzo* to be made into an orphanage in memory of my Granny Caterina. But if you think it's better to give the rest away, just tell me.'

He looked startled.

'Don't be a little idiot, Cadi.'

'I'm not. A month ago I had nothing and was happy, today I'm rich and happy, it makes no difference to me—the money, I mean. Do you want me as I was, Lucian, or as I am? All I long for is to come to you the way that you want me.'

He chewed a straw, and was silent for a long minute. Then the black eyebrows lifted and he began to laugh softly. 'It's pride, you know,' he said in a wondering voice. 'What fools men are with their stupid vanities.' He turned to me, smiling. 'Ah, Cadi, my own little fisher-girl, never stop teaching me the wisdom you were born with. Keep what's yours and do whatever you want with it. You could start by buying a beautiful motor life-boat for the Mawstone folk. And one for Bosney, perhaps. You could have Cadi Tregaron life-boats all round the coast.' He was laughing now. 'No, Cadi Farrel life-boats.' He leaned forward to kiss me, but at that moment the mare whinnied and began to foal.

For the next hour we were very busy. My happiest moments were when I worked together with Lucian, but on this occasion I knew even greater content, for I felt that Lucian had shown his love for me to be complete.

We were married at St. Mary's Church, at Wealdhurst, and for our honeymoon we took a house in Cornwall, not far from Truro. This was by Lucian's suggestion, and I joyously agreed. There would be a cook-housekeeper and two maids to come in each day and look after us. We would sail and swim, we would ride and walk through the country-side of my childhood, and we would go to Mawstone, so that I could renew old acquaintance with my friends there.

It was on the night of our wedding that I first told Lucian of the Dream that had come to me so many times over the years, and of the strange ways in which it had gradually been fulfilled. I was standing before him as he sat on the edge of the big bed. We were both in our dressing gowns and mine was a beautiful silk one that Sarah had made for me with her own hands. He looked troubled when I told him how I had walked in my sleep that night in the *Palazzo Chiavelli,* how I had seen his face in the mirror and fled from him in terror.

'Oh Cadi, sweetheart, I'm sorry. I suppose I was busy thinking myself into the part I had to play.'

'I know, Lucian dear, I know. There's nothing to be sorry about now.' I put my arms round his neck and held his head close against me. 'That was the Bad Dream, and it's finished for ever,' I whispered. 'Now come over to the door and wait for me, Lucian. I know it's silly, but I want the Good Dream to come true now. Please?'

He stood up and took my hand. 'It's not silly. I want it fulfilled for you too, Cadi.'

I went out of the room and a little way along the passage, then turned. Lucian had closed the door, and a crack of light showed beneath it.

I began to walk slowly towards the room, and as I moved I felt the warm heaviness of joy and longing spread from

315

my heart to my whole body. Before me lay the end of dreaming, for Lucian was real, and I loved him.

With a happiness almost too great to bear, I lifted my hand to the door. As I did so it swung wide, and Lucian stood there smiling, his eyes warm with a world of love and his arms open to receive me.